A Ration Book Victory

Jean Fullerton is the author of seventeen historical novels and two novellas. She is a qualified District and Queen's nurse who has spent most of her working life in the East End of London, first as a Sister in charge of a team, and then as a District Nurse tutor. She is also a qualified teacher and spent twelve years lecturing on community nursing studies at a London university. She now writes full time.

Find out more at www.jeanfullerton.com

Also by Jean Fullerton

The Ration Book Series

A Ration Book Dream

A Ration Book Christmas

A Ration Book Childhood

A Ration Book Wedding

A Ration Book Daughter

A Ration Book Christmas Kiss

A Ration Book Christmas Broadcast

A Ration Book Victory

Short Stories

A Ration Book Christmas Kiss

A Ration Book Christmas Broadcast

A Ration Book Victory

JEAN FULLERTON

Published in paperback in Great Britain in 2022 by Corvus,
an imprint of Atlantic Books Ltd.

10 9 8 7 6 5 4 3 2 1

A CIP catalogue record for this book is available from the British Library.

Paperback ISBN: 978 1 83895 094 1
E-book ISBN: 978 1 83895 095 8

Printed and bound by CPI Group (UK) Ltd, Croydon, CR0 4YY

Corvus
An imprint of Atlantic Books Ltd
Ormond House
26–27 Boswell Street
London
WC1N 3JZ

www.corvus-books.co.uk

For all the readers who have
followed the Brogan family for the
past six years and love them as
much as I do.

Prologue

Kinsale, Ireland. June 1877

WITH HER FINGERS woven together in prayer and her eyes tight shut, five-year-old Philomena Dooley shifted from one knee to the other to ease the numbness caused by the cold flagstones of the Carmelite Friary Church, which served the good and faithful in the parish of Kinsale.

Although the bright summer sunlight streaming through the church's stained-glass window dappled the stone floor with a kaleidoscope of colours, inside the whitewashed walls the air was cool. Philomena expected nothing else as, for sure, hadn't it been the same each and every time she'd ever attended? Even the blessed saints perched on their pedestals between the pillars looked chilly.

Opening one eye, Philomena squinted at her mother kneeling beside her.

Kathleen Dooley, her head bowed low, her eyes closed and the pink rosary that had been blessed by the Pope himself clasped between her hands, had the same dark brown hair and eyes as Philomena herself.

On the other side of her were Philomena's brothers and sisters, with faces scrubbed and curly hair anchored with Brilliantine and ribbons respectively, knelt in age order with their father Jeremiah Dooley at the end.

As was usual when they attended church, she and her family were dressed in their very best clothes. For her mother this was a high-necked cream blouse with her long black skirt pooling around her, and a paisley shawl draped over her head and shoulders, while her father wore his least-worn trousers, which had been laid under the mattress for three days to be rid of the creases, and a flowery waistcoat under his jacket.

Philomena's best was a flowery blue cotton dress with long puffy sleeves and a frilly button-up collar. Although her mother had made it from a gown bought from a clothes dealer and it didn't quite reach to the top of her boots, Philomena knew that any princess in the land would envy her for the wearing of it.

She and her family were sitting at the back. Her mother said it was because they hadn't been in the parish long enough to have a regular pew, but Philomena knew better.

For hadn't she seen the sideways looks and heard the word 'tinkers' whispered since she was old enough to walk beside the family's vardo while Major, their piebald horse, pulled it along the dusty highways of Munster and beyond?

And on such a day as this, with God's beauty dancing all over the meadows and streams, sure wouldn't she rather be sitting on the running board swinging her legs than stuck in this old bleak building?

'*Ite, missa est,*' said Father Parr, cutting through Philomena's musing.

'*Deo gratias,*' responded the congregation.

Shuffling themselves into the order of precedence, those in the sanctuary made their way out of the church.

Philomena and the rest of the congregation bowed their heads again for a final prayer then those at the front of the church rose to make their way out.

Philomena's family, knowing it wasn't their place to step out in front of their betters, stayed in their seats.

A well-fed farmer with his wife beside him and eight or so children following like ducklings behind started down the aisle towards the door.

They were clearly prosperous because the man's tweed suit did not bag around the knees and he sported a bowler hat instead of the cap worn by hired men. His wife's attire, too, showed they had status in the town: she wore a matching dress and jacket plus a black straw bonnet instead of the usual headscarf.

As they made their way down the aisle, the youngest of the three sons, who looked to be just a couple of years older than Philomena, caught her eye. He was dressed in short trousers and a tweed jacket very like his elder brothers. However, whereas their straight hair was neatly parted and anchored down by their father's pomade, the younger boy's springy black curls caressed his forehead.

Although her mother would have chided her for staring, Philomena couldn't take her eyes from him.

As the family drew close, the boy's blue-grey eyes met Philomena's dark brown ones.

The odd sensation of distant whispering and murmuring that came upon her from time to time suddenly filled her head.

They stared at each other for a second, or perhaps for ever, then he winked.

Dumbfounded, Philomena felt rooted to the spot as the boy followed his parents.

Her family rose to their feet and automatically Philomena did the same and made her way out of the church into the bright summer sunlight.

Watching a fat bee disappear into the purple bell of a foxglove by the churchyard wall, Philomena turned her face towards the sun.

The Mass had been over for a good while and Philomena's belly was informing her it was empty, so she guessed it was almost midday, but as it was only a short walk back to the cottage, she was content to sit on the lichen-covered gravestone at the far corner of the burial ground for a while longer.

Across the graveyard the muted sound of the congregation drifted over. Her parents were amongst them. Her mother called it being friendly but, in truth, she only stayed to chat to the other women for her husband's sake, hoping her neatly scrubbed and cleanly dressed children would indicate they were a good Christian family and that her husband was therefore worthy of employment.

'You shouldn't be sitting on that grave.'

Philomena opened her eyes to find the boy who she'd seen in church standing in front of her.

'Why?'

'Because it's where Mother Twomey's buried,' he replied.

'Is she kin of yours, then?'

He shook his head. 'She was a witch that lived hundreds of years ago.'

'If she's a witch, why was she laid to rest in the graveyard?' said Philomena.

He shrugged. 'People say if you disturb her, she'll come back to haunt you.'

'Well, let her, because I like sitting here.' Philomena gave him a sideways look. 'You can sit here, too, if you like. Unless you're afeared.'

He hesitated for a moment then jumped up on to the slab of stone beside her.

'What's your name?' he asked, shuffling along next to her.

'Philomena. What's yours?'

'Patrick,' he replied. 'I saw you in church. Your family have just taken the cottage on the Ballyvrin Road.'

She nodded. 'Three weeks back.'

Truthfully, what the boy called a cottage most would recognise as a shed. And a leaky one at that. For hadn't it taken her father a full two weeks to replace the missing slates, while her mother spent days on her knees scrubbing mouse dirt from the pantry and pigeon droppings from the windows.

'Why have you got a wagon in the garden?' he asked.

'That's what we lived in before coming here,' Philomena replied. 'But Mammy told Pa we needed to settle so we can go to school. But I already know my letters. Mammy taught me from our Bible.'

'Me too,' he said. 'When's your birthday?'

'August. When's yours?'

'September and I'll be seven,' he replied.

'I like your curly hair,' said Philomena.

He gave her a bashful smile then looked away. He drummed his heels lightly on the stonework a couple of times then his attention returned to Philomena.

'Shall we be friends?' he asked.

The world around Philomena suddenly shifted into a new pattern.

'Yes, for ever, Patrick,' she replied, certain that her words were no lie.

'Patrick!'

They both looked around.

Standing next to a monument about ten yards away stood a mousey-haired, flat-faced girl.

'Pa wants you,' she shouted.

She looked about the same age as Philomena, was wearing a brown skirt with a matching jacket, and a belligerent expression beneath her bonnet. Whereas Patrick's eyes were warm and friendly, his sister's were as cold as the depth of winter.

'Coming, Nora,' Patrick shouted back.

Jumping off the grave, he turned to face Philomena.

'Do you know the split elm on the track from the castle to Cluain Mara?' he asked in a low voice.

She nodded.

'Meet me there tomorrow afternoon,' he said.

'Patrick!' his sister yelled again.

Giving Philomena a brief smile, he ran off.

However, before Patrick reached her, Nora opened her mouth a final time. Looking straight at Philomena, and in a voice that was in danger of raising those below from their slumber, she added, 'And, Patrick, you shouldn't be bothering yourself with a dirty didicoy.'

Chapter One

'THANK YOU, QUEENIE,' said Bernadine O'Toole, taking the half a dozen eggs wrapped in newspaper from her and placing them carefully into a pudding bowl. 'Would a tin of condensed milk and a pack of Rowntree's cocoa be all right?'

'They'd be grand,' replied Queenie.

Philomena Brogan, the head of the large Brogan family and known as Queenie from Aldgate Pump to Bow Bridge, was standing in Bernadine O'Toole's kitchen. It was the first Monday in February 1945.

With its lino covering the beaten-earth floor, the large butler sink with its single cold tap and an oven that should have been in a museum, Bernadine's kitchen was very like Queenie's own a few streets away in Mafeking Terrace.

Although the bright winter sun was high in the sky, ice had still crunched under Queenie's feet when she'd walked down Watney Street Market earlier that day. Being the day after payday, the stalls and shops in the market had been full of late-morning shoppers, but Queenie had been up since before dawn. While the day was just a promise in the eastern sky, she had pulled one of her grandson Billy's old balaclavas over her head, laced up her stout day boots and wrapped herself up in her oversized seaman's duffel coat, then, as she'd done for the past thirty years, she'd set out on her rounds.

Having returned to the family home with the morning bread, she'd removed the old carpet that she draped over the chicken coop each night to keep her two dozen hens warm and the stray cats out, then let the birds into the enclosed area her son Jeremiah had knocked up with old timbers and chicken wire.

She'd only just put the kettle on and lit the parlour fire when Jeremiah came downstairs yawning.

She'd no sooner put a cup of tea in front of him than her grandsons Billy and Michael, fifteen and fourteen respectively, had crashed into the kitchen, still buttoning school shirts and tying ties. Hearing her daughter-in-law Ida dealing with Victoria, the youngest member of the Brogan tribe, in the room above, Queenie had fed the two boys and packed them off to school before putting the family's laundry in to soak. Having completed her early-morning chores, she'd left to do her deliveries just as the heavy organ tone heralding the morning God slot, 'Lift Up Your Hearts', blasted out of the wireless at five to eight. After visiting the market, she'd arrived at Bernadine's house just as the flat, throaty sound of London Dock's midday hooters sounded.

Taking the groceries from Bernadine, Queenie laid them carefully alongside the two newspaper parcels at the bottom of the basket.

'Now, will you be wanting the same next week if I have them?' Queenie asked, covering her basket with a tea towel and tucking it down firmly.

'I surely will,' said Bernadine. 'Will you stay for a brew?'

'I would,' Queenie replied, 'but Ida is covering the yard this afternoon as Jeremiah's got a delivery to Ilford, so she'll be wanting me to keep an eye on that sweet little darling Victoria.'

A fond smile lifted Bernadine's weary features. 'I saw her trotting alongside your Ida last week in the market. Taking it all in, she was. Bright as a button.'

'And with a mischievous streak that would shame a pixie.' Queenie rolled her eyes.

'Well, now, it's only to be expected that Ida would spoil her last one,' said Bernadine.

Queenie laid her work-worn hand on her friend's arm.

'As a good Christian woman, Bernadine, the saints oblige me to tell you the truth that the spoiling of the child is not to be laid at Ida's feet.' A grin spread across her wrinkled face. 'For sure, if she stood still long enough for me to butter her and eat her, so I would.'

Bernadine laughed. 'Grandchildren are the sweet balm of old age.'

'That they are,' Queenie replied, love squeezing her heart. 'And not so much of the old, Bernadine O'Toole; for like yourself, I'm just a shade over twenty-one.'

Her friend laughed louder. 'Are you sure you've not time for a cuppa?'

Queenie shook her head. 'I've still a hundred things to do before heading home, but when next I come, I promise,' she replied, re-buttoning the toggles of her coat. 'See you at Confession on Friday as usual.'

'That you will,' Bernadine answered as she opened the back door. 'God keep you until then.'

'And you,' Queenie replied as she left.

Retracing her steps between the tubs of potatoes and carrots in the yard to the back gate next to the bog, Queenie opened it and peered around the edge into the alleyway that ran along the back of the terraced houses.

Satisfied no one would see her, she stepped across a swirl of dog dirt in her path and marched swiftly to the end of the alleyway, squelching half-frozen rotting vegetation and mud under her boots as she went.

It wasn't illegal to swap your rations, but if the Food Department at the Town Hall got wind of the fact she was exchanging a few surplus eggs for groceries, they'd be round like a shot.

Reaching Cable Street, Queenie turned left at the bottom of Watney Street, then, waving a greeting to the women rearranging the display of brassieres and corsets in Shelstone's window as she passed, she walked under the railway arch and back into the market.

'Afternoon, Queenie.'

She looked around to see Sergeant Bell, the local bobby, strolling over.

Being an old soldier who'd fought for Queen and Empire against the Boers at the end of the last century, Sergeant Wilfred Bell believed in maintaining high standards and consequently his brass buttons always shone and you could see your face in his buffed toecaps. Despite being just short of his sixty-fifth birthday, he still stood ramrod straight and could make a schoolboy's ears ring with a well-aimed clip.

By rights, of course, Wapping's long-serving beat officer should have retired years ago and been pulling pints as a landlord in a country pub, but then Hitler invaded Poland.

'And to you, Sergeant Bell. And praise be for another quiet night,' Queenie replied, indicating a couple of elderly ARP wardens having a quiet smoke outside the Lord Nelson across from them.

'For us, perhaps,' he replied. 'But I heard one landed on a block of flats in Southwark last night killing fifty people in their beds.'

'Those V-2s would shame the devil himself for evil,' said Queenie, crossing herself.

'I can't argue with you there,' he replied. 'But perhaps now our boys and the Yanks are pushing Adolf's mob back in Belgium, the Allies will be knocking on the gates of the Reichstag before too long.'

'From your lips to God's ears, Sergeant,' said Queenie, as images of the four Brogan men in their khaki uniforms flashed across her mind.

He peered into her basket. 'Out doing a bit of shopping, I see.'

Queenie gave him a wide-eyed look. 'Sure now, Sergeant, with detective powers such as those, I'm surprised you've not been promoted to the CID.'

One of Sergeant Bell's shaggy grey eyebrows lifted slightly.

'The war with Hitler might be coming to an end,' he said, 'but that don't mean me and the lads at the station aren't keeping a sharp lookout for those adding a bit of something to their rations on the black market.'

'I'll bear that in mind, Sergeant,' said Queenie sweetly.

Giving her a last lookover, the officer touched the brim of his helmet and sauntered off.

Repositioning her basket over her arm, Queenie, too, continued on her way.

Watney Street Market, which had sprung up on a bit of waste ground two hundred years before, was the place where those living in the tightly packed streets of Wapping, Stepney and Shadwell did their daily shop. The many stalls sold everything from household bleach and carbolic soap to second-hand clothes and shoes. It was also the place to pick up the latest gossip, as the small groups of women dotted along the cobbled street testified. Chickens still with their innards and feathers dangled above the kosher butcher's stall, ready to be defeathered and have their innards drawn once purchased, and a hardware stall displayed hammers, saws and screwdrivers plus tin boxes of screws. There were a number of vegetable stalls, too. Well, that's to say, potatoes, carrots and parsnips mostly, as the string beans, peas in their pods and cauliflowers still had months to go before they would be ready to make their appearance.

Behind the stalls were the shops, including a couple of shoe shops, a chemist, several hairdressers, a fishmonger and a wireless shop, which also sold records to those posh enough to own a radiogram.

Harris the butchers, where the Brogan family were registered for their meat, was amongst them, as was Sainsbury's and a Home and Colonial grocers. Of course, sadly, thanks to a visit by the Luftwaffe in 1943, the Romanesque-style Christ Church that had been built a hundred years before was now just a burnt-out shell of brick and timber at the north end of the street.

Greeting acquaintances with a nod, Queenie wove her way up the middle of the market towards the place that was almost a second home to the Brogan family: St Breda and St Brendan's, which sat a few hundred yards further along Commercial Road.

However, as she reached the top of the market a sudden swirl of troubled spirits circled around her. Emptiness engulfed her briefly then the feeling vanished as quickly as it had arrived, leaving a portent of dread in its wake.

Praying to the Virgin and the saints above to keep from harm those she held dear, Queenie turned at the top of the market and looked towards the grey-stoned church. Her heart leapt into her throat.

There, parked in the road with its door open wide, was an ambulance surrounded by a cluster of women.

With her heart pounding and her basket swinging on her arm, Queenie picked up her pace.

'What in the name of all that's holy has happened?' she asked, stopping beside Mrs Dunn.

'Father Mahon collapsed, God love him,' the rectory's housekeeper replied, crossing herself.

Fear gripped Queenie's heart. 'Collapsed! How? When?'

'About twenty minutes ago in the confessional box,' Mrs Dunn replied. 'He'd just finished having his ear bent by Peggy O'Flaherty when he staggered out clutching his chest and crashed on to the floor.'

Queenie opened her mouth to speak but the words galloping around in her head refused to form themselves into a coherent sentence.

At that moment, two ambulance men came through the church's double doors carrying a stretcher between them and all eyes, including Queenie's, fixed on the supine figure lying on it. Father Mahon.

'Sweet Mary, mother of God, no,' Queenie muttered under her breath.

His wrinkled face was the colour of well-kneaded dough, his lips were blue and his eyelids were almost transparent. For a split-second Queenie thought he'd already joined the angels, but then, mercifully, she noticed his chest rising and falling under the blanket.

She crossed herself as they passed and then, without taking her eyes from his face, followed them to the ambulance.

Standing with her knees pressing against the bumper, Queenie watched as the two ambulance men laid the stretcher on to the fixed bench on the right-hand side of the vehicle. One of them strapped the stretcher firmly to the wall while the other placed an oxygen mask over the priest's face before jumping out of the back and closing one of the ambulance doors.

'Mind your back, missis.'

Reluctantly, Queenie stepped aside as he pressed the second door firmly closed and turned the handle. Taking a set of keys from his pocket, he hurried around to the front of the vehicle and clambered into the vehicle's cab.

There was a throaty roar as the driver revved the engine, then, belching out a thick fog of diesel which stung Queenie's eyes and sent those around her coughing, the ambulance pulled away. With its bell clanging, the white vehicle sped along Commercial Road on the ten-minute journey to the London Hospital.

'Here we are, kids, Nanny's house,' said Mattie McCarthy, née Brogan, to two-year-old Robert sitting on the toddler's seat of the Silver Cross pram and four-year-old Alicia walking by her side.

'Will Granny let us gather some eggs?' asked Alicia, who with brown hair and brown eyes looked like a replica of her mother at the same age.

'I'm sure she will if you ask nicely,' said Mattie, manoeuvring the front wheels to avoid a broken paving slab.

'Bicbics,' said Robert, his cheeks red and his eyes bright in the chilly air.

Mattie smiled. 'If I know Gran, she'll have a biscuit or two for you when you get there.'

She glanced past Robert at one-year-old Ian. Wrapped up like a blue knitted parcel against the cold and having had an eight-ounce bottle before they set off from home, he had nodded off almost as soon as she'd set off to walk to her parents' house twenty minutes ago.

Waiting until a grey horse and the milk float stacked high with jingling bottles had passed, Mattie pushed her coach-built pram across the road and into Mafeking Terrace.

Situated between Commercial Road and Cable Street, the row of terraced cottages with front doors that opened on to a narrow strip of pavement was very like the dozens of other streets on the Chapman Estate.

When she'd played on the cobbles as a child, all the houses had had brightly painted front doors, whitened steps and lace curtains at the windows. However, after almost six years of unrelenting pounding by the Luftwaffe, half the windows were now boarded up to save another glazier's bill, many of the doors were held together with odd bits of wood and most of the once-white steps were given just a cursory wipe over each week. Not, of course, her mother's. Regardless of everything else she did in the day, Ida would be on her knees scrubbing her front step and a half-circle of pavement just beyond first thing every morning come rain or shine.

Recognising where she was, Alicia dashed off.

'Stay on the pavement,' Mattie called after her daughter. 'Don't burst in and frighten the hens.'

Within a minute or two Alicia had reached her grandparents' front door but the youngster knew the drill, so she continued on a few steps then disappeared down the narrow alleyway between the houses that led to the rear yard.

Mattie followed, pushing the pram down the alley towards the back gate. Flipping the latch, she wheeled the pram into the backyard.

Like the front of the house, the back had also radically changed since Chamberlain had given his fateful message. Back then, when she and her brothers and sisters were all still living at home, her father Jeremiah had been the local rag-and-bone man, and their backyard had been used as an overspill from his yard under the Chapman Street railway arches. However, when, as part of the scramble to arms, the Government had taken control of the buying and selling of scrap metal, Mattie's father had had to find another way of supporting his family and so he had set up a removal and delivery company. Now, almost five years later, it was a thriving business with two three-ton Bedford lorries, a Morris van and a diary full of bookings.

Therefore, instead of the backyard being cluttered with old wash tubs and mangles and unrideable bikes, there was now a barrel planted with potatoes alongside a row of old china sinks planted with carrots and onions. However, the most notable change at the back of the family home was her grandmother's pride and joy: Queenie's chicken coop straddling the back wall, which made a welcome addition to the whole family's rations.

Alicia was standing by the wood-and-wire enclosure watching the hens pecking around in the dirt. She looked around as Mattie walked in.

'You and Robert go into the warm, sweetheart,' Mattie said, lifting her son from his perch and setting him on his feet. 'I'll get Ian out.'

Leaving the chickens, Alicia climbed the two steps to the back door and then, stretching up, let her and her brother into the house. Gently picking up the still-sleeping baby, Mattie followed them into the welcoming warmth of the kitchen, closing the door behind her.

Her mother Ida, accompanied by the soft tones of *Workers' Playtime* drifting out of the wireless on the window sill, was scraping potatoes over the sink.

Ida Brogan was just a couple of years shy of fifty and at five foot four could look Mattie pretty much in the eye. With regular applications of light-chestnut Colourtint, she still managed to keep the silver threads at her temple at bay. Although after six children she was nearer a size fourteen than a size ten, thanks to five years of rationing and running around after three-year-old Victoria, her unexpected late surprise, Mattie's mother was still pretty trim.

Unlike Mattie, who with rich brunette hair and brown eyes favoured her father's Irish side of the family, Mattie's mother was English-rose fair and wore her light brown hair in a curly bob just above her collar.

'Hello, luv,' she said, cutting a potato in half in the palm of her hand. 'Cuppa?'

'I could murder one,' Mattie replied.

'Well, you'd better pop him upstairs on the bed first,' Ida said, indicating the sleeping infant in Mattie's arms. 'Or those three are bound to wake him up with their playing.'

'I think you're right, Mum,' laughed Mattie, as the sound of children's voices drifted in from the parlour.

Leaving her mother lighting the gas under the kettle, Mattie carried Ian through to the family's main living area.

Alicia was already sitting on the hearth rug next to three-year-old Victoria, while Robert was riffling through the old toy box in the corner.

Although younger than her own daughter, dark-haired and brown-eyed Victoria was, in fact, Mattie's sister.

'Play nicely,' she said, as she strolled past them and into the square hallway at the bottom of the stairs.

After laying the sleeping baby on the blue candlewick cover of her parents' double bed, she loosened his coat and blanket a little then removed his woolly hat. Flicking the switch to turn on one bar of the electric fire in the grate, Mattie retraced her steps back to the kitchen, arriving just as her mother finished pouring tea into two mugs.

'There you are,' said Ida, placing a mug of steaming tea on the kitchen table.

'Thanks, Mum.' Mattie tucked her skirt under herself and sat on the nearest kitchen chair.

Like the backyard, her parents' kitchen had also changed in the past few years. Firstly, the old dresser that had been wedged against the wall had been replaced by a new lemon-coloured Formica one with eye-level glazed doors and a pull-down, easy-clean work surface. Thanks to a high-explosive bomb landing three streets away that had reduced the old, mismatched crockery they'd used for years to shards, the dresser also housed the new dinner and tea sets Mattie's father had bought his wife for Christmas.

However, although the furniture had changed, the warmth and love that made the room the welcoming hub of the home was still there in abundance.

'This is a nice surprise,' said her mother, dropping the potato in the saucepan beside her.

'I'm taking the kids to the mums' afternoon at the church, so I thought I'd pop in on my way,' Mattie explained. 'Gran not in?'

'She's supposed to be.' Ida glanced at the clock over the back door. 'She said she'd mind Victoria for a couple of hours this afternoon as your dad's got a delivery and I said I'd be there at half one to cover the yard.'

'Don't worry,' said Mattie. 'If she's not back, I'll hold the fort until she arrives.'

'Thanks, luv.'

Mattie frowned. 'I hope nothing's happened to her.'

'Something happened to your gran!' Ida gave a flat laugh. 'Not likely. Queenie's as tough as old boots.' She dropped another potato into the saucepan then asked, 'Good morning?'

'Not bad,' said Mattie. 'Harris's had just got a new delivery, so I managed to nab a couple of pork chops.'

'Good for you,' her mother replied, picking up another potato.

Mattie sighed. 'Of course, it took most of this week's meat rations, so we'll have to eat offal until Wednesday, but I want to give Daniel a bit of a treat before he goes back next week.'

Her mother gave her a sympathetic look.

'Still,' she continued, 'I shouldn't complain. At least being in Intelligence Daniel will be behind the lines, not like Cathy's Archie or our Charlie.'

Her mother's face took on a soft look. 'I'm glad Charlie got leave at Christmas.'

'Not as glad as Francesca,' said Mattie, thinking of her brother and her best friend, who was now his wife.

'Cathy and the kids are coming for Sunday dinner if you all want to join us?' asked Ida, swirling the knobbly spud around in her palm as she peeled it.

'Thanks, Mum,' said Mattie. 'But as it's Daniel's last Sunday at home, I think we'll spend it together.'

'As you should,' her mother replied. 'And it said on the news this morning that the Americans have got the Germans on the run in the Ardennes, so perhaps we'll have all the men home by Easter.'

'I hope so,' said Mattie, 'because those V bombs have everyone at the end of their tether.'

'One landed on the bottling factory in Limehouse yesterday,' said Ida.

'I heard,' said Mattie.

'Still,' her mother went on, forcing a bright smile, 'at least now spring's on the—'

The back door swung open and Queenie burst in.

'I thought you'd forgotten— My goodness, Queenie, what's happened?' said Ida, seeing her mother-in-law's face, which was the colour of parchment.

'It's Father Mahon,' the old woman replied. 'He's been taken away in an ambulance.'

'Is he all right, Gran?' asked Mattie, her mug hovering halfway up to her mouth.

'Was it a fall?' asked Ida, dropping another potato in the pot. 'I thought he was very wobbly on those altar steps last Sunday, didn't you, Ma—'

'For the love of God, Ida!' shouted Queenie, her white hair standing up as she whipped off the balaclava. 'Will you cease your squawking? He collapsed.'

Mattie's mother bristled. 'Pardon me for living,' she said, wielding the knife with renewed vigour.

Queenie raised her brown eyes to the ceiling. 'The spirits told me, so they did. Swirling around me like the mist over water, they were foretelling calamity.'

Ida rolled her eyes.

'A breath away from eternity, he looked, when they carried him out,' added Queenie.

Mattie stood up and helped her gran out of her coat.

'Don't worry, Gran,' she said, hooking it behind the door. 'He's in the best place.'

'It's that chest of his, I'm sure,' muttered Queenie. 'And haven't I told him a thousand times to wrap his scarf across him under his coat when he ventures out? For wasn't his mammy a martyr to her bronchials all her life.'

'I'm sure all he needs is a couple of days' rest,' said Mattie.

'Mattie's right, Queenie,' chipped in Ida. 'After all, Father Mahon is getting on a bit now.'

Queenie glared at her daughter-in-law. 'Getting on a bit? Sure, he's less than a year older than myself.'

Ida raised an eyebrow but thankfully didn't reply.

The two women glared at each other for a bit then Mattie put an arm around her grandmother's slender shoulders.

'I'm sure the doctors will have him back on his feet in a day or two,' she said, throwing a pointed look at her mother.

'Are you?' Queenie looked pleadingly at Mattie.

'I'm sure of it,' said Mattie, hoping her gran couldn't hear the uncertainty in her voice.

Although it was true there was just under a year between her gran and the good father, Queenie could still outpace a woman half her age, whereas the parish's long-serving priest struggled to climb the pulpit steps each Sunday.

Queenie looked beseechingly at Mattie for a moment then the old woman's lined face crumpled and she covered her eyes with her hand. 'Sure, isn't the devil himself cleaving my brains with an axe?'

'I tell you what, Gran,' said Mattie, giving her a little squeeze, 'why don't you go and have a lie-down and I'll bring you a nice cuppa.'

Meekly, Queenie nodded.

'You're a darling, so you are,' she said, patting Mattie's hand. 'Not like some.'

Shooting a belligerent look at her daughter-in-law, Queenie shuffled out.

'Don't worry, Mum,' said Mattie, as Ida glanced at the clock again. 'As Gran's not feeling quite the ticket I'll stay and look after Victoria for the afternoon.'

'Are you sure, luv?' said Ida, putting the last of the potatoes in the pot.

'Of course,' said Mattie. 'The kids will be as happy playing here as at the mums' club. You go when you're finished.'

Placing the pot of potatoes on the back of the stove, Ida wiped her hands on the tea towel.

'Thanks, luv,' she said, checking her hair in her husband's round shaving mirror on the window sill.

Reaching into her handbag on the kitchen table, Ida took out her lipstick and returned to the mirror.

'Poor old Gran,' said Mattie.

'True,' said Ida, her voice distorted as she ran the colour around her lips. 'But she does go a bit overboard every time Father Mahon sneezes.'

'She is very fond of him,' said Mattie.

'Aren't we all?' said Ida, dropping the lipstick back in her handbag.

'And they have known each other since they were tots in Ireland, and he's been so ill this past year with one thing and another,' Mattie went on. 'She must wonder each time if he'll pull through.'

'Are you sure you don't mind having Victoria for the afternoon?' asked Ida.

'Honestly, it's no bother,' Mattie replied. 'And I can make sure Gran's all right too.'

'And stay for tea,' said Ida, taking her coat from the back of the door and shrugging it on. 'It's liver and onions, so it'll stretch. Now I must go.'

Ida put her head around the parlour door. 'Mummy's off, Victoria, so you be a good girl for Mattie while I'm gone. You're a luv,' she said over her shoulder to Mattie as she opened the door.

The tinkle of the bell dangling in the cage of Prince Albert, her African Grey parrot, woke Queenie from her light slumber.

Mercifully, the raw pain in her head had all but gone but the grey swirl of foreboding remained.

Satisfied that the blinding headache was truly banished, she opened her eyes and surveyed the room. With a cast-iron fireplace and the window looking on to the street, by rights this should have been Ida's best room – reserved for high days and holidays. Instead, it was Queenie's bedroom and had been since her husband, Fergus Brogan, died thirteen years ago.

Truthfully, thanks to Fergus's drinking and gambling, she'd had little more than the clothes on her back, a few keepsakes from her Irish home and Prince Albert when she'd arrived at Mafeking

Terrace but, loving son that he was, Jeremiah had made sure there was always a fire in the grate when it was needed and over the years he'd furnished the room with her comfort in mind.

The brass bedstead she was lying on had been a fortuitous early find when Jeremiah had been a totter with a horse and cart. As had the dark oak double wardrobe and matching chest of drawers he'd picked up on his rounds. He'd even found her a washstand with a china bowl and jug, so she didn't have to use the kitchen sink like the rest of the family.

She watched the bird worrying at the chain for a moment then there was a light knock at the door. It opened slightly and Mattie's head appeared around the edge.

Blessed as she was with such a number of grandchildren, she could honestly say she didn't have a favourite. That said, the sight of Mattie, with the dark hair and eyes of Queenie's long-dead mother, always squeezed at her heart. The only wonder of it was that with Dooley blood running through her veins, Mattie didn't hear the call of the spirit world too.

'Are you ready for that cuppa?' Mattie said, giving Queenie a warm smile.

'That would be grand,' she replied.

Mattie stepped into the room. 'I thought I'd join you,' she said, setting two mugs of tea on the bedside cabinet. 'Are you feeling better?'

Queenie nodded. 'I rubbed a little of last Easter's holy water on my forehead and that seems to have sent my headache packing.'

'I'm pleased to hear that,' said Mattie. 'It's not like you to have a headache.'

'Ah, well, they only strike when the spirits are raging,' Queenie replied.

She shuffled up the bed, resting her back against the headboard, and Mattie adjusted the pillows behind her before handing her grandmother her tea then perching on the foot of the bed.

'Goodness,' she said, glancing around the room. 'I'd forgotten all the little bits and pieces you have.'

'Well, as your mother was kind enough to point out, I've been around a while,' Queenie replied.

'Don't take any notice of Mum,' said Mattie.

'Rest easy on that score, me darling,' Queenie replied, 'for I never do.'

Taking a sip of her tea, Mattie stood up and went over to the sideboard delicately etched with lilies and rushes that Jeremiah had acquired for Queenie just after she'd moved in.

'This is your mum and dad, isn't it?' asked Mattie, picking up the sepia photo set in pride of place amongst the half a dozen photos Queenie had brought over with her from Ireland.

'It is,' said Queenie. 'Pa had just had the domed roof of our vardo repaired and the body repainted.'

Mattie held the picture closer. 'Your dad looks very spruce in his striped waistcoat and hat set at a jaunty angle.'

'Well, there was none such in Kinsale, so Pa had to fetch the photographer from Carrigaline to make the picture,' said Queenie. 'Mammy and me spent all morning threading ribbons into Major's mane, too, so he could put on a show between the wagon's shafts. Of course, my parents had given up travelling the open road years before and were settled in Kinsale, but Pa felt the urge to wander sometimes so he'd still visit the odd market or fair when the mood took him. He was a Jeremiah, too, as was his pa, and the boy next to him is . . .' She reeled off the names of her brothers and sisters. 'And Mammy is holding baby Margaret.'

'Your mammy looks like Jo,' said Mattie.

Reaching across, Queenie picked up her tea. 'And your darling self, too.'

'Which one is you, Gran?'

'I'm the girl standing next to Mammy.' Queenie took a sip of tea. 'I was about thirteen at the time.'

Mattie replaced the photo and glanced over at a couple of

the others, including Jeremiah and Ida's wedding photo, a studio portrait of Mattie's brother Charlie in his army uniform along with ones of Mattie and her two sisters in their ARP, Ambulance and WVS uniforms respectively. There was last year's school photo of Queenie's youngest grandsons Billy and Michael next to the most recent family photo of Victoria in the christening robe her father had worn almost half a century before.

Then she spotted a photo at the back and picked it up.

'Is this you at school?' she asked.

'No, it was taken at the church picnic.'

Mattie's eyes ran over it for a minute then she looked around.

'Is that Father Mahon standing at the end of the back row,' she asked, looking across at Queenie with wide-eyed astonishment.

Queenie took another sip of tea. 'That it is.'

'Goodness, I hardly recognised him with hair. And so much of it, too,' said Mattie, studying the image. She scanned the photo again. 'And you're standing next to him.'

'Aye, I am,' Queenie replied.

'He looks so different. Very handsome, in fact,' Mattie added. 'And who's that standing on the other side of him?'

'Nora,' Queenie replied flatly. 'His sister.'

'You all look so young,' said Mattie, still studying the photo. 'When was it taken?'

'I can't quite recall,' Queenie replied, focusing on the rim of the mug.

'Mum! Robert's made Toria cry.'

Mattie rolled her eyes. 'I thought it was too good to last. I'd better go and see what Alicia wants.'

She returned the photo to its place on the sideboard and, taking her tea with her, left the room.

Queenie placed her own cup on the bedside cabinet beside the alarm clock. Swinging her legs off the bed, and slipping her feet into her slippers, she stood up. Padding across to the sideboard she picked up the photo in the silver frame that Mattie had just been looking at.

Her eyes fixed to the faded image, Queenie smiled.

Yes. Patrick Mahon had been handsome. Very handsome indeed.

Although she'd said otherwise to her granddaughter, Queenie remembered exactly when the photo was taken. It was the summer that she'd turned fifteen.

She remembered the day as if it were yesterday.

The sun was high in the sky and as bright as the future. Until one person destroyed her happiness for ever.

Kinsale, Ireland. April 1880

'QUICK,' SAID PHILOMENA, gripping Patrick's hand as she dragged him around the corner of her parents' cottage. 'For in truth this weather's fit to baptise you.'

'Are you sure your pappy won't mind, Philomena?' he asked, as they splashed through the deepening puddles on the pathway through her mother's vegetable garden.

Sending rain flying from the tip of her nose, Philomena shook her head. 'He won't be taking our wagon on the road until the hiring fairs start in a month or so.'

As always on a day when there were no chores waiting at home for either of them, she and Patrick would wander through the meadows and wood together.

Although it was a warm Thursday afternoon and a few days before April gave way to May, the wind from the south-west had been blowing soft weather their way for the best part of the last week. So as the hollows and dells where they usually lingered in the hope of glimpsing rabbits feasting on the lush spring grass or a red squirrel scampering about in the branches were more like lakes, she decided they'd have to find somewhere drier to shelter.

Diving around the back of the beanpoles, Philomena picked up speed towards the domed wagon, with its carved wooden shafts tilted back, parked at the side of the family dwelling.

Like the hundreds of other vardos carrying families as they roamed the highways and byways, scratching out a meagre living in the villages and towns of Ireland, the Dooley family wagon was about ten feet long and comprised of a domed frame covered by a grey-green tarpaulin hammered into place at the sides. Black rough-hewn planks enclosed the back but the red-painted wooden boards covering the front were set back a couple of feet and gave way halfway across to a canvas curtain that served as a door.

With her bare feet leaving muddy footprints on the handful of steps up to the van's entrance, Philomena shoved the curtain aside and they fell into the vardo's warm, dark interior.

Collapsing in a heap, they lay on their backs laughing for a moment, then, catching her breath, Philomena turned her head to look at Patrick.

He lay with his hands on his rising chest, his eyes closed and rainwater dripping from his black curls.

In the dim interior of the wagon, with the rain pitter-pattering on the canvas roof, Philomena's gaze travelled over his curly black hair, skimmed along his forehead then down to his nose, which now he was almost to the end of his tenth year had lost some of its roundness.

He opened his eyes.

'I've never been in one of these before,' he said, gazing around at the narrow planks running lengthwise that the tarpaulin roof was nailed to. He sat up. 'Don't you have a stove?'

'Too dangerous,' Philomena replied, leaning back against the cupboard. 'Once we were pitched Pa would make a circle of stones outside then set up the tripod and pot over it. Mammy hung all her pots from the ceiling.' She pointed at the empty hook above. 'And kept all our crockery in here.' She banged the empty locker she was resting against with her hand.

He looked puzzled. 'Didn't they fall out and smash as the wagon moved.'

Philomena shook her head. 'They were enamel. Mammy and Pa slept up there.' She pointed at the raised platform at the end of the carriage. 'And we bedded down here.' She patted the floor beneath them. 'Of course, there was only me, Micky, Breda and baby Cora then. It was when she arrived that me mammy told Pa we should settle somewhere.'

'What's in here?' asked Patrick, pulling open one of the doors beneath the raised bed area.

'That's where Pa kept his knife grinder and tools,' she replied.

'What's that?' he asked, as he peered into the dark empty space.

Philomena rolled over on to her knees and, scrambling forward, followed his eyeline. 'That belonged to Granny Doodoo,' she said.

Reaching in, Philomena pulled out an old biscuit tin in the shape of Dublin Castle. There were splodges of rust all over it but the grey enamel paint of the battlements and the green of the ivy were still visible.

'This van was hers and Grampa Dooley's,' Philomena explained. 'They were Pa's parents. I don't remember Grandpa as he died when I was a baby, but Granny Doodoo lived with us, too, until she joined Grandpa in heaven just after Breda was born.'

Patrick pulled a face. 'Wasn't that a bit of a jam?'

Philomena shrugged. 'I suppose, but we were never cold in the winter.'

Sitting cross-legged, Philomena dug her nail under the lid and popped the tin open, releasing a faint musky odour.

'Is that a pack of playing cards?' asked Patrick, copying her posture.

'Yes.' Reaching in, Philomena pulled out the dog-eared cards. 'Granny Doodoo used to get them out sometimes.'

Patrick studied them. 'They don't look like normal playing cards.'

'No, they're what she used to tell people what's going to happen,' Philomena replied, studying the colourful images of a sun, a wheel, a tower and a man dangling by his leg upside down.

'How?' he asked, his eyes fixed on the one with a skeleton gripping a scythe.

'I'm not sure,' said Philomena, gathering them up. She tapped them into order then handed them to Patrick. 'Gran used to get people to shuffle them . . .'

Awkwardly, Patrick divided the shabby cards in his hands and then forced them back together.

'And then she'd lay them out like this.' Philomena placed the cards in a row on the floor between the two of them. 'She studied them for a while and then . . .'

She lowered her gaze but as her eyes skimmed over the painted images the cloying heat in the van vanished and an icy shudder slithered down her spine.

Her eyes came to rest on the image of a naked man and woman with what appeared to be an angel with its wings outspread hovering above them. A soft whispering coiled in her ears as she stared unblinkingly at the card while images of another place with no fields, brick houses and children with unfamiliar smiles and dimples flooded her heart.

'Philomena!'

She looked up to find Patrick kneeling on the cards and gripping her upper arms.

'Thank all the mercies,' he said, the fearful expression on his face giving way to a look of relief.

'What happened, Mena?' he asked.

'I'm not sure,' she replied, trying to make sense of the jumble in her mind. 'But I know somehow they are telling us that we'll still be together even when we're really old with white hair.'

Patrick frowned and started gathering up the cards.

'Isn't Father Parr forever telling us that the devil is always lurking to steal the souls of those who seek to know the future?' he said, throwing the cards into the tin and snapping shut the lid.

They sat awkwardly for a moment then Patrick looked up at the roof. Smiling, his eyes returned to her. 'Sounds as if the rain has passed over.'

Jumping to his feet, he strode to the vardo's entrance then turned and grinned.

'Race you to the top field,' he said, pulling back the canvas curtain and disappearing.

Philomena stood up and followed him out.

Patrick had already reached the front gate when she emerged, but instead of rushing after him, she stood on the front board of her family's wagon.

A smile lifted her lips.

Patrick might mark her as conjuring a fanciful story, but Philomena knew it was the spirits of the old times whispering in her ear not the devil. And glad she was, too, for didn't Granny Doodoo's shabby cards tell her for sure that she and Patrick would grow old together.

Chapter Two

AS FATHER TIMOTHY, St Breda and St Brendan's assistant priest, turned to face the congregation, Jo Sweete, the second-youngest of the Brogan girls, bowed her head.

It was just after eleven thirty on the second Sunday in February and as usual she was at Mass in her family's church.

Well, truthfully, as she'd first been carried into church as a two-week-old baby by her mother Ida, the mock-medieval church was more like her second home than a place of reverent worship.

Although the church's interior still retained some of its original fixtures and fittings, such as the carved oak altar rail, the three-foot-high statue of the Virgin in her white gown was still being safely stored in the crypt along with the statue of St Peter. As the frequency and intensity of the Luftwaffe's nightly visits had petered out during the previous summer there had been talk of putting them back in the church, but the V-1 rockets falling out of the sky put paid to that idea. The high-explosive bombs had also caused the gummed paper on the stained glass to be renewed and a fresh set of sandbags to be piled around the stone cross at the front of the church.

Members of the congregation stood ready to face this new menace from the sky, so at any church service there was always a sprinkling of black ARP helmets, navy ambulance jackets and green WVS coats, plus the khaki of the Home Guard, with the odd buff-brown boilersuit of the Heavy Rescue thrown in.

Jo had been christened at two months old, taken her first communion at seven and married her childhood sweetheart Tommy here almost three years ago. And although the saints were crated up in the crypt and there was an emergency first-aid station set up in the porch, St Breda and St Brendan's would always have a special place in Jo's life and heart.

'*Benedícat vos omnípotens Deus Pater, et Filius, et Spíritus Sanctus,*' said Father Timothy.

'Amen,' chorused the congregation.

'*Ite, missa est,*' said the priest.

'*Deo gratias,*' muttered Jo, shivering. She had arrived late so, instead of sitting alongside her family in their usual place, she was freezing her rear off in the back pew near the main doors. Crossing herself, she and the rest of the congregation slid back onto the pews as the priest began to speak again.

'The notices for this week,' he said, scanning his clear blue eyes over the assembled worshippers. 'Monday . . .' He ran through the usual days and times of services along with the weekly church social clubs. '. . . and lastly, I know you are all anxious to know how Father Mahon is progressing,' Father Timothy concluded.

The congregation nodded.

'Well, I visited him yesterday afternoon and the doctors say he is stable and in good spirits. However, they also say that it would be wise for Father Mahon to remain in hospital for another week or so, just to make sure he is fully recovered. Father Mahon also wanted me to tell you how much he has valued your prayers and hopes to be back with us in time for Lent.'

There was a collective sigh of relief.

The priest smiled again. He turned and then, preceded by the altar boys and with the choir bringing up the rear, he headed to the vestry.

Bowing her head again, Jo said a quick prayer for Tommy and her family then a very personal one to the Mother of God, a prayer she'd said each day for the past two and a half years, although it had yet to be answered.

She remained still for a moment, then, collecting herself, she opened her eyes, crossed herself again and stood up.

People were already making their way to the doors behind her to leave while others, her family included, were heading for the side door to have a cup of tea in the adjacent hall.

Waiting until there was a gap in the crowd of people filing out, Jo stepped out from the pew.

Genuflecting at the brass cross gleaming in the wintry sunlight that streamed through the window on to the altar, Jo made her way to the side exit.

The small hall that sat behind the church had been built at the turn of the century and had the Edwardian green wall tiles combined with cream emulsion decor distinctive of that genteel era. The oblong windows had been covered with wire mesh in order to stop brick or bottle from shattering the glass and, like the church itself, had been further decorated with gummed tape. Jo had attended Sunday school here as a child, as well as Boys and Girls Saturday Club and the Brownies. However, as the large main hall of the Catholic Club, situated around the corner, had been turned into a WVS rest centre at the start of the war, the children of the church now had to share their space with the pensioners' lunch club and St Breda and St Brendan's Catholic Mothers' League.

Through the crowd of men and women already sitting at the dozen or so square tables enjoying their after-service cuppa, Jo spotted her two sisters: Mattie, holding baby Ian in her arms, and Cathy with her youngest, two-year-old Rory, perched on her lap.

Well, her knee truthfully, as just a week or two away from having to summon the midwife, her sister's lap had all but disappeared.

Jo's gaze shifted down to her sister's swollen stomach and the ache lurking in her chest made its presence known once more. Damping it down, she turned and joined the tea queue.

Having said a quick hello to Ida, who was filling cups from one of the church's large aluminium teapots, Jo took her cup and weaved her way between the tables to where her sisters were sitting at the back of the hall.

'Hello, Jo,' said Cathy, smiling at her as she reached the table. 'I didn't think you were here this morning.'

Unlike Jo and Mattie, who with their dark chestnut hair and brown eyes were two peas in a pod, Cathy, with light brown hair and hazel eyes, favoured their mother.

'I was late, so I slipped in at the back,' Jo replied.

'Did you oversleep?' asked Mattie, taking a sip from her tea.

Jo shook her head.

'Tommy called.' She grinned. 'He's being posted back to take charge of the army's signals branch at Northolt, so he's coming home on Friday.'

'That's wonderful,' said Mattie.

Jo's grin widened. 'I think so.'

Tucking her skirt under her, Jo sat on the chair between her sisters.

'Lucky you,' said Cathy. 'It's been six months since Archie was shipped over to Normandy and I doubt I'll see him again until we finally send Hitler and his gang of Nazis packing.'

'Well,' said Mattie, glancing across at her sister's vanished waistline, 'at least he left you something to remember him by.'

Despite the ache in her chest, Jo forced a smile.

'He did, and this little darling,' Cathy laughed and hugged the child with coffee-coloured skin and black curly hair sitting on her lap. 'Looking just as handsome as your dad, too.'

She tickled her son and he giggled.

Something on the other side of the room caught Cathy's eye. Jo turned to see Mattie's other two children, Alicia and Robert, playing with five-year-old Peter, Cathy's eldest boy, and a couple of other children in the nursery area.

'Are they all right?' asked Mattie, looking in the same direction.

Cathy nodded. 'It looked like there was going to be a fight between Peter and Alicia over a train, but Kirsty stepped in and sorted it out.'

Ten-year-old Kirsty was Cathy's stepdaughter from her husband's first marriage and had the same dusky looks as the child perched on Cathy's knee.

'Honestly,' said Mattie, turning back, 'you have to have eyes in the back of your head.'

Jo took a slurp of her tea. 'No Gran today?'

'Mum said she went to eight o'clock Mass,' said Cathy. 'So she can have dinner on the table to make sure she's not late for the start of visiting time at two.'

'I thought she went to see Father Mahon yesterday,' said Jo.

'She did,' said Cathy. 'And the day before.'

'I'm not surprised,' said Mattie. 'You should have seen Gran when she came home and told me and Mum he'd been taken away in an ambulance.'

'I'm sure,' said Jo. 'But even so, it's a bit much.'

'She even had to go and lie down,' Mattie went on.

Jo's eyes opened wide in surprise. 'Gran had a lie-down in the middle of the day?'

Mattie nodded. 'She had a headache.'

'A headache!' said Cathy.

'Well, it's not surprising given . . .' Mattie glanced around her and then leaned forward. 'You know.'

Jo frowned. 'What?'

'About Gran and Father Mahon,' said Mattie.

Jo rolled her eyes. 'What, you mean about them growing up together in the same village? Of course I know.'

'But what if it's more than just growing up together,' said Cathy, her voice low.

Jo pulled a face. 'What do you mean "more"? Like what?'

'More like them having been close,' said Mattie. 'And more than just friends close . . .'

Jo stared at her two sisters for a moment then her jaw dropped. 'You don't mean . . .?'

'It's just Daniel's theory,' said Cathy quickly.

'Daniel?' said Jo, wondering what on earth Mattie's husband had to do with her gran and Father Mahon.

'Yes, we don't really know for certain,' added Mattie. 'But ages ago he noticed that Father Mahon and Dad looked very alike.'

Jo laughed. 'For goodness' sake, Mat. I thought your other half was in Intelligence. In case no one's noticed, Dad's six foot tall with a forty-eight-inch chest and a full head of hair.'

'I don't mean now,' said her sister. 'But if you see them together you notice they have the same-coloured eyes and the shape of their face and nose is the same.'

Jo gave her sister a doubtful look. 'I think you're letting your imagination run away with you, Mattie. And he's a priest.'

'So?' said Cathy. 'Let's face it, he wouldn't be the first man of the cloth to slip off the straight and narrow.'

'And Father Mahon may be old and stooped and almost bald now,' said Mattie, 'but he wasn't always like that.'

'I must admit I had my doubts when Mattie told me, but the more I've seen Dad and Father Mahon together, the more I think she might be right,' added Cathy.

'And when I took a cup of tea into Gran the other day when she was sleeping off her headache, there was a photo of a church picnic from years ago and Father Mahon was in it and . . .' Mattie gave them both a knowing look. 'He was the image of our Charlie, who, as everyone knows, is the image of Dad.'

'It would explain why Gran's always fussing around him and is in such a state now,' added Cathy.

'Do you think Dad knows?' asked Jo.

Mattie and Cathy shook their heads.

Jo stared at her sisters for a moment and then laughed. 'So, in fact, although everyone knows us as the Brogan sisters, we might actually be the Mahon sisters.'

*

'Blimey, Mrs Brogan,' said Ernie Freidman, glancing at the clock on the white-tiled wall and clutching a tray of bread rolls. 'It's early even for you.'

'I couldn't sleep,' replied Queenie. 'And as I've a tub of laundry waiting in the bucket under the sink, I reasoned that I might as well be about my business.'

'You're not the only one, Mrs B. Even when I'm strolling in to fire up the ovens at three, I see people up and dressed. I even saw one woman last week out cleaning her windows.' Ernie chuckled as he slid the rolls into the hopper in the glass counter. 'I suppose after five years of being woken up at all hours by the Luftwaffe we've all got out of the 'abit of having a full night's kip.'

Ernie had been one of Jeremiah's schoolmates and had worked in the bakery man and boy since he'd left school at thirteen. Always smartly dressed in his white overall and apron, with a fabric cap over his thinning, pale ginger hair, his soft bread rolls and jam doughnuts had people queuing outside his shop every morning as soon as the market opened.

And Ernie was right, half five in the morning was early even for Queenie, but as she'd been lying listening to the faint snore of Jeremiah in the room above and the ticking of her mantel clock for at least an hour, she'd finally given up on sleep and got out of bed.

Now she was standing inside Anderson's the bakers in Watney Street. Wafting around her, the mouthwatering smell of baking bread mingled with the sweet aroma of confectioner's sugar.

As it was another hour and a half until the dim-out finished, the window shutters were still down, but the interior of the baker's shop was illuminated by three forty-watt bulbs hanging above their heads, each draped with a curly length of fly paper, with victims still attached.

'Well, I'm afraid you've got a bit of a wait as there's still a few minutes until I can get the first batch out of the oven,' said Ernie.

Of course, according to one of the many commands from the Ministry of Food, Ernie wasn't supposed to sell customers fresh bread because the powers that be believed it would encourage people to eat more than they needed.

However, knowing if he didn't he'd not only upset his customers but would have his friends ignoring him, his neighbours talking about him and pub landlords refusing to serve him, Ernie wisely chose not to enforce the Government's rule.

Sometimes the local food office sent people to check that shopkeepers and traders were sticking to the rationing rules. They were supposed to blend in with shoppers, but as they dressed as if they worked in a bank and often spoke with the pronounced accent of a BBC announcer, people soon twigged who they were.

'How's your lot?' asked Ernie.

'Grand,' Queenie replied.

'How many you got now?' asked Ernie.

'Seven grandchildren and eight great-grandchildren,' Queenie replied, not trying to hide the love and pride swelling her chest. 'And there'll be a couple more yet to come, no doubt.'

'Well, you should know, Mrs B,' said Ernie.

She did.

There was one wee soul biding its time before making its presence known to the world. She suspected it might be Francesca nestling a new life as Charlie had been home on leave from his heavy artillery regiment over Christmas. However, she hoped that it was Jo, who prayed daily for a baby, who was the one so blessed.

'And yours?' she asked.

Ernie thumbed towards the door behind him to the bakery's kitchen where his wife Marie and their gangly fifteen-year-old son and apprentice Russell were weighing dough for the morning's second batch, and slapping it onto the bread troughs ready to be slid into the floor-to-ceiling oven that lined the back wall of the shop. Alongside them, Rose, the shop's assistant, was laying out trays of sausage rolls.

'Hale and hearty and working hard. I hear Jerry's doing well for himself,' Ernie said, repositioning a tray of red and yellow jam tarts alongside another tray loaded with knobbly rock cakes. 'I bet you his dad, God rest his soul, would be proud of him, don't you, Mrs B?'

A memory from long ago flashed through Queenie's mind before an image of her fiery red-headed husband Fergus Brogan replaced it.

Queenie didn't reply.

Bending down, Ernie lifted some sheets of tissue paper with 'Anderson' stamped in blue across them from below the display.

'I hear poor old Father Mahon is still in hospital,' he said, slapping the tissue paper on to the counter. 'I suppose it's his chest again.'

'So Father Timothy says,' said Queenie. 'His mother was the same. Once the wind started sweeping down from the Irish Sea in autumn, she'd be coughing her lungs up.'

Ernie gave her a curious look. 'I didn't know you knew Father Mahon from before.'

'We grew up together in Kinsale, just south of Cork,' Queenie explained. 'But I blame Mrs Dunn. Calls herself the rectory housekeeper. Sure, isn't her job to care for the good father himself as well as sweep the carpets?'

'Well, to be fair,' said Ernie, 'the good father's getting on a bit – he must be nearer to seventy by now and he can't go on for ever.'

Queenie opened her mouth to reply when Marie strode out carrying a wooden tray with tin loaves stacked on it.

'Morning, Queenie,' she said, setting the tray on the ledge behind the counter.

'And here we are, Mrs B.' Grabbing a loaf, Ernie licked the index finger of his other hand and removed the top sheet off the pile of tissue paper beside him.

'All hot and floury,' he added, wrapping the tissue around the loaf and offering it to her.

Queenie placed a threepenny piece on the counter and took the solid grey slab of bread that was the government-prescribed National Loaf.

'My thanks, and I wish a good day to you both,' she said, placing the loaf in her basket.

The doorbell above the door tinkled as another woman in a check coat and headscarf entered the shop, followed by two others.

Stepping outside, Queenie turned towards the river as a train, black smoke billowing behind it, rattled from the railway arches at the far end of the market.

Greeting the odd acquaintance as she went, Queenie made her way back home.

Ernie told no more than the truth. Father Mahon couldn't go on for ever, but Queenie wasn't ready for that yet, and in her heart of hearts she knew she never would be.

Dipping her pen into the glass inkwell, Ida Brogan wrote 'six pound seven shillings' in the right-hand column of the ledger spread out before her on the desk.

It was Monday just before lunchtime and, as was usual at this time each week, she was in the office of Brogan & Sons Home Clearance, Removal and Delivery, making sure last week's invoices tallied with the money in their cashbox.

Well, 'office' was pushing it a bit as in fact she was in the enclosed area at the back of the railway arch above which ran the Blackwall-to-Minories railway.

The office had been created by sectioning off the back twenty-five feet of the arch from the rest of the yard. Her husband Jeremiah had spent all of one weekend hammering odd doors and sundry planks of wood together. As it was at the back of the space they'd rented from the railway company for the past fifteen years, Jeremiah had also inserted a large arched window that, despite being found on a bombsite, miraculously hadn't lost its glass. This helped bring some much-needed light into the dark office.

The desk Ida was working on had been bought as part of a job lot in one of the council's bomb damage sales, as had the old-fashioned swivel chair. To her left, jammed against the curved walls of the arch, were two khaki-coloured filing cabinets containing the company's order sheets and other paperwork. There was also a squat paraffin heater that struggled manfully each winter to combat the chill from the damp brickwork of the arch. Lastly, tucked alongside the cabinet was a tea trolley that looked like something a butler would have wheeled into the drawing room of a stately home. It had lost its wheels somewhere along the way but now housed equipment vital to any office: a prima stove, kettle, half a dozen mugs and a tea caddy.

Pushing her glasses back into position on her nose, Ida stuck the invoice she'd just finished with on to the spike, squashing it down on the dozen or so she'd already dealt with that morning.

However, just as she went to dab her pen into the inkwell again, a throaty roar rattled the office door. Raising her head, Ida looked through the window as a three-ton Bedford lorry with 'Brogan & Sons' painted in yellow on the side drew to a halt in the empty yard. The rumble of the engine stopped as the driver's door opened and Jeremiah leapt down.

Jeremiah Brogan still had a full head of curly hair and if it wasn't as black or as full as it used to be, there was many a man half his age who'd be happy to have it. Standing just a shade under six foot in his stockinged feet, age hadn't diminished his upright bearing while a lifetime of humping goods on and off wagons and lorries meant he'd retained his barrel chest and avoided the middle-age spread of some of his longstanding friends.

Although, as always, he was dressed in worn corduroy trousers, faded collarless shirt and a shapeless donkey jacket over his trademark colourful waistcoat, watching him stride towards her reminded Ida why she'd been so keen to marry him almost thirty years before.

The brass handle rattled as he opened the door and walked in.

'Hello, luv,' said Ida. 'I was expecting you back before now.'

'I would have been, but the foreman at Wrights and Sons caught me when I was unloading at West End Modes,' he replied. 'Seems their main printing press was at the point of running out of paper as they've had a big order from the local Labour Party for posters.'

'Posters for what?'

He grinned. 'The election, of course!'

Ida looked puzzled.

'They're hoping for one soon,' he replied.

Ida rolled her eyes. 'Well, perhaps they wouldn't mind letting our boys finish off Hitler and his cronies first before they start tub-thumping.'

His angular face lifted in a smile. 'Have you had a good morning?'

'Busy,' she replied. 'I've managed to finish off most of last week's invoices and written out some of the monthly ones ready for posting at the end of the week. On top of that I've had half a dozen phone calls booking deliveries and two from people wanting quotes for house moves, which I've booked in for you on Wednesday afternoon as they're local.'

Picking up the foolscap diary from the desk, Jeremiah flipped it open and chewed the inside of his mouth.

'I think you're right about getting another lorry,' said Ida. 'Even with using the Morris van for small orders, we've still got a full workload every day. And it's only going to get busier.'

'You're right,' he said. 'And I don't want to have to start turning people away.'

Ida glanced out of the window. 'Will you be able to get another lorry into the yard?'

Jeremiah followed her gaze. 'Just about, although we'll have to park the van outside our house. Of course, there is an answer to our lack of space . . .'

He left the sentence hanging but Ida knew what he was talking about.

'Getting another yard?' she said.

'Well, you have to admit, luv, we're like sardines now,' he said. 'And it'll only get worse once the war's finished as there'll be hundreds of families moving out of the area. And the way things are going, we might even need a fourth lorry once Charlie returns.'

'I know, but East Ham?' said Ida. 'It's miles away. And you won't be able to just stroll around the corner to work because it'll take you at least an hour or more each day to get there and back on the train.'

Jeremiah held her gaze.

Ida stared at him for a moment. 'Jerry, you know I—'

'Just think about it,' he said. 'There's some lovely houses in West Ham with four bedrooms and big gardens and just a short walk from the High Street and market.'

'But I'll be miles away from the girls and Charlie,' said Ida. 'And what about all your mates at the Catholic Club? Not to mention your mother. You'd have to tie Queenie up and gag her to get her to move – she practically lives in St Breda and St Brendan's.' Her face lit up. 'Of course, we could leave her behind.'

'Ida.' Jeremiah laughed. 'You're too soft hearted to abandon an old woman in her twilight years.'

'Twilight years!' Ida scoffed. 'I wouldn't be surprised if your mother outlives the lot of us. Still, perhaps it might give poor Father Mahon's ears a bit of a rest if she moved away – she gives the man no peace. I popped into the church hall a few weeks ago when the Darby and Joan lunch club was on and I found her giving him a right roasting for not wearing a scarf.'

'Widows of the parish always fuss over their priests,' said

Jeremiah. 'And remember, Ma and the good father have known each other since they were tots.'

'Even so,' said Ida. 'If you heard them together and you didn't know any better, you'd think they were an old married couple.'

Taking a step towards her, Jeremiah slipped his arm around her waist. 'What, like we are?'

He winked.

'Stop it,' she laughed. 'Anyone could walk in.'

'So?'

They exchanged fond looks then he let her go. Reaching across, he took her coat from the nail at the back of the door and held it out. Ida slipped her arms in and shrugged it on.

Stretching up, Ida planted a brief kiss on her husband's stubbly cheek and then walked past him, but as she took hold of the handle, she turned.

'You're not really serious about us moving out of the area, are you, Jerry?' she asked.

A sympathetic smile curled the corner of her husband's mouth.

'I'm just asking you to think about it, luv,' he said. 'That's all. Just think about it.'

Kinsale, Ireland. May 1881

BREATHING DEEPLY, PHILOMENA relished the sensation of newly sprung meadow grass under her fingers while all around her the bluebells nodded in the spring breeze.

It was the last Sunday in May and as the sun was just skimming the trees on the brow of the far hills she guessed it must be late afternoon, but it was no mind or matter to her because lying in the little dell with the blackbird and song thrushes trilling above her was . . .

Rolling her head, Philomena gazed at Patrick lying next to her and smiled.

Truly, for Philomena, while her soul still dwelt within her, being with him in their secret place was the closest thing to heaven.

He was stretched out on the lush grass next to her with his eyes closed and a small smile across his lips. It was over four years from their first meeting in the graveyard and now well into his eleventh year Patrick had grown taller, his legs sprouting from the bottom of his mid-calf-length trousers.

She studied him for a moment and then, rolling onto her side, raised herself up on to her elbow.

'What are you thinking, Patrick?'

'Nothing.'

'That's a lie, for I can see your brow furrowed from the thoughts in your head,' Philomena replied.

He sighed. Opening his eyes, he sat up.

'Well, Mena, if you must know,' he said, looking at her, 'I was thinking I'm sorry that when your pa enquired after work at the farm last week my pa didn't have need of any more field labourers.'

She knew about that. For hadn't she heard her pappy repeating Joe Mahon's words to her mammy as she pounded bread dough on the kitchen table. It had seemed odd to Philomena, as it was known throughout the county that a dozen of the farm labourers from the estate had set sail for America since the start of Lent. As Philomena's family rented a cottage on the estate, her father had been to see Patrick's father, Joseph Mahon, who managed one of the largest farms in the county, to ask for work.

Philomena shrugged. 'It's of no matter. He'll find work elsewhere, for sure. Even if he has to roam from here to Donegal, he'll find something. He always does.'

Alarm flashed across Patrick's face. 'Your pa won't up and leave, will he?'

Philomena shook her head. 'Dad's always threatening to hitch up the horse and take to the road again, but Mammy would tie his legs together if he tried. Not with us children at school and her having a regular pitch in the market.' She gave him a sideways look. 'Would you miss me, Patrick, if we did?'

Looking away, he plucked at a blade of grass but didn't answer.

She poked him in the ribs and he wriggled away from her finger but he still didn't reply.

'Would you, Patrick?'

'I suppose I might.'

Philomena felt a little squirm of happiness in the pit of her stomach.

Throwing the blade away, he turned to her. 'Cos you're not like the other girls who giggle in corners and are forever worrying about their ribbons.'

'Would that I had some,' muttered Philomena.

Patrick shifted on to his knees.

'You shall,' he said. 'For I'll buy them for you. Green for St Patrick and blue for the Virgin's cloak and red . . . and red for no other reason than it's the colour that is your own.'

They laughed.

'I'd miss you, too,' said Philomena softly.

His blue-grey eyes lit up. 'Would you?'

She studied his eager face for a moment then her gaze flickered up to his black curls.

'Well, not so much you, Patrick Mahon, but certainly your wild hair,' she said, reaching out and messing up his curls.

'Hey.'

Ducking out of her grasp, he grabbed her, and they fell back amongst the grass and bluebells.

Lying on her back, Philomena stared up at the blue sky.

Patrick lay beside her for a moment then rolled over and got up on to his elbow.

'I think we should get married,' he said, gazing down at her.

Philomena actually thought her heart would burst with happiness as all the pieces of her universe tumbled into their rightful place.

'I know we'll have to wait until you're sixteen,' he added. 'But—'

'Yes, we should,' Philomena cut in. 'And we can have lots of children.'

'Yes, we should.' He nodded and then lay on his back again, putting his hands under his head. 'Of course, we'll have to make do with a cottage . . .'

Turning on her side, Philomena snuggled into Patrick as he talked about them asking his father for one of the farm cottages and how many children they would have. The oldest boy being named for him and the eldest girl for her, as was fitting. How he would work in the fields while she kept house and cared for the children.

But as Philomena gazed into the face she'd known for ever, from out of a clear blue sky a formless sensation of pain and aching loss swum around her. Chiding herself for fanciful thinking, Philomena smiled and imagined the happy life she and Patrick would have together.

Chapter Three

'THERE WE ARE, girls,' said Queenie, throwing a handful of feed through the chicken wire just as the midday hooters in London Docks half a mile away honked across the rooftops.

'Well, that's this fine morning gone for ever,' she added, looking at the grey bird perched on the end of the three-foot-high chicken run.

Prince Albert, her African Grey parrot, raised his crest and dipped his head a couple of times in reply.

It was the second Wednesday in February – St Valentine's Day, in fact – and having washed a few bits of midweek laundry and pegged it out, Queenie had put the shin of beef stew in the oven on a very low light ready for the family's supper and then headed outside to feed the hens scratching around in the coop.

It was only after Jeremiah had brought home half a dozen hens he'd acquired during his travels three years ago, and an unfortunate run-in with the local magistrate, that she'd given up being a bookie's runner for Fat Tony and turned to the more gentle and legal occupation of keeping hens.

She'd started off hatching her own chicks but, with a bit of bartering and putting her pennies from selling surplus eggs aside, she'd switched to buying new hens each year from a registered breeder out Romford way.

Thrusting her hand into the sack of feed at her feet, she grabbed a handful and scattered it on the ground. The image of the one-room cottage with an open hearth and earth floor on the outskirts of Kinsale where her family had lived came to the front of her mind. But her memory conjured up more than just her old home. She saw a young Patrick Mahon, too, along with the aching feeling of emptiness that seemed now to be her constant companion.

With her large family around her, Queenie rarely allowed herself to look back or ponder on what might have been but, from nowhere, an uncharacteristic pang of mourning for a life that had passed rose up in her.

The click of the back-gate latch being opened cut across Queenie's musing and Jo strolled in. With their rich chestnut hair and brown eyes, her granddaughters Mattie and Jo took after Queenie's Dooley side of the family. However, whereas Jo's elder sister's figure, after having three children, had taken on a more rounded shape, Jo's was still girlishly slender.

She had been wearing her Sunday best the last time Queenie had seen her, but today she was dressed in the navy military-style jacket, trousers and soft peaked cap of her Auxiliary Ambulance Service uniform.

As it did each time her eyes rested on any one of her grandchildren or great grandchildren, Queenie's heart swelled with love. God may only have blessed her with Jeremiah, but his darling children more than made up for her lack.

'Hello, me darling,' said Queenie, scattering more feed in front of the chicken.

'Hello, Gran,' Jo replied. 'Is Mum in?'

Queenie shook her head. 'She's still at the yard and she's going to pop up to Cathy's after she collects Victoria from the WVS nursery. Were you after her for anything in particular?'

Jo shook her head. 'I just thought I'd pop by. It must feel a bit strange having the house to yourself each morning now.'

Queenie gave her a wry smile.

'Oh, I'll suffer it,' she replied, throwing in another handful of feed. 'Your little sister's a joy, to be sure, but my old bones ache chasing after her.'

Jo laughed, then closing the gate behind her, she came over and stood next to Queenie.

'How are my three new girls settling in?' she asked, watching the hens pecking around in the dirt.

Queenie had over two dozen hens in total, but you needed to hand over your weekly egg ration to get chicken feed. However, three adult and three children's rations wouldn't supply her with enough chicken feed. And, of course, the busybodies from the Ministry of Food were always sniffing around To get around the regulations, on paper, Mattie, Cathy, Jo and Charlie's wife Francesca each owned the permitted number of six chickens each, which meant that all members of the Brogan family had their full egg allocation. As well as being self-sufficient in eggs, if one of the pullets stopped laying, Queenie retired it to the oven so the family also enjoyed the occasional roast chicken.

'We had a couple of days of flying feathers, but they seem to have found the measure of things,' said Queenie. 'Now, although it's grand to see you, I can't help but think you should be on duty.'

'I should be, but Blue team's been stood down for today,' Jo replied. 'Now that the doodlebug attacks are dwindling it seems the regular ambulance service don't need us auxiliaries any more. In fact, none of the team leaders have said it yet but I wouldn't be surprised if we are stood down in the next couple of weeks. Like Dad was from the Auxiliary Fire Service in January. After all, now the Allies are moving across Germany itself, it can only be a matter of a few months until Hitler surrenders.'

Queenie raised her eyes to the billowing clouds. 'Praise Almighty God and all his saints.'

'Amen,' Jo replied.

'So you'll soon be a lady of leisure,' said Queenie.

Jo laughed. 'Not likely. Dad's already collared me to help him with some local deliveries in the Morris van.'

'Well, that'll keep you out of trouble,' said Queenie, dusting the chicken feed from her hands.

'Of course, by the end of the war I was hoping that me and Tommy would have had . . .' Disappointment flickered across Jo's pretty face.

Although an aura of motherhood had recently formed itself around her granddaughter, Queenie could not sense the echo of a child yet to be born.

After a long moment Jo forced a too-bright smile on her face and slipped her arm through Queenie's.

'Would I be right in thinking now, Gran,' she said, in a broad Irish accent, 'that that there kettle's been idle on the old stove for far too long?'

As a small hand or foot pressed up against her ribs, Cathy placed her red counter on number forty-three then handed the Bakelite beaker with the dice inside to the ten-year-old girl sitting next to her at the dinner table.

'Go on, Kirsty, throw a six,' she said, as her stepdaughter shook the dice. 'Then you can go up that ladder on number fifteen.'

Watched eagerly by Cathy's brothers, fifteen-year-old Billy and fourteen-year-old Michael, Kirsty rattled the dice.

As it was Sunday, Kirsty was in her best light blue dress, which complemented her coffee-coloured complexion; her black hair was plaited into two long braids. The boys, however, had put their school uniforms back in the wardrobe after church and were now in their usual corduroy shorts and old shirts.

It was just after three and Cathy was in her parents' back parlour having polished off one of her mother's ginormous Sunday dinners an hour before.

Her parents' family room was where she'd taken her first steps as a toddler, where she and her two sisters, Mattie and Jo, had squabbled over dolls. However, since then the room, like the rest of her family's old three-up three-down, had changed.

Before the outbreak of war – when her father's income as a rag-and-bone man was uncertain some days and non-existent on others – the furniture in the back parlour had been harvested from his daily rounds. However, in the past couple of years, as Brogan & Sons Home Clearance, Removal and Delivery had grown, much of the heavy oak Victorian furniture had been replaced by more modern pieces, most notably a new russet-coloured art deco three-piece suite. The mantelshelf, too, had been cleared of some of the old clutter her mother had accumulated over the years and now had Spelter statues of two willowy women holding a vase of flowers and a harp respectively with a brass carriage clock sitting between them.

Of course, some things remained the same, such as her father's pride and joy: a tall mahogany bookcase crammed with all manner of books, including a set of eleventh-edition *Encyclopaedia Britannica* that she and her brothers and sisters had pored over as children and that now regularly came off the shelf so the grandchildren could do the same.

After cajoling the two boys into helping him do the washing-up, Cathy's father Jeremiah had gone for a pint in the Catholic Club, but the remaining members of the Brogan family were enjoying the afternoon together. Queenie was snoozing in one of the fireside chairs while Ida sat knitting in another.

Cathy's son Peter and his three-year-old auntie Victoria were playing tea parties with their teddies and a couple of dolls on the hearth rug. Having cleaned his plate at dinner time, Rory was having his afternoon snooze tucked under a blanket on the sofa.

Cathy puffed as the baby, squeezed between her pelvis and ribcage, shifted around again.

'Is the baby moving?' asked Kirsty.

Breathing out slowly, Cathy nodded.

Her stepdaughter's eyes lit up. 'Can I feel?'

'Of course you can,' Cathy replied, smiling at her. 'Just here.'

She placed her hand on the spot where she could feel movement and Kirsty laid hers alongside.

Her eyes grew wider. 'Does it hurt?'

Cathy shook her head. 'It's a bit uncomfortable, that's all.'

'It's your go, Kirsty,' said Michael.

Taking her hand back, Kirsty shook the beaker then released the cube, which rolled across the printed snakes and ladders and stopped with the number three facing up.

'Bad luck,' said Michael, as she moved her blue counter forward.

'My turn,' said Billy, grabbing the cup.

'Don't snatch,' said Kirsty.

'Didn't.'

'Yes you did,' said Michael.

Billy rolled the dice across the board and it stopped with a single dot uppermost.

'One,' shouted Michael.

Scowling, Billy threw the cup down and folded his arms.

Michael picked it up and took his turn.

'Four,' shouted Michael, as the dice rolled across the board again.

Grabbing his green counter sitting over seventy-nine he counted along one, zipped it up the ladder to ninety-nine and then on to a hundred.

'I win,' he shouted, waving his arms in the air.

'I won last time,' said Billy.

'No, I won the last game,' said Kirsty.

'Well, I'll beat you both next time,' said Billy, setting the counters back on number one.

'For goodness' sake, boys,' said Ida, giving them both an exasperated look. 'Sunday is *supposed* to be a day of rest, so I don't want to have to listen to you two fighting all afternoon.'

'Billy started it,' said Michael.

'No I didn't,' shouted Billy. 'You did.'

Opening her eyes, Queenie pushed her upper set of dentures back into place then pulled herself upright in her armchair.

'Look, now you've woke your gran up,' said Ida.

'Waking me!' said Queenie, giving them both a hard look. 'Sure, weren't the both of you making noise enough to bring the dead from their graves?'

Suitably chastised, the boys started to reset the counters on the board.

'Count me out.' Cathy pushed herself away from the table and stood up. 'I'm putting the kettle on. Anyone for a cuppa?'

'That would be grand, luv,' said Queenie, picking up the newspaper that had slipped off her lap.

The muscle running around from Cathy's back to just above her pubic bone, which had been cramping on and off all day, made its presence known again and she stretched back to ease it.

'You go and put your feet up on the sofa, luv,' said Ida, putting her knitting aside. 'I'll do it.'

'It's all right, Mum. It's just a bit of cramp,' she said, running her right hand down her swollen stomach. 'Moving about should ease it.'

There was a knock at the front door and those in the room exchanged baffled looks.

'I'll get it,' shouted Michael, discarding the shaker and dashing for the door.

'I wonder who's calling,' said Ida. 'Maybe it's Mattie with the kids.'

'I doubt it,' said Cathy. 'Or she would have said she was popping in at church this morn—'

With that the door opened and Michael walked back into the room with Pearl, Ida's younger sister, a step behind him.

Pearl was, as the old phrase goes, well preserved. Unlike Ida, who was motherly and round, Pearl was all drawn skin and bony joints. Wearing a tight royal-blue suit with a mink stole draped over her shoulders, she tottered in on a pair of high heels that made Cathy's feet ache just to look at them. She was also holding an enormous box with jolly Santas dotted all over the wrapping paper.

A bleak expression settled on Ida's face.

Cathy moved next to her mother as Queenie rose from her chair. 'Look what the cat's dragged in,' she said, and positioned herself on the other side of her daughter-in-law.

A tremor of annoyance flickered across Pearl's heavily made-up face then her scarlet lips lifted in a smile.

'Hello,' she said. 'I was passing so I just thought I'd drop in and give my boy his Christmas present from me and Uncle Lenny.'

'Christmas!' snapped Queenie. 'You're a bit late, aren't you, considering Lent started four days ago?'

Pearl gave her a cool look. 'We've been busy.'

She offered Billy the parcel and Billy went to take it.

'Don't,' said Ida.

His bottom lip jutted out. 'But it's mi—'

'Do as your mother says, boy,' snapped Queenie. 'Or I'll tan your hide, so I will.'

Shoving his hand in his pocket, Billy glowered at the floor.

'Billy, Michael, go and play in your bedroom for a little while so we can have a chat with Aunt Pearl,' said Ida.

'Yes, Auntie Ida,' said Michael. Gathering up the counters, dice and shaker then tucking the folded board under his arm, he left the room.

'You too, Billy,' said Ida, looking pointedly at him.

He hovered for a minute, then casting her a begrudging look, he sloped out after his brother.

'Why don't you join them, Kirsty?' said Cathy.

Her stepdaughter nodded and followed the boys out of the room, closing the door behind her.

As the footsteps running up the stairs stopped, Ida folded her arms and turned to her overdressed sister.

'Billy's not your boy, Pearl. He's *my* son,' she said.

Pearl gave a hard laugh. 'Come on, Ida. Billy knows the truth now, thanks to you letting the cat out of the bag three years ago.'

'Yes, he does,' said Cathy. 'He knows you left him in the Ladies at Liverpool Street station when he was barely an hour old without so much as a backwards glance. It's Mum who fed him and clothed him and loved him.'

'While you were guzzling gin and opening your legs for any Tom, Dick or Harry with a couple of shillings,' added Queenie.

Under the layers of powder, Pearl's face went an ugly shade of puce.

'Now you listen, you old bag,' she shouted, jabbing her finger at Queenie. 'I won't be sp—'

'No, you listen to us, Pearl,' cut in Cathy. 'Mum is Billy's real mum in all the ways that count, so don't come swanning in here like Lady Muck with expensive presents and upsetting everyone. We let you get away with it before because Mum didn't want to upset the apple cart, but Billy knows now so that's an end to it.'

An odd expression flickered across Pearl's heavily mascaraed eyes as they flickered down on to Cathy's bulging stomach before the customary hard glint returned.

'I don't know what any of this has to do with you, Cathy McIntosh,' she snapped. 'Or should I say Wheeler, as I believe you're still actually married to Nazi-loving Stan Wheeler.'

Rory woke up and started crying as the baby inside Cathy shifted again. Glaring at her aunt, she picked up her son and settled him on her hip.

'People in glass houses shouldn't throw stones,' Pearl sneered at Cathy. 'Everyone knows you're shacked up with that half-caste sergeant of yours without even a hope of a ring on your finger.'

'You always were a cow, Pearl,' said Ida.

'At least I'm not a bloody mug like you, Ida,' said Pearl. 'What woman in her right mind would take in her husband's bastard son?'

'I love Michael as if he was my own,' said Ida.

Peter and Victoria, who had been happy enough watching the adults in their world arguing, now stood up and hurried to their respective mothers.

Queenie's eyes narrowed.

'How many sweet souls known only to God have you poked out of you with a knitting needle, Pearl Munday?' shouted the old woman, as Peter hugged Cathy's right leg. 'I bet a pound to a penny you can't even fecking remember, can you?'

Guilt flickered across Pearl's face for a split second and then she pulled herself up. Putting the present on the sofa, she gave Queenie a glacial look.

'You wait until I tell my Lenny about this,' she said, opening her handbag and retrieving a handkerchief.

'You do that,' shouted Queenie. 'He knows where to find me, but warn him that if he comes after me and mine he won't be the first man that I've cut down to size.'

'Billy's my boy, Ida,' Pearl said, looking past Queenie at her sister. 'And nothing you can do or say will change that.'

Pulling her fur wrap tightly around her shoulders, she turned on her heels and stomped out, slamming the door behind her.

Cathy stared after her.

'I'm surprised you didn't put one of your curses on her,' she said, feeling the baby shift again.

'There's no point,' her gran replied. 'Sure, isn't the woman's soul already owned by the devil himself?'

'Better put that away somewhere before the kids get down,' said Ida, indicating the Christmas present lying on the sofa.

'I'll get it, Mum,' said Cathy.

Untangling herself from her son's embrace she bent down, but as she did she felt a pop then the sensation of water trickling down the inside of her legs. Straightening up, she glanced at the floor to see fluid pooling on the Linoleum between her feet.

The door flew open as Billy burst back into the room, with Michael hot on his heels, but Queenie put out her arm and brought them to a halt.

'Michael,' she said, with barely concealed amusement dancing in her coal-black eyes, 'will you run around to Munroe House and tell them we're in need of one of their midwives?'

'She's so beautiful,' said Jo, gazing down at the three-day-old infant cradled in her sister's arms. 'And all that hair.'

A contented expression settled on Cathy's pretty face.

'I can't say you're wrong,' she replied, her gaze returning to her new daughter, who was blowing milky bubbles in her sleep. 'In fact, that's just what Mum and Gran said when they came yesterday and I'm sure Mattie and Francesca will say the same when they pop by tomorrow.'

It was three o'clock on the Wednesday afternoon after Aunt Pearl had pitched up, and Jo was sitting on her sister's bed in her home just off Globe Road, which was just a short walk along Whitehorse Lane from where Jo and Tommy lived.

As it was only three days since she'd had Heather, Jo had expected her sister to still be in her nightdress and dressing gown, but instead she was fully dressed in a loose-fitting navy dress, with her hair pinned up. She even had a dab of make-up and lipstick on and despite having been up feeding Heather every few hours through the night, she had been up to see the children off to school. Having had her afternoon rest before Jo arrived, her sister was now propped up on a couple of pillows with her stockinged feet up and her legs covered by a multicoloured crocheted blanket.

Unlike the two-up two-down cottage she and Tommy rented in King John's Street near St Dunstan's Church, Cathy's house had three good-sized bedrooms, two reception rooms downstairs, a kitchen and scullery plus a garden. But then with four children and Archie's softly spoken mother living with them, she needed the room.

Cathy's Archie, an electrical engineer by trade, was in France, but instead of driving a tank or manning a gun, as a newly promoted 2nd Lieutenant in Bomb Disposal, he spent all his waking hours defusing booby traps left by the retreating enemy.

'She looks like Archie, too,' said Jo.

Cathy raised an eyebrow. 'Well, she's certainly got his colouring.'

That's for sure, thought Jo, casting her gaze over the baby's coffee-coloured skin and black curly hair.

Archie was half Glaswegian and half . . . well, even he wasn't sure, as his mother never spoke of his father, but whoever he was, his ancestors obviously had their roots in Africa.

'What do the boys think of their new sister?' asked Jo.

'Rory was disappointed that he couldn't play with her, but Peter gave her lots of kisses,' said Cathy.

'How sweet,' said Jo. 'What about Kirsty?'

'With two noisy brothers, she's delighted to have a sister,' Cathy replied.

The McIntosh household was a bit of a mix.

Archie and his daughter Kirsty had moved in with his mother after his first wife had died. Aggie and Kirsty had come down to London when Cathy and Archie set up home together three years ago. The boys were five-year-old Peter from Cathy's first marriage and her and Archie's two-year-old Rory.

'How's Aggie coping with the boys?' asked Jo.

'Although she'd tear her tongue out before she'd admit it, I think they're running her ragged,' Cathy replied. 'But Kirsty's a sweetheart and pitches in to help where she can.'

Cathy pressed her lips lightly on to the baby's forehead. 'Hopefully, your daddy will get my letter in a day or two, Heather, to tell him you've made your appearance, and about his painting.'

The other reason why the McIntosh family needed all the room they could get was because of Archie's dozens of canvases, sketch pads, easel and paints, which Cathy shared her front bedroom with. They were all neatly stacked in the bedroom's large bay window, so along with the smell of milk, talcum powder and new baby, there was a faint whiff of linseed oil, too.

'Which painting?' asked Jo.

'*The War Welcome*,' Cathy replied. 'You know, his one of weary infantry troops being greeted by the inhabitants of a French village they've just liberated.'

'I love that one,' said Jo. 'You can almost feel how relieved those women crowding around the troops are.'

'Well, so does the LCC – I got a letter from them yesterday saying they've accepted it, and the one he did last year, *Christmas Gift*, showing his bomb disposal crew dismantling a German booby trap attached to a drinking fountain. Both paintings are going to be part of their forthcoming War Artist exhibition,' said Cathy, with an unmistakable note of pride in her voice.

'Well, I'm not surprised, your Archie's a blooming good artist,' said Jo. 'When's the exhibition?'

'It opens on Easter Monday for three months,' said Cathy. 'I just hope Archie gets home in time to see it.' Sadness clouded her pretty face. 'And his new daughter.'

'I'm sure he will,' said Jo. 'The writing's on the wall for Hitler. Tommy thinks now the Allies have crossed the Rhine the war can't go on much longer because—'

She pressed her lips together.

'Oh, come on, Jo, spill the beans,' said Cathy.

'Tommy heard a whisper that a couple of the generals in German High Command have made contact with our top brass,' she said, in a hushed voice.

Cathy raised her eyes to the lampshade dangling in the centre of the ceiling above.

'Thank God,' she said, with feeling.

'Amen,' added Jo.

Heather gave a little hiccup and Jo's attention returned to her new niece.

'Would you like to give her a cuddle?' asked Cathy softly.

Jo grinned. 'I thought you'd never ask.'

Shifting forwards in the chair, she gently took the infant from her sister and tucked her into the crook of her arm.

Gazing down at the new-born's tiny nose and delicate eyelashes, a familiar ache started in Jo's chest.

'You're very lucky, Jo,' said her sister softly. 'Having Tommy stationed in London.'

'I know,' Jo replied, without taking her eyes from the baby in her arms. 'Not that it's done us much good.'

Cathy gave her a sympathetic look. 'Still nothing?'

She shook her head. 'I was just getting my hopes up this month because I was a few days late, then . . .' A lump formed in her throat.

'Oh, Jo,' said Cathy, laying her hand gently on her sister's arm.

'Don't get me wrong,' said Jo quickly. 'I'm tickled pink for you and Archie, but he only had a week's leave before shipping out to France and nine months later Heather arrives. Charlie was home for a couple of weeks at Christmas so I'm waiting for Francesca to announce that she's in the family way again, whereas me and Tommy have been married for almost three years and despite us only being apart for a couple of weeks now and again when he goes to Bletchley, my Aunt Flo arrives as regular as clockwork.'

'Don't worry, you're only young and there's plenty of time yet,' said Cathy.

'That's what everyone says,' said Jo. 'But me and Tommy have decided to see a Harley Street specialist.'

'Goodness, I bet you'll have to fork out a bit for that,' said Cathy.

'We will.' Jo pressed her lips on to Heather's downy hair. 'But it will be worth every penny if we end up with a little poppet like this.'

Cathy raised her eyebrow. 'Well, not quite like Heather, I hope.'

Jo laughed.

It was true it might raise a few eyebrows if she and Tommy had a baby just like Heather, but boy or girl, blonde, redhead or brunette, blue, green or brown eyes, it didn't matter if it meant that one day she'd be able to hold Tommy's baby in her arms. The six-guinea dent in their Trustee Savings Bank account would be a small price to pay.

Kinsale, Ireland. April 1886

'WILL YOU TAKE over from me while I go and fetch some more, Philomena?' said Kathleen Dooley as Mrs Kennedy, the baker's wife, handed over a few coins.

'Yes, Mammy,' said Philomena, moving closer to her mother, who was standing behind the dwindling pile of kindling.

It was Saturday and she and her mother, dressed in her rough twill dress, with her checked shawl secured across her chest, were on their usual pitch at the end of Market Street. Surrounding them were the farmers selling vegetables, cheese and homemade pies while traders from further afield had all sorts of fancy goods from teapots to ribbons and lace.

Along with the bundles of twigs and sticks Philomena and the rest of the family had gathered and tied with twine, today she and her mother were selling eggs, at a halfpenny each, and little bags of dried lavender to sweeten clothing and dissuade moths from visiting.

Of course, tucked close behind the pile of kindling, her mother had other things on offer, such as herbs to ensure women's monthlies came to pass or to placate excitable nerves and settle acid dyspepsia. And if no clergy or sisters from the convent were nearby, for a couple of coppers, Kathleen Dooley would read palms or interpret tea leaves. Skills, now that Philomena had seen her first monthly flow, that Kathleen was passing on to her daughter each night by the fireside.

'I'll not be long,' her mother called over her shoulder. 'And it's twopence a bundle and threepence for two.'

Philomena nodded.

Pulling her shawl tighter across her, Kathleen Dooley hurried off to where her husband and son Micky and their wagon were set up at the bottom of the market.

Although the spring sunlight was warm on her face, it hadn't yet taken the chill off the cobbles. Philomena stamped her bare feet to get some warmth into them.

Idly, she gazed at the crowds milling about between the stalls, but her eyes came to rest on Patrick Mahon strolling past the Conner & Son's china shop towards her. Philomena's fourteen-year-old heart did a little dance.

Even though he was the youngest of the three Mahon brothers, he topped the other boys' height by at least three inches. He was broader, too, and while his black curly hair defied all attempts to be tamed, as when she first saw him all those years before, his once-smooth cheeks now suffered having a razor regularly scraped down them.

Like most folks in the town on a market day, Patrick was wearing his rough workaday clothes, but even though he dressed in baggy canvas trousers, a frayed-collared shirt, coarse tweed jacket and leather cap, no suit made by the Tailors' Guild in Dublin could have made him look finer.

Philomena lowered her gaze. Making a play of rearranging the top few bundles, she watched him out of the corner of her eye as he strode towards her.

'Hello, Mena,' he said, stopping in front of her.

'Oh, it's yourself, Patrick,' she said, feigning surprise. 'I didn't think to see you in town today.'

'I've come with Pa,' he replied. 'He's in the Cross Keys having a jar or two and grumbling about the prices at the Cork butter market with the other farm managers. My brothers are with him – learning the ropes, as Pa calls it. Mammy and Nora are after getting some frippery or another for her new gown, so they are somewhere around too. Is your pa here?'

Philomena nodded.

'Pa and Micky are with the handcart and their knife grinder at the other end of the market and Seamus is doing a day's work guarding Reilly's outside display from sticky fingers,' she said, wondering if her brother would get a bag of fruit as well as his wages like last time.

He glanced around. 'Where's Cora?'

'At home taking care of the three wee'uns,' Philomena replied. 'Not that she was very happy about it as she wanted to come to market.'

His eyes flickered over her. 'You look very nice today.'

'Do I?' she replied, saying a quick prayer of thanks that she'd chosen her blue gown that morning and not the brown one.

'Yes,' he replied. 'That colour really suits you. Mind, had I known it,' he said, 'I'd have bought blue instead of the red.'

Fishing in his pocket he pulled out a length of ribbon and offered it to her.

'Oh, it's lovely,' she said. 'Thank you, but how . . .?'

'General Smyth's widow gave the choir a shilling each for singing the Mass at his funeral,' said Patrick. 'And I did promise you ribbons.'

She waved his words away. 'That was years ago when we were just young 'uns; I'm surprised you even remembered.'

He winked. 'How could I forget the day when we plighted our troth?'

'Away with you now, Patrick,' she laughed, oddly pleased he remembered their childish imaginings.

'And if your mammy asks where you got it say it's an early birthday present,' he added.

Taking it from him, she pulled the long plait trailing down her back over her shoulder and tied the ribbon over the length of twine securing her hair.

'It's lovely,' she said, running her finger over the silky fabric.

Patrick glanced over his shoulder towards the crowd of farmers gathered outside the Cross Keys.

'I'd best be after finding Pa,' he said. 'He'll want to be away home soon; but before I go, I wonder if you'll be going to the dance at the town hall next Saturday?'

'I will,' said Philomena.

'Good. I'll be asking you to take a turn around the dance floor with me, Mena.'

'And I'll be considering it, Patrick,' she replied.

He beamed at her. 'I'll see you there, then.'

Touching the brim of his cap and giving her that sideways smile of his, Patrick ambled off towards the pub.

With the scarlet ribbon in the corner of her vision, Philomena sold several bundles of kindling to customers and one of her mother's strengthening potions to a pregnant woman carrying a child on her hip.

Philomena watched them go for a moment or two then returned to her task. She was just taking the money from a customer for six eggs when her mother returned, carrying an armful of tied kindling.

Plonking the sticks down on top of the rest, her mother caught sight of the ribbon wrapped around her daughter's hair and a sentimental smile spread across her face.

'So young men have started buying you ribbons, have they?'

Lowering her eyes, Philomena studied her dirty toes.

'Ah, well.' Tucking her finger under Philomena's chin she raised her head. 'You're a mite young, but with looks such as yours 'tis no wonder you're already stirring lads' hearts.' Pressing her lips on Philomena's forehead, her mother kissed her. 'But I'll tell you this and tell you no more, me darling, when you've added a few more years, you'll have so many young men trying to win your favour, you'll have ribbons enough to line the street of the town with them.'

Her mother's soft gaze ran over Philomena's face again, then a young woman with two children at her skirt came over and her mother turned to serve her.

Philomena ran her fingers over the silky fabric of the ribbon again.

Perhaps what her mother said was true, but it didn't matter how many young men tried to catch her eyes or came knocking at her father's door because for her there was only one.

Not because he was the most handsome boy that ever walked God's earth but because he was Patrick. Patrick, who would stroke any dog who was in need of affection. Patrick, who dusted down tumbling toddlers and set them back on their feet. Patrick, who always had a cheery smile for the grannies of the parish. Patrick, who would one day marry some farmer's daughter who would add a couple of acres to his father's holding. But it was no matter, for as sure as the sun rose in the east, Philomena would love him until her dying day.

Chapter Four

WITH HIS BACK pressed against the wall, Billy looked along the alleyway that ran behind the houses in Golding Street and Christian Street. It was Thursday and over a week since Aunt Pearl had visited.

Pursing his lips, he let out a low two-tone whistle. A drawstring shoe-bag flew over the wall behind Billy and landed at his feet. He scooped it up and shoved it under his school blazer out of sight just as Knobby Knowles jumped down beside him.

Clutching the sack to his chest, Billy pelted along the alleyway with Knobby just a step behind. Bursting into the street, they swerved to avoid colliding with the milkman's horse plodding along on its rounds, then headed for what had once been numbers seven to fifteen Taplow Street but was now a pile of rubble, splintered beams and mangled furniture.

Knobby reached the debris first and, scrabbling across the broken bricks, disappeared into what was once the Davis family's kitchen but was now the two boys' den.

Out of sight of passers-by, Billy lifted a square of plywood that had once been the bottom of a dresser drawer and set it on what was left of the stove. He then emptied the bag onto it.

'Is that it?' said Billy, looking at the contents of the bag. 'Just four packs of fags and a couple of lemon drops.'

'It was all I could get,' Knobby replied, taking one of the sweets from the dusty surface and popping it in his mouth.

'But there's shelves of fags out the back,' said Billy.

'Yeah and Mosher's great big dog is out the front,' Knobby replied. 'Bloody thing barked as soon as I jumped over the wall.

It's only cos the shop was busy the old man didn't come out back to take a look.' He shoved Billy in the chest. 'If you don't like it, then next time you can jump over the wall and nick the stuff.'

'All right,' Billy replied. 'I suppose it ain't too bad seeing they're proper ones and not those 'orrible ration fags that make you choke.'

Picking up a packet, he took two cigarettes out and handed one to Knobby. Taking a box of matches from his pocket, Knobby struck one and the two boys lit their cigarettes.

Billy inhaled deeply. A cough threatened to catch him, but he held it back. He'd coughed his lungs up the first time he'd had a fag, but he was an old hand now.

He filled his lungs with another long draw, then, gripping the fag between his lips, shoved the packets in his pockets and climbed back over the wreckage.

Bouncing off each other as they went, the two lads headed down the street towards the railway arches where a dozen or so boys were kicking a football about.

However, as Billy drew closer, he noticed Michael was amongst their number. The unsettling feeling he couldn't quite put a name to started in his chest. Sometimes he thought it was because although Michael was ten months younger, he was at least two inches taller. Other times he put it down to Michael being a swot and always being first with an answer in class. Whatever it was, the sight of Michael always made him feel miserable and angry at the same time.

Knobby scooted ahead and intercepted the ball, kicking it up and catching it in one smooth move.

'Anyone fancy a smoke?' he asked, bouncing the ball in his hands. 'Ha'penny a piece.'

'They're Players,' Billy said, feeling Michael's eyes on him as he stood next to Knobby. 'No rubbish.'

Fishing coppers from their shorts pockets, the boys crowded around as Billy handed out cigarettes and Knobby took the money.

Within a moment or two, they'd sold the lot. Knobby handed him his half of the takings and went to join in with the game.

Michael walked over and stopped in front of Billy. 'Where'd you nick them from?'

Irritated that he had to look up at the other boy, he blew smoke into Michael's face. 'Who said I did?'

Michael coughed and waved his hand in front of his face.

Billy sneered. 'You baby.'

'Better than being a tea leaf,' Michael replied. 'And you'll get a right telling-off if Dad knows you've been smoking.'

Billy grabbed his lapels. 'You better not tell him, or else.'

Michael shoved him away and Billy lost his grip. 'I won't have to, you thicko. He'll smell it.'

Billy balled his fist and so did Michael but then Michael's attention shifted over his right shoulder.

Billy turned to see a black Sunbeam Talbot gleaming in the late-afternoon sun. It was parked at the bottom of the street, and Aunt Pearl, wearing a cream-coloured suit with a fur collar and a wide-brimmed hat, was standing beside it.

Another unsettling feeling started in Billy, but this time it was much deeper. As if somehow inside he was still a baby and all alone. He couldn't remember feeling that way before he'd found out the truth about how he came into this world.

Pearl spotted him and waved.

Billy waved back.

'What are you doing?' asked Michael.

'Nuffink,' Billy replied casually.

Smiling, Pearl beckoned to him.

Billy started forward, but Michael grabbed his arm.

'You'll upset your mum.'

Billy shrugged him off. 'Well, she won't know, will she? Unless you squeal.'

He glared at Michael, who glared back for a moment before

running to join the rest of the boys at the other end of the street.

Billy turned back to Aunt Pearl. Taking a drag on his cigarette and holding it with the smouldering end curled into his palm like the dockers did, he bowled over.

'Hello, Billy,' she said. 'How's my best boy?'

'All right, I suppose.'

A sentimental expression crept across her powdered face. 'You look so grown up I hardly recognised you.'

Straightening his shoulders, Billy pulled himself up to his full five foot three inches.

'I'll be old enough to leave school after Easter,' he said, giving his school blazer a Jimmy Cagney shrug. 'But I'm not as I'm going to take my school certificate.'

Her eyes opened wide in awe. 'Taking a school certificate? You're so clever.'

Taking another drag on his cigarette, Billy didn't deny it.

'I suppose Michael's taking it too?'

Billy's heart sunk and he nodded.

'It must be a bit difficult having him at home,' Pearl continued. 'Especially knowing Jeremiah is Michael's proper dad.'

A crushing sensation started in Billy's chest.

'He's Dad's favourite,' he said. 'And everyone's always saying how smart he is and—'

'I bet your mum takes his side too,' she continued, as a cloud of confusion and unhappiness pressed down on Billy's young shoulders.

Dropping his cigarette stub on the pavement, he ground it under his toe by way of reply.

'You know, Billy,' she said softly, as he studied his toes, 'when I see how that family treats you, I really wish I'd never given you to my sister.'

He looked up.

'Why did you, then?' he snapped.

'Oh, Billy, believe me, I never wanted to,' she said. 'I would have done anything to keep you but you have to understand I was too young. It broke my heart to leave you like I did.'

Billy studied her anguished face for a moment then his shoulders slumped.

'I know,' he replied, wanting to believe it. 'And I know you would have kept me if you could have.'

Snapping open her handbag, she took out a packet of twenty Lucky Strike.

'You want one?' she asked, offering him the pack.

Billy took it and drew out a cigarette. Holding the end to her lighter's flame, he inhaled.

'They're American,' she told him as the smoke filled his lungs.

He handed the packet back to her.

'Naw, keep 'em,' she said, dropping her lighter back in her handbag.

'Honest?' said Billy, hardly believing his ears.

'Yeah. Lenny gets them easy enough from a Yank mate of his.'

Billy shoved them in his pocket. Holding the cigarette between his thumb and first two fingers, Billy took another drag, savouring the tingle as the nicotine entered his bloodstream.

Aunt Pearl placed her hand on his forearm. 'You know, it's not too late, Billy. Me and your Uncle Lenny have got a lovely house in Forest Gate,' she continued. 'And we're not short of a bob or two, so I could treat you to anything you fancied.'

An image of the bright blue BSA Junior bicycle in the window of Roman Cycles flashed through Billy's mind.

'So if you ever get fed up playing second fiddle to Michael and having everyone going on at you all the time, now you're old enough to make your own decisions you could come and live with me, your real mum.'

Something odd twisted through Billy. He glanced around to find the street deserted.

'I'd better get home,' he said.

'Of course.' She winked. 'You don't want to give them another excuse to start on at you.'

He gave her a weak smile.

Bending forward so her face was level with his, Aunt Pearl studied him for a moment then took hold of his upper arms.

'Oh, Billy,' she said, as tears swelled up in her mascaraed eyes. 'You are the best boy in the world to me.'

She wound her arms around him and hugged him.

With his face pressed into the soft fur trim of her jacket and her heady sweet-smelling perfume engulfing him, all sorts of strange and confusing sensations batted within Billy, but before he could make sense of any of them, she let him go.

Adjusting his satchel over his shoulder, he turned and walked away.

'Bye, Billy,' she called after him.

He turned and she waved.

Billy waved back.

'Bye, Mum,' he whispered.

'Only me,' said Ida in a sing-song voice as she walked through the back door. 'Sorry I'm a bit late but the queue outside Sainsbury's was practically to the end of the street. I only went in for some tea but as I heard that they were running short on cheese I thought I'd better get our ration for this week while I was there rather than leave it until Friday.'

'Don't you worry,' said Queenie, slicing a carrot on the chopping board. 'I'm almost done. Can I make you a cuppa?'

Victoria, who was sitting up at the table with a colouring book and crayon, jumped off her perch and trotted across the kitchen to greet her mother.

'Thanks, Queenie,' Ida replied, putting her shopping basket

on one of the kitchen chairs. 'I've been so busy I haven't had a cup since three. Have you been a good girl for Gran?' she asked Victoria, scooping up her youngest child and settling the infant on her hip.

'We had a bit of a disagreement about cabbage at dinner time,' said Queenie, relighting the gas under the kettle. 'But otherwise, she's been her darling self as always.'

'I'm pleased to hear it.' Ida gave the little girl a peck on the cheek and put her down.

Victoria ran off into the parlour and Queenie heard the sound of her granddaughter rummaging in the toy box.

'Are the boys upstairs?' Ida asked, hanging her coat on one of the nails hammered into the back door.

Queenie shook her head. 'Not unless they've sprouted wings and flown through the window.'

Ida glanced up at the kitchen clock, which showed a quarter to five. 'For goodness' sake, where on earth are they?'

'Anywhere from here to Timbuktu,' Queenie replied, picking up another carrot from the pile.

'I don't know,' said Ida with a heavy sigh. 'I used to think when I was up in the middle of the night with the kids when they were babies that it would be easier when they were older.'

Queenie gave her a crooked smile. 'I'm sure the Virgin Mary said the same herself when she left our Lord in the Temple.'

'Is there anything I can do?' asked Ida, heaving another sigh.

'Pray that the ox cheek casserole that has been in the oven since midday isn't as leathery as the one we had last week,' Queenie replied, adding two heaped spoonfuls of tea to the family's earth-brown teapot.

Ida rolled her eyes.

'I know. You'd think now cargo ships aren't getting blown out of the water by U-boats that there'd be a bit more to choose from at the butchers, but if anything, it's getting worse.'

The kettle's shrill whistle cut between them and Queenie turned off the gas as Ida put two mugs on the table and added milk.

'How's things at the yard?' asked Queenie as she made the tea.

'Good,' said Ida. 'In fact, we had two delivery orders from new customers today plus another three requests for house removal quotes.'

Stirring the brew, Queenie gave her daughter-in-law a considered look. 'Have you turned your mind to the idea of moving, Ida?'

Concern flashed across Ida's face.

'Not really,' she replied, lowering her eyes. 'The war's not over yet so perhaps when it is and Charlie comes home we can talk about it then. Anyway, I wouldn't have thought you'd be all that keen to move, not with Father Mahon still sickening in hospital.'

At the mention of Patrick Mahon's name, Queenie's heart sank further.

Picking up the saucepan of peeled and chopped carrots, she drained the dirty water into the sink.

'I'm sorry, Queenie, I know how fond you are of him and didn't mean to upset you,' Ida said softly. 'I'm sure he'll be fine in a week or so.'

With her back to her daughter-in-law, Queenie didn't reply for a moment, then, squaring her shoulders, she turned.

'For sure, Ida,' she said, forcing a smile. 'For wouldn't the spirits have told me if it were to be otherwise?'

Ida gave her a sceptical look but as she opened her mouth to speak, the back door burst open and Michael and Billy tumbled in together for once.

'About time,' said Ida, turning her attention to the two boys. 'Where've you been?'

'I stayed for chess club, Auntie Ida,' said Michael. 'I did tell you. And then Billy and I had a kick-around with a couple of mates on the way home.'

'Oh, yes, sorry, Michael, I forgot.' Ida turned her attention to the other boy. 'What about you, Billy?'

Billy's eyes flickered briefly on to Michael.

'Er . . . like Michael said, I was . . . playing football and just forgot the time. Sorry, Mum,' he said, giving her his sweetest smile.

Ida gave him a considered look for a minute then nodded towards the rest of the house. 'Go on, then. Your dad will be in in half an hour so get out of your uniform and you can make a start on your homework until your supper.'

The boys ran off.

Queenie poured their tea.

'Do you mind if I take mine through and put my feet up for five minutes while *Children's Hour* is on?' asked Ida.

'Go on with you,' said Queenie. 'I'll just finish the dinner.'

Ida went to join her daughter playing in the back parlour.

Turning back to her task, Queenie put fresh water on the carrots and placed the saucepan on the back of the stove next to the one brimming with chopped cabbage.

She reached for the tea towel to dry her hands but before her fingers touched the cloth her head filled with an unearthly rumble that seemed to come up from the very earth beneath her feet.

Grabbing the edge of the enamel sink to keep herself from falling, Queenie hung on as a cloying cloud of malevolence swirled around her.

Dizzy and nauseous, Queenie staggered through to the family's main living area and Ida stood up.

'Whatever's the matter, Queenie, you're as white as a sh—'

The ground beneath Queenie's feet shook as everything in the room leapt six inches in the air and Ida's new ornaments and smart new photo frames jumped off the mantelshelf and shattered on the tiled hearth.

Victoria screamed for an instant then her voice was obliterated by a dull boom. Queenie was lifted off her feet and flung backwards against the door post, bells ringing in her head.

Behind her came the sound of pots clattering and crockery

smashing. Queenie grasped at the sideboard to keep herself upright as a cloud of choking dust filled the room.

Although her ears were ringing, the room fell utterly silent as time froze for a second then raced forward at double speed.

Ida crunched over her shattered china and grabbed her terrified daughter, showering her with kisses as the child sobbed.

Blinking to clear the grit from her eyes, Queenie turned and went into the kitchen. The pot of carrots was now on the floor, its contents strewn across the Lino, but the gas was still spluttering in the stove.

Shoving aside an upturned chair, Queenie yanked open the pantry door and grasping the handle under the gas meter, closed it off. She then flicked the electric mains switch off too.

Hurrying back into the parlour, she found Ida standing in the middle of the wreckage holding Victoria.

They stared at each other for a moment then horror flashed across Ida's face and they both looked upwards.

'The boys!'

'I'll go,' Queenie said, her voice sounding muffled because of the thickness clogging her ears.

Ida nodded.

Leaving her daughter-in-law pacifying the terrified infant, Queenie stepped over the fruit bowl and headed towards the hall door.

Tearing it open she found an empty space where, until a few moments ago, their front door had been.

She stepped out into the hallway and looked up the stairs.

'Billy! Michael!'

No one answered.

Grabbing the handrail, Queenie hurried up the stairs. Waving away the brick dust hanging in the air, she made her way to the front bedroom and opened the door.

Queenie took in at a glance the shattered glass and piles of rubble then her eyes fixed on the two boys.

Billy was sprawled across the floor against the wall furthest from the window with a cut across his forehead. He was staring at the ceiling but looked around as she entered the room.

Michael was standing by the end of his bed, the contents of his pencil case at his feet and his fountain pen in his hand.

'Thank the merciful Virgin and all heaven's angels,' said Queenie, crossing herself swiftly.

'Gran!' Michael said, crunching a plastic Lancaster bomber under his feet as he stumbled across his schoolbooks to her.

'Are they all right?' Ida screamed up the stairs from below.

'That they are, Ida,' Queenie shouted back over her shoulder. 'A bit worse for wear but safe and sound.'

'Was it a V-2, Gran?' Michael asked.

'I expect so,' she replied, grabbing his upper arms and studying him closely. 'Are you hurt?'

He shook his head. 'But my ears!'

'That will pass soon enough,' said Queenie.

Billy scrambled to his feet and looked around at the wrecked bedroom, then his eyes travelled upwards. 'Where's the roof?'

He might well ask.

Above them, the exposed wooden beams of the roof revealed fluffy white clouds drifting by in the bright February sky.

'Somewhere between here and kingdom come, I shouldn't wonder,' Queenie replied as she took in the damage to the rest of the room.

The two school desks were lying on their sides with their lift-up tops gaping open like toothless mouths. All the Airfix model RAF planes the boys had spent hours gluing together had been ripped from their string moorings on the ceiling and lumps of plaster lay on every surface.

Mercifully, the gummed paper criss-crossing the window had prevented most of the jagged pieces of glass from flying across the room, but although the shards now dangled in the window frames, smaller fragments of glass peppered the top of the chest of drawers, the rug and the blue candlewick counterpanes on the boys' twin beds.

'Now, let's relieve your poor mother's fear and go downstairs,' Queenie said. Crossing herself, she ushered the boys out of the room.

Ten minutes later Queenie hurried down the alleyway between her house and their neighbours and out to the front of the house.

'Are the hens all right?' Ida asked as Queenie joined her in the middle of the street.

Queenie nodded. 'Unsettled, but I gave them a handful of feed so that should calm them. I let Prince Albert out as well and he's strutting about on the run.'

'You went in the house?' said Ida, adjusting her daughter on her hip.

'Of course,' Queenie replied.

'But it could have collapsed.'

'It could have, but then the bomb could have landed on us too and it didn't,' countered Queenie. 'And I couldn't leave him there, could I?'

Ida raised an eyebrow. 'What about your room? Is there much damage?'

'I think t'would be fair to say it looks as if it had been hit by a bomb,' Queenie replied. 'But nothing that can't be put right. 'Tis a pity the same can't be said for the bottom half of the street.'

Although there wasn't a pane of glass left in any of their neighbours' window frames and most of the front doors were missing, the houses at the north end of the street still had their roofs; but moving south from the Brogans' dwelling the damage got progressively worse.

Whereas they'd lost just the front few rows of tiles, the house three doors down from them was missing its whole roof. The houses at the bottom end of the street had lost parts of their front walls, too, and the houses' supporting beams had collapsed in on the bedrooms. Thankfully, the Heavy Rescue and first-aid teams were already on the scene helping people caught in the blast.

'Looks like it landed over by Swedenborg Square,' said Queenie, nodding towards the black smoke belching into the sky on the other side of the railway arches. 'It's a blessing it didn't fall half a mile sooner, or we—'

'Ida!'

Queenie turned to see Jeremiah, his jacket flying behind him, pelting up the cobbles towards them.

'Thank God,' he said, enveloping Ida and Victoria in his arms.

Closing his eyes, he embraced them then planted half a dozen swift kisses on each in rapid succession.

'I saw it fly over as I turned out of Salmon Lane,' he said, taking his daughter into his arms. 'Where are the boys?'

'They've gone to give Dick and Dolly Savage a hand to set their furniture back up – with his back he can't lift anything and she's crippled with arthritis,' said Ida.

Jeremiah nodded, then his attention turned to his mother. 'What about you, Ma?'

'I'm grand, son,' Queenie replied. 'And don't you worry none. It'll take more than one of those devil rockets to have me knocking on the Pearly Gates.'

He gave her a fond smile, then, with Victoria sitting on his forearm, Jeremiah turned to survey their house.

'Well, I think I've enough plywood in the yard to board up your window, Ma, and get the door back on to secure the house, but it looks as if you and the kids would be better off at the rest centre, Ida, until we can get tidied up and I can do something about the roof.' He looked at his wife. 'And I tell you something: it's no longer a question of *if* we move, but *when*.'

Kinsale, Ireland. April 1886

THE LONG FEATHER in the musician's hat swayed above him as he drew his bow slowly across the strings of his fiddle to signal the beginning of the next dance.

Philomena was standing in the Municipal Hall's wooden-panelled function room. At the far end, on the stage, was the five-piece band: two fiddlers, a flute player, an accordion player and a man marking the beat on a bodhrán.

They'd taken up their positions about an hour ago at six thirty and everyone who was able had been on their feet dancing ever since. Even the older members of the parish who could no longer kick up their heels were tapping their feet as they supped their ale or gin. Children too young to know the dance steps were enjoying the merriments and bobbed around beside their parents under the high, gas-lit chandeliers.

Philomena was standing on the edge of the dance floor beside one of the upright pillars that held up the arched ceiling. Watching the dancers swirl past her, she put down her empty glass on the nearest table and clapped along with the music.

'Good evening, Philomena.'

She looked around and found red-haired, generously freckled Fergus Brogan standing beside her.

'And to yourself,' she replied, still clapping along.

'I see your family are all here,' he said.

Philomena glanced across the hall to where her parents sat, her mother cradling one-year-old Colin, the newest Dooley, while her father bounced Philomena's three-year-old sister Maggie on his knee.

'They are,' she replied.

'Mine, too,' he said, indicating his mother and father surrounded by their red-headed youngsters.

He noticed the empty glass on the table.

'Would you like me to fetch you another drink, Philomena?' he asked.

The bar, a plank balanced across two empty beer barrels, had been set up in one of the adjacent rooms and Ezra McConnell, the landlord of the Anchor, was doing a brisk trade.

'Thank you, but Patrick's already gone,' she replied. 'They're a good band, aren't t—'

'And you look very pretty tonight, Philomena,' he blurted out.

She smiled.

Although she'd have to confess the sin of pride in the confessional box, Fergus didn't lie. With her long hair rippling down her back and Patrick's scarlet ribbon sweeping it back from her face, and her new emerald dress that had taken her weeks of sewing, she did indeed look pretty.

'N-not that you don't always,' he continued. 'Because you do. Look nice, that is. But . . . but . . . well, it's just that this evening you . . .'

With a crimson flush colouring his cheeks, Fergus lowered his eyes and buried his nose in his ale.

Philomena studied the top of his ginger hair for a moment.

Although three years older than her, since she'd started sprouting in the places men noticed, she'd caught him looking at her with calf-eyes across the church.

'And you look very nice too,' she replied.

He looked up, a happy expression on his face. 'Do you think so?'

Actually 'twas no lie. Although he didn't have the bristles that Patrick did or anywhere near his height, Fergus was solid enough and, unlike many boys of the same age, he had very few spots.

'Yes, you do,' she said. 'And is that a new waistcoat you're wearing?'

Beneath the garment in question, Fergus's youthful chest swelled a little.

'It is,' he replied.

'Well, it looks well on you,' Philomena added.

A joyful expression replaced Fergus's embarrassed one for a moment, then his eyes flickered towards the band.

'Er, Philomena, would you—'

'Hello, Fergus.'

He turned, revealing Nora Mahon standing right behind him.

Unlike Philomena's homemade dress, Nora's russet-colour satin gown festooned with bows had obviously been made by one of Cork's many classy dressmakers. Also, Nora wore her straight light brown hair in a mass of ringlets, which must have been in rag ties for days.

Shooting a hateful look at Philomena, Nora smiled sweetly at the young man standing between them.

'Oh, hello, Nora,' said Fergus, his face colouring again. 'I didn't see you there. I was just—'

'I've been looking for you everywhere,' Nora cut in, giving him a sugary smile.

'Have you?'

'Yes, I have.' Jutting out her lower lip, Nora frowned. 'And I should be annoyed with you, Fergus.'

'Should you?' he said, blinking rapidly.

'Yes, I should,' Nora replied, coyly batting her stubby eyelashes at him. 'Because last Sunday you promised me a half a dozen dances, but you have yet to come and claim just one.'

Nora's eyes flickered onto the red satin ribbon holding Philomena's dark hair off her face.

'What a pretty ribbon,' she said tightly. 'Is it new?'

Now it was Philomena's turn to smile sweetly. 'Yes, I was given it by a friend. Why?'

'No reason,' Nora replied, lowering her eyes and brushing a bit of imaginary dust off her sleeve.

'Well, it's very pretty,' chipped in Fergus. 'And the colour suits—'

'Is it hot in here?' said Nora, fanning herself with her hand. She slipped her arm through Fergus's. 'Would you mind taking me through to the refreshments so I can get a lemonade?'

Fergus's pale green eyes flickered from Nora to Philomena and back again. 'I suppose we—'

'Perhaps we'll see you later,' said Nora as she tugged him away.

'Yes, I'll see you later, Philomena,' said Fergus, straining around to look back at her.

She watched them go for a moment then spotted Patrick returning to the hall carrying a glass tumbler in each hand.

Dodging around the jigging couples on the dance floor he came over to where she was standing.

'For the fairest colleen in the land,' he said, handing her a glass, his eyes warm as he looked at her.

Philomena laughed. 'Have you been kissing the old Blarney Stone again, Patrick?'

'Just speaking the plain truth.' He took a sip of his drink. 'I noticed as I came through that my sister's nabbed poor Fergus Brogan.'

'Yes, he was talking to me when she came over and whisked him away. His feet barely touching the floor,' said Philomena.

'Nora's had her cap set at him since the harvest dance last year,' said Patrick. 'I even overheard her whispering to our sister Martha about marrying him a few weeks back.'

Philomena raised her eyebrows. 'I wonder if Fergus knows anything about your sister's plan.'

Patrick smiled. 'I doubt it.'

The fiddler scraped out the final bar of the dance and those on the dance floor stopped swirling about and clapped. The musicians had a brief discussion then the leader counted them into the opening bars of 'Galway Bay' and people took to the floor again for the well-known waltz.

Patrick took a sip of drink then placed it on the table behind them.

'Well now,' he said, taking her glass and setting it beside his own, ''Tis a sin to have such a fine band playing and us not dancing.'

Taking her hand, he led her out onto the dance floor. Holding her at a distance that wouldn't get the town's grannies sitting around the edge tutting, Patrick stepped off and they joined the couples already wheeling around.

With Patrick's left hand in hers and his other resting pleasantly on Philomena's waist, they glided around the dance floor, but as they passed the band for the second time, Philomena cleared her throat.

'Just to remind you, Patrick,' she said, gazing up at him, 'that almost since we met we have intended to marry when we grew up.'

'That we have, Mena,' he replied, as he steered her away from another couple.

'Don't be worrying yourself.' Philomena forced a laugh. 'For when you meet some farmer's daughter in a year or two, I won't hold you to it.'

She expected him to laugh too, but instead he looked down at her.

'Well now, Mena,' he said softly, his blue-grey eyes as soft as his voice, 'the truth is, me darling, I'm looking forward mightily to honouring that promise.'

Chapter Five

AS THE CLOCK in the stone archway over her head ticked away the last few minutes to three o'clock, Queenie reached the top of the half-dozen white stone stairs leading up to the London Hospital's main entrance then stepped through into the main lobby.

It was Wednesday afternoon, almost a week since they lost their roof, and, as it always was just before afternoon visiting hours, the Friends of the London Hospital shop to her left was busy with visitors buying magazines and cigarettes for their nearest and dearest languishing in the wards above. On the right, the waiting room at the entrance to the Casualty Department had a dozen or so people sitting outside as they waited to be called through.

Of course, there was still plenty of khaki Home Guard and black ARP uniforms around, but those wearing them weren't dashing to save life and limb. Instead, like everyone else in East London, they were going unhurriedly about their business as they waited for the Germans to bow to the inevitable.

Thankfully, while Luckes Home, the nurses' accommodation, and the Alexandra wing had each suffered a direct hit during the Blitz, the early Georgian building that sat like a benevolent maiden aunt on Whitechapel Road had survived the war more or less intact.

Although Hitler was still aiming V-2 bombs at London, everyone sensed the end of the war was in sight, and those patients needing routine care were no longer ferried out to Brentwood and Orsett in Essex to keep the wards clear for bombing casualties, as they had been during the Blitz. Also, rather than boiler suits and tin hats, the nurses were back in their lilac pinstripe uniforms with puffed sleeves and frilly caps as they tended the sick.

Passing a couple of hospital porters pushing a bed occupied by a young chap with both legs in plaster, Queenie continued along the main corridor to the stairs leading to the wards above.

Grasping the wrought-iron handrails, she made her way up the stone steps. The smell of antiseptic and floor polish greeted her as she reached the second floor. Checking the signboard briefly, Queenie turned left and made her way to the Marie Celeste Ward situated at the far end of the corridor.

There was already a cluster of relatives waiting outside the ward, but as Queenie reached them the half-glazed wooden doors were thrown back and the small crowd surged forward. Bringing up the rear, Queenie followed them in.

The ward was the standard sort, with a dozen or so beds situated down both walls, all illuminated by the high windows that looked out on to Whitechapel Road. Most of the beds were occupied, with men either sitting next to them in day chairs or laying in them, the covers having been straightened by the nurses before admitting the visitors. There were two nurses sitting at the desk in the middle of the room writing up their notes, while a couple of others tended to a patient halfway down the ward. At the far end was the airy day room from which the faint sound of the Mantovani Orchestra drifted out from the ward's wireless.

There was a doctor in a white coat and a stethoscope slung around his neck standing in the ward's office to Queenie's left. He was talking to the sister in her navy blue uniform while opposite in the sluice a student nurse was scrubbing the bedpans.

As those around her hurried to the bedside of their loved ones, with the echoes of centuries of sickness and death swirling around her, Queenie paused.

While she would be the first to admit the doctors and nurses were as close to living saints as any mortal might meet, she put her trust in the old cures and incantations passed down to her by Grandma Doodoo and the ministration of the spirits. Truth be told, she wasn't one for doctors and hospitals but, well . . . this was different.

'Can I be of some help to you?' asked a soft, lilting voice.

Queenie turned and found a young nurse with bright red hair and more than her fair share of freckles standing beside her.

Queenie smiled. 'I'm wondering how Father Mahon has been keeping today?'

'Fair to middling,' the nurse replied. 'But the doctor would be happier if he'd eat a little more.'

'Now I shall do my best to persuade the good father to do as the doctor ordered.' Queenie winked. 'County Mayo?'

The nurse nodded. 'Ballyglass.'

'Well, blessings on you and yours,' Queenie replied.

With the low hum of the visitors' voices surrounding her, Queenie made her way down the ward until she reached the bed the nurse had directed her to.

Stopping at the foot she looked at the figure lying under the neatly folded blue counterpane.

A lump caught in Queenie's throat as her gaze ran over the old man lying in faded striped pyjamas with his eyes shut. With his gnarled, blue-veined hands clasped across his chest, he looked no more than a breath or two away from eternity.

But as her gaze ran over him, she didn't see a frail old man, with wisps of grey hair and bony hands, but a strapping youth with thick, curly black hair and arms strong and tender.

At the far end of the ward a bell rang and Father Mahon opened his eyes and blinked.

'It's yourself, Queenie,' he muttered, struggling up on to his elbows.

'It is and good afternoon, Patrick,' Queenie said, settling herself into the visitor's chair and putting down her basket. 'And how are you?'

'Tired,' he replied, with a sigh. 'But well enough.'

'Are they caring for you properly?' asked Queenie.

'The nurses are all darling girls,' he replied. 'I tell you, nothing is too much for them.'

'I suppose the doctors still think it's the old trouble with your chest,' said Queenie.

'So they say,' he replied. 'Although I'm surprised that lads so young can be qualified as such.'

Queenie gave a soft laugh. 'At our age, Patrick, everyone looks too young.'

A woman, dressed in a white coat and with her hair tied up in a turban, emerged from the ward kitchen at the end pushing a tea trolley. Queenie watched her as she placed a cup on Patrick's bedside locker then her attention returned to the man in the bed.

'But didn't I tell you not to leave off your scarf until the weather was a mite warmer,' she said.

'That you did,' agreed Father Mahon as he picked up his cup.

'And not to linger in the vestry because of the fearsome draught from the windows?' she added, as he took a large mouthful of tea.

'And I've been mindful of your advice ever since,' he said, a fond expression softening his blue-grey eyes.

Queenie held his gaze for a moment then dived into the basket, pulling out a square, greaseproof packet.

'I brought you a little something in case they're not feeding you properly,' she said, placing it on the top of his bedside locker. 'They're sardine.'

'That's grand of you but the food is fine enough, although sometimes I haven't the appetite to do it justice,' he said.

Worry bubbled in Queenie's chest.

'You must try to eat, Patrick,' she said. 'For how would we manage without you?'

'Now, now, Queenie,' he said softly. 'I'm sure the lad is running St Breda and St Brendan's well enough while I'm away.'

'Father Timothy does a lovely Mass, 'tis true, but it's not the same,' said Queenie.

'So tell me, Queenie,' a kindly smile lifted the old priest's haggard features, 'how are the family?'

Queenie told him about their lucky escape after the V-2 blew the roof off the house, which had them both thanking the saints above and crossing themselves several times. She then moved on to a happier subject and gave him a quick rundown of which great-grandchild was cutting which tooth, how Michael and Billy were getting on at school, how Jeremiah was talking about buying another vehicle for when Charlie came home, Jo's ambulance station standing down, Cathy's new baby and the latest news from the Brogan men in uniform . . .

'Goodness,' he said, when she'd finished. 'Such a blessing.'

'They are that,' said Queenie.

Father Mahon gave a little rattling chuckle. 'You know, Queenie, it never ceases to amaze me that not one of your brood has Fergus's fiery red hair.'

Lowering her eyes, she brushed a bit of fluff off the hospital counterpane. 'Well, 'tis a mystery to all of us, I'm sure, how such things are decided on.'

'That's true enough,' said Father Mahon.

The ward's double doors swung open.

A young man, who looked as if he should still be in short trousers, came in. He was wearing a white coat and carrying a file. He said something to the sister who was sitting behind the desk and she indicated Queenie with her fountain pen.

With his white coat flapping behind him and the stethoscope that dangled around his neck bouncing on his chest, he strode over and stopped at the end of Father Mahon's bed.

'Good afternoon, Father,' he said, his pale grey eyes studying them both through his round, wire-rimmed spectacles.

'And to you,' Father Mahon replied.

'I'm Dr Ingram,' he said. 'How are you feeling today?'

'Better, thank you, Doctor,' Father Mahon replied.

'Good. Still coughing?' the youth asked, his Adam's apple bobbing up and down as he spoke.

'A little, but my chest doesn't feel as tight,' the priest replied.

'What you need is a few good meals and a sit in the spring sunshine. Doesn't he, Doctor?' Queenie chipped in, giving Father Mahon a fond smile.

'Mrs Brogan is a very old friend,' explained Father Mahon.

'A very old friend, who is forever reminding him to wrap up warm when he goes out,' said Queenie, giving the schoolboy in a white coat her sweetest old-lady smile. 'So when can he come home? For there's a whole parish of souls in need of his ministry.'

The doctor gave a tight smile. 'Soon perhaps, You've certainly an ongoing problem with your chest, but the consultant was concerned about some of your observations, which is why we had a second set of X-rays done yesterday. They came back this morning and I'm afraid Mr Haverstock, the consultant, is not very happy about it.'

'Is he not?' asked Queenie.

'It's nothing to worry about I'm sure, Mrs Brogan,' the doctor said in a less than convincing tone. 'It's just that we'd like to run a few more tests. Just to check your heart out, Father.' The doctor opened the file he was holding and glanced down at it.

'His heart!' said Queenie. 'Sure, I've no understanding of X-rays and the like, but even I can see it's the good father's chest not his heart that's the problem. It always has been. His mother was the same. Wasn't she, Patrick?'

'You speak no more than the truth, Queenie,' Father Mahon agreed. 'My poor mammy suffered with her chest, there's no doubt on that score.'

'Even so,' said the youthful Dr Ingram, 'we'd like to keep you with us, Father, just for a little longer so we can look into things.'

Queenie opened her mouth to assure him again that it was his chest not his heart that was the problem, but Father Mahon spoke first.

'Thank you, Doctor,' he said.

Dr Ingram gave a nod of acknowledgement then retraced his steps to the nurses' station by the entrance doors.

Queenie stared after him for a moment then looked back at the man in the bed.

'Heart! I ask you,' she huffed.

'Easy now, Queenie,' Father Mahon said softly. 'Don't be too hard on the lad; he's only doing what he thinks best and there'll be no harm in me staying a day or two longer, now, will there?'

Queenie sighed. 'You may be right.'

They sat there quietly for a moment then the bell signifying the end of visiting cut between them.

'Well, that was the quickest hour on earth,' said Queenie, retrieving her bag from the floor and standing up.

He smiled. 'Thank you for coming.'

'For sure, isn't that what old friends do?' she said. 'And who knows, one day it might be me in the bed and you visiting me.'

He gave a low chuckle. 'You in hospital, Queenie? I can't ever imagine it.'

'Well, anyway. I'll visit again in a day or two,' she replied. 'Now you rest.'

'I will.' Sinking back into the pillow, he closed his eyes.

Queenie's eyes travelled slowly over him, the frail figure bringing the lump back to her throat.

Her eyes flickered onto the hospital-issue green cup and saucer sitting on top of the locker.

She reached to grab it but then she took her hand back, fearing for once what the tea leaves might tell her.

'Cake too?' said Mattie as her sister-in-law Francesca placed a plate with a slice of Victoria sponge on it next to her cup of tea.

'Don't get too excited,' Francesca replied, settling back in her chair. 'It might be a little sticky as I had to substitute syrup for the sugar.'

It was mid-afternoon on Wednesday and Mattie was visiting Francesca at the café her father, Enrico Fabrino, owned. The two women were sitting in the family area tucked behind the main eating house.

No more than twelve by fifteen foot, the living quarters had a wrought-iron fireplace with an over-mantel mirror and rugs covering the terracotta floor tiles. The door to the backyard was still masked with a blackout curtain but, in line with the introduction of the dim-out just before Christmas, it had been pinned back, as had the curtain covering the small window beside it. Beneath the window was an ornately inlaid wooden cabinet on top of which were displayed half a dozen sepia photos showing the ancestral Fabrinos in their village dress. There was also a tinted portrait of Francesca's late mother, Rosa, and two new photos: one of Francesca and Charlie with their children and another of Francesca's brother Giovanni and his new bride.

On the circular fringed hearth rug, and surrounded by a collection of building bricks, die-cast soldiers and tin-plate cars, Robert and Ian played with Francesca's children, four-and-a-half-year-old Patrick, from Charlie's brief first marriage, and two-year-old Rosa. Alicia, Mattie's eldest, was sitting crossed-legged in one of the fireside chairs, rubbing a stubby crayon across the page of her new colouring book.

An inch or two taller than Mattie, Francesca had clear olive skin, almond-shaped ebony eyes and straight black hair so long she could sit on it, but as a busy housewife and mother of two, today she'd whirled it into a plaited bun and secured it with pins. She was dressed much as Mattie was herself, in a skirt and jumper, but whereas Mattie was wearing a Royal Stuart tartan skirt with a cream chain-pattern top, Francesca wore a navy six-panelled skirt with a periwinkle-blue cable-knit top and lacy Peter Pan collar.

Apart from being her sister-in-law, Francesca had been Mattie's best friend since Miss Gordon's infant class.

'I had to do the same last week when I made a cake,' Mattie replied. 'And Sainsbury's was so low on cooking fat the week before they were doling out just half the weekly ration.'

'You would have thought with the U-boats in the Atlantic all but out of action, the shops would have more not less,' said Francesca. 'But instead, the shelves are practically bare. And I swear, Mattie, when the war is over, I'll never eat Spam again as long as I live.'

'Or mock duck, mock marzipan, mock cream or mock anything,' added Mattie.

'And what I wouldn't give for a banana,' said Francesca in a wistful tone usually reserved for matinée idols.

They exchanged fond looks and then laughed.

'So have you heard from Charlie?' Mattie asked.

'I got a letter yesterday,' Francesca replied, pulling a pair of knitting needles and green wool from the cloth bag at her feet. 'He can't tell me where he is but says he's kept his feet dry since last week, so I guess he's crossed the Rhine by now with the rest of the Eighth Army. I just keep praying it will all be over soon.'

Mattie's brother Charlie was a bombardier on a Howitzer in the Eighth Army and having fought his way across the desert in North Africa under Montgomery, he was now doing the same across Northern Europe.

'I imagine every mother and wife in England is praying the same,' Mattie said.

'It surely can't go on much longer, not now the Allies are in Germany itself,' said Francesca.

'According to the papers, the German tanks are running out of petrol and ordinary soldiers are surrendering in droves,' added Mattie.

'I just hope that puts paid to the blooming rockets soon too,' said Francesca. 'My heart nearly stopped when Jo told me about your parents losing their roof to one.'

'I just burst into tears,' said Mattie.

'I don't blame you,' said Francesca. 'The Blitz was bad enough, but at least you had some warning, whereas these rockets ... Everyone's nerves are in shreds.'

'Any news of Gio?' asked Mattie, happily changing the subject.

Francesca nodded. 'Grace came for Sunday dinner and told us he was safe and well and working hard repairing bridges and filling up bomb craters.'

Gio – as Francesca's older brother Giovanni was known – was a corporal in the Royal Engineers and Grace was his wife of just two months.

He was also somewhere in Germany, but whereas Charlie's division was beating back the German army, Giovanni was repairing the damage the retreating enemy left in its wake.

Mattie took a sip of tea. 'What are you knitting?'

'Just a jumper for Patrick,' Francesca replied, holding up the work on her needles. 'Your mum gave me one of Billy's that he's outgrown to unwind. The pattern was in last week *Woman's Realm.*' She gave Mattie a sideways look. 'Although I might have to start knitting smaller things soon.'

Mattie's eyes flew open. 'You don't mean . . .?'

Her friend nodded. 'I'm pretty certain but don't tell anyone yet. Just in case I'm wrong.'

Mattie smiled. 'My lips are sealed but I'm so pleased.'

The door leading from the café opened and Francesca's father, wearing his long apron with his sleeves rolled up, walked in holding a cup of tea.

Enrico was no more than five foot nine, with sallow skin and thinning grey hair. Although he was probably a year or two younger than Mattie's father, he looked ten years older as he'd never fully recovered from his year-long incarceration in an aliens' internment camp.

'Look who I found in need of a cuppa,' he said, as Queenie walked in behind him.

Not one to bother too much about fashion, Mattie's gran usually wore a mismatch of clothing dictated by the weather. However, although it was the middle of the week, she'd abandoned her usual work attire and today was wearing her smart bottle-green three-quarter-length coat, the maroon dress she'd bought three years before for Jo's wedding, what looked like a new pair of lisle stockings and her Sunday hat. But the most noticeable difference was that she had her dentures in.

'Hello, Gran,' said Mattie, as the children left their toys and hurried over to her. 'This is a nice surprise.'

'I was passing and thought I'd call in. And I'm glad I did to be seeing such darlings,' Queenie replied, as she kissed the children hugging her legs.

Francesca rose to her feet, and taking Queenie's coat, she hung it up alongside the others on the pegs behind the back door.

'There you are, Mrs B,' said Enrico, placing her tea on the sideboard out of the way of little fingers.

'I'm obliged to you,' she said, settling herself back into the armchair Alicia had just vacated on her mother's instructions. 'I'll be sure to send Francesca back with half a dozen eggs when next she's down home.'

Murmuring his thanks, Enrico returned to the café.

The children went back to their abandoned toys and Mattie picked up her cup again. 'So what brings you up this way, Gran?'

'I just popped in to see Father Mahon,' Queenie replied. 'I thought I'd come and have a cuppa at the café with Francesca and see the little'uns as it's just across the road from the hospital.'

Picking up her daughter, who was having a tussle with her brother over a wooden bunny on wheels, Francesca resumed her seat.

'How is Father Mahon?' she asked, perching Rosa on her lap and giving her a rag doll she'd scooped up in passing.

'Still coughing,' Queenie replied. 'But praise Mary, to my way of thinking he's on the mend.'

'Did he say when he was going to be allowed home?' asked Mattie.

Her grandmother shook her head. 'In a few days maybe, so he'll have time to prepare for Sunday. Father Timothy does well enough but . . . no one can say the Mass like Father Mahon.'

'If they do let him out, perhaps it would be better if he rested at home for a week or two before returning to the church proper,' said Francesca.

'You're right,' said Mattie. 'After all, he is getting on a bit.'

'Getting on!' Her grandmother gave Mattie a forbidding look. 'Sure, I know at your age everyone over forty looks old, but Father Mahon is scarcely older than myself.' Reaching out, she picked up her tea from the sideboard. 'But maybe a few days more in hospital is neither mind nor matter and at least by then the tests the doctors are doing will be back.'

Mattie shared a worried look with Francesca sitting at the other end of the sofa. 'What sort of tests?'

'The doctor, who has less hair on his top lip than our Michael and looks not much older, said something about his heart,' said Queenie. 'But I told him straight it wasn't the good father's heart that was the trouble but the wetness on his chest which he got from his mother. Sure, didn't the woman sound like a pair of rusty bellows walking down the street?'

'Well,' said Mattie, 'at least now they haven't got casualties arriving day and night so the doctors can look into everything, and if they find something else wrong—'

'Haven't I just told you, Mattie?' said Queenie brightly. 'There's *nothing* wrong with Father Mahon. Nothing at all.'

'I'm sure you're right, Queenie,' said Francesca.

'Of course, I am, my dear.' The old woman's wrinkled face lifted in a cheerful smile. 'In the same way as I know that you should start knitting something pink when you've finished that jumper.'

*

Having been replenished with a further cup of tea and slice of cake by Francesca, and with five slices of cake wrapped in a greaseproof bag in her basket, Queenie left the café just as the after-school rush of mums and children started at three thirty.

Unlike many of the other cafés who catered solely for workers, Francesca's father had always provided a teatime meal for mothers and their offspring.

Queenie waited for a gap in the traffic passing along Mile End Road, letting a number 25 bus trundle past, then marched across the road and into Sidney Street. Well, what was left of Sidney Street: although the solid Midland Bank, a modest Edwardian block of flats and a few workmen's cottages were still standing, the road that joined the main East London artery to Mile End and Commercial Road looked like a war zone. Which, in truth, is what it and the rest of East London had been for the past five years.

Although, thanks to the Allies' success after D-Day, the nightly Luftwaffe raids had stopped almost a year ago, now machines had taken on the task of killing people in their houses and in their beds.

It had been the doodlebugs first, which had at least warned you death was approaching when the low buzz of their engines ceased. The V-2 rockets weren't so considerate. There was no time for a last prayer of repentance as you only knew they'd arrived after your soul had joined the light perpetual.

And if sending you to meet your maker wasn't enough, the destruction they caused resulted in children going to casualty every day with jagged splinters wedged in their arms and legs, sliced fingers from broken glass and broken bones from playing on bombsites.

Queenie walked past what had once been thriving businesses and happy homes, but were now no more than piles of charred beams and broken brick. She hurried on and turned into Mafeking Terrace twenty minutes later to find Jeremiah, hammer in hand, at the very top of a tall ladder manhandling a sheet of khaki tarpaulin.

Billy was holding the bottom of the ladder while Michael's head and shoulders were poking through the gap in the roof left by the bomb.

Jeremiah hammered in the last few nails then, after giving the tarpaulin a quick tug to ensure it was secure, he climbed down.

'Ma, you're back,' he said, stowing the hammer in his belt as she joined him. 'How's Father Mahon?'

Queenie's face formed itself into an unconcerned expression.

'Grand,' said Queenie lightly, pushing aside the hovering doubt that circled her. 'And despite the doctors insisting on some new-fangled tests, I reckon he'll be back to his old self in no time.'

'I'm sure he will,' said Jeremiah, although his tone indicated otherwise.

Irritation flared in Queenie's chest. 'I know the likes of Father Mahon and meself look like we're keeping the Grim Reaper waiting,' she snapped, 'but let me tell you, there's plenty of life in us still.'

Her son grinned. 'Which is why I'm still wary of you putting me over your knee if I give you a load of cheek,' he said, looking down at her.

'And don't think I won't,' she said, giving him a fierce look and wagging her finger at her six-foot, barrel-chested son.

They exchanged a fond look then both of them looked at their damaged house.

'The bloke from the council has said the gas mains aren't damaged, and once I've made the roof covering watertight, Ida and the kids can move back to the house.' Jeremiah looked down at her again. 'But repairs are only until we can find a house that Ida likes out East Ham way, Ma.'

Studying the packing cases boarding up the house's windows and the repaired front door, Queenie didn't answer.

'I know the war's not over yet, but when it is things will be changing, Mammy,' he continued, softly addressing her as he had as a boy. 'And we have to change with them. You know that, don't you?'

Queenie nodded.

She did.

Sure, after being a daughter, a lover, a wife, mother and a widow in her three score years and a fair few more, didn't she know that?

But Jeremiah might as well propose moving the family to China as East Ham, because until Patrick Mahon no longer walked this earth she wouldn't be going anywhere.

Kinsale, Ireland. September 1886

WITH HER ARMS tight around Patrick's neck and the smell of the fresh-cut hay they were lying on filling her nose, Philomena gave herself up to the pleasure of his mouth covering hers.

They were on top of the fifteen-foot haystack in the barn on the Mahons' farm and had been since they'd met each other after Patrick had brought the cows down for the evening milking. While Patrick had been working alongside his father and brothers in the fields all day, Philomena and her mother had been up to their elbows in diluted blood and flecks of guts, scrubbing aprons from the town's abattoir at threepence a go.

It was an unusually warm Wednesday afternoon at the very end of September, that much she knew, but as to what the time was, she wasn't completely sure. Nor, if she were to be honest, did she care. Truthfully, she didn't care about much at all at the moment other than Patrick's kisses. Well, that and his hands running over her, and his body arched over her.

After another long kiss, he released her lips.

'Oh, Mena!' he sighed.

She gave him a saucy look. 'Oh what, Patrick?'

'Sure, haven't I told you enough times already?'

'Tell me again,' she demanded, running her fingers lightly along his jaw and feeling his stubble.

He gazed down at her with that look in his eye that set her pulse racing and her stomach somersaulting. 'I love you, Mena.' He raised an eyebrow. 'Although, I'm after wondering if you can't remember—'

Grabbing his thick black curls, she pulled him towards her and silenced his words with her lips. His arms tightened around her again as she lost herself in the magic that was Patrick. Her Patrick.

After a long moment his lips left hers and then made their way along her cheekbone and then lower. Planting feather kisses on the sensitive area below her ear.

'I'll always love you, Mena,' he murmured, as his hand smothered over her bodice to cup her budding fifteen-year-old breast.

'And I'll always love you too, Patrick,' she said.

He lifted his head and looked down at her. 'I hope your father will agree to me courting you, when I ask him next summer.'

She ran her fingers through his hair again. 'I'm sure he'll be amenable to us walking out.'

Sure, wouldn't people think her father had had his wits stolen by the pixies if he did object? After all, what illiterate tinker born in a caravan would object to the son of one of the largest farmers in the area courting his eldest daughter?

'What about your mammy and pappy?' she asked.

Patrick frowned. 'I'm sure they'll be grand,' he said, in a tone that sounded hopeful rather than certain. 'I'll be seventeen, after all, and I'm sure I'll be able to prevail upon them to give us their blessing.'

To her mind, Joe and Margaret Mahon would be as mad as captured banshees when Patrick announced who he was intending to wed, but Philomena forced a reassuring smile onto her face.

His fingers brushed across the slight swell of bare flesh above her neckline.

'Although, Mena,' he said as his eyes followed, 'it seems a mighty long time until you're of an age for us to marry.'

'But it doesn't have to be.' Holding his gaze, Philomena pressed her hips into his. 'Remember how Father Parr marched Ollie Quinn out of the pub and right into church to marry Dorcas Riley when he discovered it was Ollie that had got her in the family way.'

Patrick frowned again. 'But you're not sixteen until next August so—'

'Veronica O'Dell was only a shade over fifteen when Father Parr married her and Tom Collins,' cut in Philomena. 'And everyone knows he entered her date of birth as being a full two years earlier in the parish register.' She ran her right hand over the thin fabric of his shirt and continued downwards. 'If you got me in the family way then your parents would have to let us wed because Father Parr wouldn't allow them to object.'

Philomena took hold of the hardness under his fly buttons.

Desire flashed across his face and with a low moan he lowered his mouth on to hers again in a hard demanding kiss. His hands fumbled with her bodice buttons then his hand slid beneath and closed over her breast. Bending his knee, he pressed his thighs between her legs and parted them, but just as she reached up for him, Patrick rolled back.

'What's wrong?' said Philomena, sitting up on her elbows. 'Are you not wanting to?'

'Not wanting to?' He raked his fingers through his hair. 'God, I'm fair bursting with the wanting.' Kneeling up next to her, he took her hands. 'I love you, but I want the first time we come together to be as man and wife, joined by God on our wedding night, not in a barn. And it will be.' He hooked out the small silver cross from beneath his shirt. 'Because I swear, no one on earth, including my mammy and pappy, will stop me making you my wife, Mena.'

Philomena smiled. The mute, mellow space of the barn was invaded by ethereal essences that whirled around, whispering things she didn't want to hear, but she pushed them away and looked into Patrick's loving, determined blue-grey eyes.

Her shoulders relaxed and she smiled again, knowing that no matter what, she and Patrick would be married because he'd sworn that he'd let no one on earth stop them.

Chapter Six

TAKING ANOTHER LONG breath in an attempt to steady her racing heart, Jo glanced at her husband Tommy, sitting beside her. He gave her a little nervous smile then both of them turned back to look at the man sitting across the desk from them reading the notes in a manila file.

It was the first Monday in March and two weeks since she'd visited Cathy and her new baby. According to the carriage clock ticking off the moments above the empty fireplace to the left of her, it was just before eleven o'clock.

She and Tommy were sitting in Dr Chivers' office. He was one of London's top obstetric specialists, with consulting rooms in Harley Street on the north side of Cavendish Square. The house, which had once been home to some well-to-do Regency family, was situated halfway down the street now famed for all things medical. The room they were sitting in was on the first floor and had probably seen the odd society soirée in its time, with men in morning suits and women in shimmering evening dresses swigging cocktails. Now, however, black-framed certificates with splodges of red wax lined the walls instead of watercolours and family portraits, and instead of lounge chairs and side tables loaded with canopies, there were two glass cabinets containing stainless-steel instruments next to a free-standing spotlight and the examination couch where Jo had spent the most embarrassing twenty minutes of her life last Thursday.

As befitted his status, Dr Chivers, who was somewhere north of fifty with a face like a Roman general, was wearing a black three-piece suit with a gold fob chain and spotted bowtie. Although Jo's attire couldn't match his Savile Row outfit, she looked well enough in her royal-blue going-away suit and navy Robin Hood-style hat. However, Tommy outdid them both, looking extremely dapper in his Royal Signals uniform with a three-chevron sergeant's insignia on the battle-jacket sleeves. But then, to be truthful, she always thought he outshone everyone and had done ever since she'd first laid eyes on him when she was a pigtailed schoolgirl in the first year of junior school and he was one of the big boys in year four. She'd loved him more with every passing day, which was why each month when her period arrived, the ache to carry Tommy's child grew deeper.

He'd met her at Oxford Circus station half an hour ago and they'd walked through the burnt-out shells of the elegant Victorian townhouses behind Oxford Street, past the rubble that had been John Lewis's department store before crossing Cavendish Square to Harley Street.

As a V-2 had landed somewhere west of them the day before, the ARP wardens, in their black uniforms and tin hats, and dust-covered Heavy Rescue teams, carrying picks and shovels, were much in evidence. And, as they had done for the past five years when Londoners were in desperate need of a cuppa, the green-clad women of the WVS had set up a mobile canteen and were doling out mugs of tea and slices of homemade cake.

As the mechanism of the carriage clock whirled to strike the hour, Dr Chivers looked over his half-rimmed spectacles at them.

'Well, Sergeant and Mrs Sweete,' he said, in a voice that would have made a BBC announcer sound like a Petticoat Lane barrow boy. 'We now have the results of all your tests.'

Jo's heart fluttered and she clasped her hands on her lap a little tighter.

'Infertility can be due to a variety of factors, some simple and some more complex,' the consultant continued. 'Sometimes it can be a simple thing such as anaemia, but your blood test ruled that out, Mrs Sweete. As far as I can ascertain, as your periods appear to be within the parameters of what is regarded, obstetrically, as regular, your failure to conceive isn't caused because you're not producing an egg each month. Having eliminated the most obvious cause, I had to consider the possibility that you had a misaligned or even deformed womb but, again, Mrs Sweete's reproductive organs looked healthy in the X-ray, and my examination confirmed that.'

'What about my tests?' asked Tommy.

One of Dr Chivers' substantial eyebrows rose a little.

'I have to tell you, usually I wouldn't have undertaken a fluid test on a healthy young man such as yourself as, in my experience, the failure to conceive in the vast majority of cases lies with the woman. However, as you asked for it, I'm very pleased to be able to inform you that your little chaps are both plentiful and active.' Closing the file on the desk in front of him, Dr Chivers rested his well-manicured hand on it. 'So, in conclusion, I'm delighted to be able to inform you that, as far as I can discern, there is absolutely no reason why you haven't been blessed with a bundle of joy thus far, nor why that won't happen in the very near future.'

Reaching across, Tommy took Jo's hand. 'That's good news, isn't it, luv?'

Jo smiled at him then their attention returned to the consultant.

'You're both still young; you've got plenty of time.' A lofty expression slid across the consultant's face. 'My advice to you, Sergeant and Mrs Sweete, is to relax, try to put it from your mind and just wait for nature to take its course.'

As he reached the top of the stairs, Billy rummaged around in his school-trouser pocket and pulled out the threepenny ticket he'd purchased at Stepney Green station half an hour before.

He handed it to the elderly man in the booth who was dressed in the navy uniform and peaked cap of the Great Eastern Railway.

'Cuse me,' he said. 'Can you tell me which way to Claremont Road?'

'Turn right out of the station and it's on your left before the bombed-out Methodist church,' the ticket collector replied.

Billy started towards the station's exit.

The ticket collector stuck his arm out and barred his way. 'Oi! Where are your manners?'

'Thanks; I mean, thank you,' said Billy.

From beneath his peaked cap the railway employee gave him a jaundiced look then dropped his arm.

'Bloody kids today,' the man muttered to no one in particular as Billy walked past.

It was just over a week since he'd met Aunt Pearl in the street. Michael hadn't told their parents about it and Billy had been able to sell the American cigarettes for three farthings each, so the prospect of another couple of packets of Lucky Strike was tempting, although he hadn't quite managed to pluck up the courage to actually visit Pearl until now.

Leaving Forest Gate station, he looked around. The road in front of him had the same assortment of shops and banks as anywhere else and the same sort of queues outside them. Being a Tuesday afternoon, the street was busy, mainly with women pushing prams. However, as there were a number of roughly dressed men wearing tin hats with the letter W stamped on the front and several navy-uniformed ARP wardens supping tea by the WVS mobile canteen at the junction with Romford Road, a V-2 had obviously crashed to earth somewhere nearby recently.

Straightening his school cap, Billy followed the ticket collector's directions and within a few moments he had reached Claremont Road.

A niggle of guilt bubbled in his chest as he thought about his mum chopping vegetables for the family's supper that morning, but he shoved it aside and marched on.

Like every other street in East London, the houses lining each side of the road had their fair share of cracked windows and missing tiles, but unlike his house on Mafeking Terrace, which was squashed in between two other houses, the dwellings he now walked past had a space between them that was wide enough for two people to walk down side by side. The houses were double fronted with a window on either side of the front door, and above the windows on the second floor a smaller skylight inset into the pitched roof was just visible over the castle-like brick parapets. Also, whereas his parents' front door opened straight on to the pavement, the houses in Claremont Road had small gardens at the front with a path leading to the front door.

Noting the door numbers as he went, Billy carried on until he came to one with stone pillars topped with dragons holding shields.

Stopping halfway down the black-and-white mosaic front path, Billy's gaze travelled over the black lacquered door with a shining brass knocker as big as a cabbage then up over the lace-curtained windows. But before he could continue up the path, the door opened. A man even taller and broader than Billy's father and dressed in a black suit and black tie stepped out.

'Wot you want?' he asked, the scar on the right side of his face puckering as he spoke.

'I've come to see my . . . my Aunt Pearl,' said Billy.

'Is she expecting you?'

Billy shook his head. 'But she said I could come any time I liked. I'm Billy. Billy Brogan.'

The man studied him from under his low brow for a moment.

'Wait here,' he barked, then went inside again and slammed the door.

Billy stood staring at the enormous brass lion's head gripping a ring in its mouth for a few moments until the door burst open again and Pearl stood in the doorway.

Unlike any other woman he knew, who at this time of day would be dressed in a drab wraparound pinafore, Pearl was wearing a red dress with pink mules with pompoms, and had a cigarette between her crimson lips. And instead of a scarf turban, Aunt Pearl's blonde hair was swept up into a candyfloss mound. She also had a chunky set of oversized pearls around her neck and matching pearls dangling from each ear. In short, Billy thought, she looked like one of those glamorous film stars in a copy of *Picturegoer*.

'Hello, Aunt Pearl,' he said, feeling sweat prickling between his shoulder blades. 'I hope you don't mind me just turning up like this but—'

'Course not,' she cut in, a bright smile spreading across her reddened lips. 'I said you could come any time, didn't I?'

Taking her cigarette between her first two fingers, Pearl blew a stream of smoke out of the corner of her mouth.

'Come here,' she said, jangling the overloaded charm bracelet on her wrist as she spread her arms wide. 'Give us a cuddle.'

Knocking his cap off the back of his head, Pearl smothered him in a perfumed embrace.

'Right,' she said when she finally released him. 'Let's get you inside.'

Slipping her arm through his, she smiled.

For a second Billy noted that instead of his mother's natural complexion, Pearl's was flat and powdered. Also, instead of his mother's unenhanced lashes, Pearl's were loaded with mascara, but then the notion that this was somehow not right vanished, and he smiled back.

'Shift yourself, Dodger,' she said to the man who'd opened the door to Billy.

The man stepped out of the way and Pearl led Billy inside the house. The hallway was double the width of the one in his home and at least four times as long. It was decorated with red flock wallpaper and several crystal-edged mirrors hung from the walls alongside old-fashioned paintings of country scenes.

To Billy's left was a tall coat stand with several furs hanging on it, while on the right was a narrow table with a marble sculpture of a man wearing little more than a towel around his waist, driving a chariot pulled by two galloping horses.

'That cost a hundred quid,' said Pearl. 'Do you like it?'

Billy nodded. 'Who is it?'

'Some fella with a foreign name like Archie or 'Arry or something,' she replied.

'I think I heard Mr Stamp say it was Achilles,' said Dodger.

'Oh, he was one of the Greek heroes,' said Billy, as a boring afternoon of double history popped back into his mind. 'We learned about him at school.'

Wonderment spread across Pearl's powdered face for a moment then she looked past Billy at the man still standing behind him.

'See what a little brainbox he is,' she said.

The heavy studied Billy impassively. 'Right little professor, Mrs Stamp.'

Billy squirmed under the bruiser's mocking gaze but then Pearl squeezed his arm. 'Do you like that American Coca-Cola?'

Billy's eyes lit up and he nodded.

'Fetch a couple of bottles, Dodger,' she said. 'And while you're at it, bring a Tootie bar from the box in the larder.'

Lenny Stamp's muscle headed off down the hall.

'Come on,' said Pearl with a girlish shrug of her shoulders.

Leading him past the flight of stairs, she took him through the door on the other side of the hall.

If the hallway made his eyes stretch in wonder, then the room he walked into was unlike anything he'd ever seen. For a start, he reckoned it had more furniture in it than his whole house in Mafeking Terrace. The most notable thing about the room, from the leather sofa with leopard-skin cushions scattered on it to the chrome-and-glass coffee table, was that everything in Aunt Pearl's lounge was brand spanking new.

The lounge walls had flock wallpaper, too, but purple this time, to match the velvet curtains held back by golden tassels, and at the far end of the room, behind the glass-fronted home bar, the wall was decorated with a shimmering purple-and-silver wallpaper. There was a chandelier hanging in the centre of the room and, like the hall, there were paintings of the English countryside plus a big one above the long, sleek sideboard of a racehorse with his jockey holding the reins.

'Classy, isn't it?' said Pearl, as Billy's eyes alighted on a large picture of a naked woman reclining on a chaise longue.

Swallowing, Billy nodded.

'I chose everything myself,' said Pearl, casting her eyes around the laden room. 'And I got that' – she pointed at the tiger skin with the head still attached spread out on the hearth – 'only last week.'

'Is it real?' asked Billy, his eyes glued to the tiger's glass eyes and white fangs.

'Of course it is,' laughed Pearl. 'Cost a blooming arm and a leg, but if those bloody toffs up West can have 'em then so can I.'

Dodger came into the room carrying a tray with four bottles of Coca-Cola, a bottle opener and a chocolate bar.

He set it on a spindly legged side table and, after giving Billy another scornful look, left again.

'Help yourself and park your bum.' Pearl indicated the sofa.

Popping the top off one of the fizzy drinks, he perched on one end of the leather sofa.

Pressing the bottle to his lips he took a gulp, enjoying the sweetness on his tongue and the gas bubbles in his throat.

'Nice?' asked Pearl, as she poured herself a drink at the bar.

Billy nodded. 'Mum doesn't like me drinking straight from the bottle.'

'Well, she ain't here, is she?' said Pearl, screwing the top back on the gin bottle.

The little niggle of guilt tried to reassert itself, but Billy pushed it away and took another gulp of his drink.

Taking the seat at the opposite end of the sofa, Pearl stretched forwards. She flipped open the lid of a silver box on the coffee table and took out a cigarette.

'Help yourself,' she said, picking up the chunky lighter next to it.

Putting the bottle back on the tray, Billy did. Pearl held out the flame and Billy lit his cigarette.

Holding it between his first two fingers, as he'd seen Pearl do, Billy rested back and inhaled a long draft of nicotine into his lungs.

'So,' said Aunt Pearl, taking a sip of her drink, 'have you got a day off from school?'

'Not exactly,' he replied, taking another swig of his drink and not meeting her eye.

She laughed. 'You've bunked off.'

Blinking with surprise, Billy looked up.

'Good for you,' she said, looking at him over the rim of her glass. 'And I'm guessing my sister don't know you're paying me a visit.'

Muffling his conscience again, Billy shook his head.

'Well, you know what they say?' said Pearl, blowing two streams of smoke from her nostrils. 'What the eye don't see, the heart don't grieve over. And anyway, you're fifteen already so the schoolboard man can't come knocking; there's nothing to worry about.'

'I know,' he replied. 'But I'm not leaving school cause Dad wants me and Michael to stay on to take our ordinary school certificates in the summer and then our higher one after that.'

'Whatever for?' she asked.

'Because he says a good education's the way to make something of yourself,' said Billy, repeating the phrase he'd heard for as long as he could remember.

Aunt Pearl pulled a face. 'You don't need to know all that book stuff to get on. I mean, look at my Lenny. He has businesses all over

East London. And he has shares in a couple of nightclubs up West. Right posh ones, too. Not to mention a couple of racehorses.' She thrust out her hand. 'See that.' She raised her middle finger with an enormous ring on it. 'Wot d'you think it cost?'

Billy studied the twinkling blue stone edged with white ones and shrugged.

'Twenty-five pounds?'

'Seventy-two guineas,' she replied, her lips contorting as she spoke.

Billy's eyes stretched wide in astonishment, unable to imagine what such a sum even looked like.

'That's right.' Pearl's gaze fixed on him for a moment. Putting her glass down, she stood up.

Her mules made a pattering sound as she walked across the plush carpet to the sideboard.

Taking the lid off a Chinese-patterned urn, she delved in and pulled something out. Replacing the lid, she pattered back and stopped in front of Billy.

Unfurling her red-tipped fingers she offered Billy a blue five-pound note.

'Go on, take it, Billy,' she said, smiling fondly down at him. 'There's plenty more where that came from.'

Billy stared at the money for a moment; it was more than some men earned in a week. Then he took it.

The tinkle of the ward sister's bell brought Patrick Mahon back from the light doze he'd drifted into.

As afternoon visiting had finished it was three, and just over four weeks since his breath had been taken away by what felt like a giant gripping his chest.

Thankfully, after much rest he felt greatly improved. The nurses must have thought so too, as two days earlier his bed had been moved from its position within sight of the nurses' desk to halfway down the ward.

The visitors sitting beside the beds surrounding him started to gather themselves together. Wives kissed their husbands and scolded them to get better soon, while men bidding friends or brothers farewell gave a playful punch of the shoulder and made a quip about not chasing the nurses.

As the doors at the end of the ward swung shut after the last visitor, the sound of retreating footsteps was replaced by rattling china and the occasional squeak as the Marie Celeste Ward's tea trolley started its slow progress back to the kitchen.

Father Mahon closed his eyes.

'I said would you like a tea, Father?'

Realising he must have drifted off again, Patrick blinked.

Flora Walsh, the ward's orderly, was standing at the bottom of his hospital bed holding a catering-size enamel teapot.

She had been a member of his flock until she moved in to live with her daughter at Greenbank after her husband died so now attended St Patrick's Church in Wapping.

'Sorry, Mrs Walsh, that would be grand,' he replied. 'And how are you this fine day?'

'All the better for the sun shining,' Flora replied, turning back to her task. 'And yourself?'

'I feel more like myself with every passing day,' Patrick replied. 'How's that young priest of yours faring these days?'

'Father Connor's as happy as the rest of us now the end of the war is in sight,' she said, stirring in a teaspoon of sugar. 'He's even started planning our annual church parade in honour of the Blessed Virgin.'

'I shall have to do the same myself when I get back,' Patrick replied.

'No Mrs Brogan this afternoon, Father?' she asked, placing a cup with two digestive biscuits balanced on the saucer on his bedside locker.

'No, I'm afraid not,' he replied. 'She has the care of her granddaughter for a few hours this afternoon.'

A sentimental expression stole across the orderly's wrinkled features. 'Bless her. What a joy it is to have your family around you in your old age.'

'Indeed,' said Patrick, as the image of the whole Brogan family packed into two pews each Sunday flitted through his mind.

Flora resumed her place behind the tea trolley. 'Enjoy your tea, Father.'

'Thank you, Mrs Walsh.'

Placing his hands flat on the mattress, Patrick hoisted himself straighter and the dull ache running down his left arm made its presence known again.

He rested back on the canvas backrest buckled to the headboard and took a couple of deep breaths, and mercifully the pain faded.

'Father Mahon.'

Patrick opened his eyes to see Dr Ingram standing at the end of his bed. The young man was clutching a manila file to his chest.

'I'm sorry, Father, were you asleep?'

'Not at all, I was only resting my eyes,' Patrick replied. 'What can I be doing for you, Doctor?'

'We have the results of your test. And I should like to run through them with you, if I may.'

Patrick nodded.

Pulling the visitor's chair closer to the bed, Dr Ingram sat down.

'Well, Father,' the young man said as he opened the file, 'having reviewed the X-rays and blood results and taken into account the severity of your chest pains when you were brought into Casualty, our consultant Mr Haverstock has concluded that, as we suspected at the time, you have had a cardiac incident. A heart attack,' he added, seeing Patrick's puzzled expression. 'Thankfully, since then you've stabilised, but I'm afraid your vital signs indicate that you have cardiac insufficiency. Heart failure. Because it's not pumping properly.'

'Will it get better?' Patrick asked.

'I'm afraid not, Father Mahon, because your heart has suffered too much damage.' Dr Ingram's high forehead furrowed.

The blood in Patrick's veins suddenly chilled.

'Although we can give tablets to strengthen your heart in the short term,' continued the young doctor from what seemed like a long way away, 'I'm afraid . . .'

With his pulse thundering through his ears, Patrick took a deep breath and smiled at the young man. 'Thank you, Doctor.'

Closing the file, Dr Ingram stood up and after giving him a sympathetic look, he left.

Patrick stared blindly at the cornflower-blue sky and the cotton-wool clouds slowly drifting across the tall window opposite.

After a moment he closed his eyes and tried to pray, but he had trouble gathering his frenzied thoughts.

A soft hand closed over his gnarled one and he looked around.

'I'm so sorry, Father,' said Nurse Anderson, who had taken the chair vacated by Dr Ingram. 'Is there anyone you'd like me to telephone? A colleague or someone you're particularly close to?' An image of Queenie flashed through Patrick's mind, eliciting an echo of buried emotions.

As he had done so often before, Patrick pushed it aside and smiled at the nurse in her starched lilac uniform and frilly cap.

'Thank you, my dear,' he said, 'but if you could hand me my Missal, I would count it as a kindness, and perhaps a cup of tea that's still hot.'

'Of course.' She handed him the leather-bound book perched on the top of his locker. Then she stood up and, taking his untouched cup of tea, she returned to the nurses' desk.

Patrick cradled the dog-eared prayer book that had been his constant companion for nigh on fifty years.

It had been given to him by his parents on the day the Bishop of Cork ordained him at the cathedral. He remembered as if it were yesterday, the glow of pride in their eyes.

He'd already been told he was to travel to England to take a post as the junior priest somewhere, so had been granted some time at home with his family in Kinsale.

But what he recalled most about that visit home, more than his parents' pride and the sumptuous tea the parish put on in his honour, was Queenie, or Philomena Dooley as she was back then, with her ebony black hair streaming behind her, her long slender legs moving like lightning as she ran barefoot through the meadow, and the wildflowers bobbing around them as they lay in the long grass.

Kinsale, Ireland. June 1887

STANDING WITH THE skirts of her faded cotton dress tucked up over her knees, Philomena, just two months short of her sixteenth birthday, lowered her hands into the cool water of the fast-flowing tributary that cut through the beech copse on its way to the River Bandon.

With her body blocking the bright glare of the sun, she studied the shingle riverbed through the crystal-clear water.

A few tiddlers, their scales sparkling, swam beneath her, but Philomena let them go. It was bigger fish, literally, she was after right now.

Feeling the warmth on her back, and standing unnaturally still, she waited.

'Caught anything?'

Philomena raised her head and an odd feeling bubbled in her stomach.

Patrick was standing on the bank wearing his rough work trousers and a collarless striped shirt that strained across his ever-widening shoulders. His unruly black curls were just asking to be ruffled.

'Not yet,' she replied. 'I didn't think you were coming.'

'One of Pa's cows was calving this morning and as my brother Cornelius was away at first light to take this week's butter to market, I had to lend a hand.' Plonking himself down on the lush green riverbank, he unpicked his laces. 'Is it cold?'

Philomena shook her head.

Rolling up his trousers, Patrick dipped in his toe.

'For the love of mercy,' he gasped as his toes disappeared under the gurgling water. 'I thought you said it wasn't cold.'

Philomena suppressed a smile. 'Perhaps it's a mite chilly but grand once you've been in a moment or two.'

Squaring his shoulders, he picked his way across the shingle to join her and stopped in front of her. They grinned at each other then looked down at the water swirling around their feet.

'Now let's hope a weary trout comes to take his ease beneath this overhanging rock.' He bent down to look at the riverbed.

Philomena did the same, studying the distorted image of their bare feet for a few moments. Then, without moving her head, she raised her eyes.

Patrick's face was just inches from hers and she gave in to the impulse and kissed him full on the lips.

'Oi there,' he said, pretending to be shocked. 'I thought you were here to catch fish.'

She gave him a lavish look. 'Amongst other things.'

The expression in his eyes went from tranquil to wild in an instant.

'That fish you caught long ago, Mena,' he said, in a low voice that had her stomach flipping somersaults.

They studied each other for a long moment then something caught his eye and Patrick lowered his gaze back to the water.

'We're in luck,' he whispered, as she, too, caught a flicker of movement beneath the ripples. 'I think a fish has just slipped under the rock.'

'I can see his tail,' Philomena replied in the same hushed tone.

Lowering her hand into the cool water, she curled her fingers and ran them slowly along the slippery skin of the trout's belly. However, when she reached the fish's head, instead of grabbing it, Philomena scooped a handful of water and threw it over Patrick.

He stumbled back. 'What the blue . . .?'

Philomena's other hand dived under the water's surface and laughing she threw another jet of water over him, soaking his shirt.

He retaliated by plunging his hands into the stream and splashing her, too.

Philomena shrieked and kicked water over him.

'Getting serious, are you now, Mena?' he laughed, wiping the water from his eyes.

Reaching down into the clear stream again, he threw handfuls of water at her in such quick succession that within a couple of moments she was drenched.

With her sides aching from laughing and barely able to catch her breath, Philomena made a break for the riverbank, collapsing on the lush grass as Patrick sloshed his way out of the river.

'Look at me,' she said, holding her saturated skirt away from her legs.

''Tis no more than you deserve,' he replied, wringing out the ends of his soaked shirt.

'You'll dry soon enough,' Philomena replied, leaning back on her elbows.

He flopped down beside her and gave her a playful shove. She shoved him back and they laughed.

He tilted his face to the sun and closed his eyes.

Philomena studied his profile for a few moments as the swaying leaves above dappled his face with sunlight.

Sensing her eyes on him, Patrick rolled over on to her, resting his weight on his elbows.

His gaze held hers for a moment then he lowered his mouth to her lips.

Quivering with excitement, Philomena's hands slid around him, anchoring him to her. Time stood still as his mouth worked on hers and his hands ran over her arms, shoulders and breasts.

Patrick kissed his way across to her ear then down to the sensitive area on her neck.

'Oh, Mena,' he murmured, lifting his head and gazing down at her. 'I'm mad for you, so I am.'

'I'm the same myself for you,' she whispered, enjoying the sensation of his weight. 'And you know it's only two months until you can call on me pappy so . . .' She flexed her hips against the hard area beneath his fly buttons.

Patrick groaned. 'Oh, Mena.'

'Let's,' she persisted, urged on by the throbbing sensation in the pit of her stomach. 'We're to be married, are we not?'

'We are but—'

'No one will know,' she added, scratching her finger lightly down his back. 'And I love you, so come on, Patrick, let's—'

'Patrick!'

They looked up.

Crushing newly sprung ferns and wildflowers beneath her laced-up black boots stood Patrick's sister Nora, with a tight face and red-rimmed eyes.

Giving Philomena a look of utter loathing, Nora's attention shifted to her brother.

'You're to come home, Patrick,' she said. 'Cornelius has had an accident and Father Parr has been called to give him the last rites.'

Chapter Seven

'WELL, I HEARD that the one that landed behind Stepney wash house two days ago took out every house from Nicholas Road to Rose Place,' said Minnie, her rheumy grey eyes heavy with sorrow.

'Bloody Germans,' said Nell, folding her arms across her considerable bosom. 'I tell you, those bloody rockets have shot my nerves to ribbons.'

'Inhuman, that's what they are,' Minnie replied, her lashless eyes blinking rapidly behind her thick-lensed spectacles. 'I heard thirty poor souls perished in their beds, probably without even knowing what hit them.'

'God rest and keep their souls,' said Queenie. She crossed herself and her two friends did the same.

It was midday on Friday, and Queenie was at St Breda and St Brendan's Darby and Joan lunch club.

Before the war, the weekly dinnertime chats would mainly be about who'd gone to meet their maker, whose husband was hanging his trousers on the end of a bed he shouldn't be and the genius of their grandchildren. Over the past five years, however, it had changed and now it revolved around who had been bombed out, which shops had new stock and who had received the Ministry of War telegram they all dreaded.

Around her, sitting at the dozen or so square tables that had been bleached white from regular scrubbing, sat the people Queenie had lived alongside and grown old with for over forty years. The men had been dockers, labourers and handled teams of horses as delivery drivers, while the women had fought poverty and disease as they raised families, birthed children and mourned those who departed this life before taking their first steps. Now, however, like her, they were just white-haired men and women wearing baggy trousers and collarless shirts or shapeless dresses and wrinkled lisle stockings respectively.

Queenie was at her usual table at the back of the room with Minnie Barrow, a barrel of a woman with sparse grey hair and legs swathed in bandages, and Nell Clements, a long-faced woman in her early sixties whose four daughters all lived in the same street as their mother.

'You don't have to tell Queenie about those blooming V-2s, Nell,' said Minnie. 'For didn't she nearly end up standing at the Pearly Gates when that one landed in Swedenborg Square?'

'Any idea when the landlord's going to fix the roof?' asked Nell.

'I'm thinking probably a day or two after Hell freezes over,' Queenie replied. 'But me and Ida told that shifty rent man that as we've only got half a house we're only paying half the rent and he can whistle for the rest.'

At that moment, two of the younger women of the parish who were lunchtime cooks came out of the door next to the serving hatch with Father Timothy half a step behind them.

The buzz of conversation died away as all eyes turned to the young priest standing in front of the closed shutters.

Although Father Timothy only just looked old enough to shave, he was, in fact, in his early thirties and had been at a parish over the water in Bermondsey for four years before coming to St Breda and St Brendan's. Truthfully, Father Timothy was a blessing straight from above. With his ready laugh, an athletic build, a crop of blond hair and a firm jawline, he was the sort of man many women, both young and not so young, would look twice at. It often struck Queenie that if tending to the souls in his care wasn't enough of a task to occupy his ordained servants, God felt it necessary to encumber them with the unrequitable desire of the female members of his flock.

A friendly smile lifted Father Timothy's face as his pale blue eyes travelled over the elderly members of the lunch club.

'Good afternoon, everyone,' he said in a clear voice with just a trace of a Geordie accent. 'And I hope you are all well this fine day.'

He indicated the bright spring sky visible through the gummed tape criss-crossing the committee room's sash windows.

The aged diners murmured their response.

'Now, before I say grace and the lovely ladies of the lunch club refreshment team serve you your dinners, which I understand today is the rare treat in these difficult times of fish and chips—'

A cheer went up as those in the room raised their hands in acclamation.

'Fish and chips,' whispered Minnie. 'It's so long since I had any I've forgotten what it tastes like.'

'Me too,' said Queenie, using the same hushed tone. 'There must be a glut of it in Essex if the people in the council's food department are sending it here.'

'Well, praise be it's not corned beef pie like last week,' agreed Nell. 'The blooming onions in it repeated on me all afternoon.'

'But before they do,' continued Father Timothy, 'I thought you'd like to have an update about Father Mahon.'

Queenie's heart started pounding in her chest.

'Well, I'm pleased to tell you it's good news,' said the young priest. 'The doctors have said that he can come home on Monday.'

Another cheer went up as relief flooded through Queenie.

Father Timothy waited until the noise subsided then spoke again.

'However,' he continued, his forehead furrowing a little, 'although the hospital say he's fit enough to come home, they are only allowing him to do so on the strict understanding that he continues to rest. I'm afraid, therefore, he won't be resuming his duties for the foreseeable future. Now, shall we give thanks?'

People around her bowed their heads over the knives and forks set before them and Queenie did the same.

'*Benedic, Domine, dona tua quae . . . de largitate sumus sumpturi,*' said Father Timothy above their heads.

And everyone muttered amen.

The young women standing behind Father Timothy unbolted the serving-hatch shutters and folded them back. He thanked them and the three women standing ready to dish up on the other side of the hatch then left them to their task.

'Thank goodness Father Mahon's coming home,' said Nell, as the two young women started giving out the dinners.

'Yes, but I wonder why they've let him out if he's not fully recovered,' said Minnie. 'Mrs Dunn said that he looked washed out when she went to see him last week.'

'He looked fine enough when I popped in yesterday,' said Queenie, as an image of his pale complexion flashed through her mind. 'A bit tired, perhaps, but then I wouldn't think spending so long on a hospital ward with doctors and nurses marching up and down and telephones and bells ringing all day and night is restful.'

'I'm sure you're right, Queenie,' said Nell. 'But I thought he's been looking worn out since Christmas.'

'One of the altar boys had to nudge him when he nodded off during the Epiphany Mass,' said Minnie.

'Even at the back where I sit,' added Nell, 'I can hear that old chest of his rattling like knuckles on a washboard when he is saying Mass.'

'Jesus, Mary and Joseph,' snapped Queenie, 'Father Mahon's tired and is it any wonder—'

One of the women handing out the dinners arrived at their table carrying three plates on a tray.

Queenie and her two friends sat in silence as plates of golden battered fish and crispy chips were set down in front of them. After thanking the woman, they picked up their cutlery.

'Father Mahon is tired, that's all. Tired,' Queenie said, reaching for the salt cellar that was sitting next to the bottle of vinegar in the middle of the table. 'And I'm sure once he's had his feet up for a couple of weeks, he'll be marching around the parish like he always has.'

'Would you like another one, Billy?' asked Aunt Pearl, as he noisily sucked up the dregs of Coca-Cola from the bottom of the bottle.

'Yes, please,' said Billy, putting it down on the coffee table.

Reaching below her glass-topped lounge bar, Aunt Pearl retrieved another.

It was Tuesday, just after four thirty in the afternoon, and a week since his first visit to Pearl. He'd arrived half an hour ago and had already downed two bottles of fizz as he told her about how he was getting on at school.

Of course, he'd told his mum that he was staying after school for football practice and then getting pie and mash with a couple of mates, so as long as he pitched up for choir practice at six thirty no one would be any the wiser.

Well, except Michael, of course, who'd caught him slipping off just before the last lesson of the day. But Billy wasn't bothered. Michael might be a blooming swot and a teacher's pet, but thankfully he wasn't a snitch. Billy liked to think it was because, being younger, Michael was scared of him but, annoyingly, even boys in the years above them at school didn't pick on Michael for fear of a pasting.

'From what you tell me, it sounds as though you're the top of the class,' Pearl said, popping the cap off.

Although he wasn't, not by a long chalk, Billy didn't deny it.

Returning to the chair opposite him, Aunt Pearl took a cigarette from the box on the table in between them then settled back.

'Help yourself,' she said, flicking the chunky table lighter into flame with her nail-varnished fingers.

Billy did. Lighting it, he stretched out his arm along the back of the sofa, the way he'd seen them do in the pictures, and inhaled the nicotine deep into his lungs.

'So, how's your mum?' Aunt Pearl asked, blowing a stream of smoke upwards from the corner of her mouth.

'All right,' said Billy.

'Still working in the junk yard, is she?'

'Dad's not a rag-and-bone man any more,' Billy replied.

Aunt Pearl raised a plucked eyebrow. 'Ain't he?'

'No,' Billy replied. 'Brogan and Sons is a removal and delivery business now. He's got a van and two lorries and he's going to get another one soon.'

Pearl's red mouth spread into a tight smile. 'That's nice. I suppose—' The door burst open behind Billy, cutting off her words.

Aunt Pearl's eyes lit up as she rose to her feet. 'Lenny.'

Billy swivelled around on his seat to see Lenny Stamp, with his Brylcreemed hair swept back and a cigar clamped between his teeth, filling the doorway.

Well, half filling if the truth were told: standing no more than two or three inches taller than Billy's five foot four and with the barest hint of a neck, East London's acknowledged gov'nor was never in any danger of scraping his head on any door lintel.

He was dressed in a brown double-breasted, chalk-stripe suit with wide lapels and a flowery tie, and stood chest out, legs apart, with a camel-coloured Crombie draped across his shoulders.

In contrast, standing next to him was a young man who looked to be only a few months over his twenty-one-year majority. But whereas Lenny gave the impression of being almost as tall as he was wide, the slender young man beside him looked as if a strong breeze would carry him off. He, too, was dressed in a suit, but rather than imitating an American gangster on the silver screen, the man was dressed in the sober charcoal grey of a banking clerk, the only hint of flamboyance his red, green and yellow striped tie.

Wriggling her tight skirt down, Aunt Pearl did a little hip-hoppy trot across the room on her high-heeled slippers.

'I wasn't expecting you back so soon,' she said, giving Lenny a quick peck on the cheek and leaving a smudge of lipstick.

'Well, me and Arthur finished our bit of business early,' said Lenny, shrugging off his coat and slinging it across the nearest chair.

'So we're going to have a shufty at a couple of motors,' said Arthur.

A sentimental smile spread across Lenny's ruddy face. ''Bout time my son and heir had something decent to drive around in.'

He gave Arthur a playful punch on the shoulder and then, like kids, the two of them did a couple of air punches at each other, ending with Lenny putting an ape-like arm around his son's slight shoulder.

'He's a right chip off the old block, ain't he, doll?' Lenny said, giving his son a brief hug and grinning at Pearl.

Aunt Pearl stared at him for an instant then a bright smile flashed across her face.

'He's a replica of you, Lenny, and everyone says so,' she said. 'But I didn't know you were buying him a motor.'

Lenny's bushy eyebrows rose. 'I thought I mentioned it.'

'Ain't a problem, is it?' said Arthur, his eyes fixed on Pearl as he took a packet of Benson & Hedges from his pocket.

'No . . . no . . .' She gave a brittle smile. 'Of course not, Arthur.'

His pale eyes stayed on her for a long moment then slid across to Billy.

'I didn't know it was bob-a-job week,' he said, smoothing his fair hair back into place with the flat of his hand.

'Lenny,' said Pearl, extending her arm and sidestepping towards the sofa. 'You haven't met him before but this is my Billy.'

Billy rose to his feet and stepped forward.

'Good afternoon, Mr Stamp,' he said, offering his hand. 'It's very nice to meet you.'

Arthur snorted smoke from his nostrils, but Lenny's hard-bitten expression didn't flicker.

Feeling his mouth go dry under the gangster's hard gaze, Billy dropped his hand.

'He's been telling me how well he's doing at school,' said Pearl, putting her arm around him. 'He's a right little brainbox is my Billy.'

'So he don't take after you then, Pearl,' chipped in Arthur as he strolled across to the bar.

Pearl shot him a hateful look then turned her attention back to the man beside her. 'Top of the class, he is, Lenny,' she continued.

'Is he?' Lenny replied, taking a cigar case from inside of his jacket.

'Yes,' said Pearl, with a little warble to her voice. ''E even knew who that statue of yours in the hall with the towel covering his meat and two veg was.'

'You a swot then, Billy?' asked Arthur, splashing Scotch into a couple of thick-bottomed tumblers.

Irritation jabbed at Billy but with Arthur's cold, pale eyes on him he held his peace.

''E don't need to be,' Pearl snapped, hugging Billy a little tighter. 'He's just naturally clever. Knows all about foreign countries, 'e does, and the olden days, don't you, Billy?'

'Some,' Billy replied, hoping Lenny Stamp wasn't going to ask him the capitals of Europe or the date of the French Revolution.

Jamming the cork back in the bottle, Arthur picked up the glasses and walked back to join them.

'You're a bit of a teacher's pet then, are you, Billy Boy?' he said, handing a glass to his father. 'Yes, sir; no, sir?'

Billy balled his fists.

'On top of which you don't look old enough to be out of short trousers,' added Arthur. 'What are you, ten? Eleven?'

'I'm sixteen in September,' he replied. 'And I ain't no teacher's pet.'

Arthur sniggered.

Pearl's eyes narrowed. 'And my Billy's smart enough to have a bit of business on the go.'

'Is he?' said Lenny, puffing his cigar into life.

'Don't be scared, Billy.' Pearl nudged him. 'Tell Lenny.'

'All right.' Billy gave a Jimmy Cagney shrug. 'I nicked a dozen packets of Players from a paper shop and sold the fags to my mates.'

Arthur threw back a mouthful of Scotch. 'I was doing that when I was still sucking me muver's tit so—'

Lenny raised his hand and his son's mouth clamped shut.

'Now, now, Arthur, stop pulling his ham and egg,' said Lenny, giving Billy the once-over. 'We all have to start somewhere.' Lenny chewed his cigar for a moment then snatched it from his mouth and pointed the soggy end at Billy. 'I tell you what. How'd you like to help me with a bit of business?'

'I'd like that very much,' said Billy.

'It's nothing big, just delivering a message, in fact,' Lenny continued, his deep-set eyes fixed on Billy. 'But if you show you 'ave the makings of a straight-up bloke, well, I might be able to help you out with your supplies, if you get my drift.'

He winked.

'Oh, thank you, Lenny, dear,' said Pearl, looking adoringly at the man puffing smoke in her face.

'And if your boy keeps his nose clean, you can fetch 'im along to The Rub A Dub in a couple of weeks,' Lenny added.

Pearl's heavily made-up face lifted in an ecstatic smile. 'Oh, thank you, Lenny.' She kissed him on his stubbly cheek again and then turned to Billy.

'See, I told you, Billy?' she said, beaming at him. 'You don't need all of that school rubbish.'

*

The costermongers were just starting to pack away their stalls on Whitechapel Road as Billy walked out of the station of the same name. It was just after five thirty and the sun was still visible over the tops of the houses. Because there hadn't been an enemy aircraft in the sky for months, the blackout had changed to a dim-out before Christmas. However, strolling along past the shops on either side of the underground station, it seemed strange, after five years of seeing no street or window lighting, to see lights twinkling around him now.

Truthfully, as where he was going now was a good half-hour walk from St Breda and St Brendan's, he would only just skim into choir practice on time, but having said he'd deliver Lenny's message, he couldn't very well not. Especially as Lenny had made Billy repeat it three times to make sure he'd remembered it.

But that's the way it was in Lenny Stamp's world. If the guvnor told you to do something, you did it. Even if it got you a roasting from the choirmaster. It was part of the criminal world's code. Everyone knew that.

As it was the end of the working day there were people crowding on to the buses, heading to their homes in the East. A couple of ambulances were waiting in the driveway of the London Hospital opposite while young nurses, their lilac uniforms covered by their navy capes, tripped down the hospital steps to dash to the shops before they closed.

Passing a couple of blokes winding in the awning above Lipton the grocer's front window, Billy headed toward Aldgate and within a few moments he was turning the corner into Vallance Road.

As the road ran straight through from Whitechapel Road at the south to Bethnal Green Road in the north, there were lorries and vans and the odd ARP truck speeding along it in both directions.

Straightening his cap, Billy marched on past the usual array of shops towards the eastern railway arch that carried passengers in from the leafy suburbs to Liverpool Street station each day.

Hoping a passing train wouldn't fluster the pigeons cooing in the iron girders ahead of him, which would end up with him being showered with droppings, Billy walked under the dank railway arch towards the old Victorian terraced houses, much like his own in Mafeking Terrace, on the other side.

Delving into his uniform pocket, Billy pulled out the scrap of paper with the address on it.

'He looks a bit lost, don't he, Ronnie?' said a boy's voice.

Billy turned to see two boys a few years younger than himself lolling in one of the doorways. Both had the same straight dark hair and features and were obviously twins. They were also, like him, still in their uniforms. However, although by rights at their age they should still have been in short trousers, both were in long.

'What school's that?' asked Ronnie, indicating the crest on Billy's breast pocket.

'Parmiter's,' Billy replied.

'He's proper posh, Reggie,' Ronnie sneered. 'Who you after?'

'Mr Rozinski,' said Billy.

'What'd you want Black Ivor for?' asked Reggie.

'None of your business,' Billy replied.

A snarl lifted the corner of Ronnie's lip and he went to step forward, but his brother put his arm out.

'Don't take on,' he said. 'He ain't from around here.'

Although his piggy eyes still glared at Billy, the boy didn't move any further.

'Across the road. Number 'undred and three,' said Reggie. 'But they don't answer the front door so go round the back.'

Feeling two pairs of hard black eyes boring into the space between his shoulder blades, Billy crossed the road and slipped down the alley between the houses. Picking his way past the swirls of dog dirt, brown shards of broken glass and one or two spent French letters, Billy made his way between the six-foot-high fences on either side. Finally, halfway down, he reached a battered gate with the number 103 scrawled on it.

Taking a deep breath to steady his thundering heart, Billy clicked the latch and, with an unoiled hinge heralding his arrival, walked in.

Again, like Mafeking Terrace, the backyard was no more than twenty feet by fifteen, but whereas the one behind his home had his father's vegetable tubs and his gran's chicken coop, this one seemed to be growing old bicycle wheels, rusty pails and broken china interspersed with weeds.

Skirting around the pungent brick-built lavvy and treading carefully so as not to roll his ankle on the broken concrete path, Billy crossed to the back door.

He studied the peeling green paint for a moment then rapped on it with his knuckles.

A dog barked furiously somewhere inside but after a few moments the door cracked open.

A barefooted woman who looked about thirty, dressed only in a light-blue rayon underslip, stood in the half-open doorway.

'What d'you want?'

Billy swallowed and dragged his gaze back to her face. 'I've a message for Mr Rozinski. From Mr Stamp.'

She studied him from between her heavily mascaraed lashes and Billy felt his cheeks grow warm.

'Ivor!' she screamed over her shoulder. 'Someone asking for you.'

Turning, she padded back into the house, leaving Billy standing on the back doorstep.

After what seemed like an eternity, an unshaven, heavyset man with thinning black hair and a roll-up dangling out of the side of his mouth shuffled to the door.

Although it was probably close to six in the evening now, like the young girl, Ivor Rozinski was also casually dressed in a grubby singlet and pair of saggy-kneed trousers held up by a set of red and yellow braces. He was a little older than the woman, with hooded hazel eyes, a long nose and the feature that must have given him his nickname, a grey stain on the left side of his face that was peppered with tiny black dots, like cinders on hearth tiles.

'Mr Rozinski?' said Billy.

'Yes.'

Billy took a deep breath.

'Mr Stamp said the plum duff you were after will be at the old place on Saturday. Same numbers both ways but keep your peepers peeled as there are some new acquaintances on the manor,' he concluded, not understanding one word in three of what he'd just said.

'Right,' Black Ivor replied.

He sized him up for a moment as the woman had done, then shut the door.

Billy stared at the dilapidated door for a moment, then, imagining himself as a criminal mastermind, turned and retraced his steps.

The sun was rapidly disappearing from the western sky when he reached Vallance Road and there was a decided chill in the air.

Trying to put the image of the choirmaster's angry face from his mind, Billy straightened his school tie and shrugged his blazer square on his shoulders as gangsters did in the pictures, then, running through possible nicknames for himself, he started off home.

Adjusting the basket on her arm, Queenie passed between the rectory's square-capped columns and headed up the path towards the black-lacquered door. Like the rest of the solid three-storey Victorian house, it had seen better days.

When she'd arrived in the parish as a new bride all those years ago, there had been three priests living in St Breda and St Brendan's rectory, with five servants to look after them. Now it was just Father Mahon, Father Timothy and the resident housekeeper, Mrs Dunn.

Thinking the letter box could do with a bit of a polish, Queenie grasped the knocker and banged on the door, hearing it echo through the vast house.

There was a pause and then the door opened and Mrs Dunn, with her laced-up shoes planted firmly on the coconut mat, appeared.

Although her husband had been released from this mortal coil and his wife's double-edged tongue over a decade before, Bridget Dunn still dressed in widow's weeds as if her husband had gone to his heavenly reward only a month before.

Her bosom was almost non-existent but sadly the same could not be said for her hips, which, despite five years of rationing, were in danger of scraping the side of any doorway she passed through.

At the sight of Queenie on the threshold, Bridget Dunn's pale lips pulled into a tight bud.

'Mrs Brogan,' she said, giving her a caustic look. 'I wondered how long it would be before *you* turned up.'

'And a joy so it is to see you, too, Mrs Dunn,' said Queenie, giving her the sweetest smile. 'Now, as I don't want to keep you from your duties, I'd be obliged if you would let me in.'

'The hospital said Father Mahon's to rest,' said the housekeeper, without moving.

'Well, that's a blessing indeed that you've told me,' replied Queenie, 'for wasn't I for taking him on a hike up a mountain?'

Mrs Dunn stood her ground for a moment, then she stepped aside.

'Well, as I know you'll give me no rest until you've seen him, I suppose you'd better come in.'

Queenie stepped into the bare-board hallway.

'I'll see if he's awake,' said Mrs Dunn, as she closed the door. 'But Father Mahon is still recovering.' With that she hurried towards the door at the end of the hall, leaving Queenie waiting.

As always, Queenie's attention was drawn to the small watercolour of her and Father Mahon's hometown of Kinsale.

Over the years the bright green of the fields and the crystal blue of the river had faded, but gazing at the image, Queenie could almost feel the wet meadow grass between her toes and the icy chill of the water swirling around her ankles.

After a moment, the door at the far end of the hallway opened and Mrs Dunn appeared again.

'Father Mahon is awake so will see you,' she said.

Slipping her coat from her shoulders, Queenie hung it on the hall stand, then, delving into her basket, she pulled out a paper bag.

'There's four eggs freshly laid this morning that will help set the good father back on his feet in no time,' she said, offering it to the housekeeper.

Mrs Dunn took them. 'Bear in mind that Father Mahon is still far from recovered, so make sure you don't stay too long and tire him.' She turned and headed towards the kitchen.

'In case it's slipped your mind, Mrs Dunn, I take two sugars in my tea,' Queenie called after her.

Turning the brass door handle, Queenie walked through into the rectory's south-facing parlour.

Father Mahon, who was wearing a camel-coloured dressing gown with tartan shawl collar, was sitting in his favourite armchair beside the fire with his slippered feet up on an ancient footstool. There was a multicoloured blanket over his legs and his bony hands rested on top of his open prayer book.

Gazing down at him as he dozed in the chair, fear swept over Queenie.

Sensing her presence, Father Mahon opened his eyes and smiled.

'Queenie,' he said, pushing his glasses back up his nose and sitting up a little, 'I didn't hear you come in.'

'I just thought I'd drop by to see how you were faring,' said Queenie. 'And to bring you a little something to put the colour back in your cheeks.' Dipping into her basket she took out a small pewter hipflask. Pulling out the drawer of the occasional table next to him, she slipped it in.

'It's Jameson,' she added.

'As much as I appreciate the thought, I've a feeling Mrs Dunn might not approve,' said Father Mahon.

'Well, then it would be better not to offer her any,' Queenie replied.

A smile lifted Patrick's face, showing the ghost of the man he'd once been.

'So how are you?' asked Queenie.

'Not so bad,' Father Mahon replied. 'The doctors say as long as I take it easy for a few weeks or so I might have the odd Mass or two in me yet.'

'Of course you have,' Queenie replied. 'And doesn't your cough always get easier once the sun's back in the sky?'

'Very true,' he replied. 'But the doctors said I'm not to overdo it as it might be too much for my heart.'

'Your heart?' said Queenie, feeling her own heart lurch.

'Yes, it seems that young doctor was right and it's getting a bit tired of the old pumping lark,' he replied. 'Hardly surprising really, since it's been at it for almost eighty years.'

'Don't give yourself years you haven't had,' said Queenie. 'All you need is a week or so with your feet up and a few good meals inside you and you'll be your old self.'

He smiled. 'I'm sure you're right.' A sentimental expression stole across his weary face. 'Do you think of the old days back home?'

'From time to time.'

He sighed. 'The sun always seemed to be shining.'

'Except of course when there was a howling storm from the frozen north whipping up the waves,' Queenie countered.

He gave a little wheezy chuckle. 'The devil himself trying to escape from hell couldn't have rattled the windows more than a winter storm in the Irish Sea.'

The image of fishing boats bobbing at their moorings in Kinsale's harbour flashed across Queenie's mind. 'Do you remember the smell of the quayside when the boats brought home their catch?'

'A mix of fresh fish and salty air.' He drew in a long breath through his nose. 'I can almost smell it now. And those tall arched windows in the Carmelite Friary church.'

An image of the sun shining through the stained-glass windows of her old parish church sprang into Queenie's mind.

Patrick Mahon's blue-grey eyes that could have been Jeremiah's looked into hers.

'It was there we first met, wasn't it, Philomena? Do you remember?' he asked, the sound of her name soft on his lips.

'I do.'

'You were sitting on Mother Twomey's tomb, and I said—'

'"You shouldn't be sitting on that grave,"' Queenie cut in. 'And I said, "Why?" and you said—'

'Because she was a witch that lived hundreds of years ago and if you disturb her, she'll come back to haunt you,' said Father Mahon. 'And you said, "Well, let her . . . You can sit here too, if you like, unless—"'

'"You're afeared,"' said Queenie.

'I asked you how old you were and you answered me five,' he said.

'And you were to be seven in September,' she replied. 'And I think I complimented you on your wild curly hair.'

With a twinkle in his eye, the old priest raised a bony hand and rubbed his wispy white hair.

'There's not many who would say that now,' he chuckled.

A lump formed in Queenie's throat. 'Perhaps not, but I still remember.'

'And then Nora came over,' said Father Mahon. 'You remember my sister, don't you? You and her were in the same class.'

Queenie's mouth pulled into a hard line.

'We were,' she said, as the round face and flat eyes of Patrick's younger sister loomed in her mind.

'Funny, isn't it, Queenie,' Father Mahon chuckled, 'how sometimes I can't remember what I had for breakfast yesterday, but I can recall little incidents way back then as if it were yesterday?'

'It's a strange trick of the mind, to be sure,' she agreed. 'But there are some things, like love and a moment of happiness, that remain with you for eternity.'

Kinsale, Ireland. July 1887

PHILOMENA STARED OPEN-MOUTHED at Patrick, unable to believe what she'd just heard him say.

'I know it's a shock,' he said from what seemed like a long way away. 'But I promised.'

It was almost four on a Saturday afternoon and she and Patrick were standing in the bright summer sunlight in the very spot where only a month before Nora had discovered them lying together in the long grass.

Just a foot or so from their feet, the stream babbled by while all around them, in the sweltering heat of the mid-summer, the birds sang and insects buzzed. However, Philomena heard none of this because of the voice shrieking in her head.

'But why, Patrick?' she asked, forcing her brain to work.

'Because Cornelius was a breath away from death,' he replied. 'For a month, day and night, me mammy has been on her knees praying while my sisters sobbed around her. Three times Father Parr has administered the last rites to my brother, the last being Monday past, when we were standing around his bed expecting his spirit to leave his body at any moment. Appealing to the Virgin Mary was the only hope.'

'Was it you who thought to ask St Mary?' asked Philomena softly.

He shook his head. 'No, it wasn't me who thought to promise me to the Church but me mammy,' he replied, struggling to hold her gaze. 'She vowed to the Blessed Virgin on my behalf in exchange for Cornelius's life, so what could I do? If I refused and he died I never would forgive myself for putting myself before my brother's life.'

Philomena pressed her lips together and cursed Margaret Mahon to the fires of hell in her head.

A contrite smile lifted the corner of Patrick's mouth. 'Sure, isn't it an old tradition that the youngest son should go into the Church?'

Unamused, Philomena frowned.

They stood there staring at each other for a long moment then Patrick spoke again.

'You should have seen him, Mena,' he said, tears forming in his eyes. 'Hovering there between this world and the next. We tried everything, from washing his head in holy water to laying rosaries all around him. And nothing – not even a flicker of an eyelid – but then it happened.' Patrick's expression changed from sombre to radiant in an instant. 'A miracle. I wish you'd been there to see it, Mena. After four weeks of poor Con not showing even the smallest flicker of life, two hours later he was sitting up in bed with Mammy spooning soup into him. And perhaps it's meant to be,' he went on. 'Perhaps Cornelius had his accident as a way of God telling me he wanted me to become a priest.'

'Or perhaps Cornelius falling off his cart has nothing to do with you taking holy orders and more to do with him drinking too much ale in a Cork tavern before driving home,' Philomena snapped back.

The bleak expression returned to Patrick's handsome face.

'I'm sorry,' said Philomena softly, as her heart ripped slowly apart. 'But what about us? The home we were to build, the children we were to have? You and me, Patrick, growing old together. What of all that?'

Pain and despair flashed across Patrick's face. He looked away for a long moment then raised his head.

'I'm sorry, Mena, but what else could I do?' he asked, his blue-grey eyes locking on her dark brown ones. 'Let my brother die? But how else can Con's sudden recovery be explained, if not by the Virgin herself stepping in? And now she has, I have to do my part.'

'When will you go?' she asked.

'September,' he replied. 'To St Kieran's in Kilkenny. Pa's already sent a donation for my place.'

A yawning chasm of hopelessness opened at Philomena's feet. 'So soon.'

'I'm of an age to start training,' he said.

'So instead of marrying me you'll be taking the Church for your bride,' said Philomena bitterly.

Despite the warm summer's day, like so many they'd shared together, the cold black fog of misery now pressed down on her.

Philomena lowered her eyes and studied the grass where only a few weeks before they had sworn their love and kissed. How could that be their last kiss instead of a lifetime of thousands?

Holding back her gathering tears, Philomena gave him a too-bright smile.

'Well then, Patrick,' she said desperately, 'as there's no more to be said on the subject, I'll just have to wish you all the best for your new life.'

Stifling the urge to scream, Philomena turned. Holding her head high, she marched back along the lane towards her home.

'I am sorry, Mena,' Patrick shouted after her as a fat teardrop rolled down her right cheek. 'But I had no real choice in the matter.'

No, me neither, Patrick, God forgive me, thought Philomena. *For I have no choice in the matter of loving you.*

Chapter Eight

'SO ALTHOUGH MY friends think the war isn't quite over yet,' said George Selwyn, as Jo took another sip of her G&T, 'I think the writing's on the wall for Hitler and all his goons. So we at Trafalgar Square Ambulance Station can proudly say that we did our bit to put paid to the Nazis.'

It was six o'clock in the evening on the first Wednesday in April. Jo, along with Green, Red and her own Blue team, were standing in the main hall of Trafalgar Square junior school.

Like Jo, the depot's senior officer was dressed in the navy trousers and army-style jacket of the Auxiliary Ambulance Service. In civilian life, George, who was about Jo's father's age, owned a paint shop in Burdette Road, but as a life-long member of Bow's Red Cross Brigade he'd volunteered for the Auxiliary Ambulance Service almost as soon as Chamberlain had stopped speaking on the wireless.

The three-storey, red-brick Victorian school was situated just off Whitehorse Lane, a quarter of a mile south of Mile End Road.

However, the space now filled with uniformed ambulance personnel had been without its pupils for some time. Five years, in fact, because just after it was announced that the country was at war with Germany again, its pupils had been evacuated to safety in the countryside, and the infant school had been requisitioned by Stepney Area ARP command and turned into an Auxiliary ambulance station to deal with the carnage caused by Luftwaffe raids.

Of course, there was always the possibility a V-2 rocket could fly over, but now the newspapers were reporting that the Allies had captured the Germans' rocket-launch sites in France, everyone fervently hoped they'd seen the last of the inhuman killing machines that gave no warning.

Lately, instead of phones ringing and emergency bells clanging as drivers dashed out to rescue bombing-raid casualties, Jo and her fellow ambulance men and women had been tasked with collecting patients from hospitals in the lush green Essex countryside and ferrying them back to their local London hospitals.

The dozen or so white ambulances with red crosses painted on the side were parked up neatly in the asphalt playground along with the handful of messengers' bicycles that the council was now selling off.

The interior of the ambulance station had changed over the past month, too, and many of the tatty posters urging people to 'Keep the Blackout' or showing enemy aircraft silhouettes had been taken down, leaving pale spaces on the cream emulsion.

Where there had once been three telephones on each of the two desks on the stage at the far end of the school hall, now there was just one, and although the two massive blackboards on the wall behind the desks were still up, they had been scrubbed clean weeks ago. And, as if they knew they would never be needed again, the drab blackout curtains hung forlornly at the windows.

Jo knew how they felt. Like the dusty drapes, Jo and the rest of her friends milling around in the room wouldn't be needed again either: two days ago the government had announced that the Civil Defence Service was being stood down. It was for that reason they'd all chipped in for a couple of crates of beer and a few bottles of spirits to say goodbye to the place that had been their second home for the past five years.

'But although we can now celebrate because the end is in sight,' continued George Selwyn, his round face taking on a serious expression, 'we should also remember our dear colleagues who sadly aren't here with us today.' George raised the pint in his hand. 'Absent friends.'

Jo and everyone around her raised their glasses.

'Absent friends,' she murmured.

Taking a sip, she bowed her head. The faces of her comrades who had been burned to death in their vehicles, crushed under collapsing buildings or had had their lungs destroyed in a bomb blast appeared and then faded in her mind.

After a moment or two, she wiped a tear from her eye and looked up.

'We've had some good times, too, haven't we?' said Anne Wilkins, a tall blonde with pale blue eyes, who was standing beside Jo.

She was a few years older than Jo and, like her, had joined in September 1940, just weeks before the London Blitz started. She had two school-age children and her other half was on a minesweeper somewhere in the Mediterranean.

'We certainly have,' agreed Jo.

'Do you remember the look on Old Tyler's face when Olive pulled into the yard with her tyres in shreds after she drove over all those broken bottles when Truman's warehouse was hit?' asked Ivy Bostock, who was standing opposite Jo with a half-pint of stout in her hand.

Ivy was a dark-eyed brunette like Jo, but instead of having a ring on her finger, Ivy was, as she put it herself, 'joyfully unattached'. Between dodging enemy bombs as she tore through London patching up casualties, she was doing her bit for the war effort by making any American billeted in London feel a little less homesick.

'How could I forget?' laughed Jo, sloshing the dry sherry she was holding around in the glass. 'His face went so red I thought I'd have to whisk him off to the London Hospital because he was having a stroke.'

Ivy screwed up her face.

'Guard those tyres, ladies,' she said in a gruff tone, mimicking the Green team's shift leader. 'Rubber is more precious than gold.'

They laughed.

'And there were some hairy moments, too,' said Anne. 'Remember when that tramline cable in Stratford came down just a foot in front of your ambulance, Jo?'

'I certainly do,' Jo, replied, as the image of the live cable jumping about and sparking on the rails beneath her vehicle flashed through her mind.

'And what about when you were sent to help a woman who'd broken her leg jumping down from a first-floor window in a bombing raid, Ivy, and you ended up delivering her baby.'

'I remember that,' her friend replied. 'A boy. She called him Winston.'

'I doubt he'll thank her for that when he grows up,' said Jo ruefully.

Her friends nodded. Taking another sip of their drinks, they lapsed into silence.

Someone had climbed up on to the stage and dragged out the school piano and one of Blue team's drivers was warming up on the ivories. Others joined him on the stage, gathering around the instrument as they launched into 'Roll out the Barrel'.

'I can't believe it'll soon be all over,' said Jo softly, as her gaze ran slowly over the familiar faces of those singing around her.

'I know what you mean,' said Anne, in the same wistful tone. 'We've all spent so long talking about what we were going to do after the war and now it's here.'

'What are you going to do, Anne?' asked Ivy, her foot tapping along with the tune.

'I'm not sure,' Anne replied, swilling her sherry around in the glass. 'Fred mentioned about emigrating to Australia or Canada once he was let go from the Navy in his last letter. But I'm not sure. He's a qualified mechanic so I'm sure he'd get work, but it's a long way and it's not as if you can just jump on a train and come home. And then there's Mum. She had enough to say when I moved to Bethnal Green from Poplar, so Gawd only knows what she'd say if

I told her that me, Fred and the kids were off to the other side of the world.'

'Same as my mum, I shouldn't wonder,' said Jo, as the pianist changed tempo as he moved into the next song. 'What about you, Ivy?'

Ivy shrugged. 'No idea.'

'I thought you'd go back to the City,' said Jo.

'So did I,' said Ivy, 'but typing letters, answering phones and chasing around after some toffee-nosed banker is going to be very dull after what I've been doing for the past five years. Maybe I'll try my hand at something else, like working on a newspaper. What about you?'

'Well, I'm not sure either,' Jo replied. 'I've been helping my dad out at the yard, running some local deliveries in the Morris van, so I'll carry on doing that until Tommy's demobbed and then—'

'And then she'll be too busy having babies with that handsome husband of hers to do anything else,' cut in Anne, giving Jo an exaggerated wink.

Although pain squeezed her heart, Jo forced a smile.

'And talk of the devil,' said Ivy, looking past Jo.

She turned to see Tommy standing by the door; he was wearing his Royal Signal's uniform with his battle cap tucked in his epaulette. Free from constraint, his dark brown hair had regained its curly quality. As always, the sight of Tommy, with his tall, athletic figure, blunt chin and angular face, gave Jo an excited thrill that three years of marriage had done nothing to abate.

His dark eyes scanned the room and then he spotted her. Smiling, he strode across the space between them, and Jo met him halfway.

His arms wrapped around her waist as his lips pressed briefly on hers.

'Hello, Tommy,' she said, enjoying his embrace. 'I thought you weren't getting back until tomorrow.'

'I wasn't,' he said, his arms still around her. 'But I thought I'd surprise you. They need someone back at the London HQ for a meeting tomorrow, so I volunteered. I got to Euston an hour ago and came straight here.'

'I bet you could do with a beer,' said Jo.

'I most certainly could,' he replied. 'Do you want another?'

Jo shook her head. 'I'm fine.'

'Don't go away.'

Giving her a squeeze, Tommy strolled over to the two teachers' desks that were serving as a bar. Grabbing himself a brown ale, he returned.

Anne had joined the group gathered around the piano and Ivy was chatting to a couple of people at the far side of the hall, so Jo and Tommy stood together listening to those on the stage giving a lively rendition of 'Don't Sit Under the Apple Tree'. Then the tempo changed again as the pianist played the opening chords of 'We'll Meet Again'.

The whole room joined in, including Jo and Tommy, his deep baritone voice complementing the predominantly female singers.

However, as she opened her mouth to start the second verse, Jo's throat tightened.

Putting his arm around her shoulder, Tommy drew her to him and Jo rested her head on his chest.

'Silly, isn't it?' she said, wiping a tear from her eye. 'After all, we were saying just before you turned up how we've all prayed for this day for years and now it's here . . .'

'You've all been through so much together, it's not surprising you feel emotional.' He kissed her hair. 'It's natural.'

'You know, Tommy,' said Jo, smiling up at him, 'it might seem odd to say it, but I wonder if in years to come we might look back at the war and say it was the best time of our lives.'

'It certainly was for me, Jo.' He gave her that crooked smile of his. 'Because I married you.'

They shared a private look.

'But,' said Tommy, letting her go, 'it's the future we have to think about, which is why I've booked us a table at the Three Nuns.' He looked at his watch. 'It's for seven, but if you want to stay a bit longer then I'll—'

'No, that's fine,' said Jo. 'I'm ready to go when you are.'

Tommy swallowed the last of his beer.

'Well then, Mrs Sweete,' he held out his arm, 'your carriage awaits.'

Finishing her drink, Jo took it. 'And when you say carriage, you mean . . .'

He grinned. 'A number twenty-five bus.'

'That was absolutely delicious,' said Jo, after swallowing the last mouthful of trifle.

'It was,' said Tommy, wiping his mouth with the napkin. 'Although perhaps best not to ask the chef where he got the fresh cream.'

It was just after eight thirty and they were sitting in the restaurant of the Three Nuns Hotel, which was situated almost opposite Aldgate bus garage.

With tearful farewells and promises to meet up again soon, she and Tommy had left the ambulance depot two hours before and caught a bus at Stepney station almost immediately, so they'd had enough time for a quick drink in the hotel's bar before taking their table.

Although the hotel had started life as a coaching inn, the one she and Tommy were now in was a grand red-brick Victorian building. It was three storeys high and had an impressive central entrance with heavy oak doors and brass handles. The restaurant, with its worn carpet and tables draped in white tablecloths, was on the ground floor at the rear of the premises.

The restaurant's main claim to fame was, as the brass plaque on the dark wood-panelled wall stated, that Chief Inspector Abberline, celebrated for hunting Jack the Ripper, had held his retirement bash there.

Although it was a Wednesday evening, the restaurant was almost full, mainly with men in khaki like Tommy, but there was also the odd dash of Airforce blue and even a couple of Americans in their distinctive olive jackets and fawn trousers, plus a few soberly dressed City types. On the opposite side of the room was a glass door through to the bar, where a five-piece band was playing on the small stage and a handful of couples were shuffling around on the dance floor.

Spotting Jo returning her spoon to the glass dessert bowl, the slick-haired waiter sidled over.

'Do you want a coffee, luv?' asked Tommy, as the waiter picked up their empty bowls.

'Tea for me, please,' Jo replied.

Tommy gave their order and the waiter left them.

'So,' he said, smiling across at her, 'no more early shifts or night duties for you.'

'No,' said Jo with a sigh. 'It's going to feel very strange not putting on the old uniform.'

'Are you going to carry on at your dad's?' Tommy asked.

'I might as well,' said Jo. 'At least until our Charlie is demobbed. After that, now that the Town Hall will be selling off their ARP vehicles, Dad's talking about buying another lorry and taking on another chap.' She grinned. 'And at least Dad pays me the same as his two other drivers, instead of a third like most women get.'

'Yes,' said Tommy thoughtfully. 'That will be a great help.'

The waiter reappeared and set their hot drinks before them.

'For what?' asked Jo, as the waiter left and went to the next table.

Digging his spoon in the sugar bowl, Tommy shifted forwards.

'Do you remember me telling you just after Christmas that I'd heard the army was beginning to make plans for demobbing the troops once the war was over?' he said, stirring his coffee.

'Yes, because they didn't want men returning home like last time only to find themselves in the dole queue,' said Jo.

'That's right,' said Tommy. 'Well, we've had a couple of pamphlets around about what they are planning, and I picked this one up last week.'

Delving into the front of his battle jacket, Tommy pulled out a strip of paper and handed it to her.

'I've been mulling it over for a few days and made a couple of enquiries,' he added. 'What do you think?'

Jo glanced down at the bold lettering offering training opportunities for men who had been demobbed from the army.

'Train as what?' asked Jo.

'A teacher,' said Tommy. 'A maths teacher. I know it's a bit of a surprise,' he added, seeing her startled expression. 'But it's what you said earlier. About us looking back and seeing this as the best time of our lives. We're totally different people now than we were when the war started. All of us. Take me, for example,' he continued. 'What was I before the war? A tearaway who was always dodging the truant officer and who'd already done time in borstal. Your family had a fit when they found out we were walking out. Your sister Mattie hated me, so did Cathy. Your dad punched me in the face at one point, and I can't say I blame him. If my daughter was hanging around with someone like the me I was back then, I'd have done the same.'

'But I knew you weren't really like that,' said Jo, taking a sip of tea. 'And Gran was always on your side.'

Tommy gave a wry smile. 'Yes, she was. Bless her.'

'And you couldn't help it if your brother was one of East London's most notorious guvnors,' added Jo.

'No, but I was tarred with the same brush,' said Tommy. 'Not that I blame Reggie. He's done some terrible things and is paying for them now in Parkhurst. I'm not making excuses for him, but the odds were stacked against him, too. You know what my mother was like: a drunk who'd leave her children to starve so she could throw gin down her . . .' He swallowed hard.

'I was always good at unpicking puzzles and working out figures,' he continued after taking another mouthful of coffee to collect himself. 'But if it hadn't been for the war, I'd never have discovered that I have a talent for maths or ended up at Bletchley deci— doing my bit.'

'And that's why you want to train as a teacher?' said Jo.

'It is,' he agreed. 'I know the Labour Party are promising us free doctors and better housing, but you can bet your bottom dollar there'll still be kids, kids like I was, living in damp rooms and with drunken parents. They deserve to have a better chance in life, and I want to help them have one.'

'Oh, Tommy,' said Jo, with love and pride mingling together in her chest.

'There are bound to be some colleges in London offering the two-year course,' he continued. 'And there is a grant, but with the savings we have in the bank . . .' He sucked his teeth. 'I mean, we could use that but . . .'

Putting down her cup, Jo reached across and squeezed his hand. 'That money in the bank is so we can buy a house, which will be much more possible if you're a qualified teacher,' she said. 'And if you don't qualify for a grant,' she shrugged, 'then I'll carry on working for Brogan and Sons and you can become my gigolo.'

Tommy stared at her for a moment then threw his head back and laughed.

'Oh, I do love you, Josephine Margaret Brogan,' he said, the warmth in his eyes giving truth to his words.

'The feeling's mutual, Thomas Albert Sweete.' She raised the cup to her lips. 'And it's not as if I have to stay at home and look after children just at the moment.'

An odd expression flitted across Tommy's face. He took another mouthful of coffee and then cleared his throat.

'I wasn't going to say anything just yet,' he said, 'but as you've mentioned children perhaps we ought to talk about something else I've been mulling over since our visit to Dr Chivers.'

Jo's heart gave an uncomfortable thump.

'Something else?'

'Yes. It sort of links to what we've just been talking about.' This time it was Tommy who stretched across the table to take her hand. 'Now, Jo, I hope you know I want nothing more than for us to have children.'

'So do I, Tommy,' Jo replied, feeling the familiar ache clawing at her. 'And I'm sorry I've let you down.'

His other hand clasped hers tightly.

'Oh Jo, my darling, you haven't,' he said, anguish furrowing his brow. 'And you mustn't think like that. It's not your fault.'

'But Dr Chivers said it was usually the woman's—'

'I don't care what Dr Chivers said,' Tommy cut in. 'Fifty years ago, doctors didn't understand what caused diabetes until someone discovered insulin. And it doesn't matter. I married you, Jo, because I loved you, not just so you could have children.'

'I know,' said Jo, the raw pain of their situation cutting through her. 'But how many times have we talked about how we would bring up a family, the things we'd give them, things like trips to the seaside, holidays and new instead of second-hand clothes?'

'And we can still do that,' said Tommy, gripping her hand as his dark brown eyes looked into hers. 'We still can. If we adopt.'

'Adopt!'

'Yes.' Gripping her hand tighter between his, Tommy leaned forward. 'There are thousands of children left orphaned by the war and stuck in overcrowded children's homes waiting for adoption. Waiting for a mum and dad, Jo, like us, to love them.'

*

'So,' said Baldy Oliphant, the sun shining off his bare pate as he surveyed the class like a bug-eyed insect through the thick lenses of his spectacles, 'just because the allies have crossed the Rhine doesn't mean that your essay on the causes of the Indian Mutiny shouldn't be on my desk next Monday morning.'

Billy, who was sitting in his usual place tucked in the corner at the back of the class, suppressed a yawn.

Bloody history! Who needs to know why a bunch of foreigners on the other side of the world had got the arse about something?

It was just before lunch and around him were thirty or so boys who, like him, were preparing to sit their School Certificate Examination in two months' time.

Old Oliphant never tired of telling the history class that as a boy he remembered the British Victory at Rorke's Drift, and instead of spending his well-earned retirement taking in the air on a seafront somewhere, he'd stepped forward to do his patriotic duty by filling the gap when the younger teachers in the school had been called up in 1940.

To Billy's mind, however, rather than teaching a bunch of East End kids about the moral value of the British empire, the old fart's services would have been better employed against the Nazis by sending him to the front line so he could bore them to death with lectures on the three-field rotation system or the plight of the peasantry in the late Medieval period.

David Epstein, who he shared a desk with, nudged him with his foot under the desk then slipped him a scrap of paper.

Keeping his eyes on the teacher, Billy opened it, then read it quickly.

Slipping it between the pages of his exercise book, Billy looked across to the other side of the class to find Bunny Atkinson, a goofy boy with wire-rimmed glasses held together at one corner by Elastoplast, looking back at him.

Under cover of the boy sitting in front of him, Billy gave him the thumbs-up.

Glancing at the clock above the blackboard, Billy closed his book and pulled himself up straight like the rest of the class. As he waited for the lesson to end, his gaze slid on to Michael, sitting attentively in the second row from the front.

As always, several conflicting emotions that he couldn't name began percolating in Billy's chest, but just as they threatened to rise up, the bell in the corridor rang, signifying the end of morning lessons.

'Class dismissed,' said Mr Oliphant.

The silence was instantly replaced by the sound of chair legs scraping on wood as the boys shoved their books into their satchels so as to be first in the dinner queue in the school's refectory.

Standing up, Billy gathered his exercise books together and then, under the pretence of slotting them into his satchel, he flipped open a packet of Senior Service hidden at the bottom of his school bag and took out four cigarettes.

Palming two and keeping his eyes on his brother to ensure Michael had left the classroom, Billy slid them into his blazer pocket and sauntered out.

Bunny was loitering in the crowded corridor outside, but as he saw Billy emerge, he ambled over. Turning towards the wall to shield themselves from prying eyes, Bunny gave Billy a couple of coins. Glancing at them, Billy slipped them in his pocket and pulled out the cigarettes and gave them to Bunny.

'Ta, Billy,' Bunny said, tucking them into his inside breast pocket.

'Sor right,' said Billy, giving a little gangster shrug. 'If you hear of anyone else who wants some, tell 'em they're tuppence ha'penny and you can keep the difference.'

Bunny nodded and hurried away.

Billy shifted his attention to the main staircase, which led down to the dinner hall two floors below. Michael and a couple of his swotty friends had just reached it.

Turning the other way, Billy pushed against the tide of boys making their way to the refectory and headed for the back staircase that led directly down to the playground. Shoving aside a couple of first years who went home for dinner, and with his footsteps echoing in the narrow tile-clad stairwell, Billy ran down.

His shoes skidded on the loose gravel as he came to an abrupt halt at the bottom. Casting his eyes around the playground and finding it all but empty, Billy pulled his jacket straight at the front and, as casually as he could, sauntered towards the caretaker's side gate behind the bike sheds.

Stepping out into the street, he walked briskly to the end of the school's surrounding wall then stepped into the alleyway that ran behind it.

Out of sight, he took the packet of cigarettes from his satchel and, after taking one, he slipped them into his pocket alongside Bunny's coins.

Gripping the cigarette between his lips, Billy took a strip of matches with 'Rub A Dub' in gold letters stamped on the cover that he'd picked up at Aunt Pearl's.

Tearing one off and running it along the sandpaper strip, Billy held the flame to the tip of the cigarette and inhaled. Leaning back on the brickwork, he took another drag and closed his eyes.

'Bunking off again, Billy?'

Billy looked around to see Michael standing next to him.

Shoving aside the feeling of guilt niggling at him, Billy expelled a stream of smoke from the side of his mouth and gave his brother a cool look.

'What's it to you?'

'I'll tell you what,' Michael replied. 'If Dad and Auntie Ida find out—'

'Well, they won't,' his brother cut in.

'What about when Mr Norris calls the afternoon register?' asked Michael.

'I've asked Gumdrop to tell him I've gone home because I puked up in the bogs,' Billy replied.

Truthfully, threatened was probably a better word to describe his conversation, but as Arthur Stamp put it, you don't get nowhere being soft.

'So, not only are you going to get it in the neck from the headmaster, but poor old Rowntree will be in trouble, too, for lying,' said Michael.

Billy took another drag.

'I don't know what you're making such a fuss about,' he said. 'It's only poxy RE and English Lit this afternoon, so it's not as if I'm missing anything.'

Michael's features formed themselves into hard angles.

'It's not just about playing truant, Billy,' he said, looking uncomfortably like their father. 'It's where you're skipping off to.'

'I don't know what you're talking about,' Billy replied, forcing himself to hold Michael's unwavering stare.

'Don't play the innocent,' his brother replied. 'I know you've been to see Pearl because you come back stinking of her cheap perfume.'

'It ain't cheap,' Billy snapped back, as an image of all the expensive things in Lenny Stamp's house appeared in his mind. 'Aunt Pearl buys all her stuff from the posh shops up West.'

'Or what Lenny Stamp catches as it falls off the back of a lorry,' Michael replied. 'I've seen the stash of Benson and Hedges and the pound notes you've hidden in the Hornby trainset box, so I know she's been giving you cigarettes and money,' Michael replied.

Billy grabbed his lapels. 'You'd better not have taken any.'

Michael knocked his hands away. 'Don't worry, I wouldn't touch Lenny Stamp's stolen money with a barge pole.'

'It's not nicked,' Billy snapped back. 'Mr Stamp's a businessman.'

Michael sneered. 'And we all know what that business is, don't we?'

Matching his brother's angry expression, Billy's eyes narrowed. Everything had been all right at home until Michael turned up. Since then, it had been all 'he's a chip off the old block' and 'he's going to be tall when he's grown up'.

In truth, although he and Billy were known as the Brogan brothers, they weren't, in fact, related. It was a long story, but Jeremiah Brogan was Michael's father. He hadn't known Michael existed until Michael's mother pitched up three years ago and asked Jeremiah to care for him because she was dying.

Thanks to an argument between his parents at that time, Billy had found out that despite Ida shrugging off his un-Brogan-like appearance by saying he looked like her dead brother, he was actually Ida's sister Pearl's child. Ida and Jeremiah had taken him in when he was just a few days old.

So, it was all right for tall, brown-haired, blue-grey-eyed Michael with Brogan blood pumping through his veins. Whereas it was as plain as the nose on your face that, with his russet hair, hazel eyes and stocky build, Billy was a cuckoo in the nest.

But he did have a mother – Aunt Pearl – and when he was with her the feeling in his chest faded a little. He had a mother who made a fuss of him and didn't keep harping on about stupid schoolwork and behaving properly. Granted, she'd never said who his father actually was, but given Lenny Stamp's squat stature, fair hair and deep-set green-brown eyes, Billy couldn't help but wonder if he hadn't found his real dad, too.

Kinsale, Ireland. September 1887

HALF-CLOSING HER EYES in a vain attempt to stop the daggers of pain slicing through her brain, Philomena fixed her attention on the cream surplice covering Father Parr's brown cassock as he put the used sacramental vessels in order on the altar.

Although Philomena was usually vexed at being so far back from the miracle of the Mass, today the last place she wanted to be was in the church.

Sitting in the bishop's chair just to the right of the altar was a man wearing a black cassock and a holy expression on his lean face. A stranger in their midst, but one who'd set the reverend friars sitting in the chancel behind him twitching like a flock of brown hens who'd caught the scent of a fox.

The altar boys, too, who usually needed a nudge from Father Parr, sprang forward as if the soles of their feet could feel the heat of hell.

Mass had finished a few moments before, but instead of giving the final blessing, Father Parr stepped forward.

'Please take your seats,' he said, and the congregation shuffled off the hard floor and on to the equally unforgiving pine pews.

'It is a joy to welcome Father O'Callaghan, the sub-abbot of St Kieran's presbytery, who has journeyed for three days to join us this morning to celebrate one of our number answering God's call,' he said.

A thin smile lifted the visiting cleric's lean features as he inclined his head a fraction in acknowledgement.

'As you all know only too well,' Father Parr went on, 'three months ago Mr and Mrs Mahon's eldest son, Cornelius,' he glanced to his left where the Mahon family were sitting at the front of the church, 'suffered a terrible accident whilst returning from the Cork butter market.'

A murmur ran around the congregation as people gravely nodded their heads.

'Despite the ministrations of his mother, and Mr Mahon fetching a doctor from Dublin, no less,' continued the friar, 'their dear child, who'd not murmured a sound or opened his eyes since he was carried in and laid on his bed, seemed destined to join the angels above. Preparing themselves for the worst fate that can be visited upon any parent, Mr and Mrs Mahon appealed to Our Lady the blessed Mother of God to intervene.' The priest raised his eyes to the marbled arched ceiling above. 'And lo, she answered their fervent prayers.'

Everyone in the church – all except Philomena – crossed themselves.

'However, the blessings of heaven are not bestowed without cost or obligation,' Father Parr went on, returning his eyes to the congregation. 'Which is why Father O'Callaghan has joined our humble Mass today.'

Kinsale's long-serving parish priest stepped aside.

There was a pause and then Father Parr's apostolic superior took a step forward.

With the black skirts of his cassock sweeping the dust before him, the second in command at Ireland's foremost clerical seminaries stood at the top of the sanctuary steps.

His gaze ran munificently over the congregation before settling on the family sitting in the front pew.

'Patrick Mahon,' he said, in an oddly squeaky voice for one with so sombre an appearance.

As the raw-edged knives cut deeper into Philomena's brain, Patrick, who she had loved before time itself was born, stood up.

Father O'Callaghan beckoned him forward.

With his head held high and dressed in a new Donegal-tweed suit bought especially for the occasion, Patrick made his way between the rows of brown-clad clerics sitting in the choir stall and walked towards the altar.

Stopping in front of the sub-abbot, he knelt on the flagstone.

The novice-master looked down at him for a moment then placed his hands on the wild, black curls that Philomena had ruffled a thousand times or more.

'Patrick Boniface Mahon,' continued the black-clad brother, 'did you vow to give your life to the service of God and his people by training for the priesthood, and if you are judged fit for the office to take holy orders, if the Blessed Virgin Mary restored your elder brother, Cornelius Ignatius Mahon, to health?'

'I did,' Patrick replied, his firm voice echoing around the spacious church and Philomena's head.

'And do you confirm that vow before your family and friends?' asked the novice-master.

'I do confirm that vow,' Patrick replied, 'so help me God.'

Father O'Callaghan raised his hands from Patrick's curls and made a sign of the cross over his bowed head.

Again, the people sitting around Philomena did the same. Resting his hands on Patrick's broadening shoulders, Father O'Callaghan turned him around to face the congregation.

Tears formed on Philomena's lower lids.

Why had God snatched him from her?

Through her distorted vision, she watched Patrick as his eyes skimmed over the bowed heads until they met hers.

The space between them shrank as the other-worldly whispering invaded her senses.

Past images of them together flashed through her mind but then other, half-formed pictures appeared, too faint for Philomena to hold on to. But for once it wasn't just her who was aware of the ethereal reverberations, as Patrick looked alarmed.

With her eyes fixed on Patrick, Philomena stood up and stepped out into the aisle. Without thinking she took a step forward. He did, too, but before he could take another he was surrounded by his brothers and sisters and a dozen other members of the congregation.

The pulsing air connecting them vanished.

Margaret Mahon slipped her arm through Patrick's.

Together, with Patrick's father bringing up the rear and surrounded by well-wishers, mother and son made their way down the aisle.

The brutal pain slicing through Philomena's brain returned with a vengeance and little lights started popping at the edge of her vision. Turning, and although it would earn her a severe look from her mother for barging in front of the worthies of the town, she dashed for the door and stumbled outside.

Chapter Nine

THERE WERE ALREADY a couple of women with heavy coats wrapped around them and their heads bowed low entering the church's main door when Queenie arrived. Keeping her eyes downcast and pulling her hat lower over her face, she followed them up the flagstone path and into the cool interior.

As Friday confession had started two hours ago at ten o'clock, only a handful of women remained kneeling in the pews, scarved heads down and hands clasped together in prayer while they awaited their turn in the confessional box.

As she did every Friday at around this time, Queenie stepped into an empty pew. However, instead of quietening her heart ready for her weekly absolution at St Breda and St Brendan's, today she was seeking her weekly absolution in St Anne's three miles away.

The parish church of Bethnal Green bore more than a passing resemblance to St B and B as, give or take a year or two, it was built around the same time and for the same reason: to serve the large Irish community in Spitalfields. There were obvious differences, like the marble altar and rail, the stained-glass window above the high altar depicting St Margaret Mary and the Sacred Heart, but the smell of the candles burning in the votive and the moulded Stations of the Cross fixed around the wall were very much the same. And naturally, as in every Roman Catholic church in the land, the Virgin Mary stood looking down graciously at those worshipping in her dedicated side chapel.

As well as those waiting their turn to see the priest, there were a couple of women polishing chairs in the sanctuary in preparation for the next Mass.

With her hands clasped in front of her and resting on the pew, Queenie closed her eyes and attempted to marshal her raging thoughts. A young woman carrying a baby came out of the confessional box.

Queenie waited, and when no one else stood up, she rose to her feet and side-stepped out of the pew.

Keeping her head low on the off chance that someone might recognise her, Queenie made her way across the flagstones. Opening the door, she stepped into the dimly lit box.

The smell of carbolic, cheap perfume and sweat filled her nose in the dark stillness of the closed chamber. Putting her handbag on the floor, Queenie perched on the bench and, with her heart fair crashing through her ribcage, stared ahead.

After a moment the screen covering the fretted wooden grille beside her slid open.

Clasping her hands together, Queenie closed her eyes and bowed her head.

'Bless me, Father, for I have sinned,' she murmured. 'It's been a week since my last confession.'

'You are welcome, my child, although I sense you are not a regular to our church,' said the man sitting on the other side of the screen.

Truthfully, although the screen between them was supposed to hide the identity of the transgressor, every priest knew fine well who was in the adjoining box, which was why she'd travelled three mile and two stops on the Wapping-to-Shoreditch underground line to St Anne's.

'What is it you wish to confess, my child?' he added.

'Well, Father, it's not so much confess, as guidance on a matter of conscience that I'm after,' Queenie replied.

'In that case, tell me what's weighing on your mind.'

'I'm troubled by a truth that I've been hiding from someone for over fifty years,' said Queenie. 'I'd always intended to tell them, you understand, Father, one day. When the time was right. When the knowing of it wouldn't cause trouble or hurt but . . .'

'Why haven't you, then?' the priest asked.

'Well, you know how it is,' said Queenie.

'But now time's running out,' said the priest. 'Because they're not long for this world.'

Hidden in the darkness of the confessional booth, a lump formed in her throat.

'Yes.' Pulling the handkerchief from her sleeve, Queenie blew her nose. 'But after all this time, it will just open a can of snakes that even St Patrick himself couldn't be rid of, so perhaps it would be better to let sleeping dogs lie rather than rake up a past that cannot be undone or remedied.'

There was another long pause and a rustle of fabric as the priest sitting on the other side of the screen shifted on his seat.

'Commandments tell us not to bear false witness,' he said.

'I know,' agreed Queenie. 'But I haven't lied, Father, so much as just not said.'

'My child, omission is still a mortal sin,' he said.

Queenie's fingers tightened around her rosary and she bowed her head.

'I am sorry for the sin of lying and all my many and grievous sins,' she said, reciting the words she'd said so many times over the years. 'I ask pardon of God, penance, and absolution of you, Father.'

In the quiet darkness, Queenie waited.

There was a long pause then the priest spoke again. 'I'm sorry, my child, I cannot give you penance or give you absolution.'

'But why, Father?' said Queenie. 'For I am most truly and sincerely sorry.'

'I believe you are,' he replied. 'But it's not me to whom you should be confessing, is it?'

*

'Here we are, Billy,' said Pearl as the Bentley pulled up outside a parade of shops in West Ham High Street.

Hammer, another of Lenny's heavies who'd been tasked with running Pearl around that afternoon, got out of the driver's seat, then, walking around the front of the car, opened the back door.

Swinging her legs around, Pearl planted her red stilettos on the pavement and wiggled out.

Sliding across the leather seats, Billy followed her.

'Thank you,' he said, glancing up at Lenny's muscle-bound sidekick looming over him.

It was lunchtime and around them the good citizens of West Ham were going about their usual Saturday routine. For women, clutching the family's weekly coupon books, this meant searching the shops for something to feed their family. For men, of course, it meant a pint in the pub with their mates followed by an afternoon sleeping it off while listening to the football on the wireless.

It was the last weekend in April and almost two months since Billy had finally plucked up the courage to visit Pearl. Since then he'd been a weekly visitor.

Having promised Aunt Pearl he would visit her today, he'd had a bit of a panic yesterday evening when he'd heard his father talking to his gran about taking him and Michael to help with a removal job in Ilford.

Thankfully, after gobbling down his scrambled eggs and toast and telling his gran he was meeting his mates for a kick-about in Victoria Park, he'd managed to get out of the house before his dad returned from an early-morning delivery.

'You don't 'ave to thank him,' said Pearl, straightening her tight skirt. 'That's what he's bloody well paid for.'

Although Hammer's impassive expression remained, irritation flickered in the bodyguard's eyes.

Lenny had half a dozen or so men who were always close at hand. Most went with him wherever he went. They were all ex-boxers or wrestlers, with squashed noses, missing teeth and hands like shovels. Not one of them was under six foot, which made Lenny look like a schoolboy standing between them.

Those of them still with hair wore it cropped, and none had beards or moustaches. They all dressed in square-shouldered, single-breasted suits with white shirts and dark-coloured ties.

They must have had normal names, too, like Norman, William or Eric, but if they did, Billy didn't know them because they were all referred to by their nicknames, such as Box, who had a square-shaped head, or Ape, who had hair sprouting everywhere. Billy had assumed that Hammer was a West Ham supporter until he saw him gripping a sledgehammer and piling into a van with half a dozen of Lenny's other associates, who were all equally tooled up.

Billy had turned over a few nicknames of his own. He liked Billy the Kid, but that was taken. He'd tried to think of something that would mark him out but somehow Pencil Billy – because he liked drawing – or Billy the Beef – because Sunday roast was his favourite meal – didn't have quite the same ring to them as Slash or Punch.

Although the crew of bodyguards mainly went out with Lenny when he was 'doing a bit of business', there were always a couple hanging around the house. One stood sentry outside the front door or patrolled the backyard, while the other would be at Pearl's beck and call all day. Unfortunately for Hammer, he'd pulled that short straw today.

'Well, what do you think?' asked Pearl, placing her hand on her box-shaped hat and looking up.

Billy's gaze travelled over the building they were standing in front of.

It had clearly been a large shop at some point in its hundred-year history, but now the glass in the front windows had been decorated with cartoon images of girls in short frilly skirts and high-heeled shoes carrying trays of cocktail glasses, bottles and drink shakers. Between the glass windows there was a solid-looking black door fitted with three substantial locks and with stout metal bars fixed at regular intervals down it. Above the door and stretching the width of the building was a billboard surrounded by coloured light bulbs and with the words 'Rub A Dub' painted in fat red letters across it.

'Smart, ain't it?' added Pearl.

He nodded.

Truthfully, it looked a bit dingy, but he thought it better not to say that as he didn't want Pearl to think he was a wet-behind-the-ears baby.

Pearl looped her arm through Billy's. 'Come on, then. I'll give you a tour.'

Hammer jumped forward and knocked on the door, then, clasping his hands in front of him, he stood to one side and surveyed the street.

What looked like a tiny letter box three-quarters of the way up the door flipped open. A pair of narrow eyes peered out for a moment then the letter box snapped shut. There was a rattle of locks and the door opened.

Blinking in the sunlight from the dark interior was a man in baggy tweed trousers held up by braces over a grubby light blue shirt.

'Af'noon, Missis Stamp,' he said, the roll-up stuck to his lower lip bobbing as he spoke.

'Likewise, Tucker,' Pearl replied, marching in and taking Billy with her.

Hammer followed them and closed the door, plunging them into semi-darkness save for a couple of forty-watt lights high on the walls.

'This is my boy Billy,' Pearl said, pride beaming out of her black mascaraed eyes.

Tucker gave Billy a cursory glance then his attention returned to Pearl, and he nodded towards the ceiling. 'The Boss is upstairs.' With her arm still hooked through Billy's, Pearl marched him past the cloakroom on the left and the ladies' and gents' bogs on the right then up a narrow staircase.

'Here we are,' she said, releasing her hold on him when they reached the next floor. 'What do you think?'

Truthfully, Billy didn't quite know what to think.

When Pearl had talked about Lenny's club, he'd envisaged something like the Catholic Club at the back of St Breda and St Brendan's: a place where old men with wispy white whiskers played dominoes each lunchtime and grubby dock workers relaxed with a pint after the end-of-day hooter sounded. But the room they were now in couldn't have been more different.

All the windows were blocked off for a start, so the only illumination came from the lights sunk into the dark blue ceiling. Iron columns supporting the low ceiling ran around the outside of the room at regular intervals. The area behind them was raised and carpeted, with circular booths at the back with low, dangling lights over the central tables. Spaced out between the columns were two rows of small tables with four chairs around each of them. In the centre of the room was a small dance floor and a stage with a set of drums in the middle, and beside it was a long bar with row upon row of upended bottles of spirits in optics behind. Above the bar hung rows of sparkling glasses ready for customers.

Lenny, dressed in his wide-shouldered American-style suit, was leaning on the bar with a glass in his hand and a fat cigar clenched between his teeth.

'Here they are, Arthur,' he said, straightening up as he spotted them.

Aunt Pearl trotted over to him and, leaving a splodge of Crimson Sunset, planted a noisy kiss on his cheek.

'Miss me?' she asked, batting her mascaraed eyelashes at him.

He grinned. 'Always, Doll.'

Arthur, who was sitting in one of the booths, untangled himself from the blonde draped over him and rose to his feet.

'Wotcha, Billy Boy,' he said, strolling over to them. 'New togs?'

'Yeah, Aunt— Mum bought them for me,' said Billy, forcing the word over his tongue.

'Maxi Cohen's in Aldgate,' said Pearl. 'It's the new Continental cut. Fourteen guineas.'

'Nice, ain't it, Dad?' asked Arthur, who was dressed as always in an understated lounge suit.

'You look the dog's nadgers, son,' agreed Lenny, snorting cigar smoke from both nostrils.

Arthur ran his finger under the narrow lapel. 'Might pop along and get myself one.'

Billy's chest swelled.

The Worcester suit Pearl had bought him the week before was the best he'd ever owned. The light grey tone looked good on him and the box-shoulder style made him look broader.

'Got the tie there, too,' he said, smoothing the lemon silk.

Arthur's pale eyes ran over Billy again. 'What did the old rag-and-bone man and his missis have to say about your new schmutter?'

Anger flared at Arthur's sneering remark for a second, but Billy damped it down.

'Not much,' he said, ignoring the niggle of disloyalty in his chest.

Actually, nothing would have been nearer the mark as, although he'd told Pearl otherwise, his parents hadn't seen his new clothes.

Knowing that Flo Wallace at number 3 Mafeking Terrace was bedbound and so never went into the backyard, he'd slipped down the side alley between the houses and changed back into his everyday clothes in her outside bog. He'd then stored his new togs, wrapped in newspaper, in the disused potting shed at the end of her garden.

'How'd you get on selling those fags at school?' Arthur asked, feigning a couple of punches to the side of Billy's head.

'They went like hot cakes.' Fishing into his pocket, Billy pulled out two brown ten-bob notes and a half-crown and offered them to Arthur.

Lenny's son gave him a sideways look. 'What's your skim?'

Billy looked puzzled. 'Skim?'

'How much did you keep for yourself?'

As only the week before Lenny had sent Arthur round to 'punch someone's lights out' after they'd been caught with their fingers in one of Lenny's tills, unease prickled between Billy's shoulders.

'Honest, Arthur, cross my heart,' he said, blinking rapidly. 'That's the lot.'

Arthur studied him through narrowed eyes. 'What do you think, Dad?'

'Dunno,' said Lenny, eyeing Billy and cracking his fat knuckles loudly.

Billy's mouth went dry.

Arthur studied him suspiciously for a moment or two longer then grinned.

'Go 'way, boy,' he said, grabbing Billy roughly around the back of the neck and shaking him playfully. 'I'm just pulling your plonker. Here. Treat yourself.'

He flipped the silver coin in the air.

Billy grabbed it in mid-air and turned it over in his hand. His eyes stretched wide.

Half a crown!

'Cor, thanks,' he said, looking appreciatively across at Arthur.

Pearl hooked her arm through his again and gave it a little squeeze.

'See,' she said, her red lips spread wide in a smile. 'Didn't I say you'd be better off with me?'

Billy looked down at the coin nestled in the palm of his hand again.

A whole two shillings and sixpence! That's more than he got for humping furniture on and off his dad's lorry on Saturday mornings.

Pearl was right. He was much better off with her. After all, she was his real mum.

With the pain searing into her brain like a prong from the devil's pitchfork, Queenie dropped the chopped leek into the saucepan of cold water and put her hand to her forehead.

'Are you all right, Ma?' asked Jeremiah, who was sitting opposite her at the kitchen table munching his way through a plate of bubble and squeak.

'Yes, why wouldn't I be?' she snapped, glaring at him across the condiments.

'I'm only asking, because that's the third time you've put your hand on your head in as many minutes,' he replied.

She waved his words away with the vegetable knife she was holding. 'I've a bit of a head, that's all.'

He looked alarmed, as well he might because, praise be to Mary, a headache or indeed any illness was a rare occurrence for his mother.

And she wasn't all right. Not at all, and for a very good reason.

'I tell you, Jerry, I'm grand,' she said, forcing a smile.

Her son's attention returned to the plate in front of him.

It was lunchtime on the last Monday in April and Ida and Victoria were out shopping with Mattie and Jo, so only she and Jeremiah were home. He'd been out all morning doing local deliveries and had arrived back as the one o'clock news had started.

Queenie had been about her usual early-morning business, including dispatching, drawing and plucking one of the older chickens ready for a mid-week hotpot.

Pushing his plate away, her son stood up, took his donkey jacket from the back of the chair and shrugged it on.

Queenie looked surprised. 'I thought you were done for the day?'

'I am, but there was a note slipped under the gates this morning regarding a house removal to Bow, so I thought I'd save myself a job tomorrow and pop down there now.' Crossing to the back door, he opened it. 'And I hope your headache goes soon.'

Once again, Queenie waved away his words with the vegetable knife. 'I'll be fine, and sure, isn't it fading away already?'

Frowning, he gave her a considered look, then left the house, shutting the door firmly behind him.

Turning back to her task of preparing the vegetables for the family's evening meal, Queenie scraped the knife down the edge of the potato, but it slipped and instead of cutting away the knobbly skin, the tip sliced the top of her thumb.

'Jesus, Mary and Joseph,' she cried, dropping the knife and sticking her thumb in her mouth.

With the metallic taste of blood on her tongue, dizziness whirled around Queenie's head. Muttering and whispering enveloped her and, although the words uttered were unformed, she knew what they were saying. For sure, hadn't they been saying the very same for nigh on sixty years?

Throwing open the window, Queenie dragged in a lungful of air, hoping it would clear the ethereal miasma crowding in on her.

It did not.

Instead, the presence of death joined in the dance.

'Not yet,' she shouted, as images of Patrick Mahon flickered through her mind.

Queenie stood staring blindly out of the window for a moment, then, dropping the knife on the chopping board and ripping off her apron, she hurried through to the hallway to fetch her coat.

Fifteen minutes later, and dressed in her Sunday coat and hat and with her false teeth in, Queenie turned the corner of Sutton Street. Fixing her eyes on St Breda and St Brendan's rectory, she marched towards it.

While remnants of her headache remained, the clamouring of souls from the other realm was no longer tormenting her with their goading.

Reaching the rectory's stone portals a few moments later, she paused and looked up at the solid black door.

She'd always intended to tell him. Of course she had. But somehow the moment had never seemed right and there was always later.

Straightening her hat, Queenie squared her shoulders and with her eyes firmly fixed on the door she climbed the three front steps. Taking a deep breath, she made use of the knocker, the sound echoing through the house beyond.

There was a pause then the bolt was released, and the door creaked open.

Taking another deep breath, Queenie spoke. 'Compliments of the day to you, Mrs—' She stopped. 'Nora!'

'Well, saints above in all their glory, if it isn't little Philomena Dooley,' the woman said, her flat grey eyes mocking as they studied Queenie.

In the five decades since she'd last seen Father Mahon's sister, Nora's hair had turned to steely grey and there were now wrinkles etched deep on either side of her thin mouth.

'What are you doing here?' Queenie asked.

Nora's scrubbed face formed itself into a sneer. 'Sure, where else would I be when my brother has need of me?'

'Where's Mrs Dunn?' asked Queenie.

'Gone,' Nora replied. 'And good riddance. Sure, the woman couldn't take care of a doll's house let alone a rectory, so I sent her packing.'

'So who's going to look after the rectory and Patrick?'

Nora's substantial eyebrows rose in surprise.

'Well, I am, of course,' she replied. 'Now, as you know full well why I'll not be inviting you in for tea and cake, you can be on your way.'

'But I need to see Patrick,' said Queenie.

Nora's close-set eyes narrowed. 'It's *Father Mahon* to one such as yourself, and you can't see him because he's resting.'

She went to shut the door, but Queenie put her hand on it. 'But I have something to tell him.'

'It will have to wait, as you'll not be seeing him today.' Nora's face screwed up into an ugly expression. 'You were always one for forcing your way in where you weren't wanted,' she snarled. 'You tried to make trouble for my brother once before. I stopped you then and I'll stop you now. So get you gone, Philomena Dooley, before I call the police.'

She slammed the door and the glass in the fanlight above rattled with the force of it.

Queenie stared at the peeling paint and large brass ring for a moment then turned. With her feet like lead weights at the end of her legs, she trudged down the steps.

Blindly, and with the long-forgotten images of Nora, Patrick and herself careering around in her mind, Queenie stumbled along until she found herself back in Watney Street Market, but as she passed Glinkerman's, the milliner on the corner of Brinsley Street, the strength in her legs started to desert her. Staggering past shoppers queuing outside Harris the butchers, she pushed open the saloon door of the Lord Nelson.

The pub, with wooden floorboards, half a dozen booths fixed against the walls and rough-hewn tables and chairs, was very much like the many other local pubs that had been built a century earlier. The name of the brewery that supplied the beer had once been painted on the bevelled windows, but the glass had been blown out in '41 when the Anglican parish church of Christ Church opposite the pub had suffered a direct hit. There were boards across the windows now instead of glass, which gave the smoke-stained interior an even dingier appearance.

But the regulars didn't complain. With its dartboard at the far end, piano in the corner and sticky floors, the Lord Nelson was a working man's pub, where dockers, stevedores and labourers could savour a well-earned pint at the end of the day.

Thankfully, as the public house's lunchtime stint was nearly over, there were only a few customers supping their pints.

'Wotcha, Queenie,' said Vernon, wiping a tea towel around the inside of the glass he was holding. 'Half of Guinness?'

'Double brandy,' Queenie replied, as her heart threatened to burst from her chest.

Vernon raised an eyebrow, but taking a tumbler from the rack above his head, he pressed it under one of the optics fixed to the wall behind the bar.

Handing over a shilling, Queenie took her drink. She tucked herself into the corner of one of the leather-clad booths.

With shaking hands, she raised the glass to her lips and savoured the smooth spirit rolling down her throat. Resting back, Queenie focused on one of the dust-covered light shades dangling from the ceiling and her pulse steadied.

There was no wondering as to why Patrick's sister had come to the rectory. For sure, wasn't it expected of an unmarried daughter to do her Christian duty and nurse any member of the family in need of it? But in the name of all that was holy . . .

Nora's snarling face loomed in her mind again and the pall of old hatreds and wrongs not yet righted closed in on her, but just as she feared they would suffocate her, the pub door burst open and the young assistant from Mark's Shoes, a few doors down, ran in.

'They've just told us on the wireless,' he shouted. 'Hitler's dead!'

The rattle of the bedroom door handle drove the last wisps of sleep from Patrick's mind and he opened his eyes.

'Good morning to you, Patrick,' said Nora, as she elbowed open the door and walked into his room carrying a tray. 'I've your breakfast for you to enjoy.'

'That's very kind of you,' he said. 'But Mrs Dunn usually serves me up my first meal of the day in the dining room.'

'Well, that may have been so,' Nora replied, setting the tray on the dressing table, 'but you've got me to care for you now.'

'And 'tis good of you to do so but—'

'There's no buts about it,' she cut in, grabbing a napkin and shaking it out. 'Martha and Doreen have their own families, and sure, aren't they always tending some grandchild or another with a crop of spots or a sticky ear so they have no time for their spinster sister. Whereas you, Patrick,' bending forwards she manoeuvred the bedside breakfast table over his lap then looked up at him, 'have need of me.'

She returned to the overloaded tray on the dressing table and started pouring the tea.

Patrick studied his sister's solid back and burly shoulders.

As he hadn't seen his younger sister for almost twenty-five years, when Mrs Dunn showed Nora into the rectory's parlour, it had taken him a moment to realise who she was.

Standing no more than five foot one, steely grey had replaced his sister's light brown hair, and what had been shallow furrows around her mouth and eyes were now deeply etched lines.

Although as a young girl Nora had favoured bright colours and flouncy trimmings, since she'd arrived, he'd seen her dressed only in unadorned greys and browns. Today she was wearing such a garment covered by a wraparound apron. Other than the hem of her skirt being below her solid knees instead of floor length, it was the sort of thing Sister Cecilia, the nun attached to his parish, would have worn.

He'd been somewhat puzzled as to how Nora had even known he was unwell.

It seemed that after the doctor had told him there was nothing more they could do for him and it was only a matter of time, the hospital had telephoned Father Timothy to ask if he had any family still alive, and when they were told he had, they'd phoned through to the Kinsale police to inform them. When the news reached Nora, she had organised the feeding of her cat in her absence, packed her moth-eaten portmanteau, put the shutters up on her cottage and booked the first available crossing.

'There you are,' she said, placing a cup of steaming tea in front of him. 'I've porridge, eggs and, as no one around here would know a white pudding if it strolled up and bid them good day, you'll have to make do with pork sausages and a rasher. And, of course, there's toast and what is supposed to be plum jam but surely to God looks like beetroot in jelly.' She gave him a bright smile. 'What would you like first?'

'First!'

Nora frowned. 'Well, you will need feeding if you're to return to your Holy calling, Patrick.'

'Perhaps a bit of egg on some toast, and a sausage.'

Nora turned back to the tray. She returned to his side a moment later and set down a plate laden with two fat-drenched fried eggs sitting on two lavishly buttered rounds of toast with two sausages alongside.

Patrick studied his breakfast practically floating in melted lard for a moment and then looked back at his sister.

'The doctor says that perhaps I should be cutting down a wee bit on the old greasy foods, Nora,' he said.

'Pff,' said Nora, batting his words away. 'Sure, aren't they forever telling a body that what they've eaten since Moses was a lad is bad for them? And besides,' she said, shaking out the white napkin and tucking it over the top button of his pyjama jacket, 'a man needs a full belly to do a day's work.'

Giving his sister a wan smile, he picked up his knife and fork.

Satisfied that he was doing as he should, Nora strode over to his wardrobe and opened the door.

'I thought I might go through your clothes and see what needs cleaning and repairing,' she said, pulling out one of his cassocks and hooking it over the door.

'That's good of you, Nora, but Mrs Dunn has been repairing the odd tear and dabbing off a stain as she sees them.'

Nora's thin lips pulled a little tighter.

'Has she now?' she said, as she inspected a cuff. 'Well then, she'd better invest in some new spectacles as I found two loose buttons and a pulled seam on your overcoat only yesterday along with—'

'Why don't you tell me all the news from home, Nora?' cut in Patrick, as he sliced through a sausage. 'Colleen wrote me a while back to tell me that her eldest has been blessed by the arrival of another wee girl.'

Dropping the cuff she was holding, Nora moved on to the second sleeve. 'That she has . . .'

As Patrick munched his way through his sausage and egg, Nora ran through the happenings of the Mahon family living on the other side of the Irish Sea. To be honest, there were so many Josephs and Patricks and Marthas and Marys it was hard to keep track.

'Well,' he said as she finished the long list of births, first communions and marriages, 'it seems the Mahon family has taken the Almighty at his word and gone forth and multiplied.'

The hint of a smile lifted the corner of his sister's mouth. 'That they have. Sure, the women of our family have only to have their husbands hang their trousers over the end of the bed than they are with child. Sure, aren't the men the same? For our Connie is a father of ten and Pete has eight himself who call him pappy.'

'And what about you, Nora?' he asked. 'How are you finding it being so far from home?'

'It's a mite strange, to be honest,' she replied, moving on to the half a dozen clerical shirts hanging on the rail. 'But I seem to have found all the essentials, although understanding what in God's Holy name anyone is saying to me is another matter. For the folks hereabout speak a language I'm not acquainted with.'

'It just takes a bit of getting used to,' said Patrick with a smile. 'But once your ear gets attuned to the way East Londoners speak, you'll soon get their meaning right enough. And there are plenty of us from the old country around and about. In fact, our old friend from Kinsale, Philomena Dooley, is a member of the parish, so both of you will have a mountain of news to talk about after all this time. She's known as Queenie now and has—'

'Hell will be a frozen mass below our feet before I'll be talking to the likes of Philomena Dooley,' cut in Nora.

'It's almost sixty years ago, Nora,' he said.

''Tis no mind nor matter, Patrick,' she replied. 'I'll never forgive her for what she did, and in front of the whole parish, too . . .'

Turning back to his wardrobe, Nora pulled out his everyday cassock.

Patrick studied his sister's tight shoulders for a moment then spoke again.

'Sure, what else could she do under the circumstance? And Fergus admitted it were he who'd got her in the family way,' he said.

'He would never have betrayed me had she not tempted him,' Nora said, brushing the fabric forcefully with her hand. 'Not content to have half the boys in the town trailing after her like hungry dogs, Philomena Dooley had to turn those gypsy black eyes on my Fergus.'

'But you have to lay the blame for what happened at Fergus's feet, too, Nora.'

'I will not,' snapped Nora. She jabbed her finger at him. 'And don't you be making excuses for her, Patrick Mahon, for didn't you yourself almost—' Pressing her lips together, she turned away. There was a long pause then she squared her shoulders and faced him again. 'I'll leave you to finish your breakfast in peace as I have to find my way to the Town Hall to collect my temporary ration book.'

Nora marched out of the bedroom.

Patrick stared at the door she'd just slammed behind her.

It was more than fifty years, that was true, but try as he might, he hadn't forgotten Philomena Dooley's gypsy black eyes either. How could he when he'd been gazing into them regularly each week at Mass ever since?

Kinsale, Ireland. June 1890

AS FATHER PARR raised his right hand to give the congregation the final benediction after Sunday Mass, Patrick Mahon, who towered over the elderly priest standing next to him, looked up.

His blue-grey eyes, that had drifted unbidden into Philomena's dreams, locked with hers.

For a second, or perhaps it was eternity, time stopped. Her heart did a little double beat then it rushed forward like a racehorse in sight of the winning post.

Unable to look away, Philomena was forced to admit, sin though it might be, with him in a black cassock still stiff with newness and a white dog collar beneath his square jaw, that she was still as much in love with Patrick Mahon as she had been when he'd left three years ago for St Kieran's seminary.

After he'd left, Philomena had started by telling herself that there were plenty more fish in the sea, then that theirs had been an innocent childhood friendship. Then, as the months passed and the boys from town began to call at her cottage clutching meadow flowers and sitting politely with her family on Sunday afternoons,

Philomena had almost convinced herself that she would soon enough be in love with someone else.

Even as she'd taken her place beside her mother on their usual pew just over an hour ago, she'd imagined that when she saw Patrick, she'd realise what a foolish notion it had been to think she'd ever been in love with him at all.

However, from the moment he'd strode in – tall, broad-shouldered and with the altar candle highlighting the dark richness of his black curls – she had been lost. But more than lost, because the intense and unsettling expression in his eyes as they'd met hers had ignited a yearning for his arms around her, and the feel of his lips pressed hard on to hers.

And why would she not?

For surely there wasn't a more handsome young man walking the earth than Patrick Mahon, a man that by all that was right and proper should be making vows to her not to the Almighty.

Father Parr made the sign of the cross. Philomena mumbled her response automatically and ran her fingers across her chest lightly as the congregation around her did the same.

However, instead of processing out, Father Parr stepped forwards to the edge of the dais.

'Please be at your ease,' he said, and people scrambled back on to the pews.

'As you can see,' he went on, casting his gaze over his assembled flock, 'we have a familiar face among us this morning. Patrick Mahon – or Father Mahon, as he will be soon.'

A murmur of approval ran around the assembly.

'I know it is a proud day for our dear friends and generous benefactors Margaret and Joseph to see a son received into the Church,' the parish priest continued, as Patrick's mother, in a hat that must have cost three birds their lives to beautify, preened herself in the front row. 'And, as the bishop wrote to me only the other day, Patrick, who grew from boy to a man in this very town, completed his studies at seminary in an exemplary manner.'

People around Patrick's parents murmured their congratulations and Margaret Mahon acknowledged them with a haughty nod of her head.

'He's amongst us for just a wee while,' continued the elderly parish priest, 'then he must travel to Dublin, after which he will be on the high seas and away to somewhere in England unknown to us and to Patrick, but I'm sure the Good Shepherd will send him to a place amongst the Godless English where he is sorely needed.'

Heads nodded and male voices grumbling 'proddies' could be heard.

'I'm sure Patrick, who I've known since his mother first carried him into this holy place, will keep us and his birthplace in his heart and prayers, won't you, son?'

Looking down the length of the church at Philomena, Patrick spoke.

'Always,' he replied in a rich, vibrant voice as his eyes locked with hers once more. 'My heart will always be in Kinsale.'

Father Parr said something else, and Patrick replied, but their words were blotted out by the pounding of blood through Philomena's ears as a surge of some barely understood emotion vibrated through her body.

'As if having one of our town's sons give his life to the service of God isn't enough to have us all rejoicing,' said Father Parr, his words cutting through the fog in Philomena's brain, 'the Mahons have another blessing to share with us this morning. For haven't they just given permission for their daughter Nora and Fergus Brogan to be wed?'

Another murmur went around the church as all eyes shifted on to the young couple sitting in the Mahons' family pew.

'Come out, the both of you,' Father Parr said, beckoning them to join him on the dais. 'Don't be shy.'

Nora, wearing a new gown and jacket, and with a bonnet

overloaded with artificial flowers, stood up immediately, dragging her red-haired, red-faced fiancé behind her.

Clutching tightly on to Fergus's arm and with a self-satisfied expression on her face, Nora looked out at them all. In contrast, Fergus, looking ill at ease in his hopsack jacket and best corduroy trousers, kept his eyes on the tiled floor under his feet.

Father Parr raised his hands again and mumbled something over them.

The congregation clapped loudly then Nora dragged Fergus back to their seats.

Father Parr gave a couple of other notices of things happening in the parish, then, with Patrick slotted between the choir and the half a dozen brown-clad monks from the local monastery, those in the sanctuary processed out.

The congregation sank to their knees, then, when enough time had lapsed to be respectful to God's house, the Mahons rose to their feet and made their way down the aisle towards the church's main door.

With resentment and loathing rising in her chest, Philomena watched Patrick's arrogant parents from between half-closed eyes. As the party drew closer, Fergus's gaze settled on her. The hungry look she'd seen so often flared in his pale eyes as he was swept along by Nora.

A cloud of something grey squeezed the air from Philomena's lungs. Closing her eyes, she took a couple of slow breaths to steady herself. She scratched a cross over her breastbone and rose to her feet.

Genuflecting towards the brass cross on the altar, she squared her shoulders and followed her parents slowly out of the church.

As she expected, Nora's friends, their dresses festooned with ribbons and their corkscrew curls bouncing about their plump faces, were already clustered around the soon-to-be bride, while their mothers had laid claim to Patrick.

He was standing a little way away to the right of the main door with his mother, who had a face on her as if she'd just birthed the Saviour of the World. Around them, and just as excited as Nora's overdressed friends, were the matrons of the parish. All no doubt saying they wished it had been their sons who had been chosen by God while secretly giving thanks that it wasn't.

As Philomena emerged from the church into the spring sunlight, Patrick looked at her. They gazed at each other for a moment then just as he was about to step forwards, one of the town's matriarchs blocked his path.

Ducking through the chattering families, Philomena headed down the path a little way until she was clear of the crowd.

Taking another deep breath, she turned her face to the sun and breathed in the perfume of the wildflowers growing between the moss-speckled granite gravestones.

Getting command of her racing heart, she opened her eyes and looked across at the crowd still milling about outside the church, and of their own accord, her eyes sought out Patrick.

He was still surrounded by a bustle of matrons, a fixed smile on his face, but his gaze shifted over their heads on to Philomena.

Their eyes locked again for a moment or two then she wrenched free and hurried back down the path towards the lychgate.

'Philomena!'

Although she knew who was calling, she didn't turn.

'Mena, wait, please!'

Philomena stopped.

Someone came to a halt behind her, so, taking a deep breath and with her heart fair leaping from her chest, she turned around.

Patrick had changed from a boy to a man in the two years he'd been away, his jawline and cheekbones squaring the previously boyish shape of his face. His beard, too, had thickened so that even though it was only midday, newly sprung bristles covered his chin.

Although it was a cardinal sin to desire a priest, looking up at the man she'd loved before time itself, the urge to throw herself into his arms and kiss every inch of his beloved face almost overwhelmed her.

'Hello, Mena,' he said, staring down at her with those familiar blue-grey eyes.

'Hello, Patrick,' she said, pinning her arms to her side to stop them winding themselves around him. 'How are you?'

'I'm well,' he replied, his eyes soft and warm as they held hers. 'And yourself?'

'I'm grand,' she replied, feeling anything but. 'And congratulations on—'

'When I saw you in church I knew.'

'Knew what?'

'That I should never have gone along with my mammy's vow to St Mary,' he replied, his eyes blazing with fury.

She shook her head. 'But you did, Patrick. Three years ago and you'll be gone for ever in a week so—'

'But I love you,' he cut in, his voice hoarse with emotion. 'I've done my best to convince myself that we were just children but seeing you . . .' He raked his fingers through his black curls. 'God, what was I thinking?'

Tears sprang into her eyes.

'I'll tell them—'

'It's too late.'

Turning, she ran down the path towards the stone portals of the churchyard.

'Please, Mena,' he called after her. 'I can't—'

'Leave me be, Patrick,' she shouted over her shoulder as tears streamed down her face. 'For the love of all mercies, Patrick, leave me be.'

Chapter Ten

'THERE YOU GO, me darling,' said Jeremiah, placing a glass of brandy and orange in front of Ida.

'Thanks.' Ida smiled up at her husband. 'It's busy in here for a Monday.'

'I'm not surprised,' said Jeremiah as he resumed his seat beside her. 'For haven't folks spent the whole day glued to the wireless without any reward for it.'

'Surely we won't have to wait much longer,' said Ida, taking a sip of her drink. 'I mean, Hitler's been dead for a week.'

It was just after twenty past seven and she and Jeremiah were sitting in the upstairs bar of the Catholic Club.

Situated around the corner from St Breda and St Brendan's church, this was the place where the Brogan family and the rest of the local Catholic community celebrated everything from cradle to grave.

The hall had been built fifty years ago and was a square, functional building typical of the Edwardian period.

However, although some of the wartime precautions were still in place, the club steward and committee had clearly decided to start returning the bar to its pre-war state.

The odd sign urging women to 'Come into the Factory' or to 'Back the Great Attack with War Savings' remained, but most of the posters had been taken down and replaced with framed photographs of the club's past presidents.

The same was true of the main hall below. For the past four days, dozens of women, clad in the forest-green uniform of the WVS, had been packing up the truckle beds and dismantling the rest centre they had operated for the past five years to make way for the return of the Brownies, Cubs, Irish dancing classes and the weekly baby clinic run by the nurses at Munroe House.

However, even though the woodwork was in desperate need of a lick of paint, the shine on the tables and chairs had long since vanished and some of the flock wallpaper was peeling near the ceiling, the bar where the Brogans were having a quiet drink was both comfortable and friendly.

'So do you think you'll bid for the ARP Luton lorry you saw last week?' Ida asked as her husband slurped the head off his Guinness.

'I will,' he replied, licking the creamy foam from his top lip. 'But I'll be paying no more than two hundred and thirty for it as it'll cost me a tenner on top to have Fred in Brittain's Garage paint "Brogan & Sons" on the side. I'll have to park it in front of the house until I sign the lease on the new yard.'

'So you're going to take that one you liked the look of in Canning Town?' said Ida.

'I reckon so,' Jeremiah replied. 'It's more than big enough for all the vehicles as we expand, plus it already has a brick-built office at the front, so customers don't have to walk through a grubby yard to find us. It'll probably take a few months of toing-and-froing between meself and the land agent, but I expect we'll be able to shift the business over by September.' He gave her a considered look. 'Have you given any further thought to what we spoke about before?'

Ida's heart gave a couple of uncomfortable thumps. 'What, about getting a new cooker?'

Taking another mouthful of his pint, her husband shook his head.

'Moving to East Ham,' he replied.

'I can't say I have,' said Ida airily.

Actually, that was a barefaced lie because she had, a lot. Usually staring up at the ceiling at three o'clock in the morning.

'There's plenty of time to think about that once Charlie and Archie get back from the army,' said Ida.

'East Ham's only five miles away, Ida.'

'I know, Jerry,' said Ida breathlessly. 'But with Francesca in the family way again, Cathy's Heather not yet three months and Mattie with her three, I want to be on hand in case I'm needed. And I can't desert Jo, not now she and Tommy are seeing a consultant.'

'I know you've got a lot on your mind at the moment, luv,' he replied, giving her a sympathetic look, 'but perhaps if we went and saw a couple of hou—'

'And then there's your mother,' cut in Ida.

Her husband blinked. 'My mother?'

'Yes,' said Ida, relieved to veer on to a safer subject. 'Surely you've noticed how odd she's been recently.'

He raised an eyebrow. 'Odder than usual?'

'Much,' Ida replied. 'For a start, apart from Friday confession she hasn't been to church all week and yesterday I found her sitting on the bed looking at that old photo of the church back in Ireland.'

'Well, now you mention it,' said Jeremiah, 'it was as clear as the nose on your face she had a brutal headache the other week yet she all but parted my head from my shoulders just because I asked her if she was all right.'

'Queenie had a headache?' said Ida.

He nodded. 'I should think because the spirits are worrying at her,' said Jeremiah, raising his pint to his lips again.

Ida rolled her eyes. 'I say it's more like she's getting old.'

'I wouldn't let her hear you saying that if I was you, Ida,' chuckled Jeremiah.

'Well, she is,' Ida replied. 'After all, she is seventy-four in a couple of months.'

Jeremiah swallowed another mouthful of Guinness and then put his glass on the table in front of them.

'Now, Ida,' he said, looking her in the eye, 'about us looking at a new—'

'Hold up, everyone!' shouted Pete, the club's barman, as he twiddled the knobs on the Bush wireless behind the bar. 'There's an announcement.'

The low mumble of voices ceased.

'It is understood that in accordance with the arrangement between the three great powers,' the BBC announcer's crisp tones blared out, 'an official announcement will be broadcast by the Prime Minister at three o'clock tomorrow, Tuesday afternoon, 8 May. In view of this fact, tomorrow will be treated as Victory in Europe—'

'It's over,' screamed someone, then the whole bar, including Ida and Jeremiah, jumped to their feet. Someone started singing 'Roll out the Barrel' while another opened the piano lid and sat down.

Ida stared open-mouthed for a moment then burst into tears. 'Oh, Jerry,' she sobbed.

'There, there,' he said softly, drawing her into his strong embrace. ''Tis all over now.'

'I know, I know,' she mumbled into his broad chest. 'But all the pain and suffering.'

'Indeed, and I should think the good Lord himself will weep when it's all known.' He pressed his lips on to her hair. 'But, me sweet darling girl, we survived.'

'Hurry up, Jo,' called Mattie, swinging around and walking backwards in her two-inch heels. 'If we don't get there soon, we'll be stuck at the back.'

'I'm trying, Mat,' Jo said, breaking into a trot. 'But the whole of blooming London must be here.'

'That's why we have to hurry, Jo, or we won't be able to see,' shouted Cathy, over a chorus of 'There'll Always be an England'.

Jo wasn't wrong.

It was Tuesday 8 May, and the hands on Big Ben had been showing five thirty when Mattie and her sisters had passed it fifteen minutes ago.

The three Brogan sisters, kitted out in their best togs, were marching down The Mall towards Buckingham Palace, surrounded by at least a thousand other Londoners, all waving Union Jacks and singing at the top of their voices.

Even though they'd jumped on a westbound District Line train at Stepney Green just before midday, by the time the three of them had stepped out of Trafalgar Square station the area around Nelson's Column was already chock-a-block.

Although there hadn't been an official announcement that the war was over, everyone knew the Germans had surrendered so the whole of Piccadilly, Whitehall and Westminster was filled with people milling around expectantly.

After eating their packed lunch perched on the steps leading up to the National Gallery, the sisters had headed to Whitehall where, squashed behind two burly policemen, they'd listened to the Prime Minister's speech broadcast over the loudspeakers set up for the purpose.

Jo had popped in at Mattie's the day before while she and Cathy were having a cuppa. She'd suggested that, as all their husbands were away and as the Government hadn't yet announced that the war was well and truly over, they should go up to London to hear that news first-hand rather than sitting around the wireless waiting.

Now, surrounded by people celebrating, Jo caught up with Cathy and Mattie, and Mattie hooked her free arm through her younger sister's.

'Right, the Brogan girls are here so let the celebrations commence,' she said, beaming as she turned from one sister to the other.

Her sisters grinned as they fell into step.

'There'll be blue birds over . . .' started Cathy.

'The white cliffs of Dover,' trilled Jo and Mattie as they joined in.

With the red-sky sunset cutting across the top of the Wellington Barracks, Jo, arm-in-arm with her sisters, sang at the top of her voice as they headed towards Buckingham Palace.

Reaching the end of the red-tarmacked road, the crowd around them fanned out around the statue of Queen Victoria.

'Can we get up on the statue?' asked Jo, glancing up at the Old Queen towering above them.

'I can't. Not in these heels,' said Cathy. 'We'd be better off by the railings.'

'Quick, over there,' said Cathy, grabbing Mattie's arm and heading towards the tall central gates.

The three of them ran forward. Jo reached the wrought-iron fence first and spread herself wide to block a couple of sailors from taking the space.

'Good spot,' said Mattie as she and Cathy reached her.

'That's what I thought,' said Jo, as people piled in around them. 'We'll have a clear view of the balcony when the King and Queen come out.'

'Do you think they'll come out soon?' asked Cathy.

'Well, we saw old Winston's limousine inch through the crowds in Parliament Square as we cut across Horse Guards to The Mall, so him and the King are probably cracking open a bottle of Scotch like everyone else,' said Cathy.

'Bottle of champagne more like,' said Jo. 'And some caviar, I shouldn't wonder.'

'Only if the Queen's got enough points left over on her ration card,' said Mattie.

They laughed.

'Pity Francesca couldn't come,' said Cathy, as the refrain of 'Run Rabbit Run' drifted over them.

Mattie raised an eyebrow. 'Well, as she said herself, spending all day on her feet nearly five-month gone wouldn't be the most sensible thing to do. But, as the true friend she is, she offered to have my three overnight. Just as well as Daniel is still away in conflab with his American counterparts somewhere in England, as the BBC put it.'

'Mum said he's decided to stay in the army,' said Jo.

'Yes,' said Mattie. 'He said there's a lot of mopping-up to do in Europe.'

'Tommy said the same,' said Jo. 'But he's had enough and now he's been accepted onto the teacher training programme he's counting the days till he gets his discharge.'

'Is that someone in the balcony window?' Cathy shouted, bobbing up and down on her toes.

'I don't think so,' said Mattie, shielding her eyes from the glare of the setting sun. 'It's just the reflection on the glass.'

'I tell you something,' said Cathy, 'I'm glad we had that cuppa and bun at that WVS canteen on the Embankment earlier.'

'Me too,' said Mattie. 'And spent a penny in the station.'

'Look at those idiots,' said Cathy, looking past them to the other side of the palace railings.

Mattie and Jo turned to see a couple of young lads shinning up the lamp-posts around Queen Victoria's statue.

A man somewhere bellowed, 'We want the King!'

With one voice the crowd took up the chant.

'We want the King!' screamed Jo, gripping the railings and jumping up and down.

'We want the King!' shouted Cathy.

Fixing her eyes on the empty balcony on the other side of the gravel parade ground, Mattie joined in with the chorus of voices that echoed back to them as the sound bounced off the palace walls.

'There they are,' she screamed, pointing at the balcony.

The curtain moved, then the double doors swung open and a roar of 'The King!' went up from the crowd.

'There he is,' shouted Jo, as King George, dressed in his naval uniform, stepped on to the balcony.

'And there's the Queen,' added Cathy. 'And look – Princess Elizabeth and Princess Margaret are with them.'

Without missing a beat, the crowd, who was halfway through a chorus of 'We'll Meet Again', moved effortlessly into the first few bars of 'God Save the King'.

As the familiar tune swelled to a roaring anthem, a shiver ran up Mattie's spine. She closed her eyes and drew a deep breath as the voices of a thousand Londoners boomed around her.

'Long live our gracious King,' she sang with all her might.

The King, Queen and the two princesses waved to the crowd, and a roar went up. The people pressed into the road, hanging off the railings and lamp-posts and piled up along The Mall sang the national anthem twice more, then someone started on 'Land of Hope and Glory'. Grown men and women wept and hugged each other, friends and strangers alike.

'No more screaming bombs and casualties dug from the rubble,' said Jo softly.

'Or Ministry of War telegrams delivered to mothers, wives or sweethearts,' added Cathy.

A cheer went up again as the royal family waved their farewells and left the balcony.

The sober mood changed as the opening refrain of 'We'll Meet Again' drifted up into the warm spring evening.

As the three sisters sang along, swaying to the rhythm, others standing around did the same.

A lump caught in Mattie's throat as she remembered listening to the sentimental melody as she and the children lay in their cage-like Morrison shelter, the ground shuddering as the bombs dropped around them.

She looked at her sisters and saw tears glistening in their eyes, too. Reaching across, she took their hands.

'It's over,' she said, her vision distorted by tears.

With her lips pressed together and her chin trembling, Cathy nodded.

Jo stared at them both for a moment then burst into tears.

Feeling as if her chest would burst with love and utter relief, Mattie wrapped her arms around them both as they sobbed in each other's arms.

After a few moments of unrestrained weeping, Mattie raised her head.

'Come on, you two,' she said, giving them a bright smile. 'We're supposed to be celebrating.'

'You're right,' Cathy replied, unravelling herself from Mattie's embrace.

'You're right, Mattie,' Jo agreed. 'The whole country's cried enough in the past six years.'

'And it's over,' said Mattie.

Cathy slipped her arm into hers. 'I'll drink to that.'

'I bet my mascara's run,' said Jo. She reached down to open her handbag, but someone bumped into her and she fell against Mattie.

'Come on, let's get that drink Cathy mentioned,' said Mattie, hooking her arm through her younger sister's. 'And you can fix your face in the pub.'

'Ee-aye, Ee-aye, Ee-aye-oh,' sang Jo, bobbing unsteadily on her left leg while she swung her right leg in a circle.

She staggered a little as she returned her foot to the ground, but having regained her step, she bobbed on the spot as the circle of merrymakers belted out the next few lines. Then, as everyone drew breath, Jo linked arms with the young girl and the elderly ARP warden chap on either side of her.

'So knees up, knees up, don't get a breeze up, *Knees up Mother*

Brown.' She and the rest of the prancing circle surged forwards to the centre.

In truth, after five or perhaps it was six gin and tonics, Jo didn't quite know how long they'd been in the pub. When they had finally emerged from the smoky saloon bar back into the street, you'd have been forgiven for thinking it was the middle of the rush hour.

Piccadilly had been swarming with carousers, singing and dancing as lorries and cars, horns blazing and overloaded with people waving flags and banners, drove back and forth.

After a bit of a discussion, the three sisters had decided that the night was still young, so they'd wandered back to rejoin the revellers at Buckingham Palace.

After a bit of an incident with one of the bushes in Green Park, which Mattie had to pull her out from, Jo and her two sisters had returned to the expansive area surrounding Queen Victoria's statue.

Belting out, 'Oh my, what a rotten song' at the top of her lungs, Jo now wobbled back to her starting point but then lost her balance.

Circling her arms like a windmill, she staggered back, but just as she felt the ground disappearing from under her, she collided with something.

'Sorry,' she said, sidestepping a couple of times as she regained her balance.

'That's all right, luv,' said the solid-looking naval rating who'd stopped her fall.

Dressed in his loose-fitting navy-coloured bell-bottom uniform with the traditional collar and a white flat cap, the sailor was holding a half-full bottle of Johnnie Walker and standing with a couple of other Jack Tars.

'Are you all right, sweetheart?' asked one of them. 'Cos you look a bit unsteady on your pins.'

Jo pulled herself up to her full height.

'I'm perfectly fine, thank you,' she said, wobbling slightly on her heels.

Flicking his spent roll-up on to the floor, another one of the sailors stepped forward.

'You look a bit unsteady to me,' he said, taking her arm. 'Perhaps we can see you home.'

'That won't be necessary,' Mattie's voice cut in.

The sailor let go of Jo's arm and an artless smile lifted his thin face. 'Yeah, course.'

'This is my sister,' said Jo, as Mattie took hold of her arm. 'Ahoy, shipmates,' she said, saluting the group of matelots as her sister dragged her away.

Skirting a winding line of revellers doing the conga, Jo stumbled alongside her sister, waving at people as she passed.

'Where did you find her?'

Jo looked around and Cathy's face swam into view.

'About to be press-ganged,' said Mattie.

Cathy took up position on the other side of Jo.

'Perhaps the walk to Westminster station will sober her up,' said Cathy over Jo's head.

'Hang on,' said Jo. 'I'm not drunk!'

Mattie laughed.

Jo pulled herself free of her sisters.

'I'm not,' she insisted, swaying from side to side.

Her sisters smiled and slipped their arms in hers.

'Of course not,' said Mattie, in the big-sister tone Jo hadn't heard since the playground.

Cathy raised an eyebrow and looked at Mattie. 'Home?'

'Home,' repeated her oldest sister.

Jo broke free.

'Not yet, it's only . . .' She looked at her wristwatch, but the numbers kept jumping about so she gave up. 'What time is it?'

'About twelve thirty,' said Mattie.

'And if we stay any longer, we'll miss the last train,' said Cathy.

A group of people started singing 'Down at the Old Bull and Bush', and Jo felt the urge to dance again.

'Come on, Cathy,' she said, bouncing forwards and hooking her arm in her sister's. 'Let's dance. If we miss the last train, so what? We can catch the first one in the morning.'

'We could,' said Mattie, catching hold of her arm again. 'But we've got the VE Day party in the street tomorrow and you don't want to be too tired to enjoy it.'

'No, I don't,' said Jo. 'Tommy's coming back from Bletchley especially.'

'Then you'll have to get your beauty sleep and look your best,' said Cathy.

Jo nodded emphatically. 'I do.' An image of her husband smiling at her drifted into Jo's mind. 'I love Tommy.'

'We know,' said Mattie, as she and Cathy gently walked her forward.

With her sisters holding her a little more firmly than Jo thought strictly necessary, she allowed herself to be guided through the crowd, but as a group of people moved aside, they came face to face with a young woman with short brown hair and dressed in an ATS uniform complete with cap. There were two burly soldiers standing on either side of her.

Mattie and Cathy's mouths dropped open, and they stopped dead.

With some difficulty, Jo managed to focus on the young woman. She frowned. 'I know you,' she said, as her brain scrambled to fit a name to the face.

The young woman looked amused. 'Do you?'

Jo nodded. 'I've seen you before. You don't live next to Dolly Curran in Tarling Street, do you?'

'Jo!' hissed Mattie, her eyes fixed on the trio standing in front of them.

'I'm only asking, Mat.' Jo glared at her sister for a moment then turned her attention back to the young woman. 'I know where I've seen you before,' she said, clicking her fingers. 'You serve behind the cheese counter in Sainsbury's.'

'You'll have to excuse my sister Jo, Your Highness,' said Cathy. 'She's been celebrating.'

'I am very pleased to hear it,' said the young princess, in a clear, clipped voice. 'My sister and I are, too.' She indicated towards another young woman in civilian clothes with her own pair of brawny companions. 'After all, it's not every day we win a war, is it?'

'No, Your Highness,' said Cathy.

Jo blinked and stared at the young woman again.

The young woman smiled. 'Well, we must go, but I hope you enjoy the rest of the evening.'

She walked off, with her attendants bringing up the rear.

Jo stared after her. 'So, she doesn't work in Sainsbury's?'

'No, Jo, she doesn't,' said Mattie, giving her a meaningful look. 'And she lives in Buckingham Palace not Tarling Street, because *that* was Princess Elizabeth.'

Jo turned and looked at the King's eldest daughter and her two bodyguards for a moment then she cupped her hands around her mouth.

'Me and my mum met your mum in Commercial Road,' she shouted after the heir to the throne.

'Nearly there, Jo,' said Mattie. The arm encircling Jo's waist guided her towards the kerb.

Cathy, who was on the other side, adjusted her hold on Jo's arm, which was draped over her shoulder.

Blinking, Jo looked around. She spotted the square tower of St Dunstan's Church over the rooftops and realised they'd reached Stepney Way.

Pausing to let an ATS wagon with its horn blaring and crammed with people waving Union Jacks pass, Jo and her two sisters crossed into King John's Street, where she and Tommy lived.

The street was a dog-leg shape with Stepney Green at the other end. Like Jo's parents' road, it was lined on both sides with old two-up two-down workmen's cottages, with minuscule backyards and front doors that opened straight on to the street.

'Here we are. All safe and sound,' said Cathy, as they came to a halt in front of Jo's house. 'Where are your keys, Jo?'

'In my bag.'

Looking down, she fumbled with the catch of her bag.

'Let me,' said Cathy, taking it from her.

After a bit of rummaging, Cathy pulled out the key, but just as she was reaching to fit it into the lock, the door opened and Tommy stood in the doorway.

Jo's gaze ran over her husband, dressed in his khaki shirt and combat trousers, with his Army tie loose around his neck. She freed herself from Mattie's embrace and staggered forwards.

'Tommy!' she shouted, throwing her arms around her husband and planting a noisy kiss on his cheek, leaving a smudged lipstick mark.

Encircling her waist, Tommy drew her closer and grinned. 'Looks like you lot have had a good time.'

'We certainly did,' laughed Cathy.

'Particularly your wife,' added Mattie. 'How many G&Ts was it?'

Jo glared at her eldest sister for a moment then her attention turned back to her husband.

'I'm not drunk, Tommy,' said Jo, as the memory of the joy and euphoria of the London crowds sent a tingle up her spine. 'I'm just happy.'

She flung her arms wide and lost her balance. Tommy's grip tightened around her waist.

Jo gave him a puzzled look. 'I thought you were coming back tomorrow.'

'I cadged a lift off of one of the chaps.' He raised an eyebrow.

'Well, I'm glad you did.' Mattie yawned. 'Because we've a party tomorrow down home so I need my beauty sleep.'

'If you give me a minute to get Jo sorted, I'll walk you both home,' Tommy said.

'It's all right,' said Mattie. 'My three are with Francesca so I'm staying at Cathy's. See you at Mum's tomorrow. Night, Jo.'

Jo waved at her sisters as they turned and walked away.

Tommy closed the door. As he turned back, Jo's legs buckled beneath her but before she collided with the lino he swept her up.

'Right, missis,' he said, pressing his lips on her forehead. 'It's a cup of tea and bed for you.'

Jo lay her head on Tommy's shoulder and gave herself over to the pleasure of his strong embrace as he carried her upstairs.

Sitting her on the candlewick counterpane, he took off her jacket and shoes, then plumping up the pillows behind her, he lifted her legs on to the bed. Giving her a swift kiss on the head, he went back downstairs.

Jo closed her eyes and listened to Tommy clattering about in the kitchen below. She must have nodded off because in what seemed like just a few seconds he was standing by the bed with two cups in his hands.

'Just what the doctor ordered.' Placing their tea on the bedside cabinet, he sat on the bed.

Looking up at the man she'd loved for as long as she could ever remember and who she would love into eternity and beyond, sadness rose inside Jo.

She took his hand. 'I love you, Tommy.'

He smiled that quirky little smile. 'I'm glad to hear it.'

'I'm sorry, Tommy.' Tears welled up in Jo's eyes.

He looked puzzled.

'About the baby,' she added.

Sadness flitted across Tommy's handsome face.

He looked down at her for a moment or two then tenderly gathered her to him.

'You've got nothing to be sorry about,' he said softly, pressing his lips onto her hair. 'Nothing at all.'

Closing her eyes, and as her heart ripped in two, Jo sobbed helplessly on to her husband's chest.

'Sorry I woke her,' said Mattie, gazing across at Cathy, who was sitting in the old armchair beside the bedroom fireplace feeding her daughter.

'I'm not, Mat,' said Cathy. 'Because after missing her afternoon and bedtime feeds, my charlies were just about bursting.'

Mattie, wearing one of her sister's nighties, was sitting in Cathy's double bed with a couple of pillows propped up behind her.

The alarm clock on the bedside table was showing ten past one and it was half an hour since they'd left their inebriated sister in her husband's care and retraced their steps to Mile End Road.

Although well past closing time, the Black Boy, Old Globe, the Kings Arms and the Black Horse further down Mile End Road had all still been open and were as busy as they had been when they'd passed them earlier that day.

After a short walk down Globe Road they'd crept into the house so as not to wake Cathy's children and her mother-in-law Aggie, whose bedroom was, in fact, the back parlour.

Cathy's bedroom was the largest of the upstairs rooms and was situated at the front of the house. It smelled of the somewhat odd combination of talc, flowery perfume and linseed oil. The former two courtesy of Cathy and Heather and the latter from Archie's stack of completed oil paintings and canvases.

Thankfully, although there was a boisterous party going on outside one of the houses further down the street, no one had stirred as Cathy and Mattie had crept up the stairs in their stockinged feet. Well, except Heather, who had woken as soon as her aunt opened the bedroom door. Leaving her sister to change and feed her baby, Mattie had crept back down to the kitchen and made two cups of Horlicks. These were now sitting alongside the alarm clock on Cathy's bedside cabinet.

'She's such a darling,' said Mattie, as her curly-haired niece relinquished her mother's breast.

'She is. And I know,' lifting the sleepy baby, Cathy kissed her cheek, 'the moment your dad sets eyes on you, Heather, you'll have him wrapped around your little finger.'

'And so she should,' said Mattie. 'Doesn't Dad call it "the joy of being a father of girls"?'

In the low mellow light from the bedside lamp, Mattie exchanged fond looks with her sister.

'I still can't believe it's all over,' said Cathy. 'Well, in Europe at least.'

'Yes, but we shouldn't forget about those poor soldiers stuck in the tropics,' agreed Mattie.

'Do you think the Japs will surrender now Germany has?' asked Cathy, laying her milk-sated daughter on her lap and buttoning up her nightdress.

'I hope so,' said Mattie. 'Daniel has been having lots of meetings with the Americans so I have the feeling that now Germany has surrendered, the Allies are hatching some plan to bring the war in the Far East to an end.'

'Thankfully, Archie's bomb disposal unit didn't get shipped to France until last November. There are some poor sods stuck out in Burma who haven't seen their kids for years,' said Cathy, putting her daughter over her shoulder and patting her back lightly.

'There's also a whisper going around that the Government will start releasing men from the army in a couple of weeks,' said Mattie. 'There must be thousands of mothers, wives and sweethearts all over the country counting the days until their menfolk are home. I know Francesca is. Especially with another on the way in a few months.'

The sound of people singing 'We'll Meet Again' in the street drifted into the bedroom.

Cathy's mouth drew into a hard line. 'Of course, not everyone will be pleased to see their menfolk.'

'Oh, Cathy,' said Mattie, hearing the anxiety in her sister's voice. 'Even if Stan does come back, after throwing in his lot with the so-called British Free Corps, I'm sure he'll find himself dangling alongside his Nazi chums once the Allies get their hands on him.'

'Well, I hope so,' said Cathy. 'Because even if the authorities lock him up and throw away the key, having a traitor for a husband isn't grounds for divorce, so unless Stanley ends up dangling from the end of a rope, I won't be able to be Archie's wife.'

Chapter Eleven

'THERE YOU GO, Gran,' said Jo, handing Queenie a pint of Guinness.

'Bless you,' she said, her work-worn hand closing around the cool, smooth glass. She took a sip and smiled up at her granddaughter. 'For sure, isn't this the true manna from heaven?'

'Especially with a dash of Jameson. Would you like me to fetch you a little something?'

Jo indicated the long table in the middle of the street that had been draped with bleached bed sheets which were being used as tablecloths. Not that you could see much of the white linen as the table was laden with sandwiches, cakes and jellies, which were being consumed with great gusto by the children of the street, all of whom had been scrubbed clean and were wearing their Sunday best for the occasion.

'No, I'm grand,' Queenie replied. 'But you can keep me company for a wee while if you've a mind.'

Grabbing one of the family's dining chairs that she'd brought out to the street earlier in the day, Jo sat down next to her grandmother.

'It's a glorious day, isn't it?' she asked, gazing down the street.

Jo was right.

In fact, after years huddled in damp Anderson shelters or rolled in blankets on underground station platforms while bombs rained down on them from above, it was a day that many thought would never come. VE Day.

Well, if the truth be told, it was 9 May, the day after VE Day, but the whole country was still celebrating and none with more joy than the residents of Mafeking Terrace.

Once it was clear that, with Hitler dead, the war was as good as over, Ida and the rest of the street had spent the previous few days stringing homemade bunting all along the street from bedroom window to bedroom window. To add to the festive appearance, there wasn't a house without a Union Jack either hanging out of an upstairs window or flapping on a broomstick or washing pole leaning next to the front door.

Families had brought out chairs to sit on, but apart from mothers supervising smaller children, everyone else was milling around chatting or singing around a piano that had been dragged from someone's front parlour.

Alongside the enthusiastic choir, behind an improvised bar, and opening bottles of pale ale for all she was worth, was Mo Flint from the Railway Arms around the corner. She clearly didn't have to worry about licensing laws regarding the selling of beer outside a designated premise because Sergeant Bell from Arbour Square police station was chatting to Tommy as they supped their pints.

The youngest Brogans were ranged along the table and tucking into the VE party feast, supervised by Mattie and Cathy. A section at the far end of the communal table had been separated off for the senior school children. Billy, Michael and Kirsty were having their celebratory tea there without the fear of the younger ones splattering them with jelly and custard.

As her sisters-in-law were keeping an eye on her two toddlers, Francesca was sitting chatting to a couple of neighbours with Heather on what was left of her lap; her five-month bulge was pretty much taking up the rest of it.

'Are you not having a drink yourself?' asked Queenie, noticing her granddaughter cradling a glass of lemonade between her hands.

Jo shook her head and winced. 'I went a bit over the top with the G&Ts last night, Gran.'

'Oh well, I don't suppose you're the only one who's feeling a tad delicate in the head today,' Queenie replied, suppressing a smile. 'After all, 'tis not every day we win a war.'

'I see Dad's still snapping away,' said Jo, nodding towards her father, who was standing at the end of the table and focusing the lens of his newly acquired Box Brownie on the rows of children. 'I heard Mum say that he's used up two rolls of film already.'

'I'm not surprised,' said Queenie. 'He's taken three of me.'

Jo's pretty face lifted in a warm smile.

'And so he should,' she said. 'And we'll all want a copy, Gran, when they're developed. He took one of us three girls with Francesca and another of just me and Tommy.' Jo took a sip of her drink. 'I hear there's talk of Father Mahon leading the church's annual parade in a few weeks.'

The image of Patrick's ashen complexion flashed across Queenie's mind. 'Who told you that?'

'Sister Cecilia heard about it from Father Mahon's sister.' Jo frowned. 'Surely he must have mentioned it to you when you saw him last week, Gran.'

'He . . . he did; of course he did,' said Queenie. 'It must have slipped my mind.'

Well, for sure he would have told her, had she been able to get past Nora.

Twice she'd been there in the last week and twice that sour-faced sister of Patrick's had slammed the door in her face.

Her granddaughter's brown eyes studied her for a moment then Jo reached across and took Queenie's hand.

'I know you're worried about him, Gran,' she said, squeezing Queenie's fingers gently. 'But at least his sister has come over to look after him. I bet you're relieved after all you've said about Mrs Dunn over the years. It seems strange that you all grew up together.'

'It was a long time ago,' said Queenie, as several images of Nora flashed through her mind.

Taking another sip of her lemonade, Jo laughed. 'And you must share such a lot of happy memories.'

Raising her Guinness to her lips, Queenie took a long draft of its creamy foam but didn't reply.

Skirting around a couple of toddlers running across the cobbles, Tommy strolled over.

'How are you doing, Queenie?' he asked as he stopped in front of them.

'Grand I am, as I hope you are yourself,' she replied, looking up at him fondly.

'Not bad,' he replied. 'Did Jo tell you I've been accepted for the teacher training course at Borough Polytechnic Institute? And that we've an appointment at Barnardo's next Thursday afternoon.'

'Just to talk to the matron,' added Jo, the painful longing in her voice slicing to the chords of Queenie's heart.

'Well, may God be with the two of you on both scores,' Queenie replied, aching for both of them.

Giving a final flourishing twiddle on the keys, Barney Wales, who'd been banging away on the piano for the past hour, stood up to take a break, and a couple of members of the Shamrock League, with fiddles under their arms, stepped forward. They started to play 'When Irish Eyes are Smiling', a firm favourite among those families who'd come from the Emerald Isle.

'Can I steal my wife away for a dance, Queenie?' asked Tommy.

'With such a fair tune playing it would be a sin not to,' Queenie replied.

Tommy held out his hand.

Downing the last of her drink and placing her empty glass on the floor beneath her chair, Jo stood up. She gave her husband a bright smile and took his hand. 'Lead the way.'

Tapping her foot to the beat of the music, Queenie watched Tommy take Jo into his arms.

It was the devil's own cruelty that Tommy and Jo, who would

nurture and raise a child so tenderly, should be denied the chance. Especially when, as she knew only too well herself, a man's seed could be planted even in one brief moment of never-to-be-forgotten love.

As the baby shifted inside her, Francesca placed her hand on the little foot or hand pressing out and yawned.

'Looks like Heather's not the only one who's ready for her bed,' said Cathy, as she tucked a pink blanket around her infant daughter sleeping in her pram.

Francesca nodded at her sister-in-law. They were sitting on a couple of chairs outside her parents-in-law's house. As it was almost eight in the evening, across the rooftops opposite the setting sun was cutting red streaks across the western sky. The long central table had been cleared away some time ago and the cobbled street was now filled with friends and neighbours, drinks in their hands, laughing and joking together. Jo and Tommy were over by the improvised bar chatting to Mattie and her husband Daniel.

Daniel, who was a major in the Intelligence Corps, was stationed in Whitehall. He had arrived about an hour ago and now stood holding eighteen-month-old Ian in his arms with his tie loosened and his jacket unbuttoned.

The older children, including Billy and Kirsty, were hanging around the piano at the far end of the street, giggling and fooling around with others in their early teens. Michael, on the other hand, was with his friend Jane practising their jitterbug skills amongst a handful of couples bobbing about as Barney Wales belted out 'Boogie Woogie Bugle Boy' on the ivories.

Francesca smiled. 'Yes, it has been a long day, but one to remember.'

'I'm surprised that little lot are still going,' Cathy said, indicating her and Mattie's younger children, who were still running about the street despite it being hours after their bedtime.

'It's a pity Charlie and Archie aren't here to enjoy it with us,' said Francesca.

'I know, but at least they will be coming home,' said Cathy.

Francesca nodded, and they sat quietly for a moment as they both thought of the thousands of men, both soldiers and civilians, who wouldn't be returning.

The tempo of the piano changed, and someone started singing 'I'll be Seeing You'.

'Has Archie said what he'll do when he's demobbed?' asked Francesca, as the dancers slowed to a waltz.

'In his last letter he said he'd apply for a job in Ford's new engine plant at Dagenham as soon as he gets back,' Cathy replied.

'Will you move to Essex, then?' asked Francesca, thinking of the open fields and swampy wasteland you could see from the windows of the Southend trains.

'I'm not sure we'll go that far, but perhaps East Ham or Barking,' said Cathy. 'Archie wants something with a garden for the children. And we're likely to get something with four bedrooms, too, so his mother can have an upstairs room instead of having to make do in the back parlour.' Alarm flashed across Cathy's face. 'But for goodness' sake, whatever you do don't tell Mum.'

'I won't.' Francesca frowned. 'But I had the impression from something your dad said the other week that your parents were thinking of moving that way too.'

'Dad is,' said Cathy. 'But Mum's not too keen, although with half the roof missing, I don't see she has much choice. What about you and Charlie?'

'Well, Charlie is obviously going into the family business and as your dad's looking for another yard out Canning Town way, it makes sense for us to do what you're going to do and move eastwards too.'

'What about your dad?' asked Cathy.

'He's worn out, so he's decided that once he finds someone to take on the lease of the café, he'll retire,' said Francesca. 'After all,

Gio won't take it over as I expect he'll find a job in London when he leaves the army. At least until him and Grace start a family, then who knows.'

There was a kerfuffle at the other end of the street between Victoria and another little girl until Francesca's father-in-law Jeremiah stepped forward and swept up his daughter into his arms.

He said something to the pianist, who ran his fingers up and down the keys then struck up the opening bars of an old music-hall song.

'If you were the only girl in the world . . .' Jeremiah sang, his rich baritone voice echoing between the back-to-back houses and down the street.

Balancing his daughter on his forearm, he adopted a theatrical posture.

The little girl laughed and there was a collective 'ah' as a sentimental expression spread across several faces.

'Your dad's really hamming it up,' laughed Francesca, as her father-in-law rolled his eyes Al Jolson-style at the child with her arms around his neck.

Along with the rest of the crowd, Francesca and Cathy joined in with the chorus, Jeremiah conducting them with his unoccupied arm.

Everyone applauded as he finished, and then with Victoria in his arms, he strolled over to his mother, who was sitting with another couple of grandmothers, cradling what Francesca guessed was a Jameson.

He said something to her, and she shook her head. Refusing to take no for an answer, Jeremiah said something to his three-year-old daughter who shouted, 'Come on, Gran,' at the top of her voice.

People started shouting and whistling, so, after giving her son a sharp look, Queenie downed the last of her drink and stood up.

Everyone applauded as she took her place beside the piano.

However, instead of whispering to Barney, she beckoned to one of the fiddlers standing by the bar.

They exchanged a few words and then he tucked his violin under his chin and a long plaintive chord ran out as he scraped his bow across the strings.

'When first I saw the love light in your eyes,' sang Queenie, in a clear pure voice.

The whole street hushed as Queenie's pitch-perfect tone filled the air.

The ballad was a simple one, about a couple whose love blossomed at first sight on the village green when the singer and her beloved were just sweet sixteen. It went on to explain that even though, in the passing years, they had drifted apart, he still dreamed of her and still loved her as much as when he first saw her on the village green.

Tears formed in Francesca's eyes as others took handkerchiefs from their pockets.

Queenie sang it through twice and when she finished there was a burst of applause.

'Honestly,' said Cathy, pulling her handkerchief from up her sleeve, 'I must be getting soft in my old age cos every blooming time my gran sings I'm in floods.'

'You and me both,' said Francesca, catching a fat tear with her finger as it rolled down her cheek. 'Reminds me of how I felt all those years I was in love with Charlie, and he never even noticed me.'

'Well,' said Cathy, glancing at Francesca's bulging stomach, 'it seems my brother is making up for lost time now.'

Smoothing her hand over her stomach and feeling the baby nestled within, Francesca smiled, then her gaze returned to Queenie.

The old woman was acknowledging her audience's appreciation with a forlorn smile that was at odds with the joy of the day.

Although she was at least ten years older than Francesca's father, Queenie still did the family's washing every Monday and regularly carried two full shopping bags back from the market several times a week. However, now she looked as if her years had caught up with her.

If Mattie's theory about Queenie and Father Mahon was indeed true, Francesca suspected that Queenie's choice of song meant a great deal more to her than the casual listener would suspect.

Kinsale, Ireland. June 1889

WITH THE DUST from the dry road rising in little puffs under her bare feet, Philomena picked up her pace. Not that she was in any hurry to get home, even though she'd delivered all her mother's potions to her regular customers in town.

The cloudless sky was as blue as the Virgin's cloak and the sun had been bathing Kinsale and the whole of the east coast of Ireland in a blanket of warmth for days, ripening the crops in the fields and drying washing on the line in a matter of hours. However, for Philomena, the glorious day that God had sent them did nothing to lift the black cloud that had enveloped her ever since Patrick had caught her after church two days before.

In contrast to the mellow day, inside Philomena a storm raged. A storm with Patrick at its centre.

How often had she dreamed of him coming back to Kinsale and telling her he loved her? But now his words pounded over and over in her head until she feared her skull would be split asunder with the force of them.

Feeling the invisible iron band straddling her temples tighten again, Philomena passed the last house in the town then turned off the road and on to the track alongside the river, welcoming the shade of the beech trees.

Out of the scorching heat of the sun and enjoying the cool earth beneath her toes, Philomena wandered on with her empty basket, praying the breeze from the bubbling stream close by would calm her aching head.

However, as she turned the corner by the overgrown holly bush, she saw Patrick, wearing his everyday corduroy trousers and with his collarless shirt open and the sleeves turned back, sitting on a fallen tree just off the path.

Before she could stop it, Philomena's heart did a little double step then galloped off.

Spotting her, Patrick stood up.

They gazed across the space at each other for what could have been for all time, then, although she knew 'twould be a sin for her to stay, Philomena walked towards him.

She stopped in front of him, and glancing in passing at his corded forearms and the spray of dark hair at the open front of his shirt, Philomena raised her eyes to his.

Her mind told her he was a priest and that he had made his vows to God, but her heart told her Patrick had belonged to her long before God laid claim to him.

Her mind told her to keep walking, but her heart kept her bare feet rooted to the moist earth beneath.

Her mind told her there was no future for them, and her heart countered this by saying love can overcome all.

And there was no point her trying to deny it. She did love him. She loved him now. And she would love him for ever.

Wordlessly, he gazed down at her as the sun dappled them both, then he stepped forward and his arm slid around her waist.

Drowning in his blue-grey eyes, she stood motionless for a

moment, then, dropping her basket, she wound her arms around his neck.

With her heart bursting in her chest, Philomena's eyelids fluttered down as his mouth closed over hers.

As the waves of pleasure subsided, Philomena opened her eyes and stared up at the sky. The skirts of her flowery frock and petticoat were rucked up beneath her, so she could feel the lush summer grass against the back of her thighs. Her bodice, too, was in disarray, allowing her adolescent breasts to press into Patrick's chest with its light dusting of dark hair.

Enjoying the feel of his head resting on her shoulder and his weight pressing down on her, she gazed at the leaves of the tree shading them and turned to study the delicate lilac foxgloves bobbing in the light breeze.

A happiness that she'd only ever believed possible to know in heaven itself surged up inside her so forcefully that tears formed in her eyes, blurring the wildflowers a few inches above her.

Raising his head, Patrick shifted on to his elbows and looked down at her. He frowned.

'I'm sorry, I didn't mean to hurt you,' he said, the dappled sunlight dancing on his unruly black curls.

A tear rolled down Philomena's cheek. 'You didn't.'

'Then why are you weeping, Mena?'

'Because I'm happy,' she replied, her gaze slowly travelling over the face she had loved since for ever. 'And I know, even when I'm old and grey, Patrick, I'll remember this moment and I'll love you then as fiercely as I do today.'

'And I you,' he said, the expression in his blue-grey eyes confirming his words.

He lowered his lips onto hers and kissed her deeply for a moment, then he raised his head again.

'Don't worry,' he said, smiling down at her. 'It might be a bit difficult at first but I promise everything will be all right.'

'I know,' she whispered as another tear escaped.

Reaching up, Philomena traced her index finger along his firm jawline, enjoying the sensation of his bristles.

They basked in each other's adoration for a few seconds then Patrick's eyes darkened and he lowered his head.

Philomena's eyes fluttered down as she opened her mouth and heart to receive his lips and body again.

Chapter Twelve

'WELL, IT LOOKS like the whole parish has turned out for the occasion, Ma,' said Jeremiah, as he, Ida and Queenie turned the corner into Commercial Road.

'For 'twould shame the Almighty and all his saints above if they hadn't,' Queenie replied, eyeing the crowds making their way into St Breda and St Brendan's Church.

It was twenty to ten on the Sunday after VE day, and with the air filled with the sound of every church bell in the area ringing out, the three of them were doing what they usually did this time each week, which was to take their places ready for Sunday Mass.

Well, truthfully, it was usually just her and Ida who made the fifteen-minute journey from Mafeking Terrace to the parish church. After a full working week humping furniture on and off the lorry and driving back and forth across East London, Jeremiah usually took God at his word and spent the Day of Rest sleeping, reading the papers and listening to the wireless with his feet up.

Not today.

Today was special because it was the first Sunday after six years that congregations up and down the land could kneel down to worship without fear of finding themselves standing at the Pearly Gates courtesy of the Luftwaffe.

With men dressed in their smartest suits, women modelling new summer hats and children scrubbed and buttoned into their best clothes, there was a party atmosphere as families greeted each other on the pathway leading up to the main doors.

Not to be outdone, Jeremiah had donned his best suit, newest flowery waistcoat and had traded his usual leather cap for the ancient fedora he kept in a box on the top of the wardrobe for such occasions.

'I hope Mattie and Jo are already in there or we might be hard pressed to find a seat,' said Ida.

She was walking on the other side of Jeremiah and pushing Victoria, who was sitting up in her pram wearing her new bright red coat and knitted pixie hat.

Within a moment or two they'd joined the back of the queue and slowly filed up the pathway. Reaching the door, Ida parked the pram alongside half a dozen others and lifted Victoria out.

Setting the little girl on her feet, she rejoined her husband and Queenie as they entered the Gothic splendor of their parish church.

Although gummed tape still criss-crossed the stained-glass windows and the candlesticks remained empty because of the shortage of candles, the stirrup pumps and the first-aid equipment that had done nothing for a year other than gather dust had been cleared away and the life-size statue of the Virgin Mary had been returned to its rightful place in the lady chapel after five years wrapped in sacking in the crypt.

'There they are,' said Ida, waving at her youngest and eldest daughters with their children, already seated in the family's usual pew halfway down on the left.

Seeing her playmates, Victoria twisted herself out of her mother's grip and trotted off to join them, with her parents on her heels.

Dipping her fingers in the holy water, Queenie crossed herself. She stepped aside to let others past and then looked around the crowded church.

Her gaze travelled over the heads of the congregation for a moment, then she spotted a woman sitting alone in the front row nearest to the priest's chair.

She was facing forwards and although only her tight-fitting black hat and wide shoulders were visible, Queenie knew who it was sitting as bold as brass in the pew reserved for honoured guests.

The spirits from the old country that had been her constant companions since the New Year swirled around Queenie again but, pushing them aside, she made her way down the central aisle to join her family.

'Just in time,' said Jeremiah, as the organist played the opening bars of the processional music.

The congregation stood up. Jeremiah and Ida leaned back to allow Queenie to shuffle past them to reach her seat as the opening hymn was announced.

Raising her eyes, Queenie's mouth dropped open.

'How in the name of God is Father Mahon here?' she asked, hardly believing her own eyes.

Ida rolled her eyes. 'He's the priest, Queenie.'

'Sure, don't I know that, Ida?' she snapped back. 'What I'm after understanding is why, after the doctors told him plain he should rest, he is here.'

'Well, I'm guessing as it's such a day of celebration for everyone he wanted to share it with us,' said Ida, as the congregation gave voice to 'Now Thank We All Our God'.

As Ida turned back to her hymn book, Queenie's attention returned to those leading the service.

Mercifully, Father Timothy had taken up position behind the altar so he was clearly going to say Mass, but even at this distance Queenie could see that Patrick's face was the colour of overworked pastry. Under his surplice and the broad fabric band across his chest holding his embroidered cape in place, his chest was rising and falling rapidly with each breath.

The urge to put her arms around him and hold him once more rose up in Queenie but, as she had done so many times over the years, she damped it down.

Her eyes narrowed and slid across to where Nora stood with her hymn book in her hand and a sanctimonious expression on her face.

Queenie glared at her for a moment and with desires in her heart that would break at least half of the Ten Commandments, she joined in with the rest of the congregation as they started the second verse.

As the church wardens disappeared into the vestry at the end of Mass, Queenie got off her knees.

Getting a cross look from Ida and a puzzled one from her son as she clambered past them, Queenie stepped out into the central aisle. Genuflecting, she scratched a quick cross on her chest then hurried down towards the front of the church.

Skirting around a couple of people milling about by the vestry door, Queenie headed through into the robing area where the choir were having a quick fag as they shed their cassocks. Ignoring their curious glances as she wove between them, Queenie headed for the priest's sanctum. Entering the fifteen-by-twenty room, she found Father Mahon, white faced and breathing heavily, sitting in the old Windsor chair beneath the window.

Seeing her in the doorway, he raised his free hand in greeting and Queenie hurried over.

'Don't be worrying now, Queenie,' he said as she reached him. 'I'm just a bit short of breath, that's all.'

'Short of breath! Sure, aren't you puffing like a train going up a hill?' she replied. 'Have you taken leave of what little senses you have?'

'Now, now, be so-soft . . . th- there with me, Queenie,' he said.

'Soft with you, is it?' Queenie snapped. 'When you're after killing yourself.'

'I just need to catch my breath a little and I'll be grand, Queenie, so I will,' he gasped.

As he wheezed and puffed, Queenie cast her eyes over his putty-coloured pallor and blue lips and the old spirits foreshadowing the world to come swirled around her again.

Fear tightened in Queenie's chest.

'For the love of God and all that is holy,' she said, feeling her temples starting to throb, 'whatever possessed you to attend Mass this morn—'

'Here you are again, Philomena Dooley, and butting in where you're neither required nor welcomed.'

Queenie looked around to find Nora standing in the sanctuary's doorway.

With her close-set eyes fixed on Queenie's face, she crossed the space between them. She glared at Queenie for a moment or two more, then, taking a small bottle of pills, she popped off the cork and tapped a small white pill on to Father Mahon's gnarled palm.

'Under your tongue now,' she said as he put it in his mouth.

He did as she asked and, taking a deep breath, he rested back in the chair.

Satisfied her brother had followed her instructions, Nora turned her attention back to Queenie.

'And you've no right to question a priest on such a thing,' Nora continued. 'Where else would he be on a Sunday morning than saying Mass in his church?'

'Resting in bed as the doctors said he should,' said Queenie, matching Nora's belligerent glare. 'And when you're barely able to walk the length of the church, what's this I'm hearing about you leading the church's Mary's Day parade in a few weeks, Patrick?'

'Father Mahon to you,' snapped Nora. 'And my brother knows his duty to God.'

'And if he doesn't at any time I'm sure you'll be there to tell him, right enough. You and the rest of your family were never shy of telling Patrick what he was to do, as I recall,' said Queenie.

A sanctimonious smile lifted the corners of Nora's thin lips. 'My family are faithful members of the Church, if that's what you mean, and when his duty to his family and God was made clear to Patrick we were all overjoyed that my brother entered the priesthood.'

'Bullied, don't you mean, Nora?' Queenie replied. 'As I recall it, Patrick was given no say in the matter once your mother had made that vow—'

'Peace,' gasped Patrick, placing a hand on his chest.

'You're right, Patrick, Queenie should hold her peace,' snapped Nora. Her eyes narrowed. 'You come in here pretending to be concerned for my brother's health, and yet do nothing but—'

'There you are, Ma.'

Queenie looked around again and this time it was Jeremiah filling the sanctuary's doorway.

'We wondered where you'd got to,' he said, stepping into the room and filling it with his presence.

'I was just enquiring after Father Mahon's health,' said Queenie, catching Nora gaping at Jeremiah.

'Jeremiah.' Patrick beckoned him close. 'Come. This is my sister, who has come all the way across the sea from home to care for me.'

'Pleased to meet you,' said Jeremiah, giving Nora a smile that mirrored her brother's at the same age.

'Nora,' Patrick continued, 'this is Queenie's son, Jeremiah.'

Nora stared up at Jeremiah, dumbstruck for a second, and then, with a look that would have sent her straight to her grave, she turned her attention back to Queenie.

'Your son,' she forced out between tight lips.

'Yes,' said Queenie, countering Nora's blistering expression with an unwavering one. 'Born seven months after Patrick took his final vows and five months after I married Fergus.'

As the mechanism of the grandfather clock in the corner whirled to strike one, sitting at the rectory's dining-room table, Patrick wondered if there would be a plate left to serve Sunday dinner. Through the closed hatch to the kitchen, where Nora had been slamming cupboards and crashing pots to prepare their meal, he'd already heard three crash to the floor.

Like the rest of the house, the room where he had his meals was sparsely furnished, with just an ancient sideboard, a narrow table holding a dusty bottle of sherry for visitors and the table he was sitting at, which dominated the room. It could accommodate eight people comfortably and when he'd first arrived in the parish more than fifty years ago, it regularly did. Now it was just him and, when he wasn't working his way through the many invitations to Sunday dinner from the parishioners, Father Timothy.

Reminding himself that patience was a virtue, Patrick reached for his glass of Jameson and took a sip.

The door swung open as his sister, still wearing the deeply etched scowl she had worn since they'd left church, burst into the room holding a plate in either hand.

With her lips tightly pressed together and without saying a word, she placed one in front of him.

'Thank you, Nora,' said Patrick.

She gave him a sideways glance in acknowledgement then walked around and sat opposite him.

Clasping her hands in front of her, she looked down at her lap.

Patrick did the same. '*Benedic, Domine, nos et dona tua.*'

He went to cross himself but Nora gave him a hard look, so he bowed his head again.

'*Quae de largitate . . .*' he continued.

Having completed the longer version of the prayer and given thanks for the meal, Patrick looked down at the mountain of beef, cabbage and roast potatoes smothered in gravy set before him.

'It looks delicious.' He picked up his knife and fork.

Without raising her gaze, she gave him a tight smile and jabbed her fork into a pile of cabbage.

Patrick did the same to the nearest potato. Popping it into his mouth, he bit down on it and a squirt of fat hit the back of his throat.

Dropping his cutlery, Patrick choked.

Nora's eyes flew open in alarm. 'Patrick!'

'Something caught me on the way,' he said, placing one hand over his mouth and reaching for his glass of water. 'It's nothing. I'll be grand in a while.'

Her gaze returned to her plate but not before Patrick noticed his sister's eyes.

He took a couple of sips of water then spoke. 'Have you been weeping, Nora?'

Her frown deepened. 'Of course not.'

'I ask because your eyes are a mite red at the moment,' he persisted, scooping up a forkful of cabbage.

'I've been chopping onions,' she replied, sawing at her slice of meat as if trying to cut through the china plate beneath it.

Thinking it prudent not to mention the fact that there was neither hide nor hair of an onion on their plates, Patrick turned his attention back to his dinner.

They ate in silence for a moment then Nora's cutlery clattered on the table.

'May the devil himself take her to hell!' shouted Nora.

'Who?'

With tears streaming down her face, she glared at him.

'Who? Who? Philomena Dooley, that's who,' shouted Nora.

Grabbing her napkin, his sister covered her face and sobbed.

Patrick watched Nora's shoulders shaking for a few moments then he spoke again.

'I should have told you about Jeremiah,' he said softly.

She rolled her eyes. 'Sure, wouldn't she put Jezebel herself to shame by following you here?'

He shook his head.

''Twas the other way around, Nora,' said Patrick. 'I couldn't believe it on my first morning as the junior priest at St Breda and St Brendan's when who should walk through the door but Philomena, carrying six-month-old Jeremiah in her arms. He'd been born a month early on the ferry coming over before I'd even left the seminary.'

The memory of a young Queenie, with her jet-black hair and flashing eyes, floated into his mind.

'It was pure chance that Fergus found work and a couple of rooms here, but I recall the surprised look on her face as she saw me.' His smile widened as he remembered that bright September morning. 'She was no more than a slip of a girl, like the Virgin Mary, and there she was, a mother.'

'I don't think the Pope would be happy to hear you comparing the Queen of Heaven with that floozy Philomena Dooley,' Nora replied sourly.

Pushing the vision of Queenie aside, Patrick looked back into the pain-filled eyes of his sister.

'I'm sorry, Nora,' he said. 'It must be hard for you to behold Fergus's son.'

His sister looked puzzled. 'Fergus's son?'

'Yes, even after all this time. Although, to tell the truth of it, Nora,' he gave a little laugh, 'I sometimes forget that he's Fergus's boy because, search though I have over the years, I cannot see a trace of the man himself in his son.'

Nora stared at him, incredulous, for several moments then took hold of her knife and fork again.

'As you say, it's a long time ago.' She pointed her knife at him. 'Now eat your dinner, Patrick, before it gets cold.'

Kinsale, Ireland. June 1890

'THANK YOU, MRS O'Carroll,' said Philomena, taking the cup from the elderly widow serving the refreshments. 'That looks as grand a cup of tea as was ever served to St Patrick himself.'

Bridget O'Carroll's apple-round face lifted in a smile. 'Go on with you, Philomena, you and your blarney.' She pointed at the plate next to the rows of cups. 'Don't be forgetting some of the wondrous cake. Mrs Mahon had Pete the Bread working into the night so it should be fit for the occasion.'

It was Saturday afternoon, and she was standing in the blue-and-white-striped refreshment tent on the open ground adjacent to the monastery and church along with about half the parish, all eager for their afternoon tea.

The canvas enclosure housed three refreshment tables manned by the half a dozen matronly women of the parish who spent most of their time either on their knees in the church scrubbing its floors or polishing the brass and arranging the weekly flowers.

As well as looking after the church, they were also the self-appointed providers of hospitality, whether that was serving tea at various parish meetings or catering for larger events such as today's church celebration.

The weather, as it had been all week, was scorching hot, so along with their sturdy aprons the members of the catering team each had a sheen of sweat across their downy top lip too.

Balancing a slice of currant cake on her saucer, Philomena made her way out of the crowded marquee. Finding herself a quiet spot under a crab apple tree, she took a bite of cake and looked around until she found Patrick.

He was, as ever, surrounded by the matrons and grannies of the parish, smiling and nodding as they chattered on around him. However, perhaps sensing her eyes on him, he looked over the bonnets and head-shawls and his eyes fixed on her.

As the afternoon occasion was in his honour, Patrick was dressed in his black cassock and dog collar. Wicked though many would think it, Philomena didn't see the priestly robes because in her mind's eye she was imagining the muscular torso beneath it.

In fact, she'd done nothing else since she first lay in his arms four days ago, despite having enjoyed the heat of his passion every day since.

Of course, there would be a furore the like of which had never been known before in these parts once the news got out that Patrick had turned his back on the Church to marry her, but by then she and Patrick would be far away in England.

He glanced over at her again and a fizz of excitement shot through Philomena.

'Good day to you, Philomena.'

She looked around and found Fergus Brogan standing behind her.

'And to you, Fergus,' she replied.

His pale hazel eyes flickered over her. 'You look very nice today, Philomena.'

'Thank you,' she said, swaying slightly, rustling the petticoats beneath her skirt.

When she'd spied the bolt of newly arrived cream-coloured cotton dotted with emerald and pink flowers at Cuthbertson's the haberdashers a month back, Philomena had marched straight in and bought the first five yards off the roll. She'd spent each evening for the past month sewing it into a new gown. With her long brunette hair tied back with a wide ribbon and rippling down her back to her waist, she knew Fergus wasn't telling a lie.

'Yes, you look a picture,' he added.

'You look pretty smart yourself. Quite the young farmer,' she added, casting her eye over his square-shouldered tweed jacket, new drill trousers and bowler hat.

'Nora says I have to look a bit smarter now.' Poking his finger into his collar, he tugged it away from his neck and pulled a face. 'But I doubt I'll ever be at ease with a collar and tie.'

'And congratulations on your engagement,' Philomena said, as it was expected. 'I hope you and Nora are very happy together.'

He glanced over to where his fiancée was giggling with her friends. 'I hope so. And my mammy's pleased, too,' he added.

'I'm sure she is,' said Philomena. 'You've done well for yourself, Fergus, as there's no dairy herd in these parts to match the Mahons' and not a grander house in the town square either.'

Patrick had untangled himself from the gaggle of elderly women and was now talking to a couple of men standing outside the beer tent on the other side of the green.

Fergus's gaze followed hers for a moment then his attention returned to Philomena.

'Perhaps you'll be turning your mind to wed yourself soon,' he said, the hungry look flickering on his face. 'Now that Patrick Mahon's a man of the cloth.'

Although Philomena's heart was pounding in her chest, she forced a puzzled expression on her face.

'Sure, I've no idea what you think Patrick Mahon has to do with my matrimonial plans, Fergus.'

'Because the truth of the matter is that every other boy in this town were nigh on invisible to you,' he replied.

Philomena managed a laugh. 'Oh, Fergus, I don't know how you could think that to be so.'

As the sun danced through the overhanging leaves on to his face, Fergus looked at her with sadness in his pale eyes.

'You know full well, Philomena, that your thoughts have always been filled with Patrick Mahon,' he said in a low voice.

'Fergus, there you are!'

Philomena looked over his shoulder to see Nora hurrying across the grass towards them.

'I wondered where you'd got to,' she said, slipping her arm possessively through his as she reached them.

'I was just saying what a handsome couple you make,' said Philomena, smiling her sweetest smile.

'Thank you.' Nora gave her fiancé a doe-eyed look. 'We can't wait to be wed, can we, Fergus?'

'No, Nora,' he said flatly.

Nora wrinkled her nose in a way Philomena guessed was supposed to be charming but reminded her of Joseph O'Leary's prize sow.

'I don't know,' said Nora, rolling her eyes. 'What with me and Fergus set to wed in a few months and our Patrick soon off to start his new life in the Church, my mammy's fair beside herself with joy. Still,' she sighed, 'we can't stand here passing the time of day with you all afternoon because we've got other people to talk to, haven't we, Fergus?'

'Yes, Nora.'

Nora's close-set eyes ran over Philomena and her lips curled in a smug smile, then, gripping Fergus's arm, she dragged him away.

'Lovely of you, Philomena, to come to say goodbye to my dear brother before he leaves us all for his new life in the Church,' she called over her shoulder.

Philomena watched them go for a moment then she caught Patrick looking her way. He indicated the open church door with a glance then excused himself from the men around him. He started to wander towards the church, pausing occasionally to greet well-wishers.

Sipping her tea, she waited for a moment or two, then, balancing the saucer on her hand and with a pleasant smile on her face, Philomena ambled through the chatting crowd in the same direction as Patrick.

Swallowing the last mouthful of her drink, she casually placed her cup and saucer on a nearby table then hurried into the coolness of the stone building.

It was dark inside but there was a crack of sunlight shining through the small door that led to the rear of the church. Keeping to the shadows of the side nave, Philomena hurried towards it then stepped out into the sunshine again.

She spotted Patrick tucked behind one of the buttresses at the rear of the building. Quickly glancing around, she hurried over to join him.

He enveloped her in his arms and kissed her swiftly.

'Have you a plan?' she asked, as he released her.

'I have,' he replied. 'I'll be travelling with my father to the butter market in Cork on Monday and staying overnight in a hostelry near the cathedral, as I'm supposed to be catching the early-morning train to Dublin on Tuesday. However, if you get yourself to Cork on Tuesday, we can get a room somewhere by the harbour ready to sail on the tide to Bristol on Wednesday.'

'And then where?'

'London is the safest bet,' said Patrick. 'But we might have to walk, as we'll need every penny until I can find work.'

'I've a few pennies, too,' said Philomena. 'And couldn't we save some coin by not getting a room on Tuesday night?'

He shook his head. 'It's all very well tucking yourself in the hedgerow overnight but in town the parish constables will have you in the jail for vagrancy as quick as look at you.' He frowned. 'I wish there was another way. I wish we could be married with our folks around us.'

Philomena lightly laid her hand on his cassock sleeve. 'So do I, Patrick.'

'Do you think they'll ever forgive us? Our parents, I mean,' he added.

'In time,' she replied.

Well, that was certainly true of hers, but she feared Joseph Mahon, with his eyes on the mayoral chain, and Margaret Mahon, as chairwoman of the Friends of St Mary's Society, wouldn't be giving them their blessing much before Our Saviour returned to earth.

Patrick's frown deepened.

'And?'

'And, well, what if God won't forgive us. Forgive *me* for breaking my solemn vow to him?' he said.

She squeezed his forearm. 'I'm sure he will. After all, aren't we forever being told that God loves us? So if that's true how can he or anyone hold it against us for falling in love?'

Patrick smiled down at her. 'I can't argue with your reasoning, Mena.'

'And just put this into your mind, Patrick.' She smiled up at him brightly. 'Come this time next week we'll be starting our new life in England.'

He raised an eyebrow. 'Sleeping in a ditch, don't you mean?'

Philomena took a step closer and placed her hands on his upper arms. She lost herself in his blue-grey eyes for a moment, then, sliding her hands up the barathea of his cassock sleeve, she wrapped her arms around his neck.

'But, Patrick,' stretching up, she pressed her lips on to his, 'we'll be together.'

The shadow of doubt vanished from his face and he drew her back into his embrace.

'That we will.' His eyes softened as he lowered his mouth on to hers.

As a shiver of pleasure ran through her, Philomena gave herself up to the sheer joy of his embrace.

The sound of a twig snapping and the rustle of leaves somewhere behind her broke through her dreams, but then Patrick's kiss deepened, driving all thoughts of anything and everything but becoming Mrs Patrick Mahon from her mind.

Chapter Thirteen

CROSSING AND RE-CROSSING her legs for the third time, Jo glanced at the clock on the dull biscuit-coloured wall opposite.

'Don't worry, luv,' said Tommy, who was sitting on the bench beside her and holding her hand. 'I'm sure the matron will be along shortly.'

Jo nodded. Her gaze moved to the polished half-glazed double doors at the end of the corridor then back to the line of portraits that ran along the length of the wall under the clock.

There were about twenty of them, ranging from paintings of stiff-shirted Victorian gentlemen with high collars and tight cravats to sepia photographs of fleshy-looking women with double chins dressed in pearls and furs who Jo guessed were past members of the Whitechapel and Stepney Workhouse Board.

And that's where she and Tommy were now on a Thursday morning just a week after the heady celebrations of VE Day. Sitting in the room where, a hundred years ago, those who had been forced to seek parish relief had had their names written in the workhouse register.

In contrast to the rough workhouse-grey uniforms those unfortunate souls had been given to wear, Jo had dragged her royal-blue going-away suit out of the wardrobe again for the visit and Tommy was in his Royal Signals dress uniform with his sergeant stripes on his upper arms.

Although the four-storey, brick-built building that occupied a block of land on the corner of Vallance Road and Fulbourne Street was now called St Peter's Hospital, the pervading sense of despondency and despair from its former incarnation remained. But, despite its name, it was a hospital without any patients as it had been taken over by the council when the workhouses were disbanded a decade before the war broke out and was now an orphanage.

Jo turned back to her husband. 'It'll be strange to see you out of uniform when you're demobbed.'

He smiled down at her. 'Well, you'd better get used to it – there's a rumour going around that my unit might be sent our papers next month.'

The double doors swung open.

A tall, solid-looking woman wearing a dark navy nurse's uniform with starched white collar, cuffs and an enormous wimple-shaped nurse's cap marched through it.

Jo and Tommy stood up.

'Mr Sweete, I presume,' she said, her chained spectacles bouncing on her pillowy bosom as she strode towards them.

Reaching them, she thrust out her hand. 'Miss Rowell, the hospital matron in charge of the children's wing. We've spoken on the telephone.'

'We have,' Tommy said, shaking her hand.

'Apologies for keeping you waiting,' she said. 'But I've got nurses off sick and admissions arriving every—'

'Not at all,' said Tommy. 'This is my wife.'

'Pleased to meet you, Mrs Sweete,' Miss Rowell said, giving Jo a cursory nod. 'I understand you are registered as prospective adoptive parents with the council's Welfare department.'

'We are,' said Tommy. 'We want to go through the proper channels.'

'I'm pleased to hear it,' said the Matron. 'I know not so long ago the workhouse handed over unwanted babies to more or less anyone who would take them off their hands, but with this new Welfare system that all the papers are talking about maybe coming in, the council has to be more careful.'

'And so it should with children's well-being,' said Tommy.

'Good.' The matron beamed at them. 'Now, if you're ready, we'll head to the orphans' wards?'

'Lead the way,' said Tommy.

She marched off towards the main entrance.

They headed off after the matron as she started climbing the stairs to the floors above.

'As they aren't actually sick and we haven't got room to house all of those the council has placed in our care in the infants' dormitories on the third floor, the trustees gave permission to re-open the two disused dormitories on the top floor,' she said, as they reached the first floor.

Jo, with Tommy half a step behind, trudged up the well-worn concrete stairs behind the matron.

Although it was a warmish summer day outside, as they climbed to the top of the hospital it got decidedly chilly thanks to the north-facing aspect of the windows that were covered with ill-fitting cardboard instead of glass.

'Here we are,' puffed the matron as they reached the top floor. She caught Jo eyeing the flapping cardboard. 'Had a high explosive land a mile away in 'forty-two. Took out every window at the back of the hospital, and the hospital board haven't got round to replacing them all yet.'

Giving them a jolly head-girl type of smile, she turned left and marched towards the double doors at the far end of the corridor.

'This is Fairyland Ward,' said Miss Rowell, holding open the door for them.

Taking Jo's hand, Tommy hooked it in the crook of his arm. Giving her an encouraging smile, he led her in.

The smell of cabbage and soiled nappies hit Jo in the back of the throat and the only fairyland the ward represented was the Brothers Grimm's. The run-down hallway they'd just come from could have been the reception of the Ritz compared with the high-roofed room she and Tommy now stood in.

Ancient iron cots with their paint peeling off were crammed along each side of the room. They were so tightly packed together, the gaps between them were too narrow for anyone to squeeze into. Each cot contained a baby or infant, a great number of whom were standing up and crying, clutching on to their elevated cage. As well as the cots along the walls there were others lined in pairs running down the middle of the ward, which meant the nurses' desk had been rammed in the corner. There were two staff nurses in light blue uniforms and more modest headgear on the ward, and while one was changing a squirming toddler on the raised bench against the back wall, the other was sitting in an old chair beside the desk trying to get a red-faced baby to take a bottle.

'Goodness,' said Jo, casting her gaze over the chaos around her. 'There's so many.'

'It's the war,' said the Matron. 'Most of those in our care have lost their parents in the bombing, but we have quite a few babies and children who've been abandoned.'

'Abandoned!' said Jo.

'Yes, mostly it's mothers who had a fling while their husbands were away,' explained the matron. 'But occasionally men who have come back and found their wives have been killed and don't want the responsibility.' She gave them a professional smile. 'Thankfully, we are blessed with people like yourselves who are willing to take these waifs and strays. Do you want a boy or a girl?'

'We don't mind, do we, Jo?'

Jo shook her head and her eyes returned to the ward.

'You can wander down and see if any of the little mites take your fancy, if you like,' added the matron.

'Shall we, love?' said Tommy, gently taking her arm.

He led her along the row of toddlers, the matron hovering just a few steps behind.

It was difficult to distinguish between the boys and girls because although they were clean, their clothes were a hotchpotch of hand-me-downs that repeated boiling had reduced to shades of grey. All of them had short hair, too. Having seen several older children with the same cropped hair, Jo concluded that it was the orphanage's way of minimising the chances of a nit infestation.

Pausing briefly by each cot, Jo smiled and Tommy pulled a happy face at each of the children while the matron told them the child's name and a brief history. The toddlers, for their part, stared silently back at them.

Most of the children had lost their parents in the doodlebug attacks the previous year, but there were quite a few who had been sent to the orphanage by relatives who couldn't afford or didn't want another mouth to feed. And while half a dozen or so children were adopted each month, most were waiting for a long-term place in a children's home in the country.

'And we're all excited to hear that the Government is thinking of funding a scheme for older children to have a new life in Australia,' continued the matron, as the three of them turned at the end of the ward to walk past the cots on the other side of the dormitory.

Halfway down they stopped and turned towards the cot they were standing by.

'Hello,' Tommy said to a little girl with olive skin, curly black hair and clutching an old rag doll.

The child looked solemnly at them for a moment then smiled and raised her arms to him.

'May I?' asked Tommy.

'Of course,' the matron replied.

Reaching in, Tommy picked her up and settled her on his forearm.

A lumped formed in Jo's throat.

'Hello, little lady,' Tommy said, tickling her chin. 'What's your name?'

'The writing on her label was rubbed away but we think it's Zara or Zanna or something,' the matron replied, as the little girl in his arm fiddled with his brass jacket button. 'But we've called her Sarah. We're not sure how old she is but the council doctor thinks about fourteen or fifteen months. She was left in the foyer of Mile End hospital a couple of months ago, but no one saw who left her there.'

'Hello, Zara,' he said. 'Fancy meeting you here.'

He tickled her tummy with his index finger, and she laughed.

'She's a happy little thing and sleeps all night,' said the Matron. 'It's a pity it will be difficult to place her.'

Tommy gave her a querying look.

'Well, by her colouring and the name on her label, I'd say she has a touch of the tar brush,' the matron replied. 'But people want to adopt children that look like them not ones that will have the neighbours gossiping about what the wife might have got up to while her husband's been away.'

'Well, let them gossip, that's what I say, Zara,' Tommy said, adoration shining from his eyes as he gazed at the child in his arms. 'In fact, to borrow a saying from my father-in-law, "If it wasn't for the Sweetes, people wouldn't have anything to talk about."'

The little girl babbled something in response then grabbed his bottom lip.

Tommy's smile widened.

Taking her hand, he kissed it then shifted his attention on to Jo. 'Why don't you hold her, luv?'

She didn't move for a second then put on a bright smile. Stepping forward, she took the little girl from her husband.

Jo settled her on her hip and Zara stared up at her with her enormous brown eyes.

'Isn't she a sweetheart?' said Tommy.

Jo nodded as the familiar ache for a child crushed her heart.

There was no doubt about it, Zara was completely adorable, and if they decided to apply to adopt her, she would have Tommy wrapped around her little finger within a day. And Jo knew, as sure as the sun was going to rise, that within the week, she'd have found her special place in everyone's heart. But that wasn't her problem. No, the agonising worry gnawing at Jo was could she find it in her heart to love Zara – or any child that wasn't actually hers and Tommy's – the way a mother should?

Smoothing his hand over the soft mohair fabric of his new suit jacket, Billy placed it on the open page of yesterday's *Daily Sketch*.

It was a week and a day after the VE Day street party, and he was standing among the cobwebs and discarded seed trays in Flo Wallace's unused potting shed. He should have been home after cricket practice at school an hour ago but he'd just say they started late or something. Nor had he been listening to the sound of leather on willow but Johnny Mercer's latest record on Aunt Pearl's new Bush gramophone, while guzzling Coca-Cola and smoking her Benson & Hedges.

He'd left her house in Forest Gate about an hour ago and, as he didn't want all the busybodies in the street seeing him, he had gone down the alley at the back between the houses then shinned up and over Flo's back fence.

Having retrieved the ten-bob note Pearl always gave him from his suit pocket, he'd changed back into his school uniform. Although it niggled him to have to do this, it also meant that he didn't smell of cigarettes, so it stopped his dad having a go at him for smoking.

Securing his tightly wrapped parcel with a length of string, Billy slid it alongside the other one containing his trousers, shirt and tie that he'd already stowed safely behind two large, discarded flowerpots.

Leaving the rundown outbuilding, he crossed the unkempt backyard and left via the side entrance. At the end of the dank alleyway between the houses he paused and poked his nose around the edge of the brickwork.

A couple of his mother's friends from the other side of the street were standing around Winnie Pearman's doorstep and there were a few children playing on the cobbles, but satisfied the coast was clear, Billy adjusted his satchel on his shoulder and ambled out.

Within a few moments he dipped down the narrow passageway between his own house and next door. On reaching the end, he clicked open the latch on the wooden gate and walked into the space at the back of his home.

His gran's chickens clucked their greeting as he strolled between the chipped enamel sinks with carrot tops and onion stalks sprouting from them and runner bean canes standing to attention behind.

Pulling on the handle, he opened the back door but although the air was filled with the appetising aroma of the family's evening meal, his mum wasn't standing at the stove preparing it. Instead, she was sitting, unsmiling, at the kitchen table beside his father.

However, in contrast to his mum's stony-faced expression, Billy's dad looked relaxed and affable.

'Evening,' Billy said, dropping his satchel in front of the huge crockery dresser. 'Supper smells good.'

His father smiled pleasantly. 'You're a bit late, aren't you, son?'

'Yeah, sorry,' he said, slipping his arms out of his blazer and hooking it on one of the nails hammered into the door. 'Cricket practice overran. Any tea in the pot?'

'Now perhaps my brain is remembering this wrong, Billy,' Jeremiah said, his thick eyebrows pulled together, 'but didn't hockey training do the same last Tuesday?'

Billy pretended to consider for a moment then nodded. 'It did, now you come to mention it, Dad. Is there a cuppa going?'

He looked expectantly at his mum. However, instead of jumping up to pour him one, Ida didn't move.

'And the week before that, too, as I recall,' continued Jeremiah.

Billy forced a laugh. 'You know how it is, Dad, with school stuff. People forget the time and—'

'Then there's a few weeks before that,' Jeremiah cut in, 'when the school's choir was rehearsing for the Founder's Day concert.'

Billy didn't reply.

'In fact,' continued his father, in a cheerful tone, 'by some odd reason that I'm yet to fathom, Billy, there seems to be an uncanny link between all these times when people don't consult their watches and the letter your mum and me received in the afternoon post.'

Jeremiah raised the sheet of paper that his large, work-hardened hand had been resting on.

Billy saw the embossed crest at the top right-hand corner and his mouth went dry.

'Do you know that when she opened this letter this afternoon just after one thirty,' continued his father, 'your mum came straight around to the yard? After I'd cast my eyes over it, I said that Mr Griffith must have got you mixed up with some other boy, didn't I, Ida?'

'You did, Jerry,' said his mum.

'So do you know what we did, Billy?' asked Jeremiah.

Again Billy didn't reply.

'We did no more than jump in the lorry and toddle off to your school. Mr Griffith, grand fella that he is, told us that barely a week goes by without you disappearing out of afternoon school. And, to top it all, when the headmaster sent someone to fetch you from class this very afternoon, it seems you'd vanished into thin air again.' Jeremiah's blue-grey eyes turned from warm to icy in an instant. 'So, Billy, where have you been?'

'With a couple of mates,' Billy replied, forcing himself to hold his father's withering gaze.

'Mates!' shouted Jeremiah.

Ida gripped her husband's arm. 'Jerry.'

Shaking off her small hand, Jeremiah rose to his feet and crossed the kitchen in two strides.

'And just to put you wise, Billy,' he bellowed, his six-foot towering over Billy's five foot four, 'I don't know "how it is with school stuff" because by the time I was your age I'd already been out on my father's wagon in all weathers for nigh on three years. And neither do Charlie, Mattie nor Cathy, for that matter, because as soon as they were old enough, they had to start bringing in some money to keep a roof over your head and help your mum and me put food in your mouth. And if it hadn't been for winning a scholarship to Raines, it would have been the same for Jo. For the love of God, Billy,' he said, raking his fingers through his hair, 'me and your mum fought tooth and nail to get you into a grammar school so you could get a good education and make something of yourself.'

'I can do that without having to go to school,' Billy shouted back. 'Lots of people who don't know anything about algebra or some poncy bloke who wrote about daffodils in a field have plenty of money and live in nice houses.'

Jeremiah glared down at him. 'Is that a fact?'

'Yes.' Forcing himself to look up at his father's angry face, Billy said, 'And why do you care?'

'Because I'm your dad,' Jeremiah replied firmly.

'But you're not, are you?' Billy shouted back. 'I'm not your son. Michael is. Michael who always gets top marks in school, Michael who never gets sent to the headmaster's office, "chip off the old block" Michael.' Tears sprang into his eyes but he blinked them away. 'Now you've got your precious Michael, what do you care what I do or where I go?'

Ida stood up.

'Oh Billy,' she said softly. 'We're your parents and we—'

'But you're not!' Billy shouted. 'You're not! And I hate you both!'

His mum gasped and the anger drained from his father's face.

Looking from one to the other, pain and remorse crushed Billy's chest, but he shoved them aside. 'You're not my mum and dad!'

Ripping open the back door and with tears coursing down his freckled cheeks, Billy ran out of the house.

As the final bars of 'Sentimental Journey' faded and the stylus elevated off the record with a click, Pearl glanced at the two silver-plated nymphs who were holding the clock aloft.

Six thirty!

Lenny wouldn't be back for hours, so she had plenty of time to get herself all dolled up for their usual Thursday trip to The Rub A Dub.

Uncrossing her legs, Pearl swung around on the sofa and planted her fluffy pink slippers on the carpet.

She flicked her cigarette ash into the ashtray on the coffee table, stood up and sauntered over to the walnut-veneer radiogram. Clasping her half-smoked Benson & Hedges firmly between her lipsticked lips, she lifted up the lid as the record finished its final revolution.

Easing her painted fingernails under the shellac record, Pearl lifted it off its felt pad and slipped it into its brown-paper sheath then slotted it back in the storage rack beside the turntable and picked out another. Removing the record from its protective sleeve and holding it at the edge with the tips of her fingers, she slotted it over the central arm. When she flipped the ivory Bakelite switch, the record player sprang into motion.

Swaying to the rhythm of Edmundo Ros and his Latin orchestra, she sashayed across the room to the glass-fronted bar that Lenny had acquired from somewhere or other up West. Selecting a glass, Pearl picked up the bottle of Gordon's but just as she tipped it into the glass, there was a light knock on the door.

'Yes!' she yelled, recorking the bottle.

It opened and Monkey, one of Lenny's sidekicks, appeared.

'Sorry to barge in, Mrs Stamp,' he said, studying her from under his caveman brow, 'but your kid Billy's 'ere. D'you want me to bring 'im in?'

'Don't be bloody stupid,' Pearl snapped. 'Of course I want you to bring 'im in.'

Monkey lumbered out and a minute later Billy, wearing his school uniform, with a newspaper parcel under his arm and a wretched expression on his face, stepped into the room.

'Hello, Billy,' Pearl said, topping up her gin with tonic. 'What're you doing back here? Did you forget something?'

Billy shook his head. He stared miserably at her for a moment then burst into tears.

'Oh, baby,' said Pearl, tottering across the space between them. 'What's happened?'

Holding her drink in one hand, she hugged him with the other as Billy sobbed out the story of the argument with Ida and Jeremiah.

'It's so unfair,' Billy concluded, lifting his head from her shoulder. 'They're always on at me about something or other.'

'Well, you don't have to put up with them or their bloody golden boy Michael any more, do you?' Releasing him from her embrace, Pearl straightened the crumpled leopard-print boat collar of her chocolate-brown dress. 'In fact, I'm surprised he didn't grass you up to them about seeing me.'

'Only because he knew I'd wallop him one,' Billy replied, smashing his right fist into the palm of his left hand.

'Well, as I say, you don't 'ave to put up with it any longer.'

He gave her a puzzled look. 'Don't I?'

'Course not, Billy,' laughed Pearl. Transferring her drink into the hand holding her cigarette, she ran her red-nailed fingers gently down his cheek. 'You can live here with me.'

'Are you enjoying yourself, Billy?' asked Pearl, as she perched on the bar stool next to him.

'Yeah, it's great,' he replied.

'And as I said back home,' she continued, blowing a stream of smoke upwards, 'don't you worry about nuffink. We can go up West tomorrow and kit you out from head to toe.'

'Thanks, Mum,' said Billy. 'I don't want to be any trouble.'

'Don't be daft.' Reaching across, she pinched his cheek lightly. A sentimental expression settled on her powdered face. 'I just want to make up for lost time, that's all, Billy.'

Earlier that evening, when Billy had finished blubbing like a baby, Pearl had sent one of Lenny's muscles out to fetch fish and chips for his supper. Having washed that down with three bottles of Coke, Billy had settled himself on the sofa and, relishing not having to puff away in secret, smoked a couple of cigarettes. Once Pearl had got herself ready, they'd climbed into the back of the car and had arrived at The Rub A Dub at about ten.

It was now . . . well, actually he didn't know what time it was because there were no clocks on the walls and the lights were so low that it was difficult to make out the dial on his Flash Gordon watch, but he reckoned it must be after midnight.

Pearl swallowed the last of her cocktail and waggled her empty glass in the air. 'Rita!'

The barmaid, a blonde with big eyes and a tight glittery dress, left the customer she was serving at the far end of the bar and hurried over.

'Same again, Mrs Stamp?'

Pearl gave the girl a sweet smile by way of an answer and the barmaid hurried off.

Billy stubbed his cigarette out in the ashtray and Pearl snapped open her handbag, pulled out a pack of Benson & Hedges and handed them to him.

'You know Dad said he read somewhere that smoking causes cancer,' said Billy as he took one.

Pearl rolled her eyes. 'I've never heard anything so bloody

stupid. If smoking's bad for us why do the government and the doctors tell us we should have a fag to calm our nerves?'

'I suppose,' Billy agreed, feeling foolish for mentioning it.

Rita returned with Pearl's drink and, without glancing at the barmaid, she picked it up.

'Oh, Lenny wants me,' she said, looking across the room. 'Will you be all right here by yourself, Billy?'

'Course,' Billy replied, giving the little gangster shrug he'd been perfecting over the past few weeks.

Pearl hopped off her perch. 'I'll see you later then.'

Swivelling around on the bar stool, Billy watched her make her way to where Lenny sat tucked into a dark corner with a couple of men in clean-cut suits, then his gaze returned to the floor of the club.

Now, with people squashed around tables or into booths and others bobbing around on the dance floor to the five-piece band, the nightclub looked very different from the first time he'd seen it a few weeks ago. It was very exciting – and not just because it was way past his bedtime. Here he was in a proper nightclub, sitting up at the bar, in a dapper suit, like Humphrey Bogart in *Casablanca*.

'Do you want another, luv?' asked Rita, as she wiped up a puddle of beer on the bar.

Billy threw back the last mouthful of Coca-Cola. 'Yes please,' he replied, putting down his glass.

She gave him a wrinkled-nosed smile.

'Aw, you're such a gentleman,' she said. 'Not like some.'

She went off to replenish his drink and Billy cast his eyes around again.

They came to rest on a young woman with dark hair wearing a blue dress, sitting by herself at one of the small tables by the stage.

Although there were plenty of couples in the club, there were also a dozen or so women who seemed to be on their own. Considering most women he knew wouldn't dream of walking into a public house by themselves, let alone sit drinking in one, it seemed odd. But to be fair, they weren't really by themselves as a number of men had asked them to dance or bought them a drink.

As his gaze travelled up the woman's slender crossed legs, an unsettling feeling started in Billy's stomach.

'There you go, luv,' said Rita, interrupting his peculiar thoughts.

'Thanks.'

'No trouble.' She winked. 'Anything to oblige a handsome young man like you.'

She pursed her lips and kissed the air then went to serve another customer, Billy's eyes fixing to her rear as she wiggled away.

Stifling a yawn, Billy reached for his drink but before he could grasp it a heavy arm was slung around his neck.

'What's that you're drinking, Billy Boy?' asked Arthur, crushing his shoulders briefly before taking the bar stool that Pearl had vacated.

'Coke,' said Billy.

'Oi, sweetheart!' shouted Arthur.

Closing the till, Rita came back.

'Put a rum in my mate Billy's drink and I'll have a Johnnie Walker,' Arthur said. 'And make them doubles while you're at it,' he added as she turned to the row of optics behind her.

Billy was about to say no to the spirit but he let the word die on his lips. He'd had the odd half-pint of bitter shandy at Christmas and at family parties – although his father always made sure it was never more than one – and he didn't want Arthur to think he was a baby.

Tapping his foot to the beat, Arthur watched half a dozen couples Lindy Hopping on the dance floor.

'The band's good,' said Billy, as their drinks arrived.

'Yeah, not bad.' Grabbing his glass, Arthur took a gulp of Scotch. 'So, what do you fink of the old place?'

'It's very nice.' Billy took a sip of his drink, finding the rum overlaying the previous sweetness of the fizzy drink.

'Don't be a nancy boy. Get it down yer!' said Arthur, indicating the glass in Billy's hand.

Billy swallowed another large mouthful.

'That's better,' said Arthur, as the spirit hit Billy's stomach. 'If you want to be one of the crew, you have to hold your drink. You can't let the side down.'

'Don't worry, Arthur, I won't.' Billy forced down another gulp of rum and Coke.

Arthur's lean features lifted in a grin. 'And from now on you can forget about all that poncy school rubbish, too.'

'Yeah. Who needs algebra and geo . . . geo . . . foreign countries anyway?' said Billy, abandoning the attempt to get the word geography past his front teeth.

Something peacock blue flickered in the corner of Billy's eye and he looked around.

The dark-haired young woman who had been sitting alone at the table stood up. The unsettling feeling in Billy's stomach flared up again as he watched her sidle over to the bar in her tight blue dress and high heels.

Arthur turned and grinned, seeing what had caught Billy's attention.

'Angie.'

She looked around and changed direction.

'All right, Arthur,' she said, giving him a sideways look from under her lashes as she stopped in front of them.

Although her dark hair was scooped up on her head, Billy noticed that there was a curl snaking down on to the bare skin of her right breast.

'This is Billy,' said Arthur. 'Pearl's boy.'

Angie's heavily made-up eyes slid on to Billy.

'Pleased to meet you, miss,' said Billy, offering her his hand.

She took it.

'Pleased to meet you.' She gave him the onceover and the

corners of her pink lips lifted a notch. 'Although you don't look like no boy to me.'

The ache he'd had a few weeks back when Snotty Smith had showed them all a magazine full of smiling women without any clothes caused his privates to jerk beneath his Y-fronts.

Taking a step towards him, Angie slipped her slender bare arm through his. 'Ain't you going to offer a girl a drink, Billy?'

Billy tore his gaze from the quivering mounds of her breasts and back to her face.

'Sorry,' he said, feeling suddenly quite hot.

'I'll have a Pink Lady,' said Angie, setting his heart pounding with a flutter of her eyelashes.

'Scuse me,' called Billy to the barmaid. 'A Pink Lady.'

'And another rum and Coke for my friend here,' added Arthur. 'As he's almost finished the one he's got.'

Billy hadn't, and with his brain not seeming to be working as it should, he wasn't sure he should have another, but not wanting to appear lightweight in front of Angie, he swallowed the last couple of mouthfuls in his glass.

The room went off kilter for a moment but then Rita returned with their order.

Arthur handed Billy his drink then picked up Angie's light pink drink.

'There you are, luv.' He grinned. 'A pretty drink for a pretty lady.'

Angie giggled.

Leaning forward, she pressed herself into Billy as she took the glass from Arthur.

The aching feeling at the front of his trousers flared again and Billy's eyes returned to the soft flesh spilling over the top of her dress.

'Bottoms up,' said Arthur, raising his glass.

Angie did the same and after a second or two so did Billy.

The final chords of 'Boogie Woogie Bugle Boy' brought the

dancers on the floor to a swirling halt and then 'String of Pearls' took its place.

'Why don't you take Angie for a spin, Billy?' said Arthur, nodding towards the couples on the dance floor.

Angie's eyes lit up. 'Oh, let's,' she said, putting her drink back on the bar.

'I'm not really much of a dancer,' said Billy, as the memory of Maisie Winkworth limping off the dance area at the VE Day street party flashed into his mind.

'Don't worry,' she said, taking his drink from him and placing it next to hers. 'Just follow me.'

She took Billy's hand and he stood up.

He fell against a table at the edge of the dance floor and then bounced off one of the pillars. Lights popped at the edge of his vision and laughter erupted around him.

Righting himself, Billy took Angie's hand and placed his other one lightly on her hip, the way he'd been shown at Mrs Power's Saturday-morning ballroom-dance classes at the Catholic Club.

'No, silly. Like this.' Stepping closer, Angie placed her hand on his shoulder.

Concentrating on avoiding her toes, Billy stepped off and they shuffled around for a while, then she spoke again.

'So, how old are you, Billy?'

'Nearly seventeen?' he lied, feeling his shoe scuff against hers as they turned. 'What about you?'

'Oh, Billy,' she laughed. 'Don't you know you should never ask a woman her age?'

'Sorry,' he said, staggering as they narrowly avoided colliding with another couple.

'Let's just say I'm old enough.'

'For what?'

Giving him a coy look from under her mascaraed lashes, she ran her hand along his shoulder and around his neck. 'Have you ever done it with a girl?'

Billy swallowed hard.

'Course.' He forced a laugh. 'Lots of times.'

Angie snaked herself against him, connecting her pubic bone with his groin. 'Would you like to do it with me, Billy?'

Her hand left his shoulder and, slipping it between them, she took hold of his crotch through his trousers.

'On the house, naturally,' she whispered. 'After all, any friend of Arthur's is a friend of mine.'

He opened his mouth to speak but his brain seemed to be in the grip of some invisible force from within.

She released his crotch and he stumbled back, the small band on the stage swimming in his vision as he pulled himself upright.

'There's a couple of cosy rooms upstairs,' she said, smiling at him and taking his hand. 'Don't worry, I've got some French letters in my handbag.'

Although he knew it was wrong and he shouldn't, Billy stumbled after her.

He'd barely taken two steps when a blinding light cut across his vision and screaming drilled into his ears. He blinked into the glare and, as his vision adjusted to the lights being switched on, he saw two men in trench coats and fedoras standing in front of the main door. Two dozen or so uniformed policemen, gripping truncheons, were rushing into the room.

'Detective Stone,' bellowed the stouter of the two plain-clothed officers, holding up his warrant card. 'This is a police raid so everyone stay right where you are.'

Rolling her head to the side, Queenie glanced at the old clock sitting on her dressing table.

For the love of God!

Throwing back the covers, she swung her legs out of bed and switched on the light on her bedside table. As she'd been awake since just after twelve, she might as well make herself a cuppa as lie here.

Finding her slippers amongst the folds of her patchwork counterpane, Queenie slid her feet into them and stood up. Taking her dressing gown that was draped over the brass bedknob, she shrugged it on.

Adjusting her hairnet, she opened the door, but instead of walking out into the pitch blackness of the hall, a faint light fanned out from under the closed parlour door.

She pushed it open and found Jeremiah sprawled in his fireside armchair with an open book resting on his chest, his glasses sitting at an odd angle on his nose and his feet up on the battered leather pouffe.

Queenie studied this great bear of a son of hers and joy and sadness twisted together in her chest.

Even though his dark hair was shot through with grey now and the lines around his mouth were increasingly visible, he had the man who'd sired him stamped clearly on his face.

She walked in and her son sat bolt upright, knocking his head on the lampshade of the floor lamp that stood next to his chair.

'Billy!' he said, as the book landed with a thump on the floor.

'No, it's just meself,' said Queenie, closing the door behind her. 'What are you doing up at this hour?'

Jeremiah pushed his spectacles back into place. 'What time is it?'

'Two thirty,' she replied. 'Is Billy not home yet?'

Jeremiah shook his head.

'I'm for making a cup of tea; will you join me?' Queenie asked.

He sighed. 'I might as well.'

With her slippers padding softly on the lino, Queenie headed for the kitchen. By the time she'd filled the kettle, Jeremiah had followed her in.

'Where on earth can he be until this hour?' he said, lowering himself on to one of the kitchen chairs.

Queenie struck a match and held it to the hissing gas.

'I'm sure he's grand,' she replied, praying it would be so.

Jeremiah raked his fingers through his still-thick hair, stirring a memory in Queenie from long ago. 'What if he's been set on and is lying bleeding in a gutter somewhere?'

Feeling his pain in her own heart, Queenie placed her small, birdlike hand on his massive shoulder. He gave her a wan smile. They shared a fond look and then the kettle's whistle cut between them.

Queenie took it from the flame and made the tea. After stirring in Jeremiah's two spoonfuls of sugar, she returned to the table.

She placed the cup in front of him and sat opposite. 'I'm sure Billy is all right,' she said to her son, whose eyes were fixed to the ceiling.

Ending his contemplation of the light bulb overhead, Jeremiah looked across the table at her.

'Is that what the spirits are telling you?' he asked, a hint of amusement in his weary eyes.

Queenie smiled but didn't reply.

She couldn't.

Although she loved Billy like all the others, perhaps because the Dooley blood didn't flow through his veins, the spirits weren't as forthcoming about him as they were for the rest of Ida and Jeremiah's brood.

'Anyhow, Ma,' said Jeremiah, cradling the mug of steaming tea in his large hands, 'Billy's the reason I'm still up, but what's brought you from your bed?'

'Oh, sure you know your brain sometimes just pulls you out of your slumber,' said Queenie lightly.

'Is it Father Mahon?' he asked, scrutinising her closely.

Queenie forced a puzzled expression on her face. 'Why would I be awake because of the good father?'

'Maybe because you've known him since you were a scrap of a girl, Ma,' he replied. 'And although I and many would wish it otherwise, the fact is the poor man is fading.'

It was no more than the truth, but hearing the words caught the breath in Queenie's lungs.

Looking into Patrick's blue-grey eyes gazing across the table at her out of her son's face, tears pinched at the corner of Queenie's eyes.

Reaching across, Jeremiah placed one of his paw-like hands over hers. 'Oh, Mammy.'

Queenie forced a brave little smile and nodded.

There was a knock at the door.

Jeremiah jumped up and hurried back through the house. 'Billy!'

Rising to her feet, Queenie followed him and entered the parlour just as Jeremiah walked into the room with Sergeant Bell just a step behind.

'Evening, Queenie,' he said. 'Sorry to wake you both but it's about your Billy.'

Blind panic flashed across Jeremiah's face. 'Has he had an accident? Is he in hospital somewhere? Is he all right?'

'He's safe and well,' their local bobby replied. 'That's to say, as well as you can be in a police cell. I'm afraid, Mr Brogan, your son's been arrested.'

Kinsale, Ireland. June 1890

HUMMING 'BLACK IS the Colour' to herself and swinging her empty basket at her side, Philomena turned off the dusty road and skipped up the path that led to the front door of her home.

In fact, she was surprised she wasn't flying above the ground because for sure didn't she have the very wings of love on her feet?

It was Saturday afternoon and soon she and Patrick would be heading for their new life in England and a wedding just as soon as they found a priest who would bestow God's blessing upon them in marriage.

Philomena skirted around the side of the squat whitewashed cottage, dodging around the handful of hens pecking about in the vegetable patch to her left, then ducked under the washing flapping in the salty sea breeze to reach the back door.

Grasping the handle and pressing the latch with her thumb, she pushed open the door and walked into the scullery.

Well, 'twas the scullery now but in times past the lean-to, with its low beams and a beaten-earth floor, had been the end of the cottage where the livestock would have lived. Although the wooden stalls had been removed, the posts that they had been fixed to were still nailed at regular intervals along the wall.

A previous resident had added a chimney and a brick-built stove with an iron plate above where the kettle sat. In addition, there was an iron pot dangling by a chain from the bracket over the fire.

As usual, the area where the Dooley family washed and cooked was spotless but instead of the family's mismatched crockery being neatly stacked on the pine dresser, some was missing from its usual place on the wooden shelf, as was a portion of the Saturday cake her mother had baked that morning.

But the most notable thing amiss was that her mother, who for as long as Philomena could remember spent all of Saturday afternoon cooking and baking ready for the family's day of rest the next day, wasn't at her usual place by the stove.

'Mammy, I'm home,' she called through the half-open door to the main living area.

'We're in here,' her father shouted back.

Stowing her basket under the table, Philomena bounced through to join them.

'Mrs McGonagall was asking if you'd be kind enough to—' She stopped dead.

Sitting in her father's chair was Father Parr, his bony hands gripping his sharp knees through his worn cassock and a look of thunder on his face.

To the side of him on the long bench sat Philomena's parents, her white-faced father and her red-eyed mother, who was holding a handkerchief to her mouth.

Philomena looked from her parents to the priest and back again.

'Father, what's happened?' she asked.

'Oh, Philomena,' her mother quivered. ''Tis such a—'

Father Parr raised his hand, and she lapsed into silence.

With his eyes fixed on Philomena, the lean priest unfolded himself from the chair and stood up.

'I'm here, Philomena Dooley, because you,' he jabbed his finger at her, 'have tried to tempt a servant of God and the Church into sin.'

Philomena's mouth dropped open and her heart hammered painfully in her chest.

'It wasn't like that—'

'So, you don't deny it?' bellowed the priest, his voice booming around in her head. 'You don't deny that you tried to tempt Patrick Mahon, a priest only just consecrated to God, into the sin of fornication?'

Her father stood up.

'Begging your pardon, Father,' he said, his shoulders stooped as he addressed the parish priest, 'and sure, I know it's not my place to be contrary to yourself, but Mena is but a girl and she and young Patrick have been friends since before they took their first communion, so I'm sure—'

'It wasn't friendship Miss Mahon saw between your daughter and Patrick Mahon yesterday,' Father Parr bellowed, 'but lust. The pure lu—'

Philomena's mouth pulled into a tight line. 'Are you meaning Nora, Father?'

'Indeed I am,' said the priest, his strident voice filling the low-ceilinged space.

Philomena frowned. 'She saw us behind the church?'

'She did, and I praise God for it, for had she not happened to spy you wantonly leading Patrick, a man the Bishop of Cork himself laid hands on and welcomed into the Holy Mother Church no more than a week ago, you may have drawn him into fornication and tainted him for ever.'

'Oh, Philomena, whatever made you do such a thing?' sobbed her mother, covering her face with her hands.

Father Parr's hard eyes studied her from under his overhanging brow.

'Love, Mammy,' Philomena replied. 'Patrick and I love each other.'

'Jezebel!' Drawing himself up to his full height, the priest pointed at her from a balled fist. 'Woman was ever the devil's instrument used to draw men from God, and out of your own mouth you are condemned.'

'Where is Patrick now?' asked Philomena.

'Safe from your wickedness,' Father Parr said, sneering at her down his long nose. 'He is being helped to repentance in the monastery and will be escorted to Cork on Monday and then to England, where he will be safe from your feminine deceptions and he can fulfil his vows.'

'His vows!' Philomena spat out. 'His mother's vow, don't you mean? For it was her who—'

'Silence!' shouted Father Parr, his usual sallow complexion mottled with a ruby flush. 'I'd counsel you to put aside your godless ways before the iniquity in your heart destroys your mother and father along with your sisters and brothers.'

The blood in Philomena's veins turned to ice. 'My family?'

A self-righteous smile lifted Father Parr's thin lips.

'Mr and Mrs Mahon are upstanding members of the parish,' he said. 'Joseph is a member of the town council and Margaret gives her time selflessly to overseeing the town's poorhouse. How do you think they view a tinker's daughter trying to seduce their priest son?'

Fear flashed across her father's face. 'What is it you're meaning, Father?'

'Well, naturally, when they first heard about what your daughter had done they were all for evicting you and forcing you to move on, and sure who would blame them?' Father Parr replied. 'But as I pointed out when they called me to come this morning, forcing you to move on would only raise questions.'

'Thank you, Father,' said Jeremiah Dooley, lowering his head to the priest and tugging his forelock. 'I'm obliged, for sure you're a model of Christian kindness, so you are.'

Philomena's mother let out a long sigh of relief and stood up. 'You're an example to us all,' she added, adopting the same meek posture as her husband.

A supercilious smile lifted the priest's thin features. 'And, having heard Patrick's confession, I'm assured that there has been no intimacy involved.' Philomena's parents crossed themselves rapidly. 'So I persuaded Mr and Mrs Mahon that the best course of action would be to let matters lie.'

Philomena's mother grabbed the priest's hand. 'Oh, Father, you're a saint, to be sure,' she said, pressing her lips on his thin fingers repeatedly.

Although he forced what Philomena supposed was a humble expression on his face, the priest didn't deny it.

'However,' he added, 'I wouldn't be thinking Joe Mahon will be putting work in your direction, and you'd better ensure your wife has laid plenty by for the winter as I shouldn't think Mrs Mahon will look kindly on you if you came begging for outside relief from the parish.' Father Parr's amber eyes slid onto Philomena. 'And as it would seem your daughter is showing signs of having a carnal nature, it might be as well to think about finding a husband amongst your own kind for her before too long.'

Philomena's parents nodded their agreement.

'God's blessing be upon you,' said her father, touching his forelock once more.

Father Parr's gaze ran over Philomena a final time then he turned to leave.

Her father scurried across the room before him and opened their seldom-used front door but, as he reached the threshold, the priest turned back.

'I'll see you at confession tonight, Philomena, where I expect to hear you fully confess your part in tempting one of God's holy ordained priests into mortal sin.'

'Rest assured, Father, she'll be there,' said her father.

With his cassock whirling around his legs, Father Parr swept out and Philomena's father closed the door behind him.

Philomena stared blindly at the white paint peeling off the cottage door for a moment then her mother's voice cut through.

'You will do as Father Parr says, won't you, Mena?' she said, wringing her apron in her hands.

Turning to her mother, Philomena nodded.

And she would. For her dear mammy and pappy's sake she would say the words their parish priest expected her to say, while denying each one of them in her heart.

Chapter Thirteen

WITH HIS HEAD resting on the rough grey blanket that the custody sergeant in West Ham's police station had given him, Billy watched a fat fly buzzing against the solitary window high on the opposite wall.

He didn't know what time it was but as the first streaks of sunlight had crept across the cell's clinical white tiles some time ago, he thought it must be somewhere close to six thirty in the morning.

Although he'd never been in a police cell before, he guessed the eight-by-eight room, with a hard wooden bench by way of a bed and a bucket in the corner, was pretty much standard. There was an enamel pitcher filled with water and a battered mug on the floor in the opposite corner of the room but other than that and the threadbare blanket, the cell was empty.

To be honest, what had happened after the police marched into The Rub A Dub was a bit of a blur. Some officer had taken hold of Angie's arm to lead her off the dance floor and she'd kicked off. Billy remembered trying to defend her and the next thing he knew he was being thrown in the back of the hurry-up wagon with half a dozen other blokes from the club. He'd just about kept the contents of his stomach where it was supposed to be as he bounced around in the back of the Black Mariah, but after he was dragged out and deposited on the concrete of the station's backyard, he'd lost the fight and puked up all over the shiny police boots of the officer marching him towards the back door.

With the stark light above him blinding his eyes, he'd been frogmarched into an interview room. Two hard-bitten CID officers had barked questions at him for what seemed to be forever until he slid like a jelly left in the sun off the chair and on to the floor.

The next thing he knew, he'd woken with a mouth like the bottom of a budgie's cage, a head that felt like it had an axe embedded in it, and the full enormity of what had happened the night before weighing down on him.

Someone a few cells down started cursing and swearing and thumping on the solid iron door. A distant door creaked open, and the sound of heavy boots echoed along the corridor outside Billy's cell. Keys jangled and there was some more shouting then a scream followed by silence. A heavy door banged shut, the key jangled again and the boots marched back to where they'd come from.

Feeling his bladder calling to him, Billy rolled over and eased himself upright. Taking a couple of deep breaths to stop his head from spinning, he stood up and trudged over to the bucket in the corner.

He'd just re-buttoned his flies when a distant door clanged again and heavy boots echoed along the corridor. Keys jingled and bolts turned, then the door to his cell swung open.

'William Brogan?' asked the gaunt policeman standing in the space.

Billy nodded.

'Out you come,' the officer said, marching off. 'And be quick about it.'

Grabbing his crumpled jacket, Billy hurried after him.

After being marched past half a dozen sleepy-looking officers in the front office of West Ham nick, the police officer led him into an interview room.

With peeling magnolia paint on the walls, a bare-bulb light hanging from the ceiling and a door with a small grilled window that opened into the station's lobby, the fifteen-by-fifteen room was much the same as the one he'd been interrogated in the night before.

This time, instead of there being two plain-clothes officers sitting behind the desk, there was a burly-looking sergeant with old-fashioned mutton-chop whiskers and an overhanging moustache. The granite expression on the hard-bitten senior officer alone would have been enough to set Billy's knees knocking. However, standing behind him, dressed in his rough working clothes, his brawny arms crossed tight, his eyebrows pulled into a knot in the middle of his forehead, was his dad.

Billy stepped into the room and his father looked around.

Jeremiah stared in disbelief for a moment but then as his gaze ran over Billy's vomit-splashed mohair trousers and crumpled twill shirt, an expression of undiluted fury spread across his face. Billy's heart sank to the bottom of his five-guinea calf-leather brogues.

The sergeant motioned him further into the room.

With his father's piercing blue-grey eyes fixed on him, Billy moved to the other side of the desk.

After glancing over the large ledger spread out in front of him, the policeman looked up.

'Are you William Peter Brogan?' he asked.

'Yes,' squeaked Billy.

'Of Mafeking Terrace, Stepney?'

'Yes.'

'Date of birth, thirteenth of September 1929?'

Billy nodded.

'It's because you're a minor in the eyes of the law that we asked your father to attend the police station,' said the officer. 'Your father, who was surprised to be summonsed from his bed with the news that his son had been discovered in a nightclub owned by a known criminal, in the company of a young lady who has a record as long as your arm for soliciting. Therefore, in the presence of your father, William Peter Brogan, I'm charging you with—'

'But I didn't do—' Billy caught his father's enraged expression and lapsed into silence.

The sergeant's substantial eyebrows rose. 'You are hereby charged with being drunk and disorderly and assaulting a police constable in the lawful pursuit of his duty. I'm bailing you on your father's recognisance to appear at Plaistow Juvenile Court on the first of June.' He took the pen from the inkwell at his elbow, signed the ledger, then swung the book around.

'Sign here,' he said, pointing to an empty line at the bottom of the charge sheet then offering him the pen.

Billy scribbled his name, and the officer dabbed a scruffy bit of blotting paper on both signatures. Reaching below the desk, the sergeant grasped a paper bag.

'These are yours,' he said, sliding the package across the desk.

'Thank you,' said Billy softly.

Closing the book, the sergeant stood up and tucked the ledger under his arm.

'Thank you for coming in, Mr Brogan,' he said, opening the door.

Jeremiah gave a curt nod to the officer then marched out.

Clutching the bag containing the contents of his pockets, Billy followed his father out.

Jeremiah was already pushing open the police station's main doors when Billy emerged into the lobby. Quickening his pace, Billy caught the door just as it swung back.

'Dad!' he called, as his father trudged down the stairs. 'Dad! Wait.'

But his father didn't wait. Instead, at the bottom of the steps, he turned and headed towards the Brogan & Sons lorry parked a little way along the street.

'Dad!' Billy called again as his father reached the truck.

This time Jeremiah stopped, and Billy, with his eyes fixed on his father's rigid back, trotted the final fifty feet to reach him.

'Dad, I'm—'

Jeremiah span around. 'Not a word!'

'But—'

'Not one.' Jeremiah repeated, raising a beefy finger. 'Do you understand?'

Billy opened his mouth to speak, but with his father looming over him, he thought better of it and nodded.

Jeremiah glared down at him for a few seconds then tore open the vehicle's nearside door. Billy clambered into the front cab.

Slamming the door shut, his father marched around to the driver's side and leapt in. Turning the key in the ignition, he sparked the six-cylinder engine into life, then, without glancing at Billy, he shoved the gearstick into first and they roared away.

'Goodness, Cath,' said Jo, as she and Cathy joined the queue. 'I didn't think it would be so crowded on a Tuesday afternoon.'

'Well,' said Cathy, getting into line behind her, 'Frank Sinatra *is* very dishy.'

It was two o'clock on the last Tuesday in May and she and Jo had just taken their positions at the back of the line of people trailing down the side of the ABC cinema in Mile End Road waiting to see the latest Gene Kelly film *Anchors Aweigh*.

'And thank you for suggesting we treat ourselves to an afternoon out,' she added.

'Thank Dad's Morris van,' said Jo. 'If it hadn't had to have its front wheels and steering rebalanced, then I'd be behind the wheel and buzzing around East London and Essex delivering orders, but as it is, I thought I'd take advantage of my unexpected afternoon off and drag you out to the cinema.'

Cathy laughed. 'You should know by now, Jo, you never have to drag me to the cinema.'

'That's true,' said Jo. 'While me and Mattie spent the money we'd earned lighting Saturday fires for our Jewish neighbours on gobstoppers and sherbet dips, you—'

'I dashed around to Fieldman's for the latest edition of *Picturegoer*,' added Cathy.

'I'm so pleased that Archie'll be home soon,' said Jo, as they shuffled forwards a couple of inches.

'You are?' laughed Cathy. 'You should have seen Aggie dance a jig when I read her his letter.'

In contrast to Stan's mother, Violet Wheeler, who could have matched the devil himself for evil, Archie's mother Aggie was cast from the same mould as Cathy's mum. Family, especially the children, were everything to her. Luckily, although she worked as a part-time assistant in Bancroft Road library, Tuesday was one of her days off, so when Cathy had asked her if she wouldn't mind having the four children for the afternoon, Aggie had jumped at the chance and no doubt all of them would be in the garden having a tea party when she got home.

'I bet,' said Jo, as a few people joined the queue behind them. 'And a month will just fly by.'

'Not quick enough for me,' said Cathy, the familiar ache for Archie swelling in her chest.

Thank goodness, with his demob date just a month away, he'd been taken off active front-line duty with the bomb squad. Since Easter, when it had been clear the war would soon be over, Cathy had woken at least once a week in a cold sweat imagining that, having survived defusing bombs throughout the London Blitz and the years following, Archie would be blown up by a Nazi booby trap just as peace was declared.

'I'm sure that's true,' said Jo. 'I know Francesca is counting the days off on the café's calendar. It must be the same for every wife waiting for their husband to come home.'

The image of Stan's flat face and deep-set eyes loomed into Cathy's mind.

'I suppose you're thinking about Stan?' said Jo, studying her face.

Cathy nodded. 'I just need to know what's happened to him.'

'It's early days yet,' said Jo. 'According to what Daniel was saying when I popped in to see Mattie the other day, along with feeding the starving, homeless populations of the countries they've liberated, the authorities have discovered SS officers trying to pass themselves off as civilians to avoid justice. That's why it's taking so long, because each German soldier is individually processed to make sure none of the Nazi leaders slip away.'

'Sounds like the sort of shameful thing Stan would do,' said Cathy. 'I wouldn't be surprised if he didn't try to pass himself off as an escaped prisoner of war or something. To be honest, Jo, I just want to know what's happened to him one way or the other. Even if he ends up in a military prison then at least I can try to divorce him – although on goodness knows what grounds – but at least I'd know. But . . .' A lump formed in her throat, and she pressed her lips together. Jo put her hand on her arm.

'But you really want to marry Archie,' her sister said softly.

'More than anything.' Cathy sighed, feeling the ache for the man she'd love for ever making its presence known again.

They shuffled forwards and reached the corner of the building. Jo stepped out and looked around the brickwork.

'There's a lot of people coming out,' she said, returning to her place. 'So it shouldn't be much longer now.'

Her attention shifted past Cathy, who turned to follow her sister's gaze and saw a young woman pushing a pram with a chubby-faced infant in a pink bonnet sitting in it. The mother was talking and making happy faces while the little girl waved her arms and laughed.

Cathy looked back at her sister and saw the sadness in Jo's eyes.

She slipped her arm through Jo's and, feeling totally helpless to ease her sister's heartache, gave it a little squeeze.

Jo forced a plucky little smile and the line moved forwards again.

Within a few moments of passing through the doors, she and Jo were at the ticket kiosk.

'Two nine pennies, please,' said Cathy, sliding a florin across the stainless-steel counter.

'And a bar of Cadbury's Fruit and Nut,' added Jo, offering the young woman in the maroon uniform behind the desk her ration book and half a crown. She smiled at Cathy. 'My treat for the main film.'

The cashier punched out their tickets and slid them and the bar of chocolate back along with their change and Jo's ration book.

'Right, Cathy,' said Jo, picking up their indulgent snack and grinning at her, 'Frank Sinatra, here we come.'

With her sister Cathy just a step behind her, Jo followed the light of the usherette's torch as they were shown to their seats in the packed auditorium.

'That's lucky,' whispered Cathy. 'It's only the B film.'

Jo nodded.

The B film was usually naff, after which came Pathé News, and finally the main feature film – all three shown on a continuous loop. If you were unlucky, you'd find you'd walked in smack bang in the middle of the main film. Of course, you could sit through the whole programme until that point in the film again, but it sapped all the enjoyment out of a tense, murder mystery if you already knew who the killer was.

Keeping her eyes on the glow of light marking the way down the stairs, Jo followed the usherette until she directed the torch's beam on to two free spaces in the middle of a row halfway down the auditorium. Gathering her skirts around her and trying not to tread on people's toes, Jo sidestepped along to their seats.

Tipping down the padded seat base, Jo sat down just as Cathy reached her. Slipping off her jacket, Jo folded it inwards and tucked it and her handbag down the side of her chair then settled back.

A faint fishy smell skimmed under Jo's nose. Cathy nudged her and indicated a man and woman sitting in front of them eating sandwiches.

Sardines? Jo mouthed, the silvery light from the large screen flickering across her sister's face.

Cathy pulled a face and they smiled at each other then turned their attention back to the screen. The B film today was a western with actors that Jo didn't recognise, and when the gunslinger pushed open the bar door the whole saloon wall looked as if it was about to fall on him.

'You can see why people were leaving the cinema,' whispered Cathy, as cowboys with white hats ducked back and forth behind barrels as they fired at their counterparts in black hats.

Jo nodded then looked back to the gunfight, but it failed to hold her attention and her mind wandered off. The image of the happy mother pushing her laughing little girl in the pram floated back into her mind, bringing with it the dilemma she'd been wrestling with for the past few weeks.

Although they had talked about adopting Zara since they'd visited the orphanage, Tommy had never once tried to push her to say yes. In fact, the opposite was true. Every time the subject did come up, he was at pains to tell her that it was her decision and to take as much time as she liked.

But she would have to decide, and soon, as it wasn't fair on Tommy, who she knew was desperate for her to say yes.

She had to agree with Tommy, though, because the little girl was utterly adorable. But although the greater part of Jo wanted to shout yes as Zara stared up at her with her innocent dark eyes, something – call it fear or panic – held her back.

Damping down the disquiet rising in her chest, Jo reached into her jacket pocket and took out the bar of chocolate. Unpeeling the wrapper, she offered it to Cathy.

'I thought it was for the main feature?' her sister whispered as she broke off a couple of squares.

In the muted glow of the auditorium, Jo poked out her tongue.

Mercifully, the blare of the orchestra filled the auditorium, signalling the end of the low-budget western, and as the credits started to roll, a few people around them began making their way out.

The lights went up for a few moments, but when the cock crowed, heralding the start of Pathé News, they dimmed again, and the audience settled down.

The first snippet was a short section, accompanied by an upbeat tune, showing men being greeted at Waterloo station by their wives and sweethearts, but within a couple of bars the tone of the soundtrack changed from jolly to serious.

A female Member of Parliament, in a dark dress and with an upper-class accent that could cut glass, appeared on the screen. She explained the horror she'd witnessed when she entered one of the German concentration camps as part of the government inquiry. There was a gasp as her face was replaced by images of what looked like animated skeletons walking across the screen but which were in fact human beings. The camera then panned on past the living and on to the dead, piled high and naked.

Cathy crossed herself, and staring in horror at the parchment-like faces of the bodies that had been thrown in a jumble on a cart, Jo did the same.

The picture changed to an inside shot of what looked like a huge baker's oven but instead of bread it was filled with charred bones.

The film moved outside again and on to a huddle of children, some no more than toddlers, all of them skin and bone and wearing what appeared to be striped pyjamas.

'These are the fortunate ones, alone in the world and orphaned, yes, but alive,' said the strident, upper-class tones of the woman MP.

She fell silent and the camera moved sideways to a mountain of children's shoes, of all sizes, that reached as high as the waists of the soldiers standing beside it.

Jo put her hand to her cheek and felt tears.

Although there were over two hundred people packed into the auditorium, there was utter silence.

The MP started speaking again but Jo didn't hear a word. Her eyes were fixed on the jumble of shoes that had belonged to children who had once kicked a ball, jumped a skipping rope or tottered unsteadily towards the outstretched arms of their mothers.

Time froze for a second or two, then, grabbing her coat and bag, Jo stood up.

'I'm sorry, Cathy,' she said, treading over her sister's feet as she stumbled along the row of seats. 'But I've got to see Tommy.'

As the rattle of china heralded the imminent arrival of the tea trolley, Sergeant Tommy Sweete squeezed the manila file marked 'Top Secret' alongside the two dozen others in the storage box on his desk.

Pressing on the lid, he picked up the ball of string next to it just as Ruby Trott, the department's tea lady, clip-clopped into the office on her yellow high heels.

The government supplied all their domestic staff with uniforms but, as had been the case since she'd transferred across to their department from the Ministry of Supply a few months ago, Ruby, who was probably half a decade older than Tommy's twenty-six years, had adapted the uniform to suit her own particular style. Instead of the tube-shaped pink overall being buttoned up, she'd left it open to reveal a red pencil skirt and a jumper stretched tight across her bosom. A maid's cap perched on her brassy blonde hair.

'Afternoon, Sergeant,' said the department's poor-man's Jean Harlow. 'Tea?'

'Yes please, Ruby. No sugar.' Tommy grinned. 'I'm sweet enough.'

The woman's heavily made-up face lifted in a flirtatious smile, then, gripping her glowing cigarette firmly between crimson lips, she grabbed the enamel teapot.

It was three thirty and Tommy was standing in the office he shared with four others on the third floor of a nondescript building just off Whitehall. The whole floor was listed in the foyer as being the London Signals Intelligence Centre and was sandwiched between the Department of Overseas Territories for Widows and Orphans on the floor below and the Committee for Voluntary Youth Organisation above. Tommy had no idea if that's what those organisations actually did, but the suite of rooms on his floor was, in fact, the London outpost of the Government Code and Cypher School, based in the leafy surrounds of Bletchley Park.

'You know, it won't be the same around here with you boys gone,' Ruby said wistfully, pouring tea into a fern-green government-issue cup.

'Well, now it's all over in Europe, it's time to pack up here at least,' Tommy replied, looping the sisal string beneath the box.

It never ceased to amaze him that from being a dedicated truant from school and a youthful tearaway, he'd ended up being part of one of the most clandestine operations of the entire war. So covert and secretive, in fact, that it would probably be years, if not decades, before he could even tell Jo about it.

Of course, things might have been different if he hadn't met Mr Grossman, the librarian at St George's Library, who had pointed out the puzzle competition in *The Times*. Although his motivation for filling it in had been the £50 prize, little did he know at the time that the real prize was being able now to make something of himself.

Of course, his new life was a few months away yet, but for now he was transferring all the files into boxes ready to be taken for storage to the Government Code and Cypher School's new site at Cheltenham.

'I hear tell you're to be a school master, Sergeant,' Ruby said as she placed a cup next to the telephone on the desk.

Tommy tied the knot and pulled it tight. 'I am. After I've finished my training, that is.'

Ruby's pencilled eyebrows rose. 'And 'ow long'll that take?'

'Two years,' Tommy replied. 'It's been trimmed down from three. I'm going to do it at Borough Polytechnic Institute by London Bridge.'

'And I'm sure you'll be very good,' she replied.

'Thanks,' said Tommy.

'You like kids, then?' Ruby asked.

'I really do,' he replied.

'Got any yourself?' she asked casually.

'Not yet,' said Tommy, damping down the ache to be a father that Ruby's words stirred up.

'There's plenty of time,' Ruby replied, splashing milk into his cup and cutting across his agonising thoughts.

Tommy gave her a tight smile by way of reply.

'As ignorance is one of Labour's five pillars,' he said, forcing his words over the lump wedged in his throat, 'I'm expecting them to tackle education as soon as they get into Government, so they will need more teachers.'

'You think there'll be an election, do you?'

'Blooming right, there will be,' Tommy replied. 'After what the ordinary people of this country have been through in the last six years, we deserve to have our say in how the country's run and most of us will be voting to stop a return to the old ways of doing things.'

'Seems a bit ungrateful to me – kicking Old Winston out, I mean, after all he's done,' said Ruby.

'Churchill said himself on VE Day it was the "People's Victory", and it is; so now we're going to make sure it's going to be the "People's Peace",' Tommy concluded.

'Oh well,' said the tea lady, holding her cigarette between two nail-varnished fingers and sending a stream of smoke skywards, 'I'll leave it to you lot with brains. Me, I'd be content to sleep in my own bed without worrying about waking up in heaven. But although I'm glad we've given the Nazis a right pasting, I'm still a bit sad it's all over.'

'Because of everyone's camaraderie in the face of adversity?' said Tommy, as he heaved the box off his desk and stacked it on top of the pile waiting to be collected.

Ruby rolled her eyes. 'Don't be daft,' she said, returning her cigarette to her lips. 'Cos my old man'll be back soon, so that's the end of all my fun.'

With the wheels squeaking and the cups rattling, Ruby pushed her trolley out of the office.

Tommy turned back to his task.

Of course, it was Jo's decision about Zara and he could understand why she felt hesitant, he really could. The fear of not being able to love a child that you hadn't conceived or welcomed into the world was daunting, and if she said no, then ... Well, he just fervently prayed she wouldn't.

Pulling out the next drawer of the khaki-coloured filing cabinet, Tommy removed another batch of files and laid them on his desk just as the telephone rang.

He picked up the receiver. 'Sergeant Sweete.'

'I hope I'm not disturbing you, Sergeant, but your wife is down here at the front desk,' said the receptionist.

Tommy's eyebrows rose in surprise. 'Is she?'

'Yes,' said the tinny voice at the other end. 'And she's asking if she could see you?'

'Tell her I'll be right down,' said Tommy.

Taking the stairs two at a time, he arrived in the building's spacious foyer within a few moments of leaving his office. Scanning his eyes over the dozen or so people milling around in the echoey entrance hall, he spotted Jo standing by a large oil painting on the far wall. She spotted him, too, and her face lit up.

Dodging around a couple of people, she dashed towards him and then, bouncing on the balls of her feet, threw herself into his arms.

'Jo,' he said, taking her into his arms. 'What—'

Her lips stopped his words in an enthusiastic kiss.

She released him and, somewhat bemused, he looked down at his wife's smiling face.

'Tommy, I've come to a decision,' she said, her brown eyes overflowing with love and happiness. 'Let's adopt Zara.'

Drawing her into his embrace again, Tommy closed his eyes. Yes, he'd gained £50 and a bright future, but filling in that crossword puzzle had given him the most precious thing in his life – Jo.

Chapter Fourteen

THE DOOR OPPOSITE opened and Billy's mouth went dry as a stout police officer, the sunlight from the sky light above gleaming on the silver buttons of his uniform, stepped out.

His bored gaze ran over Billy and the other four boys sitting on the long bench beside him.

'Harris!' he bellowed.

The boy next to Billy stood up and walked over to the officer, who ushered him through the door. It banged shut and the sound echoed along the empty corridor.

Billy's shoulders sagged and he leaned back against the majolica tiles that lined the wall.

It was Friday and the first day of June and he was sitting in the dimly lit corridor behind Plaistow Juvenile Court. As the large clock above the door was just ticking around to eleven o'clock, he had been waiting for the past two hours.

To be fair, considering there had been fifteen boys on the bench when the court started at nine and there were now just three of them left, the magistrates were cracking through their morning list.

His fellow accused had been a mixed bunch, from scruffy youngsters still in short trousers who were habitual shoplifters to hard-bitten youths just short of their eighteenth birthdays who were accomplished cat burglars.

Most of them had arrived together in a van from a juvenile detention centre. However, there were a couple like him, who'd been brought to court by their parents or other relatives. The bigger boys from the institution wore ill-fitting and faded clothes, but as he was the only boy wearing a blazer with an embroidered school crest on the pocket, it had caused a bit of interest amongst the other lads. Their attitude had switched from pugnacious to toadying in an instant after Billy recounted the story of his arrest and his connection to Lenny Stamp.

A few weeks ago, he would have given them his gangster shrug and smirked, but now . . . well, he just felt deeply embarrassed. Added to which, all but one of his fellow accused had been taken through a door at the far end of the corridor to the holding cells after their appearance before the magistrate. As the number of boys waiting to be dealt with dwindled, so did Billy's courage.

The door opened again and the boy who had just been called in was now marched out by another police officer and taken towards the entrance to the jail below.

'Brogan!'

Billy jumped up and stood to attention.

The stout officer with the shiny buttons jerked his head and Billy followed him through the door.

With their footsteps echoing in the narrow wood-lined passage, Billy climbed the half a dozen steps and found himself on a raised area enclosed by a waist-high railing.

Blinking at the sudden brightness, his eyes skimmed over the heads of the handful of policemen and court officials sitting at desks across to the public gallery.

In the front row, alongside a couple of women and a newspaper reporter scribbling on a pad, sat his parents, both of whom were wearing their Sunday best and looking across at him.

He smiled and his mum gave him an encouraging smile back, but the stony-faced expression that had been fixed to his father's face since he'd fetched Billy from West Ham police station didn't flicker.

A flash of navy caught Billy's eyes as the officer standing in front of the dock stood up. Billy turned his attention back to the magistrates' bench in front of him. Behind it sat three people: a smartly dressed woman wearing a close-fitting hat; a man in a sombre lounge suit with his sparse hair combed over his bulbous, bald head and, looking as if she'd muscled in between them, an older woman wearing a tweed suit with mink trim and a black hat with a brim almost as wide as her shoulders perched on her unruly steel-grey hair.

'Thank you, Sergeant,' she said, in a tone indistinguishable from a BBC announcer.

The officer, a tall chap with a hangdog face who was standing in front of Billy, cleared his throat. 'William Peter Brogan is charged with . . .'

He read the indictments as the woman in the middle of the three studied Billy from beneath her oversized hat.

'If we could hear the evidence, please,' she asked.

The officer inclined his head. 'Of course, Lady Cumberland.'

The tall officer nodded at a fresh-faced policeman with fair hair, who stood up and walked across to the witness box to the left of the magistrates' bench.

He took out his black-covered notebook and held it aloft.

Billy's head hung lower and lower as, in a clear, strong voice, the young policeman read out the events of the evening. When he got to the bit where Billy was swearing and swinging wild punches, Billy stole a look at his parents, but seeing his mum holding a handkerchief to her eyes and the look of deep disappointment on his father's face, Billy just wished the ground would give way so he could go straight to hell.

Finally, after what seemed like an eternity, the officer finished speaking.

'Thank you, Officer,' said Lady Cumberland. 'I hope you are fully recovered?'

'I am, ma'am,' he replied, closing his notepad and slipping it back in his breast pocket.

'So,' she said, looking at Billy over her half-rimmed spectacles, 'did you do what the officer says you did?' she asked.

He nodded.

She pulled a face and cupped her ear.

'Yes.' Billy squared his shoulders. 'Yes, I did but—'

She raised a hand and he lapsed into silence.

'Well, I have to say, for one moment there I thought I was back on the bench at Marlborough Road listening to an occurrence in Soho, don't you agree, Mr Ingram?'

'Indeed, I do,' the man to her right replied.

'Most shocking,' added the woman on the other side of the chief magistrate.

The wide brim of her hat obscuring her face for a moment, Lady Cumberland nodded her agreement then her eyes returned to Billy.

'Have you anything to say for yourself, young man?'

Billy stood up straight. 'I was in the wrong and I'm very sorry, miss.'

The elderly magistrate's inflexible expression softened a little. 'Mm, at least you're not trying to blame your appalling behaviour on others.' Her gaze flickered down to the badge on his chest. 'What school do you go to?'

'Parmiter's Boys Grammar School, miss,' Billy replied, feeling his father's eyes heavy on him. 'In Hackney.'

Setting the fine netting of her hat trembling, Lady Cumberland shook her head dolefully.

'Pity,' she muttered. 'However, you don't contest the evidence, so in this case I'm afraid unless there's anything else . . .'

She glanced around the room and the officer with the haggard face stood up again.

'If it pleases the court, the defendant's father, Mr Brogan, would like to say something.'

'Very well,' said the chief magistrate.

The officer beckoned Jeremiah forward and he took his place in the witness box.

'Well, Mr Brogan?' said Lady Cumberland.

Jeremiah pulled his shoulders back and looked at the magistrates.

'Listening to my son's behaviour that night in the club, I'm fit to be tied with the fury of it and agree he should be punished as a consequence, but I would say, in his defence, that he's had a rough time of it these past years.'

'Haven't we all, Mr Brogan?' said the magistrate.

A snigger went around the court.

'You'll have no argument with me on that score, ma'am,' Jeremiah replied. 'But when I say rough, I mean in his heart since he discovered the truth about his birth. And I and no other must bear the blame for that, least of all my son.' The corner of his father's mouth lifted, and he gave the woman on the bench his best roguish Irish smile. 'Now you see, although our first four children arrived in the usual way and to this day are the joy of both our hearts, sadly God, in his infinite wisdom, saw fit to call our fifth, James, to his place in Heaven at just five days old.'

'My condolences, Mr Brogan,' said Lady Cumberland, 'but if we could . . .' She tapped her wristwatch.

'Thank you, ma'am. 'Tis kind you are,' said Jeremiah. 'I'm not wanting to take up the court's time but to make matters clear to your honour. . . By a strange twist of fate, my wife's sister Pearl had also been delivered of a boy, Billy, within days of our dear James, but sadly for the sweet babe and for reasons of her own knowing, Pearl Munday abandoned her newborn infant . . .'

Although Billy had heard the story at least a dozen times, this time, as he listened to his father tell the three magistrates the circumstances around his birth, images of a newborn infant, naked and alone, lying on the cold tiles in a toilet, materialised in his mind.

'. . . and since the day we collected him from the workhouse we have loved and cared for Billy, and he is our son in all the ways that matter.'

From under her extravagant hat, Lady Cumberland gave Jeremiah a questioning look.

'I really don't see, Mr Brogan, how your son being left in a workhouse should excuse him from assaulting a policeman.'

'It doesn't,' said Jeremiah. 'But perhaps if I'd told him the truth about it instead of him finding out by chance some three years ago, Your Worship, Billy might not have been so muddled in his understanding of life when the woman who gave birth to him started luring him from the straight and narrow with promises of fancy clothes and money.'

Lady Cumberland gave him a dubious look. 'Even so . . .'

'And, Your Worship, I have here,' delving into his inside jacket pocket, Jeremiah pulled out a handful of envelopes, 'a letter from his headmaster telling as how up until the time his mother started seeing him behind our backs, Billy had a full attendance record and worked hard at his lessons.'

Billy stared in disbelief at the paperwork in his father's hand.

'I've another from Father Timothy,' continued Jeremiah, laying on the Irish charm with a trowel, 'testifying that Billy serves as an altar boy, and another from Mr Flanagan, the church's choirmaster.' Giving the magistrates a pleading look, Billy's father put his hand dramatically on his chest. 'Heart sick about the whole sorry business I am, but Billy is a well-brought-up, God-fearing, scholarly young lad led astray by those of a more disreputable temperament. I'm hoping these testimonials might persuade your worships to look kindly on him.'

'Is that it?' asked the chief magistrate.

'Yes, Your Worship,' said Jeremiah. 'And thank you for your indulgence.'

Without glancing at Billy, he stepped down from the witness box.

Watching him resume his seat beside his wife, Lady Cumberland chewed her lips for a moment then the three magistrates put their heads together.

After what seemed like an eternity, they nodded and Lady Cumberland looked up.

'William Brogan,' she said.

Billy straightened up and met her eye.

'It seems that instead of attending to your studies, you have been keeping some very bad company, have you not?' she said, her upper-class tones ringing around the wood-panelled courtroom.

Swallowing, Billy nodded.

'If,' she continued, 'being under the influence of liquor and frequenting a seedy nightclub in the company of miscreants, ne'er-do-wells and loose-moralled women weren't enough to have you brought before us, punching a police officer in the lawful execution of his duty certainly would be. It would also, in the usual run of things, cause me to sentence you to be birched followed by six months in borstal.'

Billy gripped the iron railing as his knees threatened to give way.

'However,' continued the magistrate, 'because of your father's rather flowery yet insightful thoughts on why you have become entangled with the law, and in view of the fact that other than the usual childish brushes with the local constabulary regarding the reckless kicking of footballs and playing harmless pranks on neighbours, this is the first time you've actually been up before a magistrate, I am going to impose a three-month borstal sentence suspended for two years and a twenty-pound fine payable within seven days. Next!'

Out of the corner of his eyes he saw his father put his arm around Ida's shoulder and Billy let go of the long breath he didn't know he was holding. Dizzy with relief, he stumbled out of the dock.

The tarpaulin covering the rafters at the other end of the room flapped a little in the summer breeze as Billy brushed a speck of dirt off the jacket of the mohair suit Aunt Pearl had given him two months before. He folded it carefully then slid it into a crumpled brown paper bag that had 'Woolworth' stamped diagonally across it.

Turning, he picked up the trousers that were lying next to his Hornby trainset box on his blue candlewick bedspread, but as he held the bottoms together to shake them out, he heard the unmistakable rumble of his father's voice below.

It was now just after two and he and his parents had arrived back from Plaistow Juvenile Court about an hour ago. They had sat three abreast in the cab of his father's Bedford lorry in utter silence for the whole three-quarter-of-an-hour journey and having dropped Billy and his mum off at the house, his father had sped away in a cloud of diesel smoke as he had an appointment with a solicitor regarding the yard in Canning Town that he was considering leasing.

After a quick sandwich, his mum had taken Victoria around to Mattie's for the afternoon, and Gran, having had her midday meal at the church's lunch club, was now snoozing in the parlour below. Neither of them had said very much about the morning's proceedings, instead keeping the lunchtime chat to more mundane things than him being found legless in an underworld club and punching a policeman.

After all the emotional ups and downs he'd been through during the morning, Billy had felt relieved to have the house more or less to himself but, truthfully, it was only putting off the inevitable balling-out by his father.

Well, at least he hoped it was, because rather than explode as he usually did when Billy was in his bad books, for the past two weeks his dad had maintained the same blank expression on his face and had barely said a word to him, even when he'd done his usual Saturday stint helping his father on the removal lorry.

Flicking the trousers straight, he folded them and slid them above the jacket as the sound of his father's heavy feet on the stairs grew ever nearer.

Putting his parcel on the chair by his desk, Billy turned towards the door just as his father stepped into the room.

Jeremiah's unwavering gaze ran over him and Billy's heart sank.

'Dad, I'm sorry,' he blurted out. 'I really am. I shouldn't have gone to see Aunt Pearl or got involved with Lenny Stamp. I was wrong and . . . and . . .' Tears pinched the corners of his eyes. 'I'm really, really sorry, Dad. And here.' He picked up the box with the *Flying Scotsman* on it and took the lid off. 'This is the money Aunt Pearl gave me. It's only sixteen pounds, but you can have it for the fine.'

Jeremiah studied the collection of crumpled green and brown bank notes for a moment then his attention returned to Billy.

Dragging over the chair tucked under Billy's desk, his father turned it around.

'Let's have a little chat, shall we?' he asked, sitting astride the chair and resting his arms across the back.

Gingerly, Billy sat on the edge of his bed and clasped his hands together in front of him.

'I really am sorry, Dad,' he repeated.

'I know you are, lad,' Jeremiah replied in the same hushed tone. 'And I'm mighty sorry too.'

Billy's mouth dropped open and he stared at his father.

'Sorry for not telling you sooner about Aunt Pearl. Me and your mum did it to protect you, but it's clear to me now that it was wrong. I didn't give a thought to how hard it must have been to find out that the people you thought were your true parents and brothers and sisters were no such thing. But as far as me and your mum are concerned, you are as much our son as Charlie is.'

Remorse squeezed Billy's chest.

'I know, Dad,' he replied, and his eyes felt tight again.

'Well now, Billy, perhaps you do,' his father replied. 'Let me tell you this and tell you no more. You're almost grown now, so you have to decide for yourself who you are and where you belong.'

He stood up and calmly retraced his steps to the door.

'But what about the money?' Billy called after him. 'Don't you want it?'

His father looked around and his blue-grey eyes flickered over the jumble of notes in the box.

'You'll have to decide about that, too, son, for I'll not be taking a penny of it,' he replied.

He held Billy's gaze for a second or two longer, then he turned and strolled out of the room.

Pressing down on the handle with her elbow, Nora eased the door open with her hip. Careful not to slop the milk in the jug on the tray she was carrying, she walked into the rectory's study.

Her brother, dressed as always in his black cassock and dog collar, was sitting at his desk by the window overlooking the garden.

Studying his averted face, Nora frowned.

Even in the June sunlight that cast a mellow glow over the room, Patrick's complexion still looked like a November sky.

Not for the first time, the run-in she'd had with Queenie about her brother's health sprang into her mind, but she shoved it aside.

Sure, even though her brother Cornelius was in his eightieth year now, the fact that since the day Patrick took his vows some fifty years before, Cornelius hadn't suffered more than the odd snuffle and still strode across the field each day managing his herd proved that the Blessed Virgin was still keeping her side of the bargain.

Patrick looked around and smiled. 'Goodness me, is it eleven already?'

'That it is,' Nora replied, marching across the colourless Indian rug carrying the tray and setting it on the edge of the desk. 'You're catching up on your correspondence, I see,' she said, indicating the three envelopes stood up against the base of the desk lamp.

'Indeed, Father Wren in Durham is long overdue a reply from his last letter,' he replied.

'I'm off to the butcher's to get the week's meat, so I'll drop them in at the post office to be sure they catch the midday collection,' said Nora as she poured his coffee. 'And at least letter writing is a mite less tiring than the stream of visitors you seem to be having of late. Honest to God, they give you no rest.'

'Soft now, Nora,' said Patrick. 'Sure, it's a great comfort to me having so many souls who care.'

'What is it they don't comprehend about you having to take it easy?' said Nora, stirring in his sugar. 'Are they not remembering you've got the St Breda and St Brendan's Procession Day next Sunday.'

'And I'll be grand by then, Nora,' he said, as she placed his cup next to the inkwell.

'So you will, I'm sure,' she agreed, once again damping down the niggling doubt in her mind placed there by Queenie.

'I may be old and decrepit, but I'm still at the service of my parishioners, so 'tis right they should bring their concerns to me,' Patrick said.

'Even so,' Nora replied, 'to my mind, these locals seem to lack respect for your position as God's representative. I mean, could you imagine Mammy and Pappy or anyone else in Kinsale just barging their way in on Father Parr at all hours. No, they would not.'

'That's true,' he agreed. 'But the people here are less burdened by their Christian obligation than we are back home.'

'Heathens is what they are, Patrick.'

He gave her a hard look. 'As were those our Lord himself walked among, Nora. Although,' he added, 'I am a mite surprised Queenie hasn't been one of my many visitors.'

'Well, I imagine she has enough to do running around after that wayward family of hers,' Nora said, as her life-long hatred of Queenie flared again.

Patrick pulled a face. 'I'll grant you, Nora, Queenie's brood are lively, that's for sure, but they are far from wayward, especially as all the men of the family have been fighting for King and Country for the past five years.'

'Would you not call them wayward, Patrick?' she replied. 'Not after all the shenanigans with that grandson of hers?' She rolled her eyes. 'Surely to mercy you must have heard, for wasn't the whole church buzzing with it yesterday. Found drunk, he was, in the arms of a hussy and nearly killed a police—'

Patrick raised his hand. 'Didn't St Paul write to the faithful in Corinth about hope and charity, Nora? The latter being a quality we, his followers, should have in abundance.'

Nora clasped her hands in front of her and fashioned her face into a humble expression. 'Indeed we should, Patrick.'

Her brother's affable smile returned and he picked up the envelope still lying on the blotting paper.

'Would you do me a kindness and while you're on your way around the parish could you take a note into Queenie, as I'd dearly like to see her?' he asked, offering her the letter. 'For I can't tell you what a joy it is for me to talk to her about the old days back in Kinsale.'

Rage rose in Nora's chest again but she forced a smile.

'Of course.' She took the letter and slipped it into her apron pocket. 'Well, I'd best be away to the butcher's while there's still something in the window.'

Patrick turned back to his desk and Nora left the room.

Retracing her steps along the hall to the kitchen, she took off her apron and hung it on the pantry door.

She pulled the letter from the pocket and gazed down at Queenie's name, written in her brother's shaky hand.

God curse her. Curse Philomena Dooley to burn in hell for eternity.

Grabbing the envelope with both hands, Nora tore it in half and half again, then pulling open the back door, she stomped out into the yard.

Lifting the dustbin lid, she tossed the fragments of paper on top of the dirt and rotting food then slammed it back.

Queenie had called to see Patrick almost every day, in fact, since they'd crossed swords in the sanctum, but Nora had turned her away. Talk about the old days, would they? Only over her cold dead body, they would. She'd be booking a ticket to hell herself before she let Philomena Dooley over the threshold.

Kinsale, Ireland. June 1889

AS MICHAEL BURKE brought the roan horse pulling his farm cart to a stop by the stone trough she was sitting on, Philomena stood up. Keeping her eyes fixed on Miss Cuthbertson's smart bright red door at the far end of the Market Square, she shifted her weight from leg to leg to relieve the numbness in her rear for a moment then resumed her perch.

Attracted by the sweating horse, a couple of lazy flies buzzed around her in the sultry summer heat but Philomena waved them away.

It was Wednesday and as the cooks and housekeepers from the big houses at the top of the town had finished purchasing their provisions hours ago, the poorer members of the tight-knit harbour-side community were now out in the afternoon heat hoping for a late bargain.

It was also five days since Father Parr's visit and by now Patrick Mahon, the only man she'd ever loved and ever would love while there was breath in her body, was somewhere in the Irish Sea on his way to God alone knew what in England.

Brushing down the skirts of her pale green cotton dress, Philomena re-crossed her bare ankles and glanced at the town-hall clock. Almost five. Good. Only a few more moments and the quarry she'd been stalking for the past four days would appear and hopefully this time she'd be alone.

As the first of the five chimes signalling the top of the hour rang out around the square, the red door opened and Nora Mahon, dressed in a blue candy-striped day dress and with her straw bonnet secured under her chin with a green ribbon, emerged from her piano lesson.

Hooking the drawstrings of her purse over her arm, Nora turned and headed off towards her home on St John's Hill.

Thinking that, as the penalty for murder was a hangman's noose, perhaps it was a blessing she hadn't managed to corner Nora before now, Philomena planted her bare feet on the wet cobbles and stood up.

Feeling the cool water from the trough between her toes, she headed after Nora.

Nora's stout walking shoes marching over the cobbles echoed down Main Street, but Philomena's footfall was silent as she hastened after her.

Philomena caught up with Nora as she reached the narrow passageway through to Pier Road. Grabbing Nora's arm, she span her around. 'At school you always were a one for running off to tell tales, weren't you?'

Alarm flashed across Nora's flat face for a second then she snatched her arm back and forced a laugh. 'I don't know what you're talking about.'

'Don't try to pretend it wasn't you telling tales to Father Parr,' Philomena shouted. 'Because you know full well what you've done.'

'What I've done!' Nora replied. ''Tis you who were rubbing yourself against him like the Dublin doxy you are. And him in his holy robes and all.'

'Holy robes you and your highfaluting mother forced him into,' Philomena countered.

'That's not true,' snapped Nora. 'Cornelius was all but dead when Patrick—'

'Your mother had no right to make a vow for Patrick,' shouted Philomena. 'If she was so desperate for the Virgin to perform a miracle on her behalf, why didn't she offer to become a nun instead of condemning Patrick to a life without the hope of love or children?'

'My brother has the love of God,' Nora replied, as a superior expression slid across her face. 'And his children will be God's own dear children.'

Philomena spat on the cobbles, narrowly missing the other girl's polished shoes. 'May the devil himself take you, Nora Mary Mahon.'

Above her lacy collar, a crimson flush crept up Nora's neck. Her eyes narrowed.

'Even if Patrick hadn't become a priest, don't think my family would have given their blessing to him marrying the likes of you, Philomena Dooley. Your family are no better than beggars and that mother of yours with her heathen potions and predictions would have been burned at the stake as a witch a century ago.'

Philomena pinned her balled fists to her side so as to stop them punching Nora in her ugly mouth.

'You are fortunate my mammy and pappy are God-fearing Christians,' Nora went on, 'as some would be less forgiving towards the slut who tried to lead their ordained son into the mortal sin of fornication.'

Philomena pressed her lips together.

'Now, if that's all you've to say to me,' continued Nora, putting her hand to her bonnet to straighten it, 'I'll be wishing you a good day, and don't be thinking of muttering some curse because I'll be straight to Father Parr and you and your filthy, heathen family will be turned out of the town with just the clothes on your backs.'

Giving Philomena a self-righteous look, Nora shoved past her and marched on.

Philomena's eyes bore into the space between the other girl's shoulder blades. No, she wouldn't be conjuring up the old spirits from the hills to pay Nora Mahon back, because by all the saints above, she'd be taking on that task herself.

Chapter Fifteen

'WHAT DO YOU think, Cathy?' asked Ida, standing back and studying the eighteen-inch statue of Jesus, the red sacred heart on his chest radiating gold slivers of metal.

'I think it looks fine, Mum,' said Cathy, poking a few flowers around the base of the Virgin Mary who was standing alongside her son.

Her mother stood back and ran a critical eye over the two plaster statues sitting on Queenie's outside window sill.

Of course, today it wasn't just her grandmother's window sill. Today, because it was the second Sunday in June, it had been transformed into the family's altar ready for the St Breda and St Brendan's annual St Mary's Day parade.

Ida had been up almost at the crack of dawn and had set up most of the display by the time Cathy arrived at eleven. Now, just after lunch, they were putting the statues in place ready for when the procession reached Mafeking Terrace in a few hours' time.

Jeremiah had removed the boarding that had covered the window since the glass had been blown out by the V-2 bomb, and the lace-fringed tablecloth that's only function in life was to cover the stone sill had been draped over a freshly laundered white one.

'I'm glad we went to the trouble of getting those ribbons up,' said Cathy, indicating the white, yellow and green crêpe-paper streamers around the window frame.

'And I'm glad we didn't fall off the chair doing it,' her mother replied. 'And I know it's perhaps a sin to say it, Cathy, but I think the Brogan family altar looks the best in the street.'

Her mother was right, although, truthfully, it didn't have much competition.

Except for the Cohens at number 15, the Wisemans at number 56 and a handful of families who attended St Paul's Church on the Highway, the rest of the street were members of St Breda and St Brendan's congregation. However, whereas before the war nearly every house in the street would have had a family altar set up ready to be blessed by the priest as he passed by, today Ida could count no more than a dozen and a half at most.

True, thanks to the flying bomb that had taken off their roof, the bottom end of the street was little more than rubble, but two-thirds of the street was still standing.

But perhaps that was just the way of it. After all, no one who had lived surrounded by death and destruction as they had for the past six years could ever be the same, therefore it wasn't surprising that the buildings weren't the only thing the German bombs had swept away forever.

Slipping her arm around her mother's waist, Cathy gave her a quick peck on the cheek. 'It always is.'

They exchanged fond looks then her mother's attention shifted over Cathy's shoulder.

'Here's Jo, Mattie and the children,' she said.

Cathy turned to see her two sisters heading down the street. Mattie was pushing a pram with Ian sitting in it while Jo was walking beside her holding Alicia and Robert's hands. However, when they spotted Cathy's three amongst a gang of other children they let go and dashed forwards to join their cousins further down the street.

As it was a special family day, all of them were dressed in their Sunday best, with their hair kept in order by ribbons and slides for the girls and lashings of Brilliantine for the boys.

Mattie and Jo each greeted their mother with a quick kiss on the cheek then turned to Cathy.

'Typical,' said Cathy, embracing them both. 'Turn up just when the work's done.'

Mattie and Jo grinned.

'What do you think, girls?' asked Ida, indicating the altar.

'It looks great, Mum,' said Mattie. 'And I like the ribbons.'

'Yes, that's a nice touch,' agreed Jo.

'Fieldman's around the corner were sold out, so I had to trudge all the way down to Roman Road to get the crêpe paper. Honestly, it's all very well the papers saying we've won the war, but from where I'm standing, I can't see the queues outside every blooming shop getting any shorter. I only hope things get better once the election's over.'

'Well, you're going to have to wait a while because according to the papers we won't have a result until the end of July when all the servicemen's votes have been counted,' said Mattie.

'Who are you voting for, Mum?' asked Jo.

'Labour, I suppose,' said Ida. 'I expect everyone is around here. They always have.'

'I'm surprised the Tories even bother to put up a candidate,' laughed Cathy. 'As Dad always says, "Put a chimpanzee in a suit and as long as he's got a red rosette on his chest people will vote for him."'

'Talking of your father, I was hoping he'd be back by now,' said Ida, glancing down the street.

Unlike the women, who'd spent the morning dusting off plaster statues, setting out flowers and lighting candles, having fetched the altar's frame and the prie-dieu from the shed, Jeremiah, like the rest of the men in the parish, prepared for the church's annual parish procession by having a pint or two at the Catholic Club.

'Don't worry, Dad wouldn't dare miss the parade. Anyway, never mind him, I can see Rosa and Patrick, so where's Francesca?' Mattie asked, catching sight of her brother Charlie's two children.

'Inside with Gran doing the washing-up,' said Cathy. 'Well,

Gran's doing the washing-up while Francesca's putting her feet up for an hour like the midwife said she should.'

'At least Charlie will be around when this baby's born, not like Rosa,' said Ida. 'She was almost two by the time he met her.'

Ida sighed and a soft expression crept into her eyes.

'They're all growing up so fast,' she said, watching her grandchildren laughing together as they ran around on the cobbles.

'I know,' said Mattie. 'One moment they're in nappies and the next you're waving them off to school.'

Pain flickered across Ida's face. 'At least when they're that age you don't have the police knocking on your door in the middle of the night.'

Cathy glanced at her two sisters with complete understanding.

If being found guilty and sentenced for being drunk and disorderly and assaulting a police officer in Lenny Stamp's seedy nightclub wasn't enough to send her parents into a white-hot fury, when they'd found out that Billy had been bunking off school to see Aunt Pearl, they'd been cut to the quick.

Ida pulled a handkerchief from her sleeve.

'Where did we go wrong?' she asked, dabbing her eyes.

The three sisters exchanged knowing looks and then Cathy put her hand on her mother's arm. 'You didn't, Mum.'

'And don't forget, Mum,' said Mattie, putting her arm around Jo's waist, 'we've got another new arrival coming to join us soon.'

Ida forced a brave little smile. 'We have and I can't wait to meet Zara. How's it going?'

'Me and Tommy have completed all the forms at the council and instead of just visiting Zara at the orphanage we will be allowed to take her out for the day in a week or so,' said Jo. 'If that goes all right, after a month we'll be allowed to bring her home as her foster parents until the welfare department hears our formal application to adopt her.'

'How are you feeling about it, luv?' asked Ida.

'It was a bit strange at first, but the more time I spend with her the more I feel like her real mother,' said Jo.

'Course you're her real mum,' said Ida. 'Being a mum is not just about giving birth to them but about loving them.'

'Mum's right,' said Cathy. 'I couldn't love Kirsty any more if I'd given birth to her and I know Francesca feels the same about Patrick.' She spotted her father as he appeared around the corner with a couple of their neighbours. 'Dad's coming up the street and as it's almost two o'clock we'd better make sure everything is secure on the altar before it all kicks off.'

'Here they come,' shouted Cathy, as the Shamrock League's flute, drum and fiddle band turned into the street at the far end. 'Isn't it exciting, Gran?'

No, it wasn't, it was terrifying.

From the moment she'd found out that Father Mahon was leading the annual St Breda and St Brendan's procession, spirits heavy with foreboding and menace had given Queenie no rest.

Anger sat like a furnace fire in her chest and it flared again at the thought of Nora, with a pious expression on her face, lording it over everyone by laying claim to the front pew in St Breda and St Brendan's.

It was she, that sanctimonious po-faced sister of Patrick's, who'd bullied him into the folly of walking three miles around the parish when he could barely make it from the church to the rectory gate.

It was now just after three and she along with the rest of the Brogan family were lined up along the edge of the pavement to watch the Blessed Virgin's annual parade.

Leading the parade were half a dozen young girls in white dresses with veils on their heads, each holding a bouquet of flowers in front of them. Behind them, one of the older girls carried a banner aloft with an embroidered image of the Virgin Mary. Multicoloured ribbons streamed from the ends of the banner, which were held by smaller children walking alongside. Behind them came more children, walking, solemn-faced, in two rows.

The girls all wore white dresses but the boys walking with them wore grey trousers and a green sash. Following them, two older boys, hair oiled down and shoes polished to mirrors, walked with a banner strung between them with 'Ave Marie' emblazoned across it.

'There's Kirsty,' shouted Cathy over the musicians, waving at her stepdaughter amongst a group of older children. 'And thanks again for making her dress, Mattie.'

'My pleasure,' her sister replied. 'She looks a real picture.'

Chewing the inside of her mouth, Queenie watched the Brownies and Cubs march by followed by Sister Celia and Sister Amelia, the edges of their white wimples fluttering in the summer breeze, strolling along with a handful of the Mothers' Club members. The Chairman of the Shamrock League, swirling a full-size emerald-green flag with a golden harp printed on its centre, stomped by next. Queenie barely noticed him as the ebony cross with the twisted and tortured silver figure of Christ nailed to it, held high by the church's elderly warden, honed into view.

'There are the boys,' shouted Jo, bobbing up on the balls of her feet as Michael and Billy, each dressed in a black cassock and white surplice, walked with the other members of the choir.

Queenie's gaze flitted over the row of choristers and then fixed on Father Mahon, shuffling along behind them.

The choir came to a halt and a miasma of foreboding gathered around Queenie. Without thinking, she slipped her hand into her pocket and grasped her mother's rosary resting there.

Leaning heavily on his priestly staff and with Father Timothy just behind him, Father Mahon tottered over to the O'Malleys' family altar. Kneeling on the footstool placed before it, he bowed his head for a moment then Father Timothy helped him up and the procession set off again.

He did the same at the altars outside the homes of the Byrnes, Conroys and Galloways, but when he rose from blessing the Bailey family's altar just a few doors down from where Queenie was standing, he swayed a little.

Gripping the beads of the rosary tighter, Queenie's lips moved in a silent prayer, but then Father Mahon straightened up and gave the young priest beside him a reassuring smile.

Placing a bony hand on his chest, the elderly priest paused and took a couple of deep breaths. Knowing their house would be his next stop, Francesca, who'd been sitting by the front door, stood up and joined the rest of the family.

The marching band were midway through a lively rendition of 'Be Thou my Vision' as Father Mahon stopped in front of them.

A fond smile lifted the old priest's wrinkled face. Starting with Jeremiah, who was standing behind his womenfolk, Father Mahon's gaze rested on each of the Brogan family for a moment then alighted on Queenie.

As he gazed down at her, memories of lush meadow grass, wild summer flowers and the feel of her lips, tender and sweet on his, flashed through his mind.

His blue-grey eyes, which had haunted her dreams for five decades, grew soft as they looked into hers, then he shifted his gaze back to the whole family.

He raised his hand. 'Blessings be upon you all.'

Everyone crossed themselves, then, as Cathy was rocking baby Heather on her hip, Ida, Mattie and Jo ushered the children aside.

Father Mahon moved towards the prie-dieu in front of Ida's altar, but before he could take a second step, pain contorted his face. Dropping his staff, he clutched his chest and crumpled to the ground.

'Patrick!' Queenie screamed, sinking to her knees beside him, her heart practically bursting from her chest. 'Patrick! Patrick!' she screamed again, grabbing his cold, limp hand. 'For the love of God, Patrick, will you open your eyes?'

His transparent eyelids fluttered for an instant then they rose to half-mast.

Relief flooded through Queenie so forcefully that her head span.

Forcing her dizziness away, she looked up at her son. 'Call an ambulance.'

Patrick's hand clamped around hers. 'No.'

'But—'

'No,' he repeated. 'I just need to catch my breath, that's all.'

Queenie's gaze ran over his putty-coloured face, pale lips and the mauve smudges around his eyes, and she opened her mouth to protest.

'Please, Mena,' he whispered, his eyes now fully open and alert.

The sound of her childhood name on his lips squeezed Queenie's heart.

'In my pocket,' he gasped.

Slipping her hand between the folds of his cassock, Queenie found the small bottle and popped off the cork.

Ida rushed out of the house carrying a glass of water. She gave it to Queenie who, after popping a small white pill into his mouth, held the water to Father Mahon's pale lips.

Closing his eyes again he took a couple of large mouthfuls.

'Thank you,' he gasped, looking from Queenie to Ida and back again. Then his attention shifted to the worried-looking priest standing next to Jeremiah.

'We've still a dozen streets in need of the Church's blessing, so will you take my place in the parade?' he asked softly.

'Are you sure?' said Father Timothy.

Father Mahon nodded. 'Never more so.'

Giving his senior priest another worried look, St Breda and St Brendan's junior priest reassured the gathering crowd then herded the procession back into formation. Drummers picked up the beat once more and the band picked up where they'd left off as Father Timothy crossed to the next street altar.

Father Mahon squeezed Queenie's hand. 'My old bones would count it a blessing if they could be got off these paving slabs.'

'Leave it to me, Ma,' said Jeremiah.

Stepping forwards, he helped the elderly priest back on to his feet, but as Father Mahon straightened up, his knees buckled. In one swift movement Jeremiah lifted him off his feet and carried him into the house and into the parlour, with Queenie just a step behind.

Gently, Jeremiah lowered the elderly priest on to the sofa.

'How are you feeling, Father,' he asked.

'Gra– grand,' Father Mahon replied breathlessly.

'You rest up,' said Queenie, taking her crocheted shawl from her fireside chair and draping it across his legs. 'And I'll put the kettle on.'

'I think, Ma, perhaps the good father wouldn't say no to a spot or two of Jameson. Would you, Father?' said Jeremiah.

'I wouldn't,' whispered Father Mahon. 'And 'tis kind of you to offer.'

Jeremiah gave Patrick Mahon a conspiratorial wink and Queenie's heart ached.

Whereas her son's hair was still thick and curly, Patrick's had long since vanished, and although the muscular frame of his youth had given way to the frailty of old age, the resemblance between the two men was as plain as the nose on your face. Their blue-grey eyes alone gave the game away, and Nora's reaction to Jeremiah when she'd first seen him was testament to that. And to be honest, she was surprised no one had noticed it before.

Looking from the man she'd loved for ever to his son, the emotions of the past and present dizzied Queenie's mind. Fearing she might sink to the floor, she lowered herself onto the leather pouffe next to Patrick.

'That should put the colour back in your cheeks, Father,' said

Jeremiah, handing the priest a generous measure of whiskey. 'You rest up awhile and I'll go and fetch the van from the yard and run you back to the rectory.'

Father Mahon swallowed a mouthful of whiskey. 'That's mighty kind but I wouldn't want to be putting you to any trouble.'

''Tis no trouble,' said Jeremiah. 'No trouble at all.'

Putting the bottle of whiskey back on the sideboard, Jeremiah left the room.

Father Mahon took another sip and, resting his head back, closed his eyes as the faint sound of the whistle and drum band outside drifted through the house.

The clock on the mantelshelf ticked away the minutes as Queenie sat unmoving, her gaze fixed on Patrick's gaunt face.

She thought that he'd gone to sleep but then Patrick's voice cut through the silence.

'I'm surprised you've not told me, Mena, what a brainless loon I am for taking part in the parade.'

'Sure, I've no need, Patrick, when you know full well you are,' Queenie replied.

Opening his eyes, he smiled.

'You've done a grand job raising Jeremiah,' he said.

'That's good of you to say,' said Queenie.

''Tis no more than the truth.' He took another slurp of whiskey. 'He's a credit to you, so he is. A son any man would be proud to call his own.' Patrick gave a little wheezy chuckle.

A lump formed in Queenie's throat but she swallowed it down. Indecision and doubt raged in her for a moment, then, taking a deep breath to steady her racing heart, she took his skeletal hand in her work-worn one.

'See now,' she said, holding his gaze in hers, 'there's something I need to say, Patrick. Something I'm heart sore about—'

'There's no need,' Patrick cut in. 'Sure, don't I know myself 'tis natural that a large family has first call on your time so I understand why you haven't called recently.' Stretching out, he placed his gnarled hand on hers. 'I quite understand.'

Fury rose again in Queenie's chest.

'But I have called, Patrick,' she replied, 'nearly every day for the past month but—'

He looked bemused. 'I never—'

The door burst open.

Queenie looked around to see Nora dressed in a shapeless grey gown, nondescript hat and stout lace-up shoes standing in the doorway.

Her close-set eyes flickered onto their hands joined together and her mouth and eyes narrowed.

Sending a look that if it had been a blade would have put Queenie in her grave, Nora's attention shifted to her brother and she marched across the room.

'For the love of mercy, Patrick!' she said, barging between her brother and Queenie.

'I was in need of a bit of a rest, Nora,' Patrick replied, sitting up a little straighter.

She frowned. 'And what about the procession?'

'Father Timothy has the matter in hand,' Queenie said to the back of the other woman's head.

Nora turned around and gave Queenie another hateful look.

'And although you've not yet enquired,' continued Queenie, matching Nora's hostile expression, 'Patrick is very much recovered.'

'Yes,' agreed Patrick. 'Thanks to a generous helping of Jeremiah's whiskey I'm almost my old self again.'

The door opened again.

Jeremiah strode in and Nora's expression soured still further.

'Miss Mahon,' he said, 'you've heard about your brother's little turn, then?'

'Yes, thankfully someone had the decency to tell me, his *sister*!' she replied, her hard eyes fixed on Queenie.

There was an awkward silence for a moment then Jeremiah spoke again.

'Well, Miss Mahon, I've the van outside to take him back to the rectory, but I'm afraid there's only one passenger seat so—'

'I'll walk,' Nora cut in. 'I'm in need of some fresh air.'

Jeremiah stepped between the two women. He took Father Mahon's empty glass then helped him to stand.

Father Mahon shuffled forwards a couple of steps then stopped in front of Queenie.

'God Bless you and yours, Mena,' he said, his blue-grey eyes warm as they looked into hers.

Reaching out, he gave her hand a squeeze, then clinging on to Jeremiah's arm, he tottered out, leaving the two women glaring at each other.

As the front door clicked shut, an icy smile lifted the corners of Nora's mouth.

'I suppose some would consider you've gone up in the world, Philomena Dooley,' she said, her piggy eyes flickering over the furniture, knick-knacks and family photographs in the room. 'But as far as I'm concerned, you'll always be nothing more than a dirty didicoy, so stay away from my brother.'

Lying on his bed with his eyes closed, Patrick Mahon breathed deeply, praying the ache still sitting across his chest would go but he wasn't hopeful.

In fact, when he'd collapsed outside Queenie's house, he'd thought the angels were coming for him. Truthfully, it was only a matter of time before the vicelike pain that robbed him of breath and consciousness would carry him off to meet his maker.

There was a light knock on the door followed by the rattle of the handle as the door opened.

He opened his eyes and Nora's head appeared around the door frame.

'You're awake then,' she said, coming into the room with a mug in her hand.

'I am,' he replied.

She placed the mug on his bedside table and then perched on the bed next to him.

'Mr Kelly called a little while back enquiring after you. He told me to let you know that Father Timothy managed to get around to all the altars in the parish as planned.'

'I had no doubts on the matter,' said Patrick.

'And the procession is now back to the church,' she added.

Studying his sister closely, Patrick didn't reply.

After a few minutes under his gaze, Nora spoke again.

'Don't let your tea get cold,' she said, indicating the cup beside him with her eyes.

'You didn't take the note I gave you to Queenie, did you, Nora?'

She looked puzzled. 'For sure, I took it straight there. Did she say otherwise?'

He didn't reply.

'For if she did, she's a liar,' she added.

Patrick continued to regard his sister dispassionately.

She held his gaze for a moment or two longer then straightened a fold in her apron.

'All right, I didn't,' she blurted, looking at him again. 'But 'twas for your own good. You were not yourself and the doctor himself said you were to avoid wasting your strength. I thought 'twould be better for your health not to be troubled.'

A feeling of sadness joined the pain already weighing down his chest.

'Nora,' he said softly, 'fifty years have come and gone, surely that's time enough, is it not, to put this matter between you and Philomena to rest?'

Pressing her lips together, she shook her head.

'Never,' she spat out.

They stared at each other for a second, then, gripping her hands together on her lap, Nora looked down at them.

Patrick studied the top of her head for a moment. Reaching out, he rested his hand lightly on his sister's grizzly grey hair.

'I shall pray for Our Lady to soften your heart,' he said.

He withdrew his hand and she looked up.

'However, Nora, although I am mindful of the difficulty this may occasion you, I'd be obliged if when Queenie knocks on the rectory door in future, you'll extend a welcome to her in the same way you would to any soul standing on my doorstep,' he said firmly.

For an instant, the domineering sister he'd suffered under as a boy appeared, but then she lowered her eyes.

'Thank you, Nora,' he said, relieved that she had acknowledged his wishes.

After a moment, she stood up and headed for the door, but as she reached the threshold she turned.

'But I'll tell you this and tell you no more, Patrick,' she said. 'Philomena Dooley ruined my life and you don't know the half of it.'

Kinsale, Ireland. August 1890

AS SHE SURVEYED the bowl of oatmeal she'd eaten not an hour past splattered at the bottom of the family's lavatory, Philomena realised Patrick had given her something for her birthday before he was snatched from her eight weeks ago.

Mercifully, as it had done for the past three days after her stomach had rid itself of her breakfast, the nausea that had started from the moment she'd opened her eyes subsided. Taking her handkerchief from her sleeve, she wiped her mouth. She straightened up and placed her hands on her still flat stomach.

She had a few weeks yet before the small life growing inside her would make its presence known to all the world, so she had to act fast. Grasping the old shovel in the bucket of earth beside the wooden toilet bench, she sprinkled soil over the vomit then pushed open the privy door.

Her breath formed little puffs in the crisp August air and the odd wisp of mist lingered between the tied-over onion stalks in her mother's vegetable patch at the back of the cottage. Feeling the damp soil of the pathway beneath the soles of her feet, Philomena headed back into the cottage.

Her father had left at first light to help gather in the last of the summer hay at Eli McManus's farm, but her mother was at home, giving the younger children a final lookover before packing them off on their two-mile walk to school.

Kathleen was plaiting Maggie's hair but she looked around as Philomena walked in. 'You look a bit pale,' she said, looping a ribbon around the end of her youngest daughter's long braid.

'Is it any wonder, Mammy, for it's fair freezing in the outhouse,' said Philomena, closing the door behind her.

'The weather's turned, that's for sure,' her mother replied. 'The woodland spirits were whispering of a hard winter when I was in Monks' Forest yesterday.' She smiled. 'All the more reason to take kindling bundles to market when we go tomorrow.'

Walking across to her mother, Philomena picked up one of the hessian sacks draped over the back of the kitchen chair. 'I thought I might wander over to the Shallow's Acre.'

Her mother frowned. 'That's a bit of a trek?'

Throwing the sack over her shoulder, Philomena shrugged. 'I've a fancy to stretch my legs.'

Picking up the twine-tied bundle containing the hunk of bread and cheese that would serve as her lunch, Philomena placed it in her basket beside the stoneware flask containing her mother's special elderflower brew, then headed out.

Picking up a spindly elm branch from the damp mulch of leaves on the forest floor, Philomena snapped it in two then squeezed it into the crumpled hessian sack that was pretty much straining at the seams.

Glancing at the pale sun above, she judged it to be before midday so heaving her bundle over her shoulder, she shifted it into a comfortable place on her back. Picking up her basket and crunching twigs as she went, Philomena wended her way back through the beech grove to the path that ran through the wood from Balleyregan into town.

Finding a convenient tree stump, she shrugged her burden off and on to the ground then delved into her basket and took out her midday meal.

She had just popped the last wedge of cheese in her mouth when, as she knew she would, she spotted a familiar figure through the trees making its way along the path.

Grabbing a stout branch she had spotted earlier, she pulled it closer to where she was sitting. Then, positioning herself with her head next to the branch, she lay down on the curling brown autumn leaves. Adjusting her skirt to reveal her slender calves and ankles, Philomena shut her eyes.

With her heart hammering in her chest, she lay perfectly still as the crunch of Fergus's boots grew closer and then came to an abrupt halt.

'Philomena!'

She didn't respond.

There was a rustle of leaves and his arms slid beneath her.

'Philomena,' he repeated, raising her gently.

She let her eyes flutter open. 'Fergus?'

'Yes, it's me,' he said, his amber eyes searching her face anxiously. 'Are you all right?'

'I don't know. I was just sitting finishing my midday bread and cheese when something hit . . .' She raised the back of her hand to her brow. 'I feel a bit hot. Can you unbutton my blouse a little?' she asked, giving him a doe-eyed look.

His cheeks flamed with colour for a moment, then, propping her against the log she'd just been sitting on, his chunky fingers fumbled with the pearl buttons of her blouse until he'd loosened three.

'That's a bit better but . . .' She unfastened the next two and pulled open the front of her cotton blouse.

His gaze flickered down onto her nipples made taut under the thin fabric by the cool air dancing on her breasts.

'How are you feeling?' he asked, forcing his eyes, heavy with desire, back to her face.

She gave him a wan smile.

'A mite faint still, if the truth be told,' she replied, giving him another doting look.

Taking the unfastened edges of her blouse and flapping them, popping the next button in the process, Philomena bent forwards and brushed off her skirt.

Fergus's gaze disappeared down the front of her blouse again for a moment then his hand followed, cupping her budding breast in his brawny hand.

'Oh, Fergus,' she sighed, winding her arms around his neck and pressing herself into him.

Gazing up at him, she let her mouth fall open. He accepted her invitation and pressed his lips on hers in a wet, clumsy kiss.

The feel of Patrick's kisses and the feel of his hands on her skin flashed through Philomena's mind but she shoved them aside. He was gone and now she had to protect the child she was carrying – his child – from being snatched from her as soon as the cord was cut by some vinegar-faced nun.

Releasing her mouth, he buried his face into her neck.

'Oh, Philomena,' he groaned, leaving a trail of moisture as his lips progressed along her shoulder.

With his left arm around her, his right hand fondled her breast for a moment or two as he pressed his hardened groin into her hip, then breathing hard, his hand rucked up her skirt and then disappeared beneath it.

Philomena's eyes flew open. 'Fergus!'

He snatched his hand away.

'Your pardon, Philomena,' he said, as he struggled to master himself. 'You've had a shock, I shouldn't be taking—'

'No, Fergus,' she said, grabbing his hand and looking adoringly up at him. ''Tis I that should be sorry for . . .' Tears welled up in her eyes. 'For being so stupid.'

He looked confused. 'Have you?'

She nodded and pressed his hand to her cheek.

'For being such a silly girl and not noticing what a fine young man you are,' she said, as a fat tear ran across his fingers. 'And now . . .' Her arms snaked around his neck again. 'Oh, Fergus,' she said breathlessly.

His hungry amber eyes darted over her face for a moment, then covering her mouth with his, he rolled on top of her. He fumbled with her skirts again until his hand slid up the inside of her thigh. Slipping her arms around his stout body and thinking of the small life growing in her, Philomena spread her legs wide.

Chapter Sixteen

'MORNING, QUEENIE,' SHOUTED Micky Everard, as he heaved a fresh box of cauliflowers on to the front of his vegetable stall. 'I hear your Jerry's got himself a new yard down Canning Town way.'

'That he has,' she replied.

Taking a grubby handkerchief from his back pocket, Micky, who was about Jeremiah's age and size with the addition of a beer belly, mopped his glistening brow. 'He'll be all set for when your Charlie comes home. Any news?'

'A few weeks,' she replied. 'According to his last letter they're just waiting for transport to bring them home from France.'

'Well, God bless him and all of our brave boys,' Micky said, bending down and grasping a box of carrots from under the fake plastic grass draped over the front of his stall. 'They're going to notice some changes when they are demobbed, I can tell you.'

He nodded towards the man in a scruffy pair of dungarees pasting up a poster on what was left of Christ Church's back wall. The poster showed a large V balanced on a green hill with the words 'And Now – Win the Peace' in large letters above it.

'According to some bloke standing on the back of a lorry outside the Troxy last week,' continued Micky, 'when Labour get in we won't have to shell out a tanner to see the quack and we can go to hospital for free and all. Anyhow, enough about this old politics lark, what can I do you for?'

Queenie took a step closer. 'You wouldn't by any chance have an apple or an orange somewhere about the stall, Micky?'

'I might have, ducks,' he replied cagily. 'But I'm supposed to keep them for kids, women in the family way and invalids.'

'It's for Father Mahon,' said Queenie. 'I'm away to see him now.'

'Poor old fellow,' said Mick. 'I heard about what happened at the parade yesterday. Here you are.' He delved beneath the barrow and brought out two small Cox's Pippins.

He palmed them to her and Queenie slid them beneath the tea towel draped over her basket, extracting a paper bag in the process.

'For Betty and the kids,' she said, surreptitiously glancing around as she passed the four eggs to him.

'Ta. And how are things for you, Queenie, on this fine day?'

'Never better,' she replied.

That, of course, was a complete lie.

It was close to eight thirty on the Monday after the Church's annual procession, and she doubted she'd slept more than two hours together since. And if lack of sleep and a brutal pain searing her skull wasn't torture enough, the swarms of spirits swirling around her day and night added to her purgatory.

Still, all her ills and disturbances would be gone to whence they came in but a little while.

'My regards to your Betty,' she said.

'Have a good one,' Micky replied, ripping a paper bag from the hook above his head as he spotted another customer approaching.

Adjusting her grip on the basket, Queenie continued through the crowds of early-morning shoppers towards the top end of the market.

Within a moment or two, she found herself marching up the steps to the front door of St Breda and St Brendan's rectory.

Queenie studied the polished brass knocker for a moment, then squaring her shoulders, she grasped it firmly and hammered it on the stud beneath.

The sound echoed down the hall then a bolt slid back.

The door opened and Nora, her wraparound apron pulled tight across her square frame and a turban scarf encasing her grey curls, stood in the doorway.

'Yes,' she said coolly.

'Jesus, Mary and Joseph, Nora,' said Queenie, 'will you let me in?'

'I will not, Philomena Dooley,' snapped Nora.

'But Patrick wants to see me,' said Queenie.

Nora gave her a caustic look by way of reply then went to close the door, but Queenie got her foot in the gap first.

'I'll be obliged if you'd be letting me in, Nora,' she said, putting her six and a half stone weight behind the door to keep it open.

'Well, see now the truth is I'm not inclined to, Philomena Dooley,' growled Nora, her angry face a few inches from Queenie's as she shouldered the door from the other side. 'Not while I have breath in my body.'

'I'd beware of tempting the fates now with such rash words, if I were standing in your shoes,' Queenie replied, as they glared eyeball to eyeball at each other.

'I'm a Christian woman so not afeared of any of your tinker's mumbo-jumbo,' scoffed Nora. 'Now get you gone.'

Her foot shot out and the toe of her stout lace-up shoe connected with Queenie's shin.

A stiletto of pain shot up Queenie's calf. Gasping, she staggered back, and Nora slammed the door.

Ignoring the throbbing in her leg, Queenie's mouth pulled into a tight line.

Clenching her fists together, her eyes bored into the door for a moment, then putting her basket down, she stepped back up to the door.

'Nora Mahon,' she shouted. Grasping the knocker again, she smashed it down on the door. 'You open this door.'

Although the sound reverberated through the house beyond as she crashed the brass ring down again and again, the door remained firmly closed.

Bending down, Queenie pressed open the letter box and peered along the sparsely furnished rectory hallway.

'I know you can hear me, Nora,' she bellowed, her mouth close against the cold metal of the flap. 'So you'd better open this door or, so help me God and all his saints, I'll be hammering on it until the second coming. Do you hear me?'

She peered through again and saw Nora's lace-up shoes and thick ankles marching across the black-and-white hall tiles towards her.

Straightening up and feeling more than a little pleased with herself, Queenie studied the knocker again.

The bolt was shot back again, and the door opened.

'Well, 'tis well you—'

A torrent of water hit Queenie full in the face, soaking her in an instant.

Spluttering and gagging at the putrid smell, she wiped her face. With the dampness seeping through her cardigan, Queenie gazed through her dripping hair to see Nora standing in the doorway holding an empty zinc bucket in her hand.

'Hear, Philomena Dooley, and hear it well,' Nora shouted, causing passers-by to stop and stare. 'You and your heathen family will never set one foot over the doorstep of this house.'

Placing her hand on the brass plate, Ida pushed open the half-glazed doors to the Catholic Club's main bar and, walking in, was enveloped in a cloud of tobacco smoke.

It was the fourth Friday in June, the longest day of the year, in fact, so although it was almost nine in the evening, the warm sunlight was still streaming between the gummed paper strips on the west-facing windows. At the far end of the long room someone was playing on the upright piano beside the small stage.

Jeremiah was leaning against the bar and chatting to a couple of chums, but he spotted her as she made her way to join him.

'Hello, luv,' he said, giving her a quick peck on the cheek.

'Victoria go down all right?'

Ida nodded. 'She was practically asleep when I pulled the covers over her. And the boys are doing their homework.'

Jeremiah raised an eyebrow. 'Both of them?'

'Yes, both of them,' she replied.

She could understand her husband's cynical attitude. Although Billy had been as good as gold in the past month or so, she too wondered if it would last. Especially when Pearl pitched up again, as she was bound to do sometime.

'Is Ma not with you?'

'She said she had a bit of a headache after confession so she might have an early night,' Ida replied.

'That's two this week.'

'I expect she's not the only one,' said Ida. 'The weather's been a bit muggy these last few days.'

'The usual?'

'Please.'

'You go and find us a seat and I'll bring them over,' he said.

Leaving him at the bar, Ida made her way to one of the booths and sat down. Within a moment or two, Jeremiah emerged through the crowd carrying her brandy and orange and a fresh pint of Guinness.

'It's busy tonight, isn't it?' said Ida, glancing around the Catholic Club's main bar.

'That,' said Jeremiah. 'Probably because Brendan Flannery has bought half the local Labour Party with him to drum up support for their candidate.'

'That seems a bit pointless,' said Ida, studying the dozen or so men at the far end of the bar. 'Clement Attlee's been our MP for over twenty years and it's not as if anyone around here is going to vote for anyone else.'

Her husband slurped the creamy head of his drink then sat beside her.

'So what do you say, luv?' he said, swivelling around and looking at her. 'Shall I pop around to the rent office in the morning and say we'll take it?'

Ida sighed. 'Well, I suppose it's the best house we've seen.'

'It certainly is,' her husband replied. 'And with half the houses in East London little more than rubble, if we don't put a deposit on it quick, someone else will.'

'You're right, Jerry,' Ida replied. 'After all, we can't sleep under canvas for ever and as the whole Chapman Estate has been earmarked for demolition for years, it's better to find somewhere now rather than later.'

Slipping his arm around her, he gave her a squeeze and planted a noisy kiss on her cheek.

'But you can tell your mother,' she added, as he released her from his bear-like hug.

'Don't worry, she'll be grand once she gets used to the idea,' he replied, although his tone suggested otherwise. He frowned. 'If the truth be told, I'm a bit worried about her.'

'She hasn't been herself lately, has she?' Ida placed her hand on his. 'I'm sure it's just because she's worried about Father Mahon.'

'You're probably right,' he agreed.

'Did you manage to get out of her why she came home drenched to the skin and smelling like a sewer last week?' she asked.

Jeremiah shook his head. 'I tried again yesterday, and she gave me such a look that I could say no more.'

'Ah well, I suppose like all her other secrets, it'll come out in the end,' said Ida.

The main door swung open. 'Goodness, Jerry, what's Mattie doing here?'

Peering through the haze of smoke and beer fumes, Mattie spotted her parents on the far side of the room, tucked into one of the booths lining the wall of the bar.

She waved and her mother's face lit up.

Weaving her way through the drinkers milling around, she made her way over to join them.

'Hello, luv,' her mother said, as Mattie slipped into the seat beside her.

'Drink?' Jeremiah asked, rising to his feet.

'Please, Dad. Gin and tonic, Gordon's if they have it,' she replied, smiling up at her father, who ambled off to the bar.

'No Gran?' Mattie asked.

'She's got a headache,' said Ida. 'What have you done with the children?'

'Sold them to a circus,' Mattie replied. 'Well, that's what I felt like doing by the time I put them to bed.'

Ida nodded. 'I remember those days – you girls were like three cats in a sack. You wait until you have another one.'

Mattie shifted on her seat.

'We're not having any more, Mum,' she said.

Ida looked puzzled.

'Things are going to be different now,' Mattie continued. 'After seeing how you and Dad scrimped and scraped just to keep a roof over our head and feed us, well, me and Daniel want a different life, we want to buy a house and possibly a car and have family holidays, and a smaller family means we can do just that.'

'But you know the Church forbids the use of . . .' Her mother glanced around then mouthed 'French letters' at her. 'So what about when you go to confession?'

'I shan't mention it,' Mattie replied. 'And if the Pope wants to say anything he can come and look after my three for the day and he'll soon change his mind.'

Her mother opened her mouth to speak but thankfully Jeremiah returned with Mattie's drink.

'I've just spotted Pat Mullin at the other end of the bar, Ida,' he said, placing Mattie's drink on a cardboard coaster. 'I need to have a bit of a word with him about a job. I won't be long.'

He sauntered away to join the throng of men at the bar.

'Actually, I didn't sell the kids, Mum,' continued Mattie, hoping to steer the conversation on to safer ground than the Church's teachings on contraception. 'Jo came around so I asked if she could babysit so I could come and join you for a drink. Ian's got another tooth coming so I told her she could get some practice in changing nappies that make your hair curl.'

'Has she had any news about Zara?' asked Ida.

'She and Tommy got confirmation that all the checks have gone through, they just have to wait for the panel next month to approve them as foster parents then they can bring her home pending a full adoption hearing in a few months' time,' Mattie replied.

Her mother's face lit up. 'I'm so pleased. I've looked out Victoria's old clothes and there's a whole bag that will do another turn.'

'I've got a few bits Jo can have, too,' said Mattie.

The bar door swung open again and Ida stared in disbelief. 'Oh my goodness, Mattie, it's Cathy,' she said. 'And look who's with her.'

Mattie turned and a smile spread wide across her face. Not only had her younger sister just walked in, but beside her, dressed in an ill-fitting suit and with his arm lightly around Cathy's waist, was her tall and strikingly handsome would-be husband, Archie McIntosh.

'Well, you've had quite an exciting day by the look of things,' said Mattie, shifting along the bench to make space for her sister.

'I should say,' Cathy replied. 'I nearly had a fit when he walked in at six thirty and found us all having breakfast around the kitchen table and me feeding Heather.'

Once the excitement of Archie's surprise arrival at the breakfast table had finally subsided it was established that there'd been a mix-up at the demob centre which meant he and several dozen others had been demobbed a week early. Archie had caught the milk train from Dover that morning. Now, having received a hug from everyone and a bone-rattling handshake from Jeremiah, and with several pints lined up on the bar waiting for him, he was standing with his future father-in-law.

'I bet Aggie and the kids were pleased to see him,' said Mattie, as their mother headed across the bar towards the Ladies.

'Aggie burst into tears when he walked in and she's been dabbing her eyes off and on ever since. Kirsty and Peter were all over him and Heather was happy enough to have someone pull funny faces at her.' Cathy's happy expression slipped a little. 'Rory was a bit unsure. He was only eight months old when Archie was posted, so he can't remember him.'

'I'm sure he'll be fine in a day or two,' said Mattie.

Her sister's eyes drifted across the room to where Jeremiah, pint in hand, had his arm draped around Archie's shoulder and the two men were laughing.

'I can't tell you how happy I am to have him home, Mat,' her sister sighed, love brimming in her eyes as she gazed at him.

'I can imagine,' said Mattie, following her sister's gaze. 'I don't suppose there's any news on Stan's whereabouts?'

Swallowing a mouthful of the drink her father had just bought over to her, Cathy shook her head.

'Do you want me to mention it to Daniel?' said Mattie. I'm sure he won't mind putting out a few feelers.'

'Thanks, Mat, but he's got enough on his plate,' her sister replied. 'Now they're starting to send blokes home, I'm sure I'll hear something soon.'

Reaching out, Mattie squeezed her sister's hand briefly then picked up her drink.

'I'm sure you will.' She took a sip. 'I was so lucky that Daniel was stationed in London.'

'Well, only after he'd done two stints undercover behind enemy lines in France,' said Cathy. 'Is he definitely staying in the army?'

Mattie nodded. 'He says our top brass and the Yanks' high command are a bit worried about what the Russians are planning to do next now their army's sitting across half of Europe.' She glanced across at the door. 'Do you think Mum's fallen down the pan?'

'Probably met someone on her way back from the Ladies and is nattering,' Cathy replied.

As the words left her lips, the bar's door swung open again and her mother marched in with a young man beside her.

It was Mattie's turn to open her eyes wide with surprise as her husband, wearing his khaki major's uniform and with his flat cap pinned under his arm, walked in. Her father spotted him and mimed raising a glass to his lips. Daniel nodded and then greeted Archie with a handshake and a friendly slap on the arm. Collecting his pint and after greeting a couple of others at the bar, he sidled over to where Mattie, Cathy and their mother were sitting.

'What a lovely surprise,' Mattie said, standing up.

'Hello, darling,' he replied, giving her a quick kiss.

'I wasn't expecting you until later,' she said.

'I got away earlier than expected,' he said. 'Jo told me you were here, so I thought I'd join you. When did Archie get back?'

Mattie repeated her sister's account of her husband's return that day.

Jeremiah's rumbling laughter reached them as he called Pete the barman over to get another round.

'Your dad's in good spirits,' said Daniel.

'Yes, Mum's agreed to move to the house they saw this afternoon,' said Mattie. Her mum had just told her and Cathy the news that their parents had at last found a house. 'It's down one of the roads off Green Street at the Barking Road end, a few roads back from West Ham Stadium. It's big enough for the boys and Victoria to have a room each, plus there's a half-basement kitchen and parlour that Queenie could have to herself so Mum can have her best room back. There's a sixty-foot garden, too, but I think it was the inside bathroom and lav that sold it to Mum.'

'When will they move?' he asked.

'They've just the next two weeks' rent on Mafeking Terrace so probably the back end of next month.' Mattie raised her eyebrows. 'It'll be a bit strange at first not having her around the corner, but it's only half an hour on the District Line so me and the kids can pop over to see her easy enough.'

Daniel gave a tight smile. 'Actually, I got a bit of news myself today, Mattie.' Putting his arm around her he drew her away from the table.

'I've got something to tell you, too,' she said. 'Well, more ask really.' She glanced briefly around at her sister. 'Cathy's not heard anything about Stan at all. She told me not to ask you but I know she and Archie are desperate to get married so I don't suppose you could maybe try and find out if anyone knows what's happened to him?'

'I'll try,' he replied. 'But I can't promise anything.'

'Thanks, luv.' She smiled. 'Now, what's your news?'

The tight smile returned, and he swallowed a large mouthful of beer.

'Well, Mattie, it's like this . . .' Looking her in the eye, he drew in a deep breath. 'I've been posted to Germany.'

Paddling in the salty shallows of Leigh-on-Sea while eating an ice cream, Jeremiah wondered who was shoving him from behind. Drifting up from sleep, he opened his eyes.

As the first hint of light was slithering beneath the edges of the curtains, he guessed it was probably about four in the morning.

Trying not to think about the alarm he had set for five thirty, Jeremiah rolled over and found Ida sitting up in bed with her handkerchief to her nose and her shoulders shaking under her bed jacket.

He sat up and rested back on the brass headboard.

'Is it Mattie?' he asked, forcing the last vestiges of sleep from his mind.

She nodded and started sobbing again.

'Sweetheart,' he said, putting his arm around her.

She curled into him and rested her head where she always did, between his neck and shoulder. Jeremiah held her close as she wept silently on his chest for several moments.

'I know it was a shock, luv,' he said, kissing her hair.

'Germany!' sniffed Ida. 'What if there's still a couple of Nazis around and they murder her and the children?'

'They'll be living in family quarters on an army base, so that won't happen, Ida,' he replied, feeling her tears on his skin.

'What about the children?' said Ida, her fingers playing with his chest hair. 'After a couple of months, I doubt they'll even remember us.'

'I'm sure they will,' he replied. 'And Daniel said himself it won't be for ever. Five years at most. But it's his job and he hasn't got a choice.'

Ida sighed and raised her head. 'It's not just that. There's Jo and the adoption, too.'

'But that's all going well, isn't it?' asked Jeremiah.

'Yes,' said Ida. 'But what happens when she gets Zara home. You know yourself what it's like having a new baby. What if she needs me?'

Jeremiah looked puzzled.

Ida rolled her eyes. 'I won't be able to just pop around and give her a hand if we're living miles away.'

'We're six stops along the District Line, Ida,' said Jeremiah.

'Even so.'

'And it's not as if we're in any position to stay here, are we now, luv?' he added, indicating the morning light creeping beneath the green tarpaulin.

'Yes, but—'

'And don't forget, Ida,' he said, giving her a little hug, 'Francesca has already said she and Charlie are going to look for a place near to us in Upton Park once her dad's sold the lease on the café. And there's nothing to say that Cathy and Archie won't, too. Especially if he gets that job he's after in Ford's.'

'That's another worry. What if Stan turns up?' asked Ida, untangling herself from him and twisting around. 'She has a hard enough time as it is from some mean-spirited people for having two children out of wedlock and living with Archie. And then there's Queenie.'

'Ma?'

'Well, surely even you've noticed she's been walking around like a tit in a trance these past few months,' Ida said.

This time it was Jeremiah who sighed. 'I can't argue that point, Ida.'

'Honestly, Jerry,' Ida continued, 'I'm beginning to fear for her marbles when Father Mahon does finally go to meet his maker. And then there are the boys.'

'The boys are fine,' said Jeremiah, gathering her back into his arms. 'According to their school reports both should pass their ordinary certificate and as long as they keep up the effort when they start their higher certificate next year, they should pass that, too.'

'That's true,' said Ida. 'Michael seems to have his head screwed on the right way, but I can't help worrying about Billy. What if Pearl comes back? He's already got a suspended sentence hanging over him and if he goes off with her again and then falls in with Lenny Stam—'

'Hush now, me darling girl,' said Jeremiah softly, enveloping her in his embrace. 'Let me tell you the truth of the matter, Ida. Our four eldest are all happily married with families of their own and in a year or so the two boys will be young men, too. We've worried over them all for just short of thirty years but, although I doubt I'll stop worrying about them until the day I die, my sweetheart, we have to let them be their own people now. And that means letting them make their own choices and mistakes.'

'I suppose you're right,' said Ida. 'But it's so hard.'

'I know, Ida,' he replied.

'But we're not really finished, are we, because we still have Victoria?' said Ida.

'That we do, but one day she too will be grown,' said Jeremiah. 'And then it'll be just you and me, my darling. Just like it was when we started out.' He pressed his lips on her forehead for a long moment. 'And will that be so bad?'

Raising her head, Ida looked up at him and smiled.

In the dim light of the room, Jeremiah's gaze ran slowly over his wife's face. There were a few more wrinkles around her mouth and eyes, her chestnut hair that had been tied with an emerald ribbon when he'd first set eyes on her was now shot through with grey, and he hadn't been able to span her waist with his outstretched hands for many years, but she still had a beauty all of her own and she was his Ida.

'No, Jerry,' she replied softly, tightening her arms around him. 'It's not so bad at all.'

As he reached Commercial Road, Billy paused on the kerb while a van drove slowly by. 'Vote Labour for Homes' and 'Vote Labour for the Future' blared out from the four megaphones fixed to its roof.

It was the last Monday in June, just after four thirty in the afternoon, and a full month before the end of the summer term.

It was half an hour until the factory hooters would herald the end of the working day and the sun-lit street was still filled with boys playing football and girls either skipping or hopping in and out of chalked squares. Someone had shinned up a lamp-post at the far end of the road and attached a rope, and a couple of the children were swinging on it.

Shouldering his school satchel, Billy strolled across the main road. Walking past the bombed-out row of shops he headed for Anthony Street, which ran north-south through the Chapman Estate.

However, as he reached the corner of the street, he came face to face with Knobby Knowles, who was flanked by Jono Johnson, a stick-thin youth, and Benny Tucker, who was the East End version of Billy Bunter.

Although the three of them were chalk and cheese shape-wise, they were all dressed in the street uniform of rough cord trousers, braces and a collarless shirt. Each wore a cap sitting at such an acute angle on their heads it was a surprise gravity hadn't claimed it already.

Knobby grinned.

'Look at old Billy Boy!' he said, dusting an imaginary speck of dirt off the lapel of Billy's school blazer. 'You'd think 'e was one of those posh kids from a la-di-da school somewhere.'

'Not a jail bird.'

'Wiv a criminal record,' added Jono, regarding Billy admiringly through a fringe of flaxen hair.

'Got anything lined up?' asked Knobby.

'You know, with . . .' Behind his round-rimmed spectacles Benny gave an exaggerated wink.

'Cos if you have, and you need any help, you know where we are,' added Knobby.

Billy gave them a tight smile but didn't reply.

The throaty sound of a two-litre engine filled the narrow residential street and the eyes of all three boys shifted to something over Billy's shoulder. He turned to see Lenny Stamp's Sunbeam Talbot rolling to a stop alongside the kerb.

The driver's door opened and Monkey stepped out of the car. Brushing aside a couple of boys who'd already started congregating around the vehicle, he opened the motor's back door.

Aunt Pearl unfolded herself from the car, knocking her enormous black hat slightly askew in the process.

Billy's mouth went dry as the three boys surrounding him melted away.

After straightening out the creases in her fussy yellow and black dress, she looked up and a smile spread across her crimson lips.

'Billy,' she screamed, tottering towards him.

'Hello, Aunt Pearl,' he replied.

'Aunt Pearl!' She pulled a face. 'What happened to Mum?'

She threw her arms around him, smothering him in face powder and perfume.

Billy kept his arms pinned to his sides and after a moment she released him.

'Oh, Billy, I've missed you.' Holding him at arm's length, her heavily made-up eyes ran over him. 'You know, I think you've grown another inch since I last saw you.' Letting him go, she opened her handbag and pulled out a cigarette case. 'Here, I got this for you,' she said, offering it to him. 'It's solid silver and look,' she twisted it open, 'it's got your initials on it.' She frowned. 'What's the matter?'

Looking at the lipstick bleeding into the fine lines around her mouth, Billy didn't reply.

'All right, I get it, you're pissed at me,' she continued. 'And I know it's been a couple of weeks since the raid on the club, Billy, but—'

'Six weeks,' he cut in.

'All right, six weeks,' she snapped. 'But I couldn't come before, could I? Not with the coppers crawling all over the house and Lenny's business, and that bloody detective trying to pin something on him and Arthur. But I'm here now.'

She went to embrace him again but Billy stepped back.

Pearl gave him a testy look.

'I said I'm sorry, what more can I do? Don't worry; I'll make it up to you.' Her fawning smile returned. 'Look, I've got you a present.'

Delving into her handbag, she pulled out a dark blue box and flipped it open to reveal a palm-sized petrol lighter.

'It's silver plated,' she said, taking it out and pressing her thumb on the little hammer, igniting a spark. 'And look. WPB.' She turned it over so he could see the engraving etched onto the side. 'It stands for William Peter Brogan.'

She offered it to him, but Billy didn't take it.

'I know. On top of that what about some new togs, perhaps a Crombie—'

He shook his head. 'I don't want—'

'All right,' she cut in. 'Something else, then. You name it and you can have it, now let's get in the car and go home.'

'I'm going home,' said Billy. 'But to my real mum.'

Her pencilled eyebrows drew together in an angry knot. 'Wot you talking about? I'm your bleeding real mum.'

Billy shook his head. 'You're not. You left me in the toilets because you didn't want me, and Mum and Dad collected me from the workhouse. So you can keep all your money and presents because I'm going home.'

He turned his back on her and walked away.

Kinsale, Ireland. September 1890

STARING BLINDLY AT the edge of the tapestry kneeler poking out from beneath her woollen Sunday skirt, Philomena let the words of Father Parr's final benediction wash over her. If the truth were told, she could barely hear his monotone nasal voice over the pounding of blood in her ears.

Huddled in her long winter coat against the early-winter storm lashing the boats in the harbour, Philomena was sitting alongside her parents in their usual pew at the back of the church. However, although she was supposed to be laying her soul open to God's ministrations, her mind was focused on more important matters than the Almighty's grace and mercy.

The congregation around her made the sign of the cross and kept their heads bowed, but instead of those in the sacrosanct filing out behind the raised cross as was usual, Father Parr went back to the pulpit.

Lifting the hem of his cassock, he climbed the couple of steps to the elevated platform as the congregation shuffled back on to their pews.

With her heart pounding against her breastbone, Philomena placed her hands lightly on her stomach and gave thanks to Mary the blessed Mother of God that even though her monthly flows had been missing for three months, the baby tucked within had only just started to reveal itself in a slight roundness below her navel.

Gripping the carved edge of the pulpit, Kinsale's parish priest surveyed his flock for a moment then his thin lips lifted in an indulgent smile.

'You all know and rejoice with me that in two weeks' time we will be celebrating with Mr and Mrs Mahon . . .'

Philomena looked across the heads of those seated around her and, after glancing at Margaret Mahon's monstrous hat and Joe

Mahon's overstuffed suit, her gaze fixed on Nora sitting alongside them.

She was trussed up in a dark blue fur-trimmed winter coat with a wide-brimmed hat that rivalled her mother's for pomposity.

'. . . esteemed members of the town and this congregation,' Father Parr's voice droned on. 'They have the delight every parent wishes for – that of seeing their child, in this case their daughter Nora, receive the Church's blessings in holy matrimony. It therefore gives me great joy to post their banns of marriage.' He cleared his throat. 'I publish the banns of marriage between Nora Mary Mahon and Fergus Peter Brogan, both of this parish.' His eyes skimmed the assembly again. 'This is for the third time of asking. If any of you know cause or just impediment why these persons should not be joined together in Holy Matrimony, ye are to declare it now or—'

All moisture left Philomena's mouth, but with her heart bursting from her chest she sprang to her feet.

'I do,' she shouted, her voice echoing around the vaulted ceiling.

Philomena saw her mother cover her mouth with her hands.

Squaring her shoulders, Philomena stepped out of the pew and, with every pair of eyes fixed on her, walked to the front of the church.

'I was a maid until Fergus Brogan lay with me in the woods in Shallow's Acre two months since and now I am with child, Father,' she said, looking up at the priest standing above her in the pulpit.

Nora jumped to her feet, as did Margaret and Joe Mahon.

'Liar,' Nora screamed, jabbing a gloved finger at Philomena as all three of them wished her to hell as their eyes bore into her.

With what was truly a sinful enjoyment, Philomena studied the other girl's flushed face for a moment then her attention shifted to Fergus, who sat open-mouthed in the pew.

'Is that not so, Fergus?' she asked quietly.

There was a deathly silence for a long moment then Fergus dragged himself to his feet.

'I'm sorry, Nora,' he said, looking dolefully at his fiancée.

Nora screamed again and fell sobbing into her mother's arms.

Father Parr hurried down the steps and planted himself in front of Philomena.

'Do you swear on God's holy scriptures,' he said, pointing at the open Bible lying on the altar, 'that what you say is the truth? That you were a maid, and that Fergus Brogan is the father of the child you're carrying?'

Out of the corner of her eye she saw her white-faced parents advancing down the aisle.

Taking a breath, and praying she wouldn't be smitten on the spot, Philomena stepped forwards and stretched her hand to place it on the page.

Nora screamed and flew at Fergus.

'How could you?' she cried, grabbing him by his lapels and shaking him like a rag doll.

Margaret Mahon sprang into action and pulled her daughter off Fergus, who staggered back.

'And with her,' Nora screamed at him, tears streaming down her face. 'A dirty tinker.'

Joe Mahon was now trying to calm his enraged daughter too but Nora twisted out of his grip and her eyes, burning with fury and pain, fixed on Philomena.

Philomena regarded her coolly for a moment then Nora ripped herself from her parents' clutches and planted herself in front of Philomena.

'Well, you can have him,' she shouted, flecks of spit from her lips dotting Philomena's face. 'Cos I'll not be taking no man for a husband who'd lowered himself to tup the likes of you, Philomena Dooley.'

Shoving her out of the way, Nora marched out of the church with Margaret and Joe Mahon and their younger offspring hurrying behind her, with all eyes in the church on them.

Philomena's parents stepped back to let them pass then rushed to comfort Philomena, but just as Kathleen was about to envelop her daughter in her embrace, Nora stopped and turned around. With raw hatred blazing from her eyes, she glanced down the church.

Philomena held the other girl's gaze for a moment then let a hint of a smile lift the corners of her mouth.

Chapter Seventeen

HOLDING THE LIGHTED taper to the tallest candle on the votive, Queenie waited until she was sure the flame had been transferred then blew out the spill. Laying it alongside the others at the front of the ornate metal candleholder, Queenie made her way into one of the pews halfway down on the right and sidestepped in.

There were several women already seated in the quiet church, all dressed in black and with scarves of the same colour covering their bowed heads. Although thousands of wives and mothers were joyously welcoming home their menfolk, for some women there would now always be an empty place at the table and a cold side of the bed.

Pulling out the tapestry kneeler, Queenie eased herself on to it. She clasped her hands together and rested them on the back of the pew in front then bowed her head.

However, although she tried to force her mind into prayer, as Queenie closed her eyes her thoughts took her away from war-torn East London and back to another church and to Patrick. It moved to them running hand in hand as children through their homeland's lush green fields and sheltering in the lee of an old tree as the rain fair threatened to wash them away. After showing her images through all the seasons of hers and Patrick's guiltless childhood, Queenie's mind moved on to less innocent moments and a long-forgotten yearning ached in her chest.

The corners of Queenie's mouth lifted slightly.

The young thought only they could feel the heat of passion and the shock of desire, but it wasn't so. Though her once-rich chestnut hair was thin and snow white, she could still taste Patrick's lips on hers and feel the warmth of his strong arms around her. And even now her body, withered and dry as it was, remembered the unimaginable joy of her and Patrick making love, with the wildflowers playing in the warm spring air, over fifty years ago.

A lump formed in Queenie's throat as tears pinched the corners of her eyes.

The wordless whispering of the ancient spirits started to swirl around her again, echoing the exhortation they'd been plaguing her with for months, but Queenie pushed them away.

After a lifetime of holding her peace, what good would it do to tell Patrick the truth about Jeremiah? And on his death bed, too. Surely it would be wrong to unsettle him so when he was at peace? And what if he reviled her for keeping the truth from him for so long?

A solitary tear escaped and rolled down her cheek.

Going on living without Patrick would be struggle enough, but Queenie knew she wouldn't be able to walk another day on this earth if the man she loved as fiercely now as she did when she first laid eyes on him slipped from this world to the next hating her in his heart.

Raising her eyes, Queenie's gaze rested on the statue of the Queen of Heaven on her pedestal next to the altar. Draped in her traditional white and blue gown, she'd recently been liberated from the crypt where she had been stored. Now back where she belonged, she looked serenely down on her followers once more.

Studying the alabaster face of Our Lord's mother, Queenie couldn't help but wonder had the angel of the Lord not appeared to Joseph, would the Virgin Mary have kept her secret, too.

Pushing the pram with his two children sitting in it, Charlie turned the corner into Mafeking Terrace.

'My goodness,' he said, casting his eyes over the sight before him. 'You weren't exaggerating about the state of the street.'

'That was the V-2 that landed behind Swedenborg Square,' Francesca replied. 'It took most of the roofs with it.'

'And all the windows, too, by the look of it,' Charlie replied. 'Although it hasn't stopped everyone getting election fever,' he noted, as they passed a house with a Labour Party poster pasted on to the brickwork.

It was the middle of the afternoon on the first Saturday in July and a fair few of his parents' neighbours were out enjoying the good weather, chatting on doorsteps while their children played on the cobbles.

A couple of them spotted him and shouted their greeting. Charlie waved in response, but his eyes soon returned to the street that had been as familiar to him as the back of his hand but was now little more than piles of rubble. In fact, had he not known he was walking through East London, he could have imagined himself in some of the towns and cities he'd passed through in France and Germany as the Allies pushed on to Berlin.

Casting aside the memories of death and destruction he'd witnessed in the past five years, Charlie's gaze shifted to Francesca.

'By the way,' he said, his heart filling with love at the sight of her, 'have I told you how lovely you look in that dress?'

'About a dozen times,' Francesca replied, the emotion in her dark brown eyes matching his own. 'I don't think I'll fit into it for much longer.'

His gaze drifted down on to the red fabric stretched tight across his wife's swollen stomach.

'And your gran says it's a girl,' she added.

Looking back at her, Charlie grinned.

'As my dad has often remarked, "'Tis one of life's great joys to be the father of girls,"' he replied, with a broad Irish lilt.

Francesca's eyes ran over him and she giggled.

'What?'

'Nothing really. But after five years of looking at you in uniform, it's just odd seeing you in ordinary clothes. And in a suit, too,' she added.

'Not as odd as it feels to be wearing it. Still,' said Charlie, brushing the sleeve of his chocolate-brown pinstriped demob suit, 'as the army was kind enough to give me a new set of togs, the least I can do is wear them.'

'Nanny,' shouted Patrick, pointing towards his grandparents' door.

'That's right, we're going to see Nanny and Granddad,' said Francesca.

Charlie's attention turned to the two children in the pram, and pride swelled in his chest. His mother had dozens of photos of him growing up and anyone who didn't know better would have been forgiven for thinking all of them were of Patrick. However, Rosa was a very different matter. Olive-skinned and almond-eyed like her mother, Charlie knew she would break many a young man's heart.

Within a few moments they were at his parents' front door, but as always they walked past and turned into the narrow, dank alleyway between the house and its neighbour.

Guiding the pram with one hand, Charlie slipped his arm around Francesca's expanded waist.

'Do you remember, sweetheart, we had our first kiss here?' he said, in a low voice.

Francesca turned and her dark eyes looked into his. 'I do and I think I told you to push off.'

He gave her a little squeeze. 'You didn't say that last night.'

She gave him a pulse-racing look then raised an eyebrow. 'Just open the gate, Charlie.'

He grinned and, reaching out, flipped the latch.

When he'd been on leave at Christmas all the tubs, pots and old butler sinks his father used to grow vegetables in had been bare, but now the whole yard was bursting with greenery from the row of cabbages alongside the path to the runner bean canes standing tall against the side wall.

Parking the pram under the kitchen window, Charlie lifted his son out and then turned his attention to Rosa who, seeing her brother talking to the hens, was wriggling her hands and kicking her heels to join him.

Lifting her up, Charlie set her on her feet, and she toddled over to join her brother by the chicken run.

'Come on, you two,' Charlie called after them. 'Let's go and say hello to everyone.'

The children left the hens to their scratching and pecking and ran back to the house. Patrick dashed in through the open back door and, after helping Rosa up the back step, Charlie and Francesca followed.

The faint smell of the family's midday meal was still lingering in the air as Charlie walked into the familiar kitchen. Seeing the kettle sitting on the stove, standing ready to make a cuppa for anyone who arrived, a sense of contentment washed over him.

'Oh, hello, you two,' he heard his mother call from the parlour as she saw Patrick and Rosa.

Francesca started to follow them, but Charlie caught her arm gently and, as she turned, he took her in his arms and kissed her.

'It's good to be home,' he said.

Francesca smiled and they walked in.

His mum and dad were sitting in their chairs either side of the fireplace, knitting and reading the paper respectively. On the arrival of her playmates, Victoria was already diving into the toy box in the corner with the other two children.

Charlie grinned. 'Hello, Mum.'

'Charlie!' Ida screamed, bursting into tears.

Dashing across the room, she enveloped him in a motherly embrace.

His father rose to his feet and, still with his arm around his sobbing mother, Charlie turned to his father and all three of them hugged for a moment.

'Welcome home, son,' Jeremiah said, tears visible in his eyes as he squeezed Charlie's shoulder with his paw-like hand.

'I'll put the kettle on,' said Francesca.

'No you won't, my love,' said Ida, extracting a handkerchief from her sleeve and blowing her nose. 'You'll put your feet up.'

Francesca took the chair Ida had just vacated and put her feet up on the pouffe.

'Where are the boys and Gran?' Charlie asked as he made himself comfortable on the sofa.

'Michael's around at Jane's house, Billy's gone to the library and your gran's at the church,' said Jeremiah. 'You heard how it is with poor Father Mahon?'

'Yes,' said Charlie. 'Francesca told me and sorry I am to hear it as there couldn't be a kinder soul this side of heaven.'

'Indeed, and according to Father Timothy, it's only a matter of time.'

'Poor Father Mahon,' said Charlie.

'Your gran's taken it hard, as you can imagine,' continued his father. 'For they've known each other since they were young, so she's been fair wearing her knees to the bone in church in recent days.'

Ida returned carrying a tray of tea and cake.

'So, when did you get back?' Jeremiah asked, as his wife handed him a cup.

'Yesterday evening,' Charlie replied. 'We were all loaded on a truck yesterday morning and . . .'

He ran through the events of the previous day, describing how he and the rest of those who'd signed on at the outbreak of war and were therefore earmarked for early discharge had been driven from their barracks in Folkestone to a demob centre outside Tunbridge Wells. Having made his father roll his eyes at the amount of paperwork he'd had to go through and made his mother blush as he described his discharge medical, he had them all laughing as he relayed the debacle of trying to find a demob suit with trousers that reached his ankles and didn't make him look like Max Miller. 'So after they finally sent me on my way I jumped on the three-thirty to London Bridge and walked through the back door of the café as Francesca was giving the kids their tea at five,' he concluded as the emotion of that moment caught in his throat again.

'Well, it's grand to have you back,' said his father.

Charlie raised an eyebrow. 'And I hear you've already got a spare lorry waiting for me.'

'I have,' Jeremiah replied. 'And a new yard come September, but there's no rush.'

'I know, but I'll be there on Wednesday,' Charlie replied. 'I want to get back into things and now it looks like Francesca's dad has someone interested in the café, we'll be looking for a new place to live soon.'

'There's some lovely houses near where we're moving, isn't there, Jerry?' Ida added.

'That there is,' Jeremiah agreed. 'And 'twould ease my life considerably if you were to consider your mother's suggestion.'

They laughed, then Charlie heard the side gate being opened and shut, followed by footsteps on the kitchen lino.

'That sounds like your gran now, Charlie,' said his father.

All eyes turned to the door leading to the kitchen as Queenie appeared, dressed in a flowery cotton dress that sat just an inch or two above the laces of her Sunday shoes. The finely knitted shawl that must be almost half a century old was draped around her shoulders.

Charlie rose to his feet. 'Hello, Gran.'

She looked up at him and when her tortured coal-black eyes met his blue-grey ones an unnerving shiver ran through him.

She stared at him for a long moment then her face screwed into something resembling what could only be described as an angry walnut.

Pressing her lips together, she marched past Charlie and out into the front hall, returning in the blink of an eye carrying his grandfather's old knobbly shillelagh which spent its life in the umbrella stand.

Gripping it firmly in her right hand, and with everyone in the room staring incredulously at her, she headed to the kitchen.

'Queenie,' said Ida, as her mother-in-law reached the kitchen door, 'Charlie's come home.'

'And glad I am too,' Queenie replied, half-turning to face them. 'But I'll be seeing him when I return and, please God, for many a day after, but now I have a matter that won't wait for the sun to move further across the sky to be attended to.'

With the unquiet spirits that had been plaguing her for the past months surging around her, and oblivious of the stares of passers-by, Queenie marched up St Breda and St Brendan's rectory path within ten minutes of leaving Mafeking Terrace.

Reaching the top step, she paused for a moment, then, gripping her husband Fergus's old fighting club in her right hand, she grabbed the brass knocker and hammered it against the door until she heard the bolt being drawn back on the other side.

The door creaked open and Nora, a frown etched deep into her forehead and in a dress that would have made a nun look like a chorus girl, stood in the doorway.

'Have you no consideration for—' She saw Queenie and she went to shut the door. 'Haven't I told you plain enough that—'

Swinging the wooden club in her hand, Queenie whacked it on Nora's fingers as they curled around the edge of the door.

Nora screamed and let go.

Queenie barged the door open with her shoulder, throwing the other woman against the wall in the process.

Stepping into the house, Queenie slammed the door behind her.

'You've broken my fingers,' said Nora, glaring at her as she nursed her injured hand.

'Where's Patrick?'

Nora's eyes flickered upwards.

Queenie strode past her towards the staircase, but Nora scurried after her and darted in front of her as she reached the bottom step.

'Don't think I don't know what you're about,' Nora said, spread-eagling herself between the wall and the newel post. 'My brother is preparing for his just reward, and I'll not let the likes of you—'

Queenie swung her husband's shillelagh again and it connected with the other woman's left knee.

Nora yelped and staggered sideways. Queenie pushed past her and headed up the stairs.

'I'll have the police after you for this, Philomena Dooley,' shouted Nora, gripping tight on the banister as she limped up after her. 'Assault and battery, that's what it is.'

Ignoring her, Queenie strode up the stairs but about three steps from the top a hand closed around her right ankle. Queenie missed her footing and sprawled across the stairs. She pushed herself upright just as Nora hobbled past and on to the first floor.

Getting to her feet, Queenie hurried after her. Reaching the landing she turned and saw Nora standing sentry outside the door at the far end of the corridor.

Gripping the gnarled club firmly, Queenie advanced on her.

'Will you stand aside?' she said, stopping in front of Nora.

'I will not, Philomena Dooley.' Scrambling under her clothes, Nora pulled out a silver cross. 'And may God strike you dead where you stand if you take one foot over this threshold.'

She thrust the crucifix into Queenie's face.

Queenie glanced at it then raised her gaze and looked into Nora's hate-filled, close-set eyes.

'Is that you, Nora?' called Patrick from the other side of the door.

'That it is,' Nora replied over her shoulder. 'I'll not be more than a moment.'

'And who is it you're talking to?'

''Tis no one of any importance,' Nora replied, her eyes boring into Queenie's.

'I thought it might be that Queenie's come,' he replied in a quivery voice.

Adjusting her grip on Fergus's shillelagh, Queenie took a step closer until her nose was but an inch from the other woman's.

'Now, I'll tell you this, Nora Mahon, and tell you no more,' she said, in a soft, lilting tone. 'Don't mistake my intentions here; if I swing from the gallows or rot in hell, I'll be going through that door. So will you be stepping aside or will you have me make you?'

A puce flush crept above Nora's unadorned white collar. With fury boiling in her face, she glared at Queenie for a moment then sidestepped away from the door.

Grasping the handle, Queenie opened the door.

'The devil take you, Philomena Dooley,' Nora muttered.

'He can try,' she replied, marching past her.

The room was sparsely furnished, as befitted a man whose mind was on heavenly rather than worldly matters.

On the faded rug that covered most of the floor stood a wardrobe and a chest of drawers so rickety that had Jeremiah acquired them in a house clearance he would have used them for firewood. The only other furniture was a hard Windsor chair with woodworm and an armchair someone had brought up from the study. However, all this barely registered as Queenie's gaze fixed immediately on the man lying on the single bed with his eyes closed.

Although it had been only a few weeks since she'd last seen Patrick, the old man with sunken cheeks and the blue veins visible under his transparent skin stopped her in her tracks.

It wasn't just how he looked but the rattling sound that filled the room as his chest rose and fell that caused her heart to lurch in her chest.

He opened his eyes and smiled. Damping down the urge to throw herself on to him and sob, Queenie smiled back.

'Queenie,' he said, raising a skeletal right hand and beckoning her closer.

Queenie walked across the room and sat in the armchair alongside him.

'Glad I am—' He broke off and started coughing.

Snatching a handkerchief from the bedside cabinet as she passed, Nora ran forwards.

'You can see how it is with my brother,' she said, glaring at Queenie and giving the handkerchief to Patrick. 'If you had an ounce of Christian feeling in you, Philomena Dooley, you wouldn't be barging yourself into places you've no right to—'

'Hush, hush, Nora,' croaked Patrick, wiping a smear of frothy spit from his mouth. 'I've been wanting . . . to . . . see Queenie . . . for many . . . a . . . long . . .'

He sank back into the pillow, his chest rising and falling as it battled to keep his soul in his body.

'You shouldn't be tiring yourself, Patrick,' said Nora, patting her brother's pillows.

Unable to speak, he waved away her words and his head rolled towards Queenie.

'Tell me, Mena,' he rasped, 'how it . . . is with . . . you . . .'

He put the handkerchief back to his mouth as another cough raked his body.

'You and . . . yours,' he added, as the spasm subsided.

'They are all well, praise be, but I have something I need to tell you, Patrick.' Queenie half turned towards where Nora still lurked by the chair. 'And you alone.'

She gave Nora a hard look, but the other woman didn't move.

'Thank you, Nora,' whispered Patrick.

She remained motionless for a moment then stomped across to the door.

'And Nora,' Patrick spoke again, 'Queenie's to stay.'

Giving Queenie another caustic look, Nora left, banging the door behind her.

Patrick's gaze returned to Queenie.

'Forgive me, Patrick,' she said, looking him in the eye. 'I should have told you long before now but . . .'

As he lay amongst the mountain of pillows, his gaze never leaving her face, Queenie sobbed out the true circumstances surrounding Jeremiah's birth.

'So, Patrick,' she concluded, tears welling up again in her eyes, 'now you know the full truth of the matter. I should have told you before and for that I ask your forgiveness. I'm sorry.'

Patrick stared incredulously at her for a moment then his head fell back into the pillows, and he closed his eyes.

Clasping her hands together on her lap to stop them from shaking, Queenie waited. After what seemed like for ever, Patrick turned his head and looked at her.

'Although I entered the priesthood to fulfil Mother's vow, I know now that it was always God's plan that my life should be lived in his service,' Patrick said. 'But I've also come to understand that he is a merciful God who forgives our transgressions and blesses us in unexpected ways.' Tears welled up in his eyes as, reaching out, he clasped her hand in his shaky pale one. 'Jeremiah is my son.' He squeezed her hand. 'We have a son, Mena.'

Queenie smiled. 'A great big bear of one who is so like you in all his ways, it fair breaks my heart each time my eyes rest on him.'

'And all those children,' he said.

'Yes,' said Queenie. 'He and Ida have seven of their own and another nine darling grandchildren who are the joy of my heart.'

A smile lifted Patrick's bloodless lips for a moment then he frowned.

'But 'tis I who . . . should be asking your . . . forgiveness, Mena,' he said softly. 'For breaking my promise and—'

'Now, now, Patrick.' Queenie patted his hand gently. 'This is no time for either of us to be saying what should have been done and what might have been, because life is as it is.'

He sighed. 'You . . . you have the truth of—' Gasping, he put the handkerchief to his mouth again as a raw cough racked his body, after which he fell back on the wall of pillows keeping him upright.

Rising from the chair, Queenie grabbed the glass of water on the bedside cabinet and, cradling his head in her hand, held it to his lips.

He took a couple of sips and his breathing steadied.

Resting back, he looked at her. 'You must make . . . your confession . . . to Father Timothy.'

'I will.'

'And hatred eats at the soul so will you make your . . . peace with Nora, too?'

Queenie nodded and resumed her seat. 'I'll try for your sake, Patrick.'

Patrick shut his eyes. Fighting back tears, Queenie sat quietly beside him as the battered clock next to the water jug ticked away the minutes.

Then he smiled, giving her a glimpse of the boy she'd fallen in love with over sixty years before.

'I'll say this for your grandma's old tarot card, Mena,' he said. 'There was no lie in their telling that you and I would grow old and grey together.'

Queenie tried to reply but she couldn't get her words past the lump in her throat.

He covered his mouth and coughed again, then, gathering his breath, he reached for her hand.

She took it and he gripped it tightly.

'I've always loved you, Mena.'

'And I've always loved you, Patrick,' she replied, looking into the blue-grey eyes she'd lived her life gazing into.

'Don't leave me, Mena.'

With tears streaming down her face, Queenie shook her head. 'Never.'

Still holding her hand and with his laboured breathing echoing around the room, Patrick closed his eyes.

Chapter Eighteen

WITH THE FIRST ray of the Sunday-morning sun creeping beneath the curtains, Queenie watched Patrick's chest rise and fall steadily beneath the bedcovers.

He was still enthroned amongst a multitude of pillows and with his hands resting on the white sheet, but he hadn't moved for some time.

Nora sat on the other side of the bed in the easy chair that she'd commandeered when she'd returned to the room a little while after Patrick had drifted off to sleep.

That's to say, Nora was slumped in the chair, mouth gaping open and snoring, as she had been since just after midnight four hours ago.

The district nurses had come to freshen Patrick up and make him comfortable for the night at about seven o'clock the previous evening. Philomena and Nora had stood outside, glaring at each other, for twenty minutes before being allowed back into the room.

Father Timothy had arrived just after eight o'clock and given his senior priest the last rites for the final time and then, led by the young priest, the three of them had spent half an hour praying for Patrick as he moved towards his eternal reward.

As Nora couldn't very well offer Father Timothy refreshment without including Queenie, they'd all had a cup of tea and a slab of cake as unyielding and unappetising as a house brick as St Breda and St Brendan's clock had rung out for nine o'clock.

After the priest had left, the two women had sat in resentful silence for another few hours until Nora's eyes had closed and her chin had sunk on to her chest.

Awakened by the promise of dawn, the birds perched on chimneys and washing lines nearby started chirping their greeting to the rising sun.

As it had lately, Queenie's mind summoned up images of other dawns in her life. Early ones snuggling into her sisters' warmth to snatch a few more precious moments before her pa called them to breakfast. Her bare feet on the icy mud on a walk to market with her mother. Heavily pregnant and waiting on a damp Dublin dockside for Fergus to secure them passage to England. Pushing Jeremiah into the world while the storm tossed the ferry around. There were countless others, like Jeremiah pitching up to tell her of Charlie's arrival and long nights sitting beside Ida as they nursed one of the girls through a fever. And those more recent dawns when she lay staring at the ceiling wondering if this was the day she would lose Patrick all over again.

A wet rasping sound dragged Queenie's mind back from its wandering and onto the man lying on the bed. Although Patrick's chest still rose and fell, there were now long pauses between each breath and the unmistakable rattle that heralded the soul's imminent departure. Leaning forward, Queenie slipped her hand into his lifeless one.

With her heart slowly ripping apart, she gazed at the man she'd loved since forever. Valiantly, Patrick's body dragged in its last few breaths and then his chest stilled.

A yawning chasm of desolation opened at Queenie's feet and although tears tightened the corners of her eyes, none came because her grief was too deep to break the surface. Even the ancient spirits around her were stilled by the depth of it.

Queenie rested in the space between life and death for a moment then she stood up. Leaning across, she closed her eyes, and pressed her lips on to Patrick's still warm forehead.

With her eyes never leaving his face, Queenie resumed her seat as the morning light slowly illuminated the room.

As St Breda and St Brendan's clock chimed the first of five bells, Nora gave an almighty snort and woke herself up. Blinking, she looked around and her attention fixed on her brother.

'He slipped away peacefully about an hour ago,' said Queenie.

'You should have woken me to catch his last breath.' Nora glanced at the small hand mirror on the bedside table.

'I didn't like to as you looked so peaceful,' Queenie replied.

Nora glared at her. 'You were ever without shame, Philomena Dooley, and only you would sully a priest's final hours on earth by sitting by his death bed to remind him of his sin.'

Queenie regarded her coolly. 'I loved Patrick from the first moment I saw him and will do until I take my last breath.' She stood up. 'Before he died he asked me that I should make my peace with you.'

'Make peace?' Nora spat. 'You ruined my life, so I'd sooner embrace the devil in hell than make peace with you.'

'Glad I am that on that we agree,' said Queenie. 'For as much as I'd like to honour his last wish, I can't in this regard for 'twould mean I'd be telling you I was sorry for what I did all those years ago. But I'm not. And never will be. But despite you and your arrogant family's efforts to separate us, we did spend our lives caring for each other and sharing good times and bad. And although he didn't know it until a few hours ago, he held all our grandchildren over the font as they entered into God's Grace, and our great-grandchildren, too. He lives on in my heart and in Jeremiah, the son we made one blissful sunny afternoon. As we lay there with the wildflowers bobbing around us, I told Patrick that I'd love him as fiercely when I was old and grey as I did on that day, and I do.' Gathering herself together she stood up and walked towards the door but as she reached it, she turned back.

'And as for ruining your life . . .' She looked Nora straight in the eye. 'I'd say 'tis your own bitter and twisted soul that has done that.'

Gazing for one last time at Patrick, the man who'd held her heart for over sixty years and with her happiness ripped into a million pieces, Queenie left the room.

As the milkman's cart turned into Mafeking Terrace, Queenie ducked into the cool of the side alley and headed towards the back gate. Clicking it open, she dragged herself into the yard and was greeted by the clucking of the hens eager to be let out of the coop.

Walking over to the wooden and wire structure, Queenie grasped the flap and raised it. There was a flurry of feathers followed by a waft of bird droppings as the dozen or so chickens scurried out. Going to the food bin, Queenie stretched in, took out a scoop of feed and scattered it through the top of the cage.

'What are you doing, Ma?'

Queenie looked around to see Jeremiah in his dressing gown and slippers standing in the back door.

She gave him a testy look. 'What I'm always after doing this time in the morning. Feeding the chickens.'

'But where have you been all night?' he replied, padding across the concrete. 'When you didn't come home for supper, me and Charlie scoured half the pubs in Wapping looking for you.'

Queenie opened her mouth to explain but as she raised her eyes to her son's face her heart faltered and then she spewed out all the pain and loss within it.

'He's dead,' she wailed, tears coursing down her cheeks. 'Patrick's dead.'

Jeremiah frowned. 'Father Mahon?'

She nodded. 'I can't—'

Suddenly her knees collapsed beneath her but before she hit the earth, Jeremiah had his arms around her.

'Come inside, Ma,' he said softly, taking the scoop from her and guiding her towards the back door.

With her emotions clogging up her thoughts and tears continuing to fall, Queenie let herself be led into the house. Clinging tightly to her son's arm, she staggered through to the kitchen and into the parlour. Collapsing on her old chair, her head fell back and she stared blindly at the fringed lampshade hanging in the middle of the room.

Jeremiah dragged the pouffe across and lifted her legs up and on to it, then taking the shawl from the back of his wife's chair, he draped it over her.

Pulling across a chair, Jeremiah took her hand and squeezed it gently. Queenie left her contemplation of the light fitting and, lowering her eyes, looked at her son.

'I'm so sorry, Ma,' he said. 'I know how close you and he were.' The quirky smile so like his father's spread across Jeremiah's face. 'Sometimes me and Ida used to say you were like an old married couple.'

Another wave of grief washed over Queenie, but this time she held back the tears.

Clasping her son's large work-worn hand in hers she looked him square in the eye. 'Jeremiah,' she said. 'I have to tell you something.'

'And that I swear is the whole truth of it,' Queenie concluded, twenty minutes later.

Folding her hands on her lap, she waited.

Jeremiah stared wordlessly at her for another couple of moments then he spoke.

'Well, that certainly explains why Father Mahon's sister was barely civil to us,' he said. 'Did Pa know?'

Queenie shook her head. 'Or if he did, he never mentioned it. I know he wasn't the best husband and father but—'

'Are any of us?' Jeremiah cut in. 'But Pa worked hard and even in the lean times there was always something on the table each night and he taught me his trade. I grant you, he had a weakness for the drink, which took him in the end, but that vice isn't a rarity around here. Father Mahon was one of the kindest people who has ever walked this earth, but for all his faults, Fergus Brogan was my pa in the same way I'm Billy's. You only have to look at Pearl, Ma, to understand that being a parent isn't about bringing children into the world but loving them through it.'

As she looked at her son, Queenie felt love pouring balm over the raw grief in her heart.

'Will you tell the children?' she asked.

'I will.' That quirky smile of Jeremiah's returned. 'Although, after such a tale of love and romance, they'll not be looking at you in quite the same way from now on.'

Despite her heavy heart, Queenie smiled.

Footsteps sounded above them on the stairs and Ida, also in her dressing gown and slippers, walked in.

'Thank goodness you're back, Queenie,' she said as she saw her sitting in the chair. 'We were going to go to the police if you hadn't come home by the time we were ready to go to church.'

'Ma's been at the rectory all night,' said Jeremiah. 'Father Mahon has died.'

'I'm so sorry,' said Ida, sympathy all over her face. 'He was such a lovely man. I'll put the kettle on as I expect you could do with a cuppa.'

Queenie opened her mouth to speak but then from nowhere an otherworldly sense of joyfulness swirled around her.

The back gate clicked open and within a few moments two-year-old Rory, with Peter on his heels, ran into the parlour from the kitchen. A few steps behind was his big sister Kirsty, followed by Archie with Heather on one arm and Cathy on the other. All of them were in their Sunday best and all had wide smiles spread across their faces.

'Hello,' said Ida. 'This is a nice surprise so early on a Sunday morning. I was just putting the kettle on.'

'That would be very nice, I'm sure,' said Archie. 'But perhaps, although I ken it might be considered a mite early in the day, I wonder, Jerry, if we could perhaps crack open the Jameson?'

'Yes,' said Cathy, her eyes sparkling with love and happiness as she hugged his arm. 'We need to celebrate because we're getting married.'

Chapter Nineteen

TAKING A SIP of her G&T, Mattie sidled over to where Francesca was sitting and slipped into the booth beside her.

'Doesn't Cathy look lovely?' she said, settling beside her friend.

'Every bit the radiant bride,' Francesca agreed. 'In fact, she and Archie make a very handsome couple.'

'They certainly do,' agreed Mattie.

It was true.

And not because the mint-green dress and jacket her sister was wearing highlighted her hazel eyes, nor that Archie, with his striking good looks, could have stepped straight out of the silver screen.

No, they were a handsome couple because of the love and happiness radiating from them, and now they were together in law as well as in their hearts. Mr and Mrs McIntosh.

It was about four thirty in the afternoon on the last Saturday in July and two hours since Father Timothy had pronounced Cathy and Archie, with their children watching from the front row, man and wife.

After various members of the family and friends had clustered around the happy couple for the usual sets of wedding photos, the whole party had decamped back to the Catholic Club's upstairs bar. As Mattie, Jo and Ida had set up the wedding spread earlier that morning, everything had been ready when everyone arrived so it only needed Father Timothy to say grace and Jeremiah to put some money behind the bar for the celebrations to kick off.

Now all that was left of the mountain of sandwiches, rabbit pies dressed up to resemble the pork variety and sausage rolls was the odd crumbled biscuit or a curled slice of bread. The only food untouched was the ten-inch boiled-fruit wedding cake. As it was still hard to get hold of enough sugar to make the icing, the cake was cunningly concealed beneath a fancy cardboard mock-up of an iced one, complete with glued paper scallops and piping, which they'd hired from the baker.

The happy couple were standing together by the small stage, with Heather in Archie's arms and Rory holding Cathy's hand as they accepted people's congratulations and best wishes for the future.

After cramming food in their mouths, the children of the family, having been cleaned up with a spit-and-handkerchief wipe by their mothers, were now stomping around at the far end of the room. The older ones – Michael, Billy and Kirsty, along with Michael's friend Jane – were loitering at the far end of the bar as they sucked their lemonade from bottles with straws.

Meanwhile, although everyone else was now sitting back to let their lunch go down, Ida, the sleeves of her mulberry dress rolled up to her elbows, was tidying away some of the debris on the table. Archie's mother Aggie, smartly dressed for her son's wedding in a box-shouldered navy suit, was helping her and the two of them were chatting away, no doubt trading anecdotes about their mutual grandchildren.

At the bar, Mattie's husband Daniel, out of uniform for once; Jeremiah, looking dapper in a new flowery waistcoat; Charlie, in his demob suit; and Jo's husband Tommy were having a beer with Father Timothy.

'I suppose they're still talking about the election result,' said Francesca, as Jeremiah's booming laughter rolled over to them.

'Aren't we all?' said Mattie. 'It's not every day you get a landslide Labour victory.'

After what had seemed like months of posters being stuck everywhere urging people to vote Labour, and loudspeakers on the back of lorries instructing voters to do the same, yesterday the country had woken up to the news that the men and women who'd given their blood, sweat and tears fighting Hitler for the past six years had kicked Churchill out and voted for the first ever majority Labour government.

'I wonder if we will get free hospitals and better houses like they promised,' said Francesca.

'We'd better,' said Mattie. 'Or they'll be out next time around.'

'I must say, I can't imagine not paying the doctor when you visit, or that the council will provide you with a new house.'

'Well, don't hold your breath, Fran,' said Mattie. 'I don't think anything will be changing overnight because we're still fighting in Burma and goodness knows how long that will go on for.'

'You're right. We shouldn't forget that while we're all celebrating the end of the war here, there's plenty of our poor soldiers stuck out in the Siamese jungle,' said Francesca. 'But I hope it's over soon before our Billy and Michael are old enough to be called up.'

'From your lips to God's ears,' said Mattie, glancing across at her brothers, who, dressed in two-piece suits and ties, were looking very grown up.

Her youngest son, Ian, trotted over, his arms outstretched. As Mattie picked him up, Francesca pulled a face and placed her hand on her swollen stomach.

'Baby shifting?' asked Mattie, settling her son on her lap.

Breathing out slowly, Francesca nodded.

'How long have you got?' asked Mattie.

'Another six to eight weeks, according to the midwives at Munroe House,' Francesca replied.

'Isn't that when your dad's signing over the lease of the café?' said Mattie.

Francesca nodded again. 'And knowing my luck, I'll go into labour just as we've loaded all the furniture into the back of the van.'

'Have you found somewhere?' asked Mattie, moving her glass out of Ian's grasp.

'Not yet,' Francesca replied. 'But we're going to look at a couple of houses around the corner from where your mum and dad are going this week. They're a bit pricey but they're big enough for all of us and they have a garden.'

The door opened and Jo came in carrying baby Zara on her hip and a basket filled with nappies and extra clothes in her spare hand.

Spotting Mattie and Francesca, she came over and, tucking the basket under the bench Mattie was sitting on, she perched on one of the chairs.

'Now you smell a bit sweeter, Zara, let's sit with Auntie Mattie and Auntie Francesca,' she said to the little girl.

Ian gave the newcomer a blank-faced stare, but Mattie made a happy face at the newest member of the Brogan family. 'Hello, Zara,' she said.

The child curled into Jo, who pressed her lips to the little girl's curly black hair. 'She's a bit shy.'

'I'm not surprised. Meeting all of us at once must be a bit overwhelming for her,' said Francesca.

'I'm sure.' The expression in Jo's eyes softened as she gazed down at the child on her lap. 'We're so lucky to have her.'

'And she's lucky to have such loving parents,' said Mattie, as a lump formed in her throat.

'Has she settled in all right?' asked Francesca.

'She was a bit upset when we first brought her home but once we got into a routine, she was a lot happier,' said Jo. 'Having spent months in a ward full of other babies, I think it must have been a bit strange for her sleeping in a room by herself.'

'Is she staying with you now?' asked Francesca.

Jo nodded. 'As of two weeks ago we are her official foster parents pending an adoption hearing in October, after which she will be our daughter.' She beamed at them. 'And once Tommy's finished his teacher training in two years, we're going back to the orphanage and adopting another baby.'

'That's wonderful,' said Francesca.

Ian started to fidget, and Mattie let him climb down. He ran off towards the other children. Zara's eyes followed him for a moment then she too started squirming. Jo set her on her feet, and she trotted after him.

As she watched the children go, she noticed that Queenie, who had been talking to one of the old women from the Darby and Joan lunch club, was now sitting by herself in the corner nursing her Guinness.

She was wearing a mauve crushed-velvet dress that was designed to sit just below the knee but, on her four foot ten inches, skimmed her ankles. Mattie couldn't recall seeing it before so it must have been at the back of her gran's wardrobe since the end of the last war with Germany. Queenie was also wearing her single string of pearls and matching drop earrings, and they adorned her modest bosom and ears respectively. Although she'd taken off the black armband she'd been wearing since Father Mahon died for such a joyous day, her face showed her heartbreak and sorrow more starkly than any mourning paraphernalia ever could.

Jeremiah noticed her too and, leaving the bar, he ambled over to join his mother. He said something and she forced a smile.

'Poor Gran,' said Mattie.

'Mum said she sobbed so much when they got back from Father Mahon's funeral on Monday that she feared they would have to call the doctor to give her something,' said Jo, looking across at Queenie.

'Father Timothy did a lovely Mass for him, though,' said Francesca. 'And the church was packed.'

'And so it should be,' said Jo. 'There's no one around here who would have anything but a good word to say about Father Mahon. Everyone loved him.'

'They did,' agreed Francesca. 'Although I overheard Miss Mahon complaining to Father Timothy that the bishop didn't come.'

'I've heard more than a few people say they'll be glad when she catches the boat back to Ireland,' added Mattie.

Jo raised an eyebrow. 'So your Daniel was right after all, then, about Father Mahon being Dad's—'

'Shhh,' cut in Mattie.

'What?' said Jo, giving her a wide-eyed, innocent look.

'You know we promised Dad and Gran that we would keep it to ourselves,' said Mattie, suppressing a smile. 'Father Mahon's gone now, God rest his soul.' She crossed herself and the other two did the same. 'And it would upset Gran if people started gossiping about him now.'

'True,' said Jo. 'But it's so sad.'

'Yes, it is,' agreed Francesca. 'To be in love with someone for so long but never able to be with them.'

'Although,' Jo arched an eyebrow, 'I can't quite imagine Gran as a young girl stealing away to the woods for a bit of you know what . . .' She winked.

Mattie laughed. 'I'm sure our grandchildren will say the same about us one day when they find out what we've got up to these past six years.'

'You speak for yourself,' said Francesca. 'I was always a good girl.'

'Until you met our Charlie,' Jo added, giving her a sideways look.

Francesca glanced across at her husband standing at the bar, his jacket off and sleeves rolled up, and a slight flush coloured her cheeks.

Covering Queenie's hand with his large one, Jeremiah gave his mother a swift kiss on the forehead then stood up. He beckoned Cathy and Archie back to the refreshment table.

'Looks like Dad's going to do the toasts in a minute,' said Mattie, as people started ordering their drinks in readiness.

'I'd better get myself another,' said Jo, rising to her feet. 'You two all right?'

Mattie and Francesca nodded.

Jo walked over to the bar just as Tommy caught hold of Zara as she ran past. Hoisting her up with one arm, he put the other one around Jo as she joined them.

Carrying a pint in one hand and a smaller glass in the other, Charlie wove his way between the guests to where they were sitting.

'Here, take my place,' said Mattie, standing up as her brother reached them. 'I'm going to join Daniel for the speeches.'

Taking her drink with her, Mattie wandered across to join her husband at the bar.

Slipping his arm around her waist, Daniel gave his wife a little squeeze as they shared a fond look.

Although they had been married for five years and had three children, Mattie's heart fluttered at the sight of him. No, it wasn't easy imagining Queenie, with her eccentric fashion sense and false teeth, as a young girl running through an Irish meadow to meet her lover, but loving Daniel as she did, Mattie could quite understand how her gran could love one man for a lifetime.

Shifting her attention from her husband's rugged profile, Mattie looked across at Cathy and Archie, who were gathering their children together to sit with Aggie for the speeches.

'Do you think Cathy will tell Peter?' Daniel asked, as Cathy's son ran across the room.

'Eventually,' Mattie replied. 'When he's old enough to understand.'

'I don't imagine it will be an easy conversation. I wouldn't relish telling him that his father was an officer in Hitler's British Free Corps and hanged by the Allies as a traitor,' said Daniel.

'I wouldn't either,' said Mattie. 'But the truth can't be denied.

And better that Cathy and Archie tell him than he finds out some other way. But thank you for finding out about Stan.'

'Glad to be of help.' He gave her a sideways smile. 'Although I gave them a bit of a shock turning up at midnight to tell them.'

Mattie laughed, then Jeremiah picked up the long-bladed knife beside the cardboard facsimile of a cake and tapped it against his glass.

'Ladies and gentlemen,' he began, 'I hope you've replenished your glasses, for 'tis that time in the proceedings where in exchange for the fine spread my own sweet darling Ida' – he blew her an exaggerated kiss which set off a couple of wolf whistles – 'has set before us, you have to listen to meself blather on for a moment or two.'

Everyone laughed.

He did the usual bits of thanking Father Timothy for a lovely service and Pete behind the bar for making sure everyone's glasses never ran dry, then he turned to the happy couple.

'Now, just to remind you all,' he said, tucking his thumbs in the armholes of his flowery waistcoat as he cast his eyes around the assembled company. 'I am truly one of the most fortunate men that ever walked on God's green earth. Because not only have I meself a darling wife but she has blessed me with no less than seven lovely children. My boys, Charlie' – Jeremiah's eldest son raised his glass – 'and those whippersnappers, Billy and Michael.' He indicated the boys standing at the end of the bar, who nudged each other. 'But, in addition, my sweet Ida has given me four,' he held up the required number of large fingers, 'yes, four, beautiful daughters. All named after empresses as all of them are a rare wonder.'

This brought forth another round of wolf whistles, with both Tommy and Charlie joining in.

Jeremiah's face took on a mournful expression and he placed his hand dramatically on his chest.

'But with the blissful joy of being the father of girls there is the pain too,' he continued. 'The pain of having to relinquish their care to another.'

He put his hand over his eyes and shook his head as laughter filled the room.

Victoria, seeing her father looking unhappy, trotted over and tugged at his trouser leg.

Grinning, he scooped her up in his arms and planted a noisy kiss on her cheek.

Settling her on his forearm, he looked around. 'Now, my friends, I have to tell you that in this regard I have been mightily blessed, too, because my eldest Mattie found true love with the lad Daniel over there.' Jeremiah raised his glass and Daniel returned the favour. 'My youngest Jo has done the same with Stepney's very own mathematical genius Tommy.' Jeremiah toasted towards Jo's husband, who copied his father-in-law's gesture. 'And now,' he turned to face the newly married couple standing beside him, 'my joy is complete, for my darling Cathy had the great good sense to say yes to Archie McIntosh, a man who has an eye for beauty and a rare talent with a paintbrush, and I'm not talking about emulsioning the parlour ceiling.' Everyone laughed. 'But I have to warn you, son,' he continued, looking at Archie. 'As all of us who are here can testify, being married to one of the Brogan girls is not for the faint-hearted. If you think dismantling a thousand-kilo German bomb is dangerous, God help you, boy, should you forget a birthday or anniversary.' Everyone laughed again. Jeremiah's gaze shifted to Cathy and his face took on a sentimental expression. 'I know you'll love and take care of my darling Cathy, Archie, so it gives me the greatest of pleasure to welcome you into the Brogan family.' Stretching out his hand he shook Archie's. 'And can I just add, Cathy and Archie,' Jeremiah continued as the commotion settled down, 'when troubles come your way, as they surely will, remember this: if it wasn't for the Brogans, the street-corner gossips would be short of a thing or two to talk about.'

There was a roar of laughter as everyone clapped, whooped or whistled.

Holding his wife's hand, Archie stepped forwards. As he thanked Jeremiah for his welcome into the family, Mattie's gaze ran around the room and her heart strings tightened.

The familiar room where she and her family had shared so many happy times looked different somehow.

Frowning, Mattie wondered at it for a moment then she realised. Although the criss-cross tape on the windows had been scraped off and the images of the Shamrock League's past presidents had been returned to their places on the wall, it wasn't the room that was different but she and everyone in it. How could they not be?

And this is where it had started, the day before war broke out. Cathy was a bride then, too. And now here they were again. Mum, Dad and Gran. Along with the old and new friends they'd shared the last six years with, as they'd done their bit as part of the country's home defence.

Back then, it had just been her, Cathy, Jo, Charlie and Billy, but now Michael and Victoria had been added to their number. Daniel, Tommy, Francesca and Archie were part of the family, too. Not to mention all the children who'd been born as bombs dropped around them and who had never known a world at peace.

And now what?

Mum and Dad would be loading their home and their memories on to the back of a lorry in a week's time and leaving the house in Mafeking Terrace for ever. Gran, with her chickens and her parrot, Prince Albert, would be going too, taking the memory of her secret love with her. Jo and Tommy were starting a new life as adoptive parents, while Cathy would walk beside Archie as he pursued his dream of becoming a recognised artist. As for Billy, Michael and Victoria, who knew what opportunities there might be for them in the future? And what of her? Off to live in Germany. Daniel had already reminded her of her desire to study for an English degree. Perhaps, rather than become a bored army wife, she could take a university correspondence course, like others stationed overseas did.

The world had changed, and the Brogans had changed with it.

If the new government stood by their promises, soon the old East End neighbourhoods, with their squalid houses and cobbled streets, would be swept away and modern dwellings with proper sanitation and dry walls would replace them.

And what would survive? The pubs with someone bashing out a tune on an old piano? The street markets and their raucous stallholders? What about all the churches' annual processions? Would people still have a string dangling behind their letter boxes with their front door key attached? Perhaps not. But what would survive in this shining new world that millions of people like her had fought so hard to preserve was love and family. The two strands of her life were woven so tightly together, nothing this side of heaven could pull them apart.

The sound of clapping brought Mattie's mind back from its wandering.

Looking around she saw Archie, with his arm around Cathy and a smile on his face, raising his glass.

'Ladies and gentlemen, lads and lasses,' he said, grinning at everyone as he cast his eyes over them. 'I give you the future.'

Mattie held her G&T high.

'The future,' she chorused with everyone else.

Perhaps people would cheer when the bulldozers moved in but then later forget the rats lurking in the outhouses and the bed bugs feasting on you while you slept, and instead remember the friendliness of the overcrowded houses and the neighbours always ready to lend a hand or a cup of sugar when asked. Who knew?

But whatever the future held, one thing was certain. The Brogan family would face it, as they had always done, together.

The End

Acknowledgements

AS ALWAYS, I would like to mention a few books, authors and people, to whom I am particularly indebted.

In order to set my characters' thoughts and worldviews of the final days of WW2 authentically, I returned to *Wartime Britain 1939-1945* (Gardner) and *The East End at War* (Taylor & Lloyd).

In *A Ration Book Victory*, I've had to look beyond the bombs and hardship to the brighter future that people in 1945 were hoping for. I dipped into *Austerity Britain* (Kynaston) and *Our Hidden Lives 1945-1948* (Garfield), which features extracts from post-war mass observation diaries.

I would also like to thank a few more people. Firstly, my very own Hero-at-Home, Kelvin, for his unwavering support, and my three daughters, Janet, Fiona and Amy, who listened patiently as I worried endlessly about whether the dual timeline in *A Ration Book Victory* would work.

Once again, a big thanks goes to Sarah Hodgson and the editorial team at Atlantic, who turned my 400+ page manuscript into a beautiful book, and last, but by no means least, a big thank you to the wonderful team at Atlantic Books, Karen Duffy, Poppy Mostyn-Owen, Jamie Forrest, Patrick Hunter, Sophie Walker and Hanna Kenne for all their support and innovation.